THE UNUSUAL MAYOR MARHEART

Book four

of

The Cassie Black Trilogy

TAMMIE PAINTER

Yes, book four, because trilogies (like sourdough starters) refuse to be tamed.

The Unusual Mayor Marheart
Book Four of The Cassie Black Trilogy

Copyright © 2024 by Tammie Painter, All Rights Reserved

Daisy Dog Media supports copyright. Copyright fuels and encourages creativity, free speech, and legal commerce. Thank you for purchasing an authorized copy of this book and supporting the hard work of the author. To comply with copyright law you agree to not reproduce, scan, distribute, or upload any part of this work in any form without permission from the author.

This book is a work of fiction. Names, characters, places, and incidents either are the product of the author's imagination or are used fictitiously. Any resemblance to persons, living or dead, business establishments, events, or locales is entirely coincidental.

You may contact the author by email at
Tammie@tammiepainter.com

Daisy Dog Media
Portland, Oregon 97222, USA

First Edition, July 2024
also available as an ebook

ALSO BY TAMMIE PAINTER

The Undead Mr. Tenpenny: Cassie Black #1
The Uncanny Raven Winston: Cassie Black #2
The Untangled Cassie Black: Cassie Black #3
The Unwanted Inheritance of the Bookman Brothers
Hoard It All Before (A Circus of Unusual Creatures Mystery)
Tipping the Scales (A Circus of Unusual Creatures Mystery)
Fangs A Million (A Circus of Unusual Creatures Mystery)
Beast or Famine (A Circus of Unusual Creatures Mystery)
The Great Escape: 15 Tales of Humor, Myth, and Magic
Day Sixteen: A Supernatural Thriller
Domna: A Serialized Novel of Osteria (Six-Part Series)
The Trials of Hercules: Book One of the Osteria Chronicles
The Voyage of Heroes: Book Two of the Osteria Chronicles
The Maze of Minos: Book Three of the Osteria Chronicles
The Bonds of Osteria: Book Four of the Osteria Chronicles
The Battle of Ares: Book Five of the Osteria Chronicles
The Return of Odysseus: Book Six of the Osteria Chronicles
13th Hour: Tales from Light to Midnight

WHAT READERS ARE SAYING...

ABOUT THE UNDEAD MR TENPENNY...

"...a clever, hilarious romp through a new magical universe..."

—Sarah Angleton, author of Gentleman of Misfortune

"Wow and wow again! I absolutely loved this book! You get such a feel for the characters and the story is so fast paced you don't want to put it down."

—Goodreads Reviewer

"Man oh man, did I love this book!"

—Jonathan Pongratz, author of Reaper

"...suffused with dark humor and witty dialogue, of the sort that Painter excels at..."

—Berthold Gambrel, author of Vespasian Moon's Fabulous Autumn Carnival

"...a fun and entertaining read. Great wit too."

—Carrie Rubin, author of The Bone Curse

ABOUT THE UNCANNY RAVEN WINSTON...

"More, please!"

—Goodreads Reviewer

"…quirky with a capital Q, and I mean that in the best way! …I laughed out loud several times while reading this…"

—Bookbub Reviewer

"Magic, mayhem, mystery, it's all here."

—Bookbub Reviewer

ABOUT THE UNTANGLED CASSIE BLACK...

"…a great ending to a truly delightful ride."

—Bookbub Reviewer

"…super captivating! If you love magical hijinks, punny witticisms, and crazy adventure, then this is the series for you!"

—Bookbub Reviewer

"A truly satisfying end to a charming, funny, action-filled trilogy."

—Goodreads Reviewer

"You can never have too much sugar."

—Jodi Taylor
Lies, Damned Lies, and History

THE UNUSUAL MAYOR MARHEART

A QUICK NOTE BEFORE WE BEGIN

Just a little housekeeping before we jump into Cassie's new adventure…

First, although this story begins just a couple of months (August, to be exact) after the third Cassie Black book (*The Untangled Cassie Black*), it was written about three years after that "final" book of the trilogy.

As such, there might be some minor inconsistencies between the "summing up" bit at the end of *The Untangled Cassie Black* and things at the beginning of *The Unusual Mayor Marheart*. These should be only a few, very minor inconsistencies, but I just wanted to mention them to (hopefully) avoid any angry emails.

Second, *The Unusual Mayor Marheart* is the start to a completely new Cassie Black trilogy (Trilogy 2.0).

Yes, it's still set in MagicLand, Real Portland, and London. And yes, it features Cassie, Mr Tenpenny, Morelli, Alastair, and loads of other characters from the first trilogy, but this new trilogy is a separate story in itself, not a continuation from *The Untangled Cassie Black*.

What that means is, if you haven't read Trilogy 1.0 yet, you should have no problem enjoying and understanding Trilogy 2.0. Although, reading the original trilogy first will give you far more insight into how the characters got to where they are now and how MagicLand works.

And if you have read Trilogy 1.0? Then thank you! I'm so glad you're back, and I hope you enjoy seeing all those familiar faces and what they get up to in Trilogy 2.0.

Alright, let's go see what trouble Cassie is falling into these days…

PROLOGUE
A SQUISHY, SQUIDGY MEETING

"Wordsworth would like to speak to you," Rafi told Olivia, his dark eyes glancing respectfully away from the involuntary shudder that danced across his boss's shoulders.

"Why is he here? I thought he'd wriggled off to that Magical Book…" Olivia fluttered her slim hand "…whatever-it's-called."

"The Magics' International Library Consortium Conference. And he's back. Just returned."

"I don't need this now, Rafi. I really don't." Olivia, who always carried herself with posture so perfect that Rafi often wondered if she slept with her shoulders back and head held high, slumped in her swivel chair. "Doesn't he need to go sniff the library books for food stains or something?"

"Already has. That's why he wants to see you." Rafi started to pour Olivia a cup of tea, then thought better of it. If you were going to deal with Wordsworth, you needed something stronger. He snapped his fingers over the mug, instantly changing the ruby-brown Earl Grey into a crystal clear gin and tonic.

When Rafi slid the drink across her desk, Olivia, director of Magical HeadQuarters, didn't hesitate to take a sip. She then downed the entire cupful in three deep gulps.

"Send him in." Indicating her mug, she added, "But have another one of these ready for me when he leaves."

Rafi nodded then opened the massive oak door of Olivia's office — a stone-walled, tapestry-lined space within the Tower of London — and told Wordsworth that Olivia could see him now.

Finding no Dutch courage in the gin, Olivia sought strength in the framed photo on her desk. It was of herself and Runa at the Harry Potter theme park in Los Angeles. It had been such a wonderful holiday that, even before they'd returned, they'd made plans to visit the one in Osaka.

Like someone unable to avoid gawking at a car wreck, Olivia's gaze drifted to the reports on her desk. If they were correct, that Potter-themed trip to Japan was going to have to wait.

Still, there was Wordsworth to deal with, and the only way to get through a meeting with him was to cling to her happy, Runa-filled memories as tenaciously as a spider clings to its web in a hurricane. Olivia looked once more at the photo before she stood to greet her guest.

"Wordsworth, how was the conference?" Olivia asked with forced warmth before begrudgingly offering her guest a seat.

The lumpy, squishy, and squat creature stretched himself upward, causing two or three segments of his body to extend until he was at a height where he could slither onto one of the two designer chairs before Olivia's desk. When he sat, the segments contracted again with a rather slushy sound. Olivia tensed every muscle in her upper body. It was the only way to keep from cringing.

"It was awful," the Tower's head librarian stated.

"I'm sorry to hear that. Were the talks not to your—"

"The talks were perfect. Being in the company of other bookworms was perfect. What was not perfect was the state of my library upon my return."

This was news to Olivia. At Wordsworth's request, she had closed down the library during his absence and had seen to the protective spells on the locks herself. She'd gotten no sense of the spells having been broken. Although, she had been spending a lot of time with Runa up until these latest reports had reached her. Since then, she'd been occupied with their possible implications.

Still, if there had been a breach, surely Chester, the Tower's most dedicated security troll, would have noticed, or the surveillance gnomes, or even the cleaning pixies.

"The state of your library?" prodded Olivia.

"It's very upset," the Bookworm said gravely.

The beads at the end of Olivia's braids clicked against themselves as she shook her head in exasperation. The library might be full of magical books, some of which could be rather lively, but for Wordsworth to believe the library itself had feelings… well, maybe it was time for him to consider retirement.

"Upset?" she asked dubiously.

"You would be too if a book was missing from your collection."

"One missing book? But otherwise the library is okay?"

Wordsworth extended three of his upper segments as he leaned over Olivia's desk, his muddy-green eyes fixed on hers. "A piece of the collection went missing while I was at the convention. I would hardly call that okay. Think how you would feel if you woke up tomorrow morning to find one of your limbs gone."

The segments contracted, jiggling like something from a gelatin commercial, and the Bookworm eased back. But only slightly.

"Now, Wordsworth, please don't take this the wrong way. You have been the librarian here at the Tower for longer than most Magics have been alive, and you are very... *dedicated* to your work." An observation Olivia could hear Cassie Black calling the Understatement of the Century. "But can you be sure this book is missing? Perhaps it's been checked out. Or misplaced."

"I do not misplace books. I have no record of the book being checked out in decades. It is indeed missing. And before you ask, yes, I am certain."

"How?" Olivia might run Magic HQ, but she honestly had no idea how the Bookworm went about his work. She doubted anyone did. Likely because they were too afraid to ask.

"Because I can sense the weight of the library is off. It is what we do," he said, emphasizing each word. "Perhaps you should attend the next Magics' International Library Consortium Conference to enlighten yourself on these matters."

The very idea of being in a room— No, an entire building full of bookworms was enough for Olivia to believe there really was something worse than what was in the files on her desk.

"That's a very generous offer, but perhaps we should stick to the issue at hand. This missing book, do you have any idea how it went astray?"

For the first time in Olivia's memory, Wordsworth's face slackened with guilt.

"My fault, I suppose. I should have known to keep the book with me at all times. Any item removed from the library should be treated with all the attention of a visiting dignitary."

"You took it to the conference?"

"It was a request. Given there's only a few copies in existence, most librarians have never seen one. Rather than transport it home in my luggage— It is rather large, you see." Olivia nodded in understanding. "I sent it on ahead with the courier service the conference provided. When I got back, I assumed it had been re-shelved. Then I noticed the—" the Bookworm sucked in a shaky breath through his broad nostrils, then struggled to speak the final word "—absence."

"Is there anything I can do?"

"You must take on the responsibility of finding it." For a moment, Olivia had actually felt sorry for the Bookworm. But her compassion died a quick death at the return of his imperious, demanding tone. "Or, if need be, obtain a replacement. I cannot have the collection compromised."

Rafi stepped forward, for which Olivia was grateful. First, even if she had the time, she had no idea how to locate a missing book. Second, she was teetering on the edge of an overwhelming desire to scream at Wordsworth, and with the drop of banshee blood in her veins, that scream would be the last thing Wordsworth ever heard. A problem solved, but the pixies would complain to no end if they had to clean up a dead bookworm.

"If I may," Rafi said, full of the obsequious deference he was so good at feigning. "There is someone who could help you find your missing item. Or a replacement."

"Who?" the Bookworm asked peevishly as he peered at Rafi over his half-moon spectacles.

"Cassie Black."

Olivia brightened at this. Rafi was a genius. Cassie was a detective, or would be soon enough. And despite her anti-social attitude, she was keen to prove herself. For a brief moment Olivia wondered if it was fair to heap her own problems onto someone else's shoulders, but she would do anything to get Wordsworth out of her office.

"Yes, Miss Black has—" Olivia began.

"The one who blew up a commercial kitchen, melted a girl, snuck out of the Tower through an illegal portal when you were trying to keep her safe, and who has yet to obtain her library card for the Magic collection?" Wordsworth added as if this were the worst fault in Cassie's list of misdemeanors.

Olivia closed her eyes. She should have had two gin and tonics before letting this pest in. She inhaled through her nostrils and deep into her belly. Thankfully, Rafi spoke first.

"That was all just a little misunderstanding. She's very good at what she does." Rafi then paused as if considering the accuracy of his words. "Well, she will be once she gets some practice in."

"She refused to follow the rules. I don't think this is someone I can work with. There must be order. Respect is mandatory. Things need to be in their place, and that includes people."

The Bookworm slipped off the chair, and Olivia half-expected to see a trail of slime left behind. Rafi eyed her pleadingly over the Bookworm's lumpy head.

"What can I do to convince you that Miss Black is the best person for this job?" Olivia called.

"Well," Wordsworth said, in a rather calculating manner to Olivia's ears, "there is something."

Olivia agreed to the creature's demand. Really, she'd have promised him the moon to be done with this meeting.

As soon as Wordsworth had crossed the threshold and the office door was closed once more, Rafi snapped his fingers. A fresh gin and tonic popped into Olivia's hand.

"You're sure she's able to handle this?" Olivia asked after downing the drink.

"How hard could it be to find an enormous book?" Olivia gave him a look that spoke volumes about how impossible she thought it could be. Rafi responded by tapping the file on Olivia's desk. "You've got other matters to deal with. Leave this to me."

Once Rafi had slipped out of the office, Olivia dragged her finger upward along the empty cup to fill it again. She put Wordsworth and Cassie from her mind. Rafi was right, there really were far more troubling issues to deal with than a missing book.

CHAPTER ONE
HE IS THE WALRUS

THREE WEEKS EARLIER

How could I have been so stupid? It was a simple Ink Shifting Spell. A spell I've done... well, I probably shouldn't incriminate myself by saying how often I'd done that particular bit of magic. Let's just say, enough times that I knew I had a natural talent for being able to simply flick my fingers to alter the existing words on any page.

And stupidly, I'd just performed a few of those handy flicks during a test at the Academy. That would be Rosaria's Magic Academy of Detective Science, one of seven law enforcement and detective training schools across the world's magic communities.

Really, though, that pop quiz? No one in class had been prepared for it. Also, for a pop quiz, it had been asking some pretty advanced questions. Like final exam questions. So, yes, I'd panicked, peered over at Tobey's paper during test time, and done a little answer-changing magic. It hadn't been the first time. In fact, I'd done it during every pop quiz, unit test, and weekly exam Tobey and I had been given since joining up a few weeks ago.

Trouble was, this time, Inspector Oberlin, chief of police and head instructor at the Academy, had been paying close attention to my every move.

Which is why it was next-level idiotic of me to do anything against the rules during that pop quiz. And why, at the barest whiff of my magic in action, Oberlin had ordered me to put down my pencil and wait for him in his office.

Detective Inspector Wesley Oberlin sported a thick bristly mustache, had weirdly large front teeth, and carried a fair bit of extra weight that spoke more of "hours at the all-you-can-eat buffet" than "hours at the gym." He was also the bane of my magical education existence. But don't worry, the feeling was entirely mutual. And since I'd recently compared him to a certain sea mammal, I'd earned myself a spot at the top of his Least Favorite Students list.

I've never been the teacher's pet. Far from it. Pair my disrespect for authority with a mouth that will whip out a phrase such as "a pregnant walrus suffering from heat stroke would make a better teacher than you," and I've seen the inside of plenty of teachers' offices.

Like the one I was in now, these offices always came with agonizingly stiff-backed chairs, the faint smell of dismay and musty gym socks, walls painted taupe (even if they didn't start out that color, they somehow always managed to fade to it), and posters meant either to warn or encourage.

Oberlin had opted for the warning variety.

To the left of the room's only window was a reminder that 'Not Every Witch is to be Trusted,' featuring the snarling, green face of the Wicked Witch from *The Wizard of Oz*. To the window's right, you had a mugshot of a vampire of the non-sparkly variety stamped with 'Tolerate But Never Forget' in deep red boldface. Flanking the ornately framed diploma behind Oberlin's desk were two more mood-boosting pieces of wall art. One, an image of a headstone carved with the words 'Magic Meth is Death.' The other, a red placard stating 'Keep Calm and Carry On… With Handcuffs, Warrants, and Backup.'

I twirled my finger, changing that particular placard to read 'Keep Calm and Hug a Cat.'

Unable to tame my curiosity, I turned the frame perched on the corner of Oberlin's desk to see a photo of him, his wife, and Rosaria's new mayor, Matilda Marheart. Oberlin looked so displeased to be standing next to her, I considered what I could do to liven up his portrait. Surely a toothy grin complete with walrus tusks wouldn't go amiss.

The door's latch clicked. I hurriedly returned the frame to its place and jerked back in my seat. My spine went rigid, driving the rails of the chair into several vertebrae.

Oberlin marched over to stand behind his desk. He didn't bother to sit. Speaking from experience, this is never a good sign.

After giving me a hard stare that was probably meant to be intimidating, he flipped open the file he'd carried in.

"Miss Black, you were caught cheating on a test. Do you have anything to say for yourself?"

I considered reminding him about the evil wizard I'd defeated, of telling him I'd recently faced more harrowing events in a handful of weeks than he probably had in his entire career, of insisting that his training was merely a formality I had to endure to get my badge and officially join HQ's Magic Detective Squad.

But I didn't. Because even though I had a good reason for doing so, I *had* cheated.

"No, sir," I said stiffly.

"And to think you came highly recommended."

That's right, I did. See evil wizard comment above. Did I

mention I also helped save the world? I mean, really, that alone deserves—

Oh, sorry, he's not done scolding me.

"Which is why I put up with so much from you these past weeks. But cheating will not be tolerated."

Should I have explained? Should I have told him the truth? No, that would only drag more than just me into this office. And it would still be considered cheating. Besides, I could handle the punishment. How bad could it be? A failed class? A fine? A delay in graduation? I was Cassie Black. I had a medal from HQ for my service to Magics and Norms alike. This walking walrus couldn't possibly—

"—I'm dismissing you."

Wait. What?

"Sorry?" I asked, meaning for him to repeat himself.

"It's too late for apologies, Miss Black. I have no choice but to kick you out of the Academy. And don't think your little friends at HeadQuarters can pull strings this time. My decision is final. Regardless of recommendations.

"You may collect your things from your locker. After that, you will not be welcome back into this building." He eyed me levelly, a slight smirk underneath his brushy mustache. "Not as a student, anyway. Farewell, Miss Black. You will not be missed."

Oh, I would be.

Especially the next time he handed out a pop quiz, unit test, or weekly exam.

* * *

With my satchel full of the few items I'd had in my locker, I exited the Academy's main doors and trudged down the entry stairs.

Even though the whole building is referred to as *The Academy*, it's only the top floor that's dedicated to education. The other two floors serve as the police station for MagicLand — my name for Rosaria, the "other" side of Portland. A side accessed through enchanted doors, closets, and mail slots. A side the magically challenged (aka "Norms") are completely unaware of.

I was nearly to the pavement when I was half blinded by a flash, causing me to stumble down the last step. Another flash pierced through my eyelids as I righted myself, but by the time the bright floaty things cleared from my vision, the photo snapper was loping down the street.

Six foot, slim build, dark hair, human-shaped, my Academy-trained brain rattled off.

I considered a Stunning Spell, but throwing attack spells on the street without just cause is illegal, and I figured, just this once, I should avoid falling under the ire of Inspector Oberlin twice in less than an hour.

Instead, I headed in the opposite direction with no idea of what to do or where to go. It took exactly twenty-three paces for the shock of realization to stop me in my tracks.

I'd been kicked out.

I wouldn't graduate.

I wouldn't become a detective.

What Oberlin had said was true. I had come highly recommended, as had Tobey Tenpenny, who's not only a pain in the backside but also my cousin to some degree I still wasn't able to sort out.

After defeating the Mauvais (that would be the evil wizard mentioned above) Tobey and I were on the road to becoming future detectives who would eventually serve Magic HQ under Busby Tenpenny — former dead guy, Tobey's grandfather, and my uncle, again to a degree my genealogically challenged neurons struggle to untangle.

Following the whole Mauvais thing, Busby had spent a month mentoring me and Tobey, putting us through our paces to get us up to speed on legal procedure, magic police tactics, and all manner of sleuthing stuff. I thought that was it. That once he deemed us trained up, we'd get a certificate and a badge and be sent on our crime-solving ways.

I know, what kind of delusional dust had I been snorting?

Because one day, Mr T says, "I think you're ready."

I brushed down my Ramones t-shirt and pointed to where he could pin my badge. What would be my first case? Cracking down on illegal flying cat races? Rooting out an underground pixie powder trade? Thwarting a goblin gang's extortion racket?

"Cassie, come along. Inspector Oberlin is waiting," Mr T had said impatiently as he and Tobey headed toward Mr T's garage door — one of the portals that lead from Real Portland to MagicLand.

"Where are we going?" I asked, thinking that perhaps there was a ceremony this Inspector Oberlin conducted for new detectives. Maybe that's when I got my badge?

"I can't believe you don't know," said Tobey in that condescending tone he seems to reserve especially for me.

"Well, excuse me, but I have only known about Magics and all this for, what, three and a half months now?"

"Yeah, but Grandad told us about this next step last week."

He did? Maybe I'd been distracted by doodling my very own badge design.

"Next step?"

According to Tetchy Tobey, Mr T's mentorship had only been to catch us up to Oberlin's current cohort of student recruits. To become an official detective and handle cases for HQ, you had to attend and graduate from the Academy.

Why, you might ask, couldn't HQ simply hire Tobey and me based on our stellar performance at defeating evil? Because Magics, in addition to thriving on gossip and sugary treats, also require a steady diet of paperwork, rules, and bureaucracy.

Oberlin wasn't thrilled about taking on two students who he claimed hadn't done the grunt work of basic training. Even though Mr T reasserted his recommendation and explained the rigorous work he'd already put us through, Oberlin muttered complaints about fairness, entitlement, and bias. But, since Mr Tenpenny is pretty high up at HQ and outranks Oberlin by a mile, guess which two newbies got into the Academy even though the current cohort was nearly two-thirds of the way through their curriculum.

Despite Oberlin's grumbling about privilege, Tobey had quickly become the teacher's pet, while I… well, let's just say I did not. Having a lifetime of experience of withstanding others' vitriol and disdain, I had no trouble ignoring Oberlin's unfair treatment. Besides, I only had to complete a few easy weeks of schooling that would culminate in a final exam, after which I would finally be dubbed Detective Cassie Black.

You know, with a badge and everything.

But since the universe loves using me as the birdie in its badminton game, here I was, standing dumbstruck at the corner of the Academy, booted out and badge-less. And since the Academy pays its students a stipend, I was also out of a paying job.

Not wanting to risk a loitering citation, I lumbered down the block to get away from the building. Two blocks later, I dialed Alastair's number.

"Zeller's Magical Mechanisms," he answered. While he

worked, his attention was always on the mechanical doodads he handcrafted, and he never bothered to check the caller ID.

"Hey, just me."

"Hey, Cass, how's school?" He then cursed. Not at me (I assumed) but at something that was squawking with a mechanical twang. "Hold on a sec." I heard the snap of fingers and the noise immediately stopped. "Sorry. I've been trying to make a rooster timer, but the thing has decided it wants to be a blue jay."

"We all have dreams, I suppose," I said, rather dejectedly, if I'm being honest.

"What's wrong? Oberlin being a jerk today?"

"You could say that. He kicked me out of the Academy."

"He can't do that. You're smart, you're clever, and you're one of the strongest Magics I've ever met." Not having received much of it in my life, I wasn't exactly good with praise, and a big lump of emotion filled my throat at his indignant confidence in me. "Wait, you didn't call him a pregnant walrus again, did you?"

"Not today. I got caught cheating."

"But you were only—"

"I know, but I can't tell him that."

"You're really going to take the full blame for this?"

"Already have. Taking one for the team, I guess."

"That's why I love you. You want to go drown your sorrows at Spellbound?"

Despite the temptation to plop my face into a slice of molten lava cake for the next hour, I didn't want to pull Alastair away from his work. One of us had to keep bringing in a paycheck, right?

"Maybe later. Besides, I've got an appointment with Runa soon."

"How much longer—?" The squawking came again and then the sound of something metal crashing to the floor. "Pablo! Sorry, Cass, your cat has found his way into the workroom again, and he's— No, Pablo, not the wings! Gotta go."

The phone went silent. At least I wasn't the only one getting into trouble today.

CHAPTER TWO
SAMPLES AND SWEEPERS

Propped up on an easel near the door to Dr Runa Dunwiddle's clinic was a sign reminding everyone that it was time to get their annual RetroHex Vaccines. When I stepped into the robin-egg blue interior of the pharmacy that fronted MagicLand's medical clinic, Runa herself was at the cashier's counter taking payment from a tiny, twenty-something Japanese woman with purple streaks in her hair.

The stout doctor, her glasses diving back into the breast pocket of her white lab coat, handed the patient a tube and told her, "Use it twice daily, and the rash will clear up within the week."

The lady, shamefacedly not meeting my eye, scurried out the door, flinching at the ting-a-linging of the bell as she went.

I gave Runa a quizzical look. It was probably rude to want to know what had caused the woman's rash, but her guilty behavior had my morbid curiosity running as out of control as an unleashed labradoodle who's just scented a squirrel. I wasn't sure about doctor-patient confidentiality rules in MagicLand, but if it was something too personal, I was sure Dr Dunwiddle would remain tight-lipped about it.

"Mrs Kawasara," Runa explained. "She meant to conjure a honeysuckle for a trellis in her garden. Problem is, she's new to gardening and doesn't really know what honeysuckle is, so she ended up conjuring a tangle of poison oak instead. I told her, next time, just go to Gorgon's Garden Center and pick up the plant she's after." Runa glanced at her watch. "Why are you early? You're never early."

"I was in the area," I said, the statement rising into a question. Runa crossed her arms over her ample chest and gave me her most out-with-it look. "I have suddenly found myself with some free time."

"Because…?"

"Because I got kicked out of the Academy."

Runa barked a laugh. "I'd have thought you'd be kicked out long before now. Were you—?" Knowing about the adjustments I'd been making during test time, she waggled her fingers. I nodded. "Well, at least you tried."

"I need to do more than try. I need a purpose here. I can't just roam aimlessly around MagicLand being known as nothing more than the Starlings' kid, the person who brought Busby Tenpenny back, the girl who defeated the Mauvais."

"You do realize there are people who would kill for that resume?"

"You know what I mean. I need a profession, a place here, not to mention a paycheck, since Morelli still expects rent every month."

"You really want a job?"

I perked up. Did Runa need an assistant? I didn't have any training in witch doctoring, but I'd be more than willing to learn.

"I know it's not glamorous, but there's this." She pulled a folded sheet of paper from her pocket. "It was stuck to my window this morning."

Once I'd unfolded it, I arched an eyebrow questioningly.

Runa's glasses wiggled out of her pocket to hover an inch in front of her eyes. Her face pinched, and she snatched the scrawled note out of my hand, wadded it up, and threw it in a blue recycle bin.

"Every year I put up with the same handful of idiots claiming the RetroHex Vaccine leaves people unable to perform defense spells. Ridiculous superstition." Runa dug in her pocket again and glanced over what she'd pulled out before handing it to me. "It's a job, and look here," she tapped a finger on the listed requirements, "it uses your skills. So? Ready for your checkup?"

"No," I said, grudgingly slipping the notice into my bag.

"Good. If you started looking forward to these appointments, I'd think something was wrong with you. Go through."

Knowing the routine by now, once in the exam room, I hopped onto the table. I hated this. I thought once I'd been trained, once I'd gotten my magic under control, I'd no longer feel like a freak. But it wouldn't be the first time in my life I'd been wrong.

See, back in the spring, not long after I'd been dragged into the world of Magics, Runa had drained me of most of the magic I hadn't even been aware I possessed. Soon after, I sucked up a whole hunk of power, including some of the evil variety, from an enchanted watch. Not long after that, I was drained again. This time, the job was better done, leaving me running on a completely empty magical tank. But, thanks to people liking me more than I ever expected, my magic had been restored.

Needless to say, this yo-yo dieting isn't something most Magics go through. As such, ever since getting my tank refilled, Runa had been keeping a close eye on my magic levels. Which had all been perfectly stable and quite top-notch, I'm happy to report.

But there was a second reason for Runa's close scrutiny: She was transfusing regular donations of my magic to my parents. Sort of like a magical booster shot to restore the power that the Mauvais had slowly sucked out of them over the two decades he'd held them captive.

"Find anything wrong with me yet?" I asked as Dr D removed the first vial, the test sample, from my arm and attached ten more for donating to my parents.

"You want me to lie?"

"Why start now?" Because Runa, if nothing else, has always been brutally honest with me. Like sledgehammer-to-the-face honest.

Runa sat on a leather-seated wheelie stool and faced me, an agonized grimace on her face. My stomach flipped. She'd found something, hadn't she? Something bad. Very bad.

"Oh, get that worried look off your face," she said as she crossed her left foot over her right knee then began rotating her ankle. "It's these new shoes." She had on a pair of bright white canvas sneakers from a high-end brand. "They might be in style, but they are murder."

"Then why wear them?"

"Olivia gave them to me. She saw an ad for them and told me they'd be perfect for all the walking we'd be doing on our vacation."

This vacation was a trip to the Japanese Harry Potter Land, or whatever they were calling it. As a little getaway after all the trouble with the Mauvais, she and Olivia had recently been to the one in Los Angeles, and they'd had a blast. Especially when they'd delighted a few kids with a version of the Solas Charm that sent rainbow-colored flames shooting from both ends of a fake dragon. Although impressive, hilarious, and in no way harmful to life, limb, or animatronics, the blaze had sent the park employees into a panic-stricken attempt at emergency measures that included spraying fire extinguishers in a way Runa had compared to a Keystone Cops skit.

The two had barely been back a week before they'd booked a trip to another of the Potter-centric theme parks.

"Olivia'd be upset if she thought I didn't like them," Runa said, removing the vials from my arm and lining them up in a rack.

"I think she'd like it less if she knew you were in pain."

"Oh, so now you're doling out relationship advice? Perhaps you should give me the job notice back, since apparently you've undertaken a career as a couple's counselor."

"Then just wear the shoes when Olivia's around. Or why not magic them into a different size?"

"Olivia would know. Sometimes I swear she knows everything," Runa said, her tone disgruntled, but the impish smile on her face spoke volumes about how she really felt. "Now, back to you."

"My shoes are fine. There, we done?" I made to slide off the table. Runa held up a hand, signaling me to sit back down.

"I've been monitoring your parents. The regular infusions have made an improvement, but their cells are being stubbornly leaky, so the magic isn't sticking as well as I'd prefer. It's like a supernatural three steps forward, two steps back kind of thing. Still, the percentage that is sticking is increasing, and since your magic levels seem to be stable, I see no problem with you keeping up with this intense level of donations. It's taking longer than I expected, but I think we're getting there."

Magic, by the way, resides in everyone's cells. Somewhere in the mitochondria, I'm guessing. But only Magics have the ability to access this power. Runa explained to me once that the in-and-out torrent of magic I'd been through was the equivalent of my cells running two ultramarathons back to back. Add to that my donating far more magic than is normally recommended, and I was putting myself at risk for what was essentially magic anemia in my desire to rush my parents back to full health.

"Terrific. So, we're done now?" Again, I made to hop off the table, but the doctor's hand went up once more.

"I'm sure your magic will stay steady, but your cells have experienced something no one has seen before. Which means I still want to do regular tests on you. If nothing else, your results could make for an interesting study."

"And by regular, you mean....?"

"Weekly, at the very least." She twisted around to glance at a calendar on the wall behind her. Several days at the end of the month had the words *Trip with Olivia* written across them. "How about the same time next Wednesday?"

* * *

Once outside, I pulled the sheet Runa had given me from my bag. It certainly wasn't what I'd envisioned doing, but I told myself it would at least be a job. It would be a way to keep the money coming in until I could find something else. I read the notice again.

> *Street sweeper needed. Start immediately.*
> *Must be good at Shoving Charm to push the mess into its rightful place.*

Runa had a point: I certainly was qualified. The Shoving Charm was my go-to trick. It had saved my butt more than once, and it had been the first spell I'd mastered. Well, besides my surprising ability to wake the dead. But that had been pure accident and rarely comes in handy, so I'm not sure if it counts.

I pulled out my phone and dialed the number. A man with a scratchy voice answered.

"I was calling about the street sweeper job."

"Already been filled," he said curtly.

"But you posted a notice at Dr Dunwiddle's just this morning."

"Been filled. Just this morning," he repeated mockingly.

"Can I put my name on a list in case your new hire doesn't work out?"

"Nah, got a stack of applications. Be a good girl and pull that sign down for me, will ya?"

I hung up the phone, wadded up the flyer, and was tempted to throw it into the street for this new hire to tidy up. Instead, I crammed it into my bag, determined to put it in the recycling bin at home. Not out of community spirit, but in the vengeful hope that if I kept the streets of MagicLand clean enough, I might just put this street-sweeping, job-stealing newbie out of a job.

What? I was feeling petty.

I was also feeling the need for some flaky pastry with fruit filling. Or chocolate filling. Maybe one of each. After all, I had to keep up my strength for all these magic transfusions, didn't I?

Deciding it was medically necessary, I turned onto MagicLand's Main Street and headed for Spellbound Patisserie.

CHAPTER THREE
WORKING WITH FRED

As if the universe was finally cutting me some slack, the first thing that caught my attention when I reached Spellbound was the sign hanging in the window.

Okay, if I'm being honest, the first thing that caught my attention was the mouth-watering smell of the apple strudel that must have just come out of the oven, and then I ogled the various forms of delectable desserts in the window. But you know, the sign got my attention eventually.

Help was wanted.

Sure, I didn't have the best track record with the behind-the-scenes area of Spellbound. Really, though, how was I to know a simple potion could cause such a big explosion? But that was in the past. My magic was under control now, and I counted Spellbound's owner, Gwendolyn Morgan, as a friend. A friend who might just cut me a break and give me a job. Granted, the position didn't come with a badge (or did it?), but it would help pay the bills while Mr T checked to see if one of the other magic police academies would take me as a student.

Or maybe I would give up on the detective business altogether. Maybe I, Cassie Black, would find my true calling as a baker. Look how much people loved Gwendolyn, how wholeheartedly they accepted her, what an integral part of MagicLand she was. Perhaps if I learned my way around a commercial oven, Gwendolyn's big mixing thingamajig, and all that other kitchen stuff beyond a fridge and a microwave, I could find my niche in Rosaria.

And no, I don't know why I was so determined to find a job that very day. After all, it was one of those lovely dog days of summer where the sun is playing nicely and warming the air without trying to melt your brain. I could have just kicked back at the park and lost myself in a good book. But this is what I'd done all my life. One job's door would be slammed in my face, and I'd find another one to open as soon as possible. Typically in less than twenty-four hours. Seize the day and all that. Plus, I wanted to go home with good news that would put a roadblock in front of any pity parades Alastair might be planning.

Gwendolyn beamed a smile at me when I entered the bakery's addictively scented interior.

"Cassie, what can I get you?"

I pointed to the sign in the window. "You're hiring?"

Gwendolyn has red cheeks from spending her days in a warm kitchen, pulling delicious things out of hot ovens. But even this deep, ever-present color paled when her eyes darted from me to the sign, then back to me.

"You've not exactly got the best track record in this kitchen."

So I guess she hadn't conveniently forgotten the time I blew up her prep area, which also served as a classroom for her potions lessons.

"Well, no, but I could clean up, tend the register. I wouldn't have to work in the kitchen."

"But that's what I need. A baker's assistant. Barry, the last one, well, he had to leave on account of some distress he couldn't get over. So unless you know anything about dough preparation..." She trailed off in a way that made it clear she really hoped I didn't know my biga from my boules.

I was about to concede that my bread baking skills only extended to toast (which I often burnt), when Gwendolyn quirked her face, put on a look of grim resolution, and told me, "You know what? With your stubborn streak and way with animals, I bet you and Fred will get along. Let's give you a trial run, shall we?"

"Fred?" I was pretty sure the head baker for Gwendolyn was called Guillaume, but maybe this was a nickname.

"Yes, he's usually a darling, but they can get so grumpy in their old age. He bit into poor Barry's wrist. Damaged some important tendons, according to Dr Dunwiddle. I told Barry he could always use a Kneading Charm, but I think the trauma's been too much for him. Apparently, he's so afraid of bread now, he's gone gluten-free."

I hesitated. Fred didn't sound like someone who should be allowed loose in public, let alone to manage underlings. Plus, since learning about the existence of MagicLand, my hands had already been mangled more than once. My desire to work took a back seat as phantom pain tingled from my wrists to my fingertips.

"I don't know," I said, backing away from the counter. "Maybe we should leave bread wrangling to the experts."

"Believe me, I've put ads in the papers of various magic communities, and it's the weirdest thing, but as soon as I tell applicants the job description, they suddenly remember they have gainful employment. Come on, then." She lifted a hinged portion of the counter, hooked her arm in mine, and pulled me into the kitchen.

Memories flooded back. None of them good. What had I been thinking? And clearly, I wasn't the only one recalling the explosion, the unplanned melting of a student, or my many

35

potion failures, because several members of the kitchen staff were already eyeing up the fire extinguishers and emergency exits.

"Everyone, you remember Cassie. She's going to be working with Fred. I hope." Their wary expressions changed far too quickly to looks of commiseration.

"Here you go. All official," Gwendolyn said as she handed me a full-body apron and a white baker's cap before leading me to a door I'd always thought was a housekeeping closet. I now noticed a sign on it with 'Fred's Room' etched in swooping cursive letters. Below this, in heavy block print, were the words 'KEEP OUT'.

Gwendolyn glanced at me. Perhaps seeing the how-can-I-escape look on my face, she smiled weakly and said, "Just a little staff joke. Fred's really a sweetie once you get to know him. Oh, and you'll want these." She passed me a pair of safety goggles and gauntlet gloves better suited to falconry than baking. "Just until you get to know each other. Now, in you pop."

The door opened onto a chef's pantry. Goggles fogging and gloves barely on, I was shoved in, and the door slammed shut behind me.

The pantry was lit by little more than a bare bulb. The shelf-lined walls held various kinds of flour in opaque containers. No one was in the small space, but centered on a wooden counter in a gallon-sized glass jar was a creamy, wet mass. On the side of the jar was a label: *Fred, Best Sourdough Starter in the World*.

Sourdough starter.

From flicking through a few of my dad's cooking magazines, I knew this was little more than a fermented mixture of yeast, water, and flour. I laughed. This whole setup was probably some sort of initiation joke, a little fun with the newbie. I grinned. This was already more my style than the stupid Academy.

On the wall above the counter was a sheet titled 'Fred's Feeding Instructions'. Today was Thursday, which meant Little Freddie got a serving of rye and barley, plus an equal amount of bottled artisan spring water that cost more than a six-pack of my favorite microbrew.

I gave up on the gloves and crammed them into the apron's pockets so I could crack open the bottle and measure out the day's serving of water. As I poured the liquid into the jar, I cooed, "You're very spoiled, aren't you, Fred?"

Something rumbled. And it wasn't a happy rumble like when Pablo hears his bag of Kitty Crunch Cat Treats being opened. No, this was a rumble that sent an instant message of "Run!" to my gut. I watched Fred a moment. The rumbling had stopped. I chided myself for being silly. I'd probably just heard water running through the bakery's pipes.

"Are you going to play nice?" I asked. And yes, somehow I'd gone from receiving honors from HQ to speaking to fermented dough. Oh how the mighty have fallen, right?

As I got the rye flour from the shelf, I checked the sheet again for the amount to weigh out. "Wouldn't want Freddie Poo to get an upset tummy, would we?"

I then noticed a scrawled note at the bottom of the sheet under Saturday's instructions which stated, "Feed flour first, THEN gradually stir in water... if you know what's good for you."

Who knew bakers had such sinister senses of humor? I really was beginning to see myself fitting in here.

I weighed out the rye and was about to grab the barley when the rumbling started again. The rational part of my brain said, *Pipes*, but an image of a hunger-crazed lion flashed through the instinct-driven part of my brain. Instinct won out, and I darted a glance at the jar.

Fred, who had previously occupied only a third of the container's space, now mounded up toward the rim. Carbon dioxide, Rational Brain stubbornly insisted. Just the water stirring up the fermentation process, right?

I hurriedly grabbed the jar with both hands and thumped the base of it on the countertop, hoping to knock the gas out of Fred and make room for the flour, after which I would be hightailing it out of the confined space.

The knocking didn't work. Like poking a stick at an already snarling mastiff, I'd only riled up Fred more. He swelled out of the jar and began glopping his way toward me.

Fred may have been nothing more than flour, yeast, and water, but I swear the mass formed together into something worryingly solid with a well placed horizontal gash that looked far too much like a monster mouth for my taste. Fred lurched toward me. I hurled a handful of rye flour at him. The split opened to reveal teeth. Sharp, tendon-munching teeth.

It was when four glutinous, tentacle-like appendages stretched out toward me that Instinct Brain shouted, "Enough of this," kicked Rational Brain aside, and fully took control of the helm.

I hurled a Stunning Spell at the satanic sourdough.

Faster than you can say *baguette*, Fred went from carnivorous monster to cooked mound. Apparently, Instinct had added some heat to my Stunning Spell. Still, I've seen too many movies where the supposedly dead bad guy grunts his way back to life, so I kept my eyes on Fred (who now smelled amazing, by the way) and my magic at the ready as I unlatched the door and backed out of the room.

Gwendolyn was waiting outside.

"How did it—?" She took a whiff, catching the unmistakable scent of freshly baked Fred. The look on her face reminded me of someone stepping into the garden to find their prize-winning koi being munched on by a raccoon. "What did you do?"

"I— He— I mean, it— I had to defend myself."

I expected snickers from the staff, but they only nodded in solidarity. The guy shaping croissants wore a look of relief.

"But he was over a hundred years old!" cried Gwendolyn. "He was family."

"He was a cantankerous psychopath," said a woman who was squeezing a frosting rosette onto a cupcake. Gwendolyn seemed not to hear her.

"I'm sorry, Cassie, but this really won't work. You and this kitchen are simply two ingredients that don't belong together."

I nodded my agreement and understanding, then pulled off the goggles, cap, and apron and handed them back to her.

I made my way out of the kitchen. Not without a few pats on the back and whispered thank yous, I might add.

Before I left, the clerk tending the counter slipped me a large sack of ginger-molasses cookies on the house.

* * *

My parents were indignant about my dismissal from the Academy. Mr Tenpenny was indignant about my dismissal from the Academy. Alastair, well, he was indignant about it too, but he also wished someone had filmed my adventures with Fred.

Regardless, four days after my meeting with Oberlin, I still had no job, and rent was due in six days, ten hours, and eleven minutes. Yes, Alastair now lived with me, so finances were a little less wobbly, but he relied mainly on commission work for his earnings, and I couldn't rid myself of the pessimistically nagging voice in the back of my head telling me that we were always one cancelled project away from ruin.

It really wasn't that dire, but after barely making it from paycheck to paycheck for most of my life, that voice has very little experience with the power of positive thinking.

For all their tricks and talent, Magics have somehow missed the whole concept of creating a job posting website. Morelli, my landlord, told me this is because Magics can't risk some bored hacker coming across a listing for "Someone who can work independently, types seventy words per minute, and knows their way around a BrainSweeping Charm."

Instead, as you've seen, Magics rely on flyers, signs in windows, and the classified section of the local paper.

Which is why I'd popped out that morning to pick up a copy of the *Rosaria Herald*. By the time I got back, my parents had dropped by. As usually happened when they came over, Alastair had already dragged my dad down to the ground-floor workroom.

"What are you two up to this morning?" I asked as I sat at the table with a bowl of yogurt and a red pen ready to circle all the amazing job opportunities I hoped would be hidden in the newsprint.

Completely failing to fight back a grin, my mom said, "Oh, we just have a little something to show you."

"Something?"

"You're busy," she indicated the paper. "How about we wait until your dad gets back up here with Allie?" My mom, having known Alastair since he was a tween, couldn't get out of the habit of using his childhood nickname. "Tea?" she asked, as she puttered impatiently around the kitchen.

"Sure, thanks," I muttered as my eyes skimmed an article about a Magic having gone missing from the Seattle community, and a plea for anyone with any information to come forward. When my mom placed a mug of dark black tea on the table next to me, I took a sip and turned to the next page, thinking it was the paper's help wanted section.

Instead of an ad for my next career, a picture filled a third of the page. A picture of me. In it, my face was twisted into a grimace as I squinted away from the camera's flash, and my ungainly legs were shooting out at contortionist angles as I stumbled down the Academy's steps.

If I thought the photo was unflattering, it was nothing compared to the accompanying article.

An article that was definitely *not* going to help my job-hunting efforts.

CHAPTER FOUR
THE ROSARIA HERALD

Cassie "Cheater" Black: Scandal Exposed

It's like a bad story we can't seem to escape. As I've brought to your attention a few times over the past several weeks, after more than two decades of Rosaria doing fine without her, Cassie Black has joined our community.

Did anyone ask our opinion in the matter? Did anyone screen her for any previous acts of hooliganism? No, but they should have.

You've heard of her "defeating" the Mauvais (where's the evidence, I say). You've heard of her "rescuing" Simon and Chloe Starling (going against all the rules and advice she had been given by HQ). And you've even heard of her getting fast-tracked into our very own Magic Academy of Detective Sciences, making a mockery of all the effort and hard work the real recruits put in to get there.

We're all supposed to be enamored of her, but can we really trust this interloper?

Because I'm starting to wonder if she's had us under a Confounding Charm all this time.

After all, does a hero, a person who we're told is a

strong and clever Magic, cheat on a simple quiz? No. But that's exactly what the glorious Cassie Black was caught doing only a few days ago, making it abundantly clear she never had what it takes to be in the Academy in the first place.

Thankfully, our own Inspector Oberlin isn't as fooled by Cassie Black as others have been. And we must remember that, from day one, this well-respected head of the Academy and leader of Rosaria's police force protested her joining his elite training program. And he has now been proven correct in his resistance.

After enduring Miss Black's verbal attacks involving words and names no young person should ever use to refer to their betters, Inspector Oberlin caught her cheating right under his nose during what he called "a very basic quiz that even an uneducated Norm could pass." He then showed an impressive amount of restraint by not throwing a Stunning Spell at her to stop her undignified behavior.

Personally, I don't think I'd have had such self control.

You can breathe a sigh of relief, though, residents of Rosaria. Inspector Oberlin has booted Cassie Black from the Academy. While I would enjoy seeing her permanently kicked out of Rosaria, at least we can rest easy knowing that this scoundrel won't play any part in solving crimes, enforcing the law, or playing detective in this community.

Fingers crossed that she takes the hint, leaves Rosaria, and goes back to being a makeup artist to the dead — although, refer to my earlier piece about her illegal, authority-defying behavior in that situation as well.

Face it, folks, Cassie Black has a pattern of cheating and ignoring the basic tenets of society. How much longer can we let this continue? How much longer can we allow a cheat, a scoundrel, a flouter of the rules to wander our streets?

All I can say is that I'm avoiding Cassie Black at all costs.

You might want to do the same.

"Grrrunnghhhh!"

Which, in case you aren't fluent in Frustrated Female-ese, translates to: *What kind of jerk is such a coward that he can't even put his byline on this vicious piece of slander?*

I slapped the paper down on the kitchen table, scaring Pablo so much he jerked out of his nap and tumbled to the floor. But really, he should know better than to be on the table.

My mom stopped her examination of the new paint job Alastair and I had given the kitchen. We couldn't settle on a color, and since changing wall colors was now as simple as a swish and a flick, we'd been trying a different color scheme every week or so. As such, my mom would follow the scent of paint to whichever room had gotten the makeover treatment almost the instant she and my dad emerged from my coat closet.

And no, although I worry about them and prefer to keep them close at hand, I don't store my parents in the closet.

First off, they have their own place in MagicLand — a little townhouse that's quite cozy.

Two, my parents had already vanished once in my life, and any object that spends more than a couple minutes in my closet runs the risk of never being found again.

Despite my repeated attempts to organize the tangle of coats and shoes and other random stuff, that small space remained a mess. I'm convinced it's dedicated its life to being a visual demonstration of the laws of entropy, and I'm sure if I could find some physics students to show it off to, they'd marvel at it. After they tripped over several pairs of secondhand sneakers, of course.

But besides the clutter, my closet also contains the nearest portal from my parents' home in MagicLand to my apartment in Real Portland.

My mom picked up the paper I was scowling at and scanned the article. "Oh, dear. That's not very nice."

Meet Chloe Starling, everyone, Queen of the Understatement.

"No, it's not." I stooped down to pick up a groggy and confused Pablo. He instantly began purring. "Is this even legal?"

"I asked around when the first of these started showing up, and apparently it is if the *Herald* prints them in the opinion section. Here, let me." She sat down at the table with the paper in front of her. "Your dad's better at this than I am, but…" She waved a fragile hand over the article, glanced at it, then gave a nod of approval before pushing it toward me. "Better?"

Pablo curled onto my lap as I read the new headline: *Cassie "Charming" Black, Superstar.*

Using an Ink Shifting Spell to rearrange the printed words, my mom had changed the article's first paragraph into several lines of glowing praise of what a wonderful daughter I was, what a fast learner I was, how amazing I was with magic I didn't even know I had until a few months ago, and how anyone who didn't agree "could go stick a dozen rotten troll toes up their backside."

"Rotten troll toes?" I asked, grinning.

"Best I could do on short notice. Should I have made it clear the toenails hadn't been trimmed in at least six years?" My mom then gave the apartment's front door a perturbed stare. "What is keeping those two? Your dad knows this is important."

"I've warned you about letting them go down there. Alastair's probably showing dad every bolt and bracket he's ever built."

"I do find it strange, though."

"Boys and their toys," I said by way of explanation as Pablo launched himself off my lap and pounced on Fuzzy Mouse.

"No, I mean the articles. They're pretty awful, and you've really done nothing to deserve them. You should be commended by everyone in MagicLand." My mom had quickly adopted the name I'd given the community, preferring it to the overly formal *Rosaria*. "After all, Allie's making mechanical things, even getting commissions for his creations, and no one bats an eye, even though he nearly ruined us all with that watch of his. I know he didn't do it on purpose, but if they're going to harass you just for being here, why not harass him for continuing to build things?"

It was a fair point. One I'd tried not to consider because that way lies resentment. As a tween, Alastair had invented a certain watch as a way to prove his magical and mechanical prowess, and the thing ended up containing unprecedented levels of dark magic within its gears.

Alastair didn't intentionally make the timepiece evil, but his making it did set off a whole string of horrible events, deaths, and near disasters, and yet no one was writing scathing sentences suggesting people smash up his workshop like a bunch of wizardly Luddites.

"They'll be down there all day if we don't fetch them," I said, needing a change of subject.

We headed down the building's interior stairwell. Standing guard outside the workroom was one of Morelli's pair of garden gnomes dressed in his conical red hat and blue trousers, and sporting a chest-length white beard.

This particular one was named Rosencrantz. Or was it Guildenstern? I could never tell. Like all garden gnomes, he worked security by keeping a steadfast and seemingly unmoving eye on his surroundings. The instant he saw us, he gave three quick raps on the door. From inside came a rush of footsteps and a gruff voice hissing, "Hurry, put it away!"

I gave my mom a look, we rolled our eyes, then I feigned to dart past the gnome. He waved a tiny shovel at me, but his attack was thwarted when the tip of his hat flopped over his eyes. With the gnome distracted, my mom whipped open the door, and we barreled in to find Alastair and my dad standing nonchalantly (or so they probably thought) in front of Alastair's worktable.

Pointing dramatically to a screwdriver, my dad asked, "And this does what exactly?"

Morelli, meanwhile, was tapping some flakes of food into a goldfish bowl as he asked, "Do those taste good? Yes, they do."

And just in case you were worried about his mental state, he was directing this baby talk at a goldfish by the name of Gary, not to an empty bowl of water. Although, I doubt sweet talking a miniature carp is any way to prove your sanity.

Also, if you're wondering why Morelli is in Alastair's workroom and not holed up in his apartment watching reruns of *The Beverly Hillbillies*, it's because the two had started plotting soon after Alastair moved in with me. Which I wouldn't normally consider a good thing, but in this case, it worked out for the best.

Alastair's workshop was in his own home when we'd first met. But after he and Morelli got to scheming, they figured Alastair commuting back and forth was silly, so they magically expanded an empty apartment on the ground floor of Morelli's building and turned it into an enviably vast workroom they now shared for their creative endeavors.

For Morelli, this was knitting and crochet. He still churned out variations of the doilies and cushion covers that decorated his own home, but he'd also gotten into kawaii and amigurumi over the past couple of months, which meant his side of the workroom contained piles of colorful, yarn-based body parts that would eventually become irresistibly cute bunnies, frogs, and smiling fruits and vegetables. Judging from the form now taking shape on his worktable, Morelli was nearly done with a dragon with a pink body and half-finished, amethyst-colored wings.

Alastair, on the other hand, spent his time building complex mechanical doodads, such as his animal-shaped timers that waddled, hopped, or crawled around until the time was up. Alastair also did repairs around Rosaria, took commissions, taught a sort of Magic Social Studies to the older kids of MagicLand, and had lately been flaunting his superior time management skills by also taking on part of a research project for Magic HQ.

Now, though, he was holding his hand at an awkward angle with his palm facing something fuzzy on the workbench. And I don't mean *fuzzy* as in a hamster suffering the effects of static electricity. I mean, *fuzzy* as in I could tell something was on the table, but I couldn't make out its shape, size, or form in any way.

My dad then scurried over and flung a sheet over the fuzziness. This was followed by him beaming an innocently bright smile at me.

"Is it time?" he asked.

Alastair, relieved of whatever combination of Shield Charm and Mirage Hex he'd been using, walked over and slipped his hand into mine. A spark of magic flowed through my palm at his touch and I've yet to figure out if that's the effects of love or my innate ability to absorb power from other Magics.

"Past time," my mom told my dad as he gave her a peck on a cheek that was still hollow and bony from the emaciation they'd both been left with after their lengthy leave of absence courtesy of the Mauvais. This time off included loads of fun activities such as starvation, magic draining, and torture, and also explained why my parents still weren't the poster children for healthy living.

But there were signs of improvement: the dark circles under my dad's eyes were gone, and my mom was regaining magical strength by the day. She'd never have been able to manage that Ink Shifting Spell a month ago.

"What's this all about?" I asked.

"Well, we know you've been a little out of sorts since the whole Academy thing—" said my dad.

"If only I'd known you could just kick her out," interjected Morelli as he stuck a meaty finger into Gary's bowl and stroked the fish on its head. "My life would have been so much better."

He was kidding, of course. Well, sort of. In my time as his tenant, I had caused him more than a little trouble. But since he'd been magically bound by a promise to protect me, and since magic promises can't be broken without certain conditions being met, he'd been stuck with me regardless of how late I'd been with the rent or the occasional evil wizard problems I'd invited into the building.

"We just thought a little surprise would cheer you up," said my mom, finishing my dad's interrupted sentence.

I'm not one for surprises. I had more than my share a few months ago when the dead started waking up (my fault), an evil wizard set his sights on me (not my fault), and I'd learned I had far more magic in me than is healthy and had to do something about it before I was turned into a human battery (also not my fault, except for when it was).

But these were my parents, namely my dad, offering up surprises, so I had a good idea of what it involved.

See, the moment my mom and dad had returned to MagicLand, Dr Dunwiddle had advised them to eat as many sweets as possible. Obviously, the extra calories would help pack some fat onto their gaunt frames, but it would also boost the power in their cells, as sugar did for all Magics.

My dad had seized ahold of these doctor's orders more tenaciously than a terrier with a buttercream-covered rat, so any time he mentioned an outing that included 'a little surprise,' I knew we were off to Spellbound Patisserie.

Since a hunk of lemon drizzle cake sounded like just the thing I needed to counteract the mood the article had put me in, I wasn't about to complain.

* * *

Passing through my closet portal put us on a side street at the end of which, if you turn right, you're only a few steps away from Spellbound. In fact, the enticing scent of baked goods was already filling the air before we reached the end of the block. But when I turned right, Alastair tugged at my hand and pulled me to the left.

Okay, so maybe instead of Spellbound's sugary surprises, we were going to the Wandering Wizard Pub for their full English breakfast.

Or maybe *in addition* to Spellbound's sugary surprises. Merlin be praised!

Nope, we were passing the street the Wandering Wizard was on. We also passed Mr Tenpenny's street.

"Are you two lost?" I asked, my tone flippantly teasing to hide my worry. What the Mauvais had done to them had left them babbling idiots who couldn't even remember how to speak or feed themselves. Could residual memory issues crop up now and then? Maybe I shouldn't have let them move into their own home without round-the-clock care.

My mom giggled, and my dad, stifling his own laughter, whispered to her to shush.

"We know exactly where we're headed," he told me.

I looked to Alastair, but he was doing a fair poker face. Was there a new cake shop in town? I felt bad for Gwendolyn, but I was sure Spellbound could handle the competition.

The new place just better have lemon drizzle cake.

Distracted by thoughts of cake, I hadn't been paying attention to where we were going until we turned a corner.

My legs froze.

Alastair tugged on my hand, encouraging me to step forward like an owner tugging on the leash of a dog who's just realized she's being taken to the vet and not to the dog park as promised.

"Come on, Cass," he whispered. "They're really excited to show you this."

I didn't care. Even if this new place was handing out award-winning pastries for free, I wanted nothing to do with it.

Goaded to move only by Alastair's insistence, I staggered forward until I saw where my parents had stopped. I pulled out of Alastair's grip, refusing to get any closer to the very last place in MagicLand I wanted to be.

Seriously, I'd have rather fought naked against a Sumo wrestler who was suffering from a highly contagious skin rash than be anywhere near this street, this shopfront.

CHAPTER FIVE
THE SURPRISE

"Just remember this, when you wake up tomorrow morning and find you can't pull your head from the pillow because I've put a Rooting Hex on your hair," I grumbled, since, as if I wasn't already hating this experience enough, Alastair had stepped behind me and cupped his hands over my eyes.

"Trust me," he whispered, sending a delightful shiver down my back.

With Alastair walking behind me and blocking my vision with his palms, the final stretch was an awkward shuffle. Once we came to a stop, my dad let out a triumphant "Voila!" and Alastair whisked his hands away from my face.

If stunned into speechlessness was the effect everyone was going for, I certainly wasn't disappointing them. I stepped back from the building, my hand throbbing with the memory of what had happened the last time I'd been there.

My parents, glee on their faces, watched me expectantly. Behind them, Alastair silently goaded me to say something.

"This is a joke, right?" I asked.

I instantly hated myself for the question. Clearly, you don't drag someone away from their yogurt, make them walk several blocks while hinting about some wonderful secret the whole way, then rip off the proverbial blindfold with expectant delight if it's a joke.

At least I don't think you do. I have been known for having the social IQ of a three-toed sloth.

"You don't like it?" my mom asked, and if I could have managed it without falling over, I'd have kicked myself at the dismay in her voice.

"It's just... I mean..." I floundered.

The shopfront we were standing in front of was where, not long ago, I'd been stupid enough to overestimate my magical powers — and my own cleverness, if I'm being honest — and ended up fighting the Mauvais. I'd sort of won that battle when he turned tail and ran off, but not before he'd broken my hand into half a million pieces and pummeled my kidneys into mincemeat.

So, to say I was thrilled about this return to Vivian's Boutique, would be like saying there was nothing better in the world than drizzling battery acid into your eyeballs.

"Maybe you should explain," Alastair told my parents as he tried to take my hand. With the bone-crushing grip of the Mauvais still playing on a loop in my mind, I jerked my fingers away. Then, realizing Alastair meant to comfort and support, not smash into smithereens, I slipped my hand back into his.

Which, as it always did, elicited a simpering, lovey-dovey look from my parents.

"We own this building," declared my dad.

Which, as far as surprises go, didn't exactly seem worth all this drama.

"This is yours?" I asked, trying to sound interested, and now desperately craving that slice of lemon drizzle cake.

"Yes. Well, technically, it's your mother's. She inherited it from her parents. The lower level has always been rented out as a shop, but we lived up there," he pointed to the upper story, "with your grandparents for a short time after we had you. Just until we got our own place."

"I lived here?" I asked dumbly.

This was all coming too fast, and if I was the swooning type, I might have dropped to the pavement right then. As far as my memory banks were concerned, my first time in MagicLand had only been this past spring when I stepped through a garage door/portal with Tobey and Mr Tenpenny. But to think I lived and might even have been happy in the very building that held one of my most physically painful memories? That was just Weird with a capital W.

"Only for a few months," said my mom. Turning to my dad with a look of delight, she asked him, "Do you remember our last tenant?"

"The pet shop!" my dad enthused. "Cassie, you loved it. We used to take you here so you could play with the flying iguanas."

"Although your grandfather did once find the nesting place of a razzamatazz rat who must have gotten loose," my mom said regretfully. "Their glitter-laced poo is the worst to clean up. I found an old t-shirt of his that still had sparkly bits on it."

Okay, head very much reeling now. I had been a kid whose parents rented out and whose grandparents lived above a pet shop? I'd played with flying iguanas? If the Mauvais weren't already dead, I'd have killed him for robbing me of that sort of childhood happiness.

"Lola told us the owner died soon after we went missing," my dad said. "Apparently, the shop remained vacant until that Vivian character moved in."

"So, now you're renting it out again?" I asked, still not getting the whole 'surprise' aspect of this outing.

"Not exactly," my mother said, a playful gleam in her eyes.

"You know how HQ is giving us all that backpay from our

time away?" asked my dad. I nodded. "That, and the salary they're giving us now, means we don't need the rent from this place. Of course, I did dream of perhaps convincing Gwendolyn to take it and open up another branch of Spellbound. She could have paid me in pastries." A dreamy and very relatable look filled my dad's face until my mom elbowed him. "But we decided it might have a better use…"

As he trailed off he made an expansive sweep with his arms. This wasn't simply the limb flapping of a wannabe showman. The move, likely some variation of a Shoving Charm, lowered the drop cloth that had been tacked up over the shop's façade.

The out-of-season display of winter wear that had filled the window the last time I'd been here was gone. In its place was a tasteful display that included an artful arrangement of a dozen old Agatha Christie, Sherlock Holmes, and other classic detective novels, an antique fingerprinting kit, several time-yellowed sheets of what looked like secret code scattered around an Enigma machine, and even a deerstalker cap on a hat rack. On the window itself was a stenciled decal of a magnifying glass enlarging the first few letters of the words *Detective Agency*.

"Once you pick out a name," my mom explained, "we can add it to the decal."

"But this was a clothing shop," I said, picturing myself interviewing clients as they sifted through a rack of ironically ugly Christmas sweaters.

"We're aware of what this place was before," my dad said bitterly. "And what happened here with you and a certain someone. But that's been taken care of."

"Oh, let's stop this," my mom said, her face glowing with pleasure. "Go on, step inside. You'll see."

I took a deep breath, pulled my hand out of Alastair's, and opened the door.

Did you hear that? That was my jaw dropping to the wood flooring.

The interior, which had previously contained several clothing racks, a sales counter, and changing rooms in the rear — and which had been an absolute wreck after my little scuffle with the Mauvais — was now a bright and tidy open office space complete with desk, a plush swivel chair, bookshelves (stocked with more mystery novels, I noted), filing cabinets, and, where the changing rooms had once been, was a kitchenette with shelves stocked with cookies and tins of tea.

"You did all this since Oberlin gave me the boot?" I asked.

"We had a little help," my dad said and waggled his fingers in that way we Magics like to do when we're being cheeky. "Lola, Morelli, and Alastair chipped in as well. And, of course, Runa kept an eye on us."

"But why?"

"Because she wanted to monitor our magic levels."

"I mean, why this?" I spread my hands to indicate the office. No. The *agency*.

"Because you got kicked out of the Academy."

"Not usually something that deserves rewarding," I said while Alastair strolled around as if double-checking everything was in its proper place.

"No, but we were talking to Busby about your... well, your early departure from the Academy, and he couldn't believe it. He insisted you were a natural at detecting, finding clues, and all that. Even if you do go about it in unconventional ways, he went on and on about what a great detective you'd make, so we got to thinking..."

"Mr T said all that?" Again, a direct assault with a Stunning Spell could not have knocked me for a larger loop.

"He did, and we agree. After all, you found us when no one

else could," my mom said, lifting her chin with pride. "So, education or not, we think you deserve every chance at sleuthing success. This," she gestured at the office, "is the least we could do to see you on your way to that success."

"So, what are you going to name the place?" my dad prodded.

"DetectiveLand?" I said lamely.

"Might want to work on that," said Alastair.

"Go on, let's see you at work," my mom gushed, pointing to the desk.

Not knowing what I'd done to deserve these people (okay, yes, rescue them from a slow and agonizing death) I stepped around the desk to a leather chair — the fancy executive kind that has wheels and leans back when you want to prop your feet up. With three pairs of eyes on me, I took a seat behind the desk.

Or tried to.

The moment my backside touched the edge of the chair, it rolled away. Unfortunately, I was already on the downward slope. Momentum had me in its grip and there was no time to recover. I fell to the floor with a butt-aching *thump*.

Alastair, used to my clumsy ways, couldn't help but snort a laugh. Which sounds like he's the worst boyfriend in the world, but he knew I could take a fall like a seasoned stuntman. And really, with as many times as I'd tripped my way through our time together, my pratfalls had become the humorous glue of our relationship. He held out a hand as he fought back his giggles.

Before I could accept his offer of help, a flash brightened the room. A couple dark spots floated in my eyes, but I didn't miss a tall, slim figure stalking away from the window and carrying a camera with a lens that looked too expensive not to be a piece of professional kit. I had no doubt that picture would highlight the *Herald's* next anti-Cassie article.

With Alastair holding the chair steady, I climbed into it and rolled up to my desk.

Who needed some stupid diploma from some stupid Academy?

I, Cassie Black, was a detective.

And let's just say there were tears of gratitude, protests of me saying it was too much, and plenty of super sappy hugs. But since that is so un-Cassie-like, let's just skip ahead to the next day.

You know, right before the whole idea of me starting my own detective agency seemed about as smart as licking a light socket.

CHAPTER SIX
THE BUNNY & THE VACUUM

The first full day of my new career as a private detective started out amazing. Alastair had donuts and tea waiting when I woke up, and he'd even fed Pablo, who was quite pleased since Alastair forgets that Pablo only gets half a can of food, not the whole thing.

Even my closet seemed to sense a new beginning as it let me through its portal without a single shoe tripping me up. Feeling confident, sugared up, and ready for my crime-fighting future to begin, I hurried to the agency. And since Pablo kept sneaking into Alastair's workroom and causing trouble anytime I wasn't around to entertain him (Pablo, that is, not Alastair), my cat joined me on my commute.

It took about ten minutes of sitting at my desk before pessimism and reality took hold. I'd always worked for other people. What did I know about running a business? What did I know about luring in clients, writing up contracts, and doing the whole nicey-nice customer service thing? Hell, I didn't even know when garbage day was for this section of MagicLand.

I dropped my forehead onto my desk. Three or four times.

My forehead was just beginning to go numb when the latch on the door clicked.

Heart hammering with hope, I looked up to see a short, dark-skinned woman with fluffy, grey-streaked hair approaching my desk. I instantly went from wanting to wallow in self-doubt to wanting to wrap everyone in a friendly hug.

Pablo trotted out from the kitchenette. At the sight of Lola LeMieux, he dashed over to slink between her stocky legs and gave one of his barking meows that were half greeting and half demand for attention.

"Hello, handsome. I have a vampire costume I think would fit you perfectly," she said, because the one time I'd left town and let Lola cat-sit Pablo, she'd dressed him up in an array of outfits that no self-respecting cat should be proud to wear. Pablo, it turns out, is not self-respecting.

Before I even had a chance to say hello, Lola sat in one of the guest chairs and declared, "I have a case for you. Oh, and I brought you a little agency-warming gift."

She reached into her oversized, brightly colored patchwork bag and pulled out a small paper sack. My mouth instantly began watering. You didn't need a Magic's sense of smell to detect the scent of Lola's swoon-worthy coconut-almond cookies. I thanked her, and to avoid losing the treats to my sugar-addicted father, I locked the bag in my desk drawer.

"Have you picked out a name yet?" she asked, looking around the place. "The window, well, it does look a little empty with just 'detective agency' on it." Before I could answer, Lola added, "Because I was thinking, if you had some business cards, I could hand them out to friends, neighbors."

My jaw nearly thudded onto the desktop. Lola handing out my cards would be a boon. As you just saw above with my uncharacteristic desire to hug everyone, Lola has a unique effect on people. It's her magic. Or, more precisely, her scent.

See, all Magics have a scent. And I don't mean a bad case of

B.O. It's just the way a Magic's power affects the molecules around them.

Alastair, for example, smells of chocolate and raspberries to me; Mr Tenpenny smells of Earl Grey tea; and Runa Dunwiddle emanates a citrusy fragrance. Lola's scent has a warm cumin hint to it. But, due to her being an elf, it also brings along with it a soothing effect, like a tender hug just when you need it most, followed up by a plate of just-from-the-oven chocolate chip cookies.

And that special elven influence meant whoever she gave my cards to would trust her implicitly and wouldn't hesitate to take her recommendation. I might know nothing about running a business, but I did know only an idiot would turn down that kind of marketing.

"The Black Magic Detective Agency," I responded. Lola winced critically. "It's a pun."

"Right, well, if you've already got business cards made up…"

With this new venture being less than a day old, I didn't have any of my own cards. But I did have a half-empty box of old business cards from Wood's Funeral Home in my desk drawer. I'd brought them in yesterday evening along with a few other personal items and supplies. They were cast offs from when Mr Wood had gone on a cleaning spree last winter. Seeing their potential as future bookmarks, rather than tossing them into the recycling bin, I'd kept the cards for myself.

Now, I pulled out a couple dozen of them from the box and, using the same ink-shifting magic that had gotten me kicked out of the Academy, waved my hand over them. The text quickly changed from 'Wood's Funeral Home' with its contact details to 'Black Magic Detective Agency' with my address and phone number. Another brush of my hand altered the lily embossed on the left-hand side into a magnifying glass over a fingerprint.

I handed Lola the stack of cards. She examined them, murmuring the agency's name disapprovingly.

"Well, at least you can change these in the future." She waggled her fingers to clarify her meaning. "Do give the name a think, child. You need to seem professional, especially given those nasty articles in the *Herald*."

Pablo let out a gurgling growl, precisely summing up my feelings about the paper.

"So," I said, ready to build my detecting resume, "a case? What is it? Murder? Blackmail? Kidnapping?"

I had only been joking, but when the warmth drained from Lola's cheeks, I cursed myself for the stupid slip up. Lola was supposed to have been minding me when I'd vanished from MagicLand as a toddler. Even though she'd been cleared of any wrongdoing, and even though it was explained to her that none of it had been her fault, she still blamed herself for me not growing up in the company of other Magics.

"No, nothing like that," replied Lola. "Some hooligan has stolen my vacuum, and I'd like it back."

Because I'm learning a few things about interacting with other people, I did not ask why she would care about a missing vacuum or any cleaning tool for that matter. Still, it was on the tip of my tongue. That's not to imply Lola's a slob. In fact, although her home is full of cozy cushions and homey nicknacks, it is impeccably clean. It's just those cleanliness levels aren't maintained by Lola herself.

"Did you hire a maid service? Maybe they accidentally took it with them."

"You know darn well I do not hire out for any help," she said indignantly.

Which was true. After all, why pay for housekeepers when you had students? See, Lola taught what was essentially a

Magic's version of physical education. She'd arrange for you, her unwitting pupil, to show up to her home for lessons in gaining precise control over your magic. What you soon learned was that these lessons involved hours of using your power to polish floors, dust shelves, put away dishes, and even clean the chimney.

"Then, have you taken on any new students lately?"

"Of course. Every quarter I get at least three new recruits. And with Fiona so busy lately, I've taken on a higher number of students than usual."

"I didn't think the married life would add that much work for her."

"Oh, it's not Busby. She's managing him just fine. But HQ has her researching something, and it's gobbling up her time like your dad gobbles up cookies."

"What sort of something?"

"Research into some historical records. I think with Banna gone, well, she kept so much of our history in her head, now we've got to replace it."

Normally, Magics keep meticulous records, but Lola had a point. With Banna — one of the oldest and most powerful of Magics — gone, the historical knowledge she'd built over the centuries had vanished with her. Alastair was part of this research team, but he hadn't mentioned Fiona was on it as well.

Still, while interesting, HQ's research had nothing to do with my agency's first case.

"Do any of these new students seem especially disgruntled with the, um… *classwork* you give them?" I asked.

"If they are, they shouldn't be. Practical work is very important. Far more useful than background work, that's for sure."

Practical work being the pizazz of magic, the tricks, the spells, the charms and hexes. Background work was the book-learning realm of a Magic's education. Not that the history and cultural aspects of magic aren't important and interesting, but I couldn't agree more with Lola about the practical stuff. I mean, did knowing the legal aspects of magical wills help me fight the Mauvais? No, but a Shoving Charm, perfected in Lola's own living room, sure came in handy.

"Still," I continued, "is there anyone who would, say, rather mix up a potion than magically push a vacuum around?"

"Everyone seems very happy to attend my in-home classes."

"That's because it's you, Lola. You do have a tendency to put even the biggest grump in a better mood."

"Why, thank you," she said and gave her hair a prim little fluff. Pablo then jumped onto the desk, purring as loudly as a poorly tuned lawnmower as he gazed at my guest. Lola obeyed the non-verbal command and scratched him under the chin, then moved her fingers up his jaw to rub the base of his ears. She suddenly dropped her hand and gave a resolute nod.

"Earl," she said, with rarely heard irritation in her voice.

"Earl…?"

"Earl Thorpe. Fifteen-year-old. He's had three lessons with me, and even though he was eager to do whatever chore— I mean, *assignment* I asked of him during our first lesson, the past two classes he's refused to do any work with the vacuum, the mop, or the dust cloth because he said his dad told him that such things are women's work. As if a Shoving Charm has anything to do with whether you've got a dingle dangle or a hoohoo. Earl was more than willing to do the chimney and the windows, though," she added, because she's Lola and will find something good in even the most dreadful of students.

"Let's take a little walk, shall we?" Pablo leapt off my desk and trotted to the door, eager as any Watson to help solve this case.

The Unusual Mayor Marheart

* * *

Lola's street was in a lively Caribbean-themed neighborhood with houses painted in aqua blues, fuchsia pinks, and canary yellows. Smells of rich, spicy food wafted from kitchens, and from inside the house next to Lola's came the sound of someone practicing the steel drums. *Practice* being the key word.

"I do wish they'd move Bunny on to a different instrument," complained Lola. "I'm sure that child's got musical talent in him somewhere, but it's doing a darn good job at hiding itself. As most of the street will agree."

"It's actually Bunny's house I want to visit. Do you think his parents will mind?"

"No," Lola replied, drawing the word out as if I'd just asked a rather odd question, "I wouldn't think so,"

My knock on the door stopped Bunny's practice session. I swear the street gave a collective sigh of relief at the momentary silence, and a few neighbors even dared to open windows that had been firmly shut... likely ever since this Bunny kid took up the drums.

I'd been expecting Bunny to be a child, a teenager at most, but he turned out to be a thirty-something-year-old man. A bright smile lit up his almond-shaped eyes and spread across his broad face.

"Help you?" he asked in a friendly way as he took care to annunciate the words carefully. "Lola!" His long arms reached out and wrapped around Lola.

"Bunny," said Lola after backing out of the hug, "this is my friend Cassie Black."

"Hello, Cassie Black." Bunny reached out to shake my hand, then quickly withdrew after a brief touch. "You absorb. I've never met another absorber before."

"She is, Bunny. She's special like you, and she'd like to ask you a question or two."

"Cool. Then I can get back to my drums."

"Yes, well…" Lola said uncomfortably.

"Bunny," I said, "have you seen anyone at Lola's house when you've been practicing your drums? Or any other time?"

"Lots of people go to Lola's house."

"You have to be specific with Bunny," Lola whispered as Bunny began drumming his fingers on his thigh.

"Right," I began, trying to think how to frame my inquiry. "I know Lola is pretty popular, but did you see anyone at her house when she wasn't home two days ago?"

On the walk over I'd gotten a few more details about the case. Lola had told me the vacuum had gone missing sometime on Sunday. When I blurted out my surprise that she'd noticed its absence, she told me she hadn't. It was only when her first student arrived Monday morning that she realized it was gone.

Bunny scrunched up his face and looked to the sky, searching for an answer. I was tempted to give him the description of my suspect, but even in my limited time at the Academy I'd learned not to lead the witness. Bunny suddenly snapped his fingers, then pointed his index finger at me, thumb up like a kid making an imaginary gun for a game of cops and robbers.

"Earl Thorpe. He went in Lola's front door and he came out a little later."

"Was he carrying anything?"

"A vacuum. So I asked him if he was a sheriff."

"Why would you ask that?"

"That's what he said. It's so obvious, right?" He looked at both of us expectantly. "He had a vacuum. He was going to clean up this town," Bunny said with the drawl of a cowhand in a spaghetti western.

Lame as the joke was, Lola and I couldn't help but chuckle. We thanked Bunny for his help. Before we got to the end of the street, the sharp *ting* and heavy *clang* of poorly played steel drums started up again. Much to the disappointment of the neighbors, who began closing up their windows once more.

* * *

Earl Thorpe's house was located one block over from Lola's street. With an encouraging nod from Lola, I knocked on the scuff-marked door.

"Help ya?" the woman who answered barked at me. I didn't take it personally. This woman had the harried look of someone nearing the end of their tether. The frizzy, home-perm hair sticking out from her headband only added to her frazzled appearance. When she saw who was with me, her curt tone instantly warmed, although it still sounded weary. "Oh, hello, Lola."

"Stella, this is Cassie Black. She's helping me with a little something."

The woman turned her shrewd, blue eyes back to me with a look that told me not to beat about the bush.

"Have you gotten any new household appliances lately?" I asked.

Her thin lips pinched tight as her head shook slowly back and forth. Not in denial, but in frustration.

"I should have known. You want to arrest that son of mine?" she asked hopefully.

"I'm not with the police." And I was pretty sure Inspector Oberlin would laugh me out of the station if I brought in a fifteen-year-old vacuum rustler. "Is the vacuum here, then?"

"It is. Earl told me it was an early Witch's Day present. Of all the terrible gifts he could have come up with, he goes for a vacuum. A *used* vacuum— No, wait. A *stolen* vacuum. Am I right?" I nodded. "Should have gone with my first instinct and walloped him over the head with it. So whose is it?"

"It'd be mine," Lola said, almost apologetically.

"From a neighbor of all things," Mrs Thorpe sighed. "I tell you what, that boy is going to get a nasty surprise come this evening. I still remember my potions. A Pustule Profusion Infusion might be just the thing before he goes out tonight with his buddies. I'll go get your vacuum." Mrs Thorpe fetched the gift and apologized for her son. "You sure you don't want to report him to the police? I could use a break from that kid."

"I'm sure whatever you come up with will be punishment enough," Lola replied.

"Damn right it will be," she grumbled, then apologized once more for her offspring before closing the door and shouting for Earl to get his "butt down here right this instant!"

"You really are quite the detective, Cassie," said Lola as we rolled the vacuum away. Even from the next block we could hear Mrs Thorpe's tirade.

"Well, I don't think Hercule Poirot would be impressed, but I'm glad to have helped."

"You did help. My students will be so happy to see this fellow back," she said, patting the purple vacuum canister. "And now, your fee."

"I don't need payment."

"Girl, that's the biggest lie I've heard since someone told me I had the body of Halle Barry." Lola's a tad on the plump side. "I took the compliment, but told him he might want to see Dr Dunwiddle about an eye exam. Now, your fee…"

"You gave me cookies."

"No, you have a business to launch from the ground up, and I will not allow you to be the stubborn child you have always been. If you're determined to make a go of this career, you must be paid."

From her pocket she extracted two twenty-dollar bills.

"I will not take no for an answer," she said sternly when I started to protest that it was too much. "You earned this. Besides, it's more than worth it. You wouldn't believe how hard it is to find new vacuums that take orders from beginners as readily as this one." Which raised so many questions, I didn't know where to begin. "And don't you worry. I'm going to recommend you to everyone I meet who has a problem to be solved." She patted her purse where she'd stashed the business cards.

A wave of relief washed over me. With Lola's magic having the ability to lull anyone she came near into a sense of agreeable tranquility, I'd have clients lining up around the block in no time.

CHAPTER SEVEN
AGENCY DOLDRUMS

Two Weeks Later...

 I made a lifting motion with my hands, palm up. What small specks of dust were left in the desk drawer floated into the air then scattered to wherever they went when no one was looking. I followed up this textbook-perfect demonstration of a Vacuum Charm with a flawlessly precise Shoving Charm to place, one by one, three dozen paperclips back into the drawer's organizer tray.

 Once the paperclips had been sorted, I glanced to the door again. You know, just in case a client was out there and hadn't yet figured out how the doorknob worked.

 I knew it wasn't the door's fault I hadn't had a client since The Case of the Vanishing Vacuum, but I accusingly narrowed my eyes at it anyway. I also knew from the several times I'd checked it that the door was working fine. Still, best to make sure it hadn't suddenly gotten itself up to any trouble. I mean, this was once the retail premises of my own personal Voldemort. Who knew what anti-Cassie hexes he might have left strewn about the place?

 Plus, checking the door was better than alphabetizing the boxes of cookies in the kitchenette. Again.

I strode over to the door and checked the lock. Nope, not engaged. I turned the knob. Yep, still rotating smoothly. Then, just to be sure, I opened the door to verify that the hinges hadn't suddenly seized up with rust. The entry bell Alastair had made and installed for me chirruped with a songbird's trill as I swung the door fully open.

Pablo adjusted his position on my desk and meowed back at the twittering, while I sighed at the realization that all aspects of the door were perfectly functional.

Perhaps seeing he wasn't needed for a client meet-and-greet, Pablo arched his back into a stretch then flopped onto his side, liquifying as only cats can do. His lanky body now puddled over a poster-sized desk calendar Runa had given me as an agency-warming gift. The same calendar that remained stubbornly empty of any client appointments. The only reminder, written in bright red ink and peeking out from between Pablo's back feet, was my next appointment with Dr Dunwiddle.

I considered Vacuum Charming the three orange hairs Pablo had dropped onto the dark surface of the desk, but then came up with an even better time-killing idea. After all, I'd read about feng shui. What if my pens and pencils were throwing off the whole ready-for-clients vibe of the agency?

I removed my cluster of writing implements from the drawer and rearranged them alphabetically by color: black, blue, green, pink, purple, red. It was when I caught myself pondering if I shouldn't arrange them by their brand names, not their ink color, that I pushed myself away from the desk.

This couldn't go on. My desk— No, the entire agency was the cleanest, most color-coordinated, and most rigorously alphabetized place in all of MagicLand.

Clearly, something besides the position of the potted plants or the angle of my desk lamp needed to change if this agency was going to succeed. And it had to succeed if I was ever going to find my place in this community where everyone seemed to have a calling. Come hell or high wizards, I refused to fail at this endeavor.

Just then, the bell above the door let out a cheep. Pablo perked up and meowed cheerily at the woman who'd just entered.

"Busy?" my mom asked.

"Oh, yes." I swept my arm to indicate the waiting area. "As you can see, I'm overwhelmed with clients. Weird thing is, they all just happen to be invisible."

My mom, after giving me a rueful glance, stepped over to my desk to pet Pablo. I didn't miss the sympathetic look that crossed her face when her gaze landed on my obsessively tidy desk drawer.

"Well, I hope they don't mind waiting, because your father — he'll be on his way shortly — and I might just have a case for you."

"A case? Are you serious?" My heart kicked up from a slow-paced ballad to a high-energy techno-funk beat. I scrambled for my notepad and grabbed a pen from my drawer, ruining my orderly handiwork. Pen poised, I asked, "So, what are the details?"

My mom began to speak, but no sooner had she opened her mouth than my door's bell tweeted. Pablo stood at attention, kneading his feet as his purrs ratcheted up from a gentle rumble to a noise louder than a freight train chugging over poorly laid tracks.

I, however, considered sliding under my desk. Because, if I had to guess, Busby Tenpenny probably hadn't dropped by to give me belly rubs and cat treats.

CHAPTER EIGHT
NOT FOR THE FIRST TIME

"Chloe, you're doing well?" asked Mr Tenpenny, greeting my mom in his smooth as soapstone accent that oozed more British upper class than a diploma from Eton College. Despite the August morning already promising near-record heat for the day, he wore an immaculate three-piece suit. The only nod to Fiona's efforts to get him to dress a little more casually was his waistcoat: deep pink with a subtle paisley pattern that perfectly matched his pocket square.

Before my mom could answer, the agency door whisked open for the third time in less than ten minutes. If this kept up, I'd have to check the hinges again. After all, they weren't used to this much of a workout.

"Hello, Busby," my dad said as he held up a paper bag that was dotted with grease spots. "Care for a fritter? Divination Donuts just put out a fresh batch."

Mr T eyed up the greasy sack. "While that sounds delightful, I'm afraid I'm here on official business." And from the way he said this, I was pretty sure he wasn't here to give me my New Detective of the Year award.

After a few pleasantries, my parents excused themselves and went into the kitchenette. "Am I seeing things," my dad whispered, "or has she arranged the tea bags by country of origin?"

Busby finally turned his attention to me, and although the look on his face was as welcoming as his sharp features could get, there was something in the way he was scrutinizing my desk that made my gut feel heavier than if I'd eaten every one of the grease bombs my dad had just brought.

Mr Tenpenny's gaze shifted to the kitchenette. "Are they doing well? Improving? Runa informs me the magic isn't taking hold as readily as she'd expected."

"They're improving, and I'm still making magic donations." I pointed to the appointment with Dr Dunwiddle marked on my calendar. "I'm sure it's just a matter of time."

"That's good to hear. We could use them fully back on the team, but I wouldn't want to put them under any unnecessary strain. Once they're better, though…" Mr T trailed off, his jaw stiff with tension.

Mr T then examined the office, taking in the jewel-toned walls, gleaming oak floors, and the tidy bookshelves. "It's surprisingly organized," he said, and I just knew he was recalling the state of my apartment when I'd first met him. You know, when I'd sort of accidentally brought him back to life.

"Well, I haven't been here long. Give it time."

"I've no doubt you'll work your haphazard wonders on the place soon enough."

After offering him tea, which he refused, I took a seat behind my desk. Perhaps trying to be on its best behavior for our visitor, the chair made no attempt to roll away.

I clicked my pen, notebook at the ready. "So, have you come about a case? Something I can assist HQ with?" Although desperate for him to say yes, I worked a good deal of flippancy into my questions.

"No, not exactly." Before sitting down, Busby pulled a file folder from an inner pocket of his jacket. Yes, an entire file folder, because, you know, magic. "You've set up a detective agency."

"What gave it away? The big 'Detective Agency' stencil on the front window?"

"That, and information trickling along the grapevine." I was surprised it had taken so long. Gossip amongst Magics usually defies the laws of physics it spreads so fast. "And I need to know if you've had any cases."

"Just one. Two weeks ago," I added, feeling completely stupid that I wasn't an instant success. I'd been recommended for detective training by Busby Tenpenny himself. My parents had revitalized this space because they believed in me. Were they now regretting not just renting it out to a new branch of The Conjurer's Cookie Club?

"That's good. At least you haven't wasted your time."

"Wasted my time on what? Detectives, last I checked, take and solve cases when clients come to them."

More like *if* clients come, in my case.

"No, no, not what I meant. As I've said, I believe this is an excellent career choice. You're inquisitive, clever, and dig your heels in to solve a problem. The trouble is — and this is partially my fault for being distracted with other affairs — you've set up a private detective agency without having obtained the proper license."

"Wouldn't be the first time."

See, when I'd first met Mr Tenpenny, I'd been working at Mr Wood's Funeral Home where it was my job to hang out with dead people and do their makeup for their final show. While this sounds like an extraordinarily fun pastime that should be free for anyone to enjoy, the State of Oregon can be a real killjoy and expects you to have a mortuary license to swish foundation and eyeshadow on the recently deceased.

But because I'd been broke and needed to work, I'd failed to finish the schooling required to get that license. Thankfully, Mr Wood had overlooked this little detail and hired me on the pretense that I was merely filing documents and answering phone calls.

Busby Tenpenny, as I was guessing from the stern way he was watching me, was not going to show such leniency. Magics can be so persnickety, am I right?

"Be that as it may," said Mr T after letting out a long exhale, "such rules can't be skirted when it comes to detecting. You've been in business now for," he flipped open the file and scanned the top sheet, "fourteen days. Which means you should have already completed this application," he pulled a sheet from the file and handed it to me, "and submitted the required documentation. A failure to do so would normally require this place to be shut down."

Okay, right then, I did wish I had a little more control over my monster of a chair, because I would have very much liked to sic it on a certain British gentleman.

"And you couldn't have told me this sooner?" I was no fan of paperwork, but I'd been sitting around bored out of my skull for two weeks. At least filling out a stupid form would have been something to do.

"I must offer my apologies for that. There's been—" He twisted his lips in frustration. "There are some matters going on at HQ that have been stealing my attention. Matters which, if you get your license, we might request your help with. In fact, I would very much like you to get this submitted and approved as soon as possible."

I started to complain, but Mr T held up a hand to stop me. "Again, I am sorry. I knew your parents had been toying with the idea of turning this place over to you, but until yesterday, I was unaware they'd actually done so, and that you'd already been taking on clients."

"Well, not really," I muttered, then asked, "Why didn't my parents know anything about this?"

"The license requirement was only enacted about six months after their disappearance. We didn't like the added bureaucracy, but at that time there were many charlatans luring people in with false hope, scamming those desperate to find their friends and relatives who had gone missing during the Mauvais's most active period. Rules had to be put into place, and I'm afraid your parents haven't been briefed on all the changes. Again, an oversight on my part."

"So you're shutting me down?"

I hate to admit this, especially after my I'm-gonna-make-it bit in the previous chapter, but a tiny piece of me was hoping he was here to do just that. A piece that wanted the easy way out. Because while I might have envisioned clients lining up at my door, the past couple of weeks of Everest-sized boredom were proof that making this business a success was going to be an uphill battle. In blizzard conditions.

"No, I've been assigned to be the case manager for your license process. Not a difficult argument to win since Olivia has other issues to focus on. As it was my fault for not realizing your agency had already opened its doors, you've been granted an exception."

"Exception?" I asked skeptically, because I'd seen how Magics went about official things. Exceptions were rarely better than the problem they were excepting.

"As with any applicant, until you have your license, you won't be allowed to work with any official agencies. But you may continue to take on cases from the general public. In fact, you *will* have to take them on as that is one of the requirements of the application. Which, by the way, is due in six days, today included."

Mr Tenpenny made a flicking motion with his fingers, and License Due Date appeared on my calendar in his precise copperplate handwriting.

"Is this all really necessary?"

"It is indeed. Once you have your license, you will not only be able to take on assignments with and be provided certain protections by HQ, but you'll also be allowed in on more, shall we say, undercover information that we are not at liberty to divulge to unlicensed individuals."

"I know you Magics thrive on making up non-sensical rules, but it seems like if you really wanted to, you could just tell me this information."

Mr T shook his head. "Unfortunately, we can't. Most details for HQ's cases are much like a Confidentiality Spell. You recall how those work, right?"

I did. A Confidentiality Spell was a charm put on a group of people who shared a secret. If any of them divulged the secret to someone not part of the group, the revealer risked having his or her magic permanently extracted.

"A license," Mr T continued, "allows you to be one of the people in on the secret. Believe me when I say it is very much in your best interest to complete this form. Now," he said brightly, signaling the lecture part of the conversation was over, "have you selected a name for the agency so I can add that to your case file?"

Licenses. Forms. Business names. All these silly expectations. I mean, seriously, why did no one appreciate a perfectly organized desk drawer?

"The Black Magic Detective Agency?" I said doubtfully. Yes, I'd had two weeks to think of something better, but boredom had crushed my creativity like a boulder squashing a cartoon coyote.

Mr T's steely grey eyes fixed me with one of those looks. You know, the that's-at-least-fifty-miles-away-from-the-right-answer look you dread getting from teachers, parents, and government officials. Especially government officials.

"I don't think that name sends the right message. What's wrong with simply naming it the Cassie Black Detective Agency?"

I pulled out a copy of the *Herald* from my desk drawer. Dated the day of my grand opening, it featured an article full of scathing comments about my dogged disrespect for the rules, even HQ's rules. At least now I understood what the anonymous author meant.

"This is quite unfair," Mr T stated, scowling at the page.

"It's far from the only one," I told him. "You don't read the *Herald's* opinion pieces?"

"I've avoided the *Herald* ever since they started denouncing the RetroHex vaccine a decade ago," he replied, distaste filling his words. "*The Preternatural Times of London* has far more journalistic integrity."

"Well, the *Herald's* done an excellent job at swaying public opinion. More and more people in this community think I'm a flake or a downright criminal, so I don't think having my name on the door is going to pull people in."

"I'm quite certain people don't think you're a flake." I stared at him. He wasn't the kind of guy to turn a blind eye. Regardless of how busy he was, he and Fiona spent what little free time they had in MagicLand. He had to know what people were saying.

"Mr T—"

"Busby, please. We're family."

"Sorry, but I think you'll always be Mr T to me." He gave the eyebrow version of a shrug, as if to say, *So be it*. "As for being a flake, it's pretty hard to miss the sneers and whispers when I'm out and about."

"Admittedly, there is talk about you in some circles, but I know the real you, and I'm confident you'll prove them wrong." I dropped my attention to my calendar as heat flared into my cheeks at his heartfelt conviction. "But whether you call yourself the Cassie Black Agency or the MagicLand Zoo, it won't matter if you don't turn in this application and submit the proper paperwork to obtain your license."

"So, what does this paperwork entail?" I gave the form a cursory glance. It didn't seem terribly complicated.

"In addition to filling that in, you merely need one of these statements," he moved aside the application form and tapped the sheet underneath, "signed by a single client to show you've completed a case to their satisfaction."

My heart jolted with delight. This was great news. I'd already solved The Case of the Vanishing Vacuum for Lola, and I knew she wouldn't hesitate to throw her signature onto one of these silly forms. I had to say, detective licensing was far easier than mortuary licensing, and I was glad to finally find one MagicLand matter that involved less bureaucracy than Real Portland.

"That's simple. On my first day, I solved Lola's—"

Why did I not like the look on Mr T's face? Oh, that's right, because it was reminding me that optimism is the world's stupidest invention.

"It doesn't work like that," he said.

"Sure it does. Case solved. Client happy. I'll just pop over and have her sign—"

"You have to write up the contract," he turned the sheet over to reveal the outline of a contract on the other side, "beforehand. Then they sign off at the end of the job." I gave him my most intense you've-got-to-be-kidding stare. "Go on," he urged. "Try to fill it out with Lola's case information."

I filled in the form with my details, then Lola's. Under *Case Details*, I began jotting down, *Missing vacuum*. Before I'd even finished the second U, the letters vanished. I tried again, and the pen launched from my grip. Before I could retrieve the pen, the form had gone blank again.

Because I'm more stubborn than a geriatric mule, I put pen to paper once more. The form was done with being subtle. It began shouting, "Solved already! Solved already! Falsified document!" And then it burst into flames. Cold flames, mind you, that affected nothing else other than dusting my desk with ash. A fresh form popped into existence a moment later.

"Fine. I got the point," I said, shoving the file away from me. "New case needed."

"There's also the fee."

Fee? As if flaming forms and ridiculous rules weren't bad enough?

"And this fee is how much?" I asked, imagining, as I'm prone to do, the worst. You know, like several hundred dollars for the privilege of filling in and handing over a piece of paperwork. With no new clients, I was strapped for cash. Lola's forty dollars hadn't gone far, and after all the cleaning and organizing I'd done, I knew there were no thousand-dollar bills hiding amongst the agency's shelves and cabinets. Which is why Mr Tenpenny's next words nearly had me falling out of my seat without any help from my misbehaving chair.

"Twenty dollars."

I was too stunned over the bargain price to reply.

"I'm more than willing to loan you the money." He started to reach into his jacket's inner pocket where I knew he kept a slim stack of cash held together with a money clip Fiona had purchased for him from Alastair's workshop. A specialty item, it had been enchanted to convert any bills it held from dollars to pounds to euros, depending on which Magic community he happened to be visiting.

"Put it away," I said. His empty hand slipped from his jacket as if I'd just coerced him with a Voice Modulation Charm. "I'll do this on my own."

Shaking his head, Mr T said, "Stubborn as ever."

"No, simply trying to prove myself. You can understand that, can't you?"

My guest nodded solemnly. "Indeed, I can. Now, will you have everything you need to get the application in on time?" He glanced at my open desk drawer. "I see you have plenty of pens for filling in the form. As for clients…"

I grimaced. I could scrounge up twenty bucks. I could tick boxes on a form. I could even come up with a pithy business name. But I could not magically force people to hire me. Well, I could, but that sort of thing is frowned upon whether you're Magic or Norm.

In a gentle tone, Mr T added, "There's no shame in asking for help when you need it. As I said, I'm impressed by your skills and would very much like you in on certain matters with HQ."

"Is it to do with the missing Magics I keep reading about?"

"You're not licensed, so unfortunately, I cannot say."

"If that's the case, then why not convince HQ to forget the whole license thing altogether?" I plucked a pen from my drawer. "I can still fill in all these little boxes if it'll make them happy."

"There are rules, Cassie. We must not ignore them."

"You know you're very unappreciative for someone who owes his life to me."

"I also owe my death to you."

Which was technically true. Had I been able to make one final delivery during my brief stint as a bike messenger, Busby

Tenpenny would never have been walloped with an Exploding Heart Charm. Unless, of course, someone got really miffed when he began pestering them about fees and forms and such.

"Sure, but look at you now. Walking, living, breathing, harassing people about applications, and," I said cheekily, "happily hitched to Fiona. All thanks to me."

"I am not 'hitched' to Fiona. We are married, joined together as man and wife. And I am appreciative for this second chance at life, but that doesn't mean the license requirement will disappear. So, what is the status of your caseload?"

From the kitchenette I heard the crinkling of a cookie box's wrapper being torn open.

"Business is booming," I said. Never mind it was the cookie business that would be seeing record profits this quarter.

"Good to hear. But don't get in over your head. Even the highest ranking, most experienced detectives are advised to take on no more than three cases at a time. Oh, and I have a gift. Something no agency should be without." From his jacket pocket he pulled out what looked like a small mint tin.

"Fresh breath?"

Mr T gave me a scolding look and placed the tin behind my desk. He held his hands together, then opened them to the side, then moved them up and down. The tin expanded into a safe about the size of the kitchenette's microwave oven.

"For keeping clients' items and documents secure. Now," he said, brushing down his suit jacket and adjusting his pocket square since it had shifted an entire millimeter off center, "I must be off. And do get that application filled in. Believe me when I say sooner would be better than later."

He held out his hand. I shook it, still surprised to feel warmth in his fingers.

CHAPTER NINE
CRACKING THE CASE

Once Mr Tenpenny had passed out of view, I pushed the papers away and slumped back in my seat.

Of course, now that it was no longer under the scrutiny of a representative from HQ, my chair decided it was time for an impromptu jaunt. It shot straight back, and I was flipped off the slick leather seat like an egg from a non-stick frying pan.

Pablo peered over the edge of the desk, quizzically staring at me on the floor and tilting his head as if to say, "Why, human, whatever will you think of next for my entertainment?"

Concerned voices were raised, cabinets were snapped shut, and my parents emerged from the kitchenette..

My mom hurried around to help me up. Not that her stick-thin arms had much strength in them, but with a simple Lighten the Load Spell, she had me up and on my feet faster than gravity could throw me back down.

"Is it our turn now?" my mom asked. "The case I mentioned, I think it will really help with that little problem Busby spoke to you about."

"Will it?" I perked up, nabbed a blue pen, and grabbed one of the client forms from Busby's file, ready and pathetically eager to delve into my second case. "I mean, please, go ahead. Who's the client? What's happened?"

"You handle this," my dad told her. "I'll be right back." He gave her a quick peck on the cheek, then dashed back into the kitchenette.

"So…" I prodded. Too wary to get back into the Chair from Hell, I perched on the edge of the desk.

"Well," my mom began, slipping into one of the guest chairs in front of my desk. Okay, her desk. Also, her chair. At least the pens were mine. "It's a missing object case, and the client is not only willing to sign off on that silly form, but is more than willing to pay top dollar for your services."

This raised my skeptical hackles. I arched an eyebrow at her, an expression she insisted was an exact imitation of my father. "And why would they pay more than the usual rate?"

"For the honor of being your first official client, of course. Just think about it. One day, you'll be Rosaria's most famous magic detective. Who wouldn't pay to say theirs was the case that earned you your license? Now," she leaned in as if ready to whisper an unconfirmed rumor that had been flying around MagicLand, "I can't say exactly, but I heard a pretty hefty figure being tossed around for the bragging rights."

"So what does this amazing case involve?" I said, as if she wasn't as transparent as a strip of plastic wrap.

"Now, don't be sarcastic. I can be a client as well as anyone else." She plucked the form from my fingers and began filling it out as we spoke.

"And what is it you're missing?"

"A pencil," she replied with breathy seriousness, like she had just asked me to find Amelia Earhart.

"And can you describe this pencil?" I asked, playing her game as she neared the end of the form. "I mean, it must be very valuable for you to hire a detective to find it. Perhaps it's made of gold?"

"No, it's your run-of-the-mill pencil, but it does have a unicorn pattern on the barrel, so it's very meaningful to me."

"Unicorn pattern? You mean like the one you've stuck through your hair?"

Her hand went to the messy bun at the top of her head. Her fingers touched the pencil, then slid it out. With poorly feigned amazement, she examined the unicorns prancing around its shaft.

"You are an absolute marvel. I mean, without any clues, barely a description, you managed to solve this. Miss Marple has nothing on you. Now," she said, flourishing a signature at the bottom of the form, "I am a client and my case has been solved to my satisfaction. Oh, and your fee," she enthused, reaching into a pocket of the cardigan she wore over her dress.

My fingers were itching to take both the form and the cash. The signed contract was tempting, but the pestering voice of my admirer at the *Herald* was bleating something about taking an overly simple case, of cheating the system, of gaining a license through questionable means. I placed my hands firmly in my lap.

"Put it away, Mom. I can do this without your help," I said, with no conviction whatsoever. Two weeks without a single client. Three more disparaging articles in the *Herald* in just the past few days. Dozens of snide looks whenever I walked the streets of MagicLand. None of that added up to success.

My dad stepped out from the kitchenette carrying a platter piled with fritters, maple bars, glazed rings, and cinnamon swirls. As I mentioned, he had taken whole-heatedly to Dr Dunwiddle's pastry prescription, and after spending most mornings at Divination Donuts and most afternoons at Spellbound Patisserie, he had filled in slightly more than my mom had. Still, I'd inherited my lanky frame from him, so he would likely always stay slender, regardless of his attempts to persuade Gwendolyn to introduce a bottomless scone basket for loyal customers.

"Simon, our daughter is a genius." My mom held up the pencil to show him the lost treasure had been recovered. "It's like she was born to this."

"She won't accept the form, though, will she?" he stated as he set the platter on my desk. My mom grumbled that I hadn't. He placed a kiss on the top of her head then grabbed a maple-bacon bar from the top of the donut pile. "Told you she wouldn't fall for it." To me, he explained, "We overheard Busby, and we feel so stupid for not knowing about the license thing before getting you all excited about the detective agency. There's so much that's changed since we've been away. That's the only reason we want to help. We know you'll be great once you get some momentum."

"We're not trying to be patronizing or coddling," my mom added as she picked the crispy bits off a blueberry fritter. "We just want to help. You know that, right?"

"Of course I know that. But I have to do this on my own. If I take handouts, well…" My eyes flicked to the newspaper still on my desk. "You know what people are saying about me getting kicked out of the Academy. That I didn't belong there in the first place."

"Well, they don't know the whole truth, so they should mind their own business," my mom huffed.

"Not knowing the whole story is exactly what people feed on," said my dad. "Although, maybe it is better they don't know about *all* of the names you called Oberlin." Reaching for a sprinkle-coated donut, he chuckled, "Pregnant walrus."

"There's no sense dwelling on that," my mom asserted in a chipper tone as she handed me a cinnamon swirl the size of a small planet. "Now, let's tackle the first step of that application: Have you come up with a name yet?"

I groaned. I was terrible at naming things. If Pablo hadn't already come with a name when I'd rescued him from Mrs Escobar's evil sister, he'd probably still be wandering around being called Kitty.

"I like the sound of Starling, Starling, and Black," said my dad.

"That makes it sound like a law office," I said. "Besides, you two are officially on leave."

Before the Mauvais had snatched them out of my life when I was a toddler, my parents had moved up the police ranks with surprising speed to become two of Mr Tenpenny's top agents. Since returning, their positions with HQ had been reinstated. Sort of. Being understandably concerned for her patients, Dr Dunwiddle refused to allow them to return to active duty until she gave the okay. And even then she advised them to serve only as consultants, insisting it would be ridiculous of HQ to put them in the field again after all they'd endured.

My mom, in a way that seemed very much like my own, rolled her eyes and gave a dismissive shrug. "We'll see about that. Busby said if we regained our strength and could pass the physical tests, he'd consider putting us back to work sooner rather than later."

"In the meantime, though," my dad cut in, possibly seeing my disapproval at this notion, "you need a name for this place for your application."

The stupid application. The stupid forms. And the stupid license. Why couldn't I just detect? Okay, besides the lack of any clients I wasn't related to.

"I don't need a name. I need cases," I said. My mom glanced at her unicorn pencil, then started pushing her form toward me.

It was unbearably tempting, and I know to most normal people such help sounds ideal, but I had to do this on my own.

Call it stubbornness, call it a skewed sense of independence, call it a need to prove myself, but my self-worth wouldn't let my mom and dad sign a form for me like a school kid hoping to go on a field trip.

Still, I didn't want to be tempted.

I took the form from my mom, wadded it up, and sent it flying. While it was still in the air, Pablo sprang from a cardboard box he'd claimed as his own and gave chase to his prey. Once he'd pounced on his victim, he ripped the sheet apart. Who needs a paper shredder when you've got feline claws and fangs, right?

"But we want to. We've missed out on providing you so many things. Bicycles, coloring books, prom dresses. Just let us do this." She started reaching for the file as if to grab a new form to fill out. With cinnamon-sticky fingers and reflexes that were faster than hers, I grabbed Mr T's folder and put it out of her reach.

"First off, I never went to or wanted to go to prom. Second, you don't need to make up for anything." Most of the time this was true. Sometimes, though, I blamed them for the abuse I'd endured at the foster places I'd landed in. But as soon as this line of thinking would pop up, I told myself it wasn't fair. They'd made arrangements for me to be protected if anything happened to them in the line of duty. Things just got sort of mixed up by someone else's good intentions. Unfortunately, this set into motion a curse I'd been saddled with, so I soon became the punching bag for more than one messed up individual. "Besides, you *have* helped. I mean," I gestured around me, "this whole place?"

The agency really was generous, it was more than I could have expected, and I secretly swore to myself that I would start paying them rent as soon as I got the business up and running.

But amongst my detractors in MagicLand the gift of the agency had also become fuel for whispers about me taking handouts, and of not being able to make it on my own in the real world.

The real Magic world, that is.

I wasn't about to take anything more.

"Another cinnamon swirl?" my dad offered, lifting a massive carb bomb from the box.

Okay, maybe I could take a little something more.

I'd eaten all the outer layers of the sweet treat and was just about to dedicate my gooey fingers to the task of unraveling the center swirl, when Pablo meowed and the bell above the door chirruped.

You know, the main door.

Like the one a client might use.

CHAPTER TEN
THE REAL REASON

I stood, ready to greet my customer. Ready to show MagicLand Cassie Black was going to succeed. Ready to—

"Oh, it's just you."

Licking cinnamon and sugar from my fingers, I dropped back onto the edge of my desk. Or tried to. I'd missed the mark and, needless to say, ended up sprawled on the floor. I was beginning to suspect all my office furniture had a grudge against me.

My dad strode over to shake Tobey's hand.

That's right. Tobey Tenpenny. Not a client.

The disappointment almost made me want to stay on the floor and crawl under my desk. Perhaps I could spend the day searching for any hairs Pablo had shed and sorting them by length.

"Donut?" my dad offered, pointing to the now half-empty platter.

"I'm good," Tobey said as he held up the burger he'd been munching on when he'd walked in.

"How's the Academy?"

"Simon," my mom hissed admonishingly while emphatically darting her eyes toward me.

"Oh right," my dad sputtered. "I meant the movie, of course. The *Police Academy* DVD I loaned you? Did you enjoy it?"

"I liked the guy who made funny noises," Tobey replied awkwardly. My dad quizzed him more about the film, even though Tobey responded with only the shortest answers to my father's deep dive into the finer points of the farcical comedy.

Finally, my mom butted in and asked after Daisy. This stirred Tobey out of his hesitant reverie and he barreled on with glee about… well, to be honest, I stopped paying attention at that point since I have no interest in my cousin's love life.

While they were distracted, I hurriedly swapped my desk chair for one of the guest chairs. You know, the ones that had no mind of their own and kept all four legs firmly on the ground. I then scattered a dozen pieces of printer paper across my desk to make it look like I was drowning in work.

"We'll leave you two to it," said my mom, putting a halt to the conversation when my dad tried to launch into a compare-and-contrast speech about the *Airplane* movies. She slipped her arm through my dad's and tugged him out the door.

"Place looks nice," said Tobey, scanning the whole of my office. His mouth full of the bite of burger he'd just taken, he asked, "What's with the printer paper, though?"

"It's…" I floundered "…paperwork. Obviously. Messy desk, busy schedule, as they say."

"They do?" He dropped into the rollie chair from hell, which not only put up with this assault, but practically taunted me with its stability when Tobey rocked back in it. "If you want, I could help you with your cases. It'd be good practice."

I pushed a few pieces of paper into a tidier pile and gave up my ruse.

"That'd be great. If I had any cases."

"None?" Tobey said, leaning forward. And of course the damn chair moved with him like they were a pair of figure skaters who'd trained together for years.

"None. I mean, unless you count the Case of the Purloined Pencil my mom presented to me this morning."

"Tough one?"

"Took at least ten seconds to solve."

"What about the missing Magics the *Herald's* been reporting on? You could see if people need help with that."

"Nice idea, but none of the Magics have vanished from Rosaria. Any chance that crime spree might be popping up here? It'd be great for business."

"We've been asking Oberlin about it." Tobey took the last bite of his burger, tossed the wrapper in my bin, then helped himself to a glazed donut. "You know, whether he thinks the problem might come to Rosaria, and what we'd do about it if it did, but he doesn't want to divert from the syllabus."

"Figures."

Tobey's shoulders hunched. He seemed to suddenly have trouble meeting my eye.

"Look, Cass, I'm sorry about all this. That's why I came by."

"You're sorry?" I scoffed. "It's been two weeks. And don't tell me you didn't drop by because you couldn't get through the throngs of people lining up outside my door."

"I've just been busy. Oberlin's really piling on the homework."

"What's he teaching now? How to polish your badge?"

"Nah, it's a whole unit he's come up with himself on spotting vampires and how to take them into custody safely. It's pretty intense. Plus, I feel awful and figured you'd be furious with me, but Daisy's been pushing me to clear the air with you," he added, almost under his breath. "It's not right you getting kicked out. I should have said something then, but—"

I waved my hand to dismiss his groveling apology. Tobey and I had a more verbal-sparring-tossing-of-insults kind of relationship than a let's-dig-deep-into-our-feelings one.

"What's done is done," I told him, and I even meant it. "If you'd told Oberlin what was really going on, you'd be out of the Academy too. And who knows, I might need a contact on the force if I ever get this shindig up and running."

"You really think I'll graduate? Even without... Well, you know."

"Sure," I said, and I think even lunkheaded Tobey Tenpenny could sense my hesitation.

After all, without me there, I wasn't sure how Tobey was going to make it through the Academy.

Let me explain.

You remember the whole "cheating" thing back in the first chapter that got me booted out of the Academy and doomed my chances of earning a Magic Detective Squad badge? It wasn't me who'd been cheating.

Well, I had been, but I was cheating *for* Tobey Tenpenny, not *from* him.

Because unbeknownst even to Mr T, somewhere between high school graduation and admittance to the Academy, Tobey had developed this thing about test taking. Basically, when he sits down to any exam, it's like his skull has been hit with a Sieve Spell and all the information leaks right out the holes.

It's ridiculous really, because for being such a lunkhead, Tobey really is smart and picks up on things quickly. He's easily trainable. Sort of like a labrador.

If Tobey didn't know his stuff, if he was nothing but another of the many wannabe sleuths in our cohort who couldn't detect a hole in a brick of Swiss cheese, I wouldn't have helped him. In fact, I'd probably have done a little Dance of Superiority.

But Tobey — and please don't tell him I ever said this — well, he does have a talent for sussing out clues, making connections, and, as he demonstrated when he showed up to my showdown with the Mauvais, he's either too brave or too stupid to hesitate going into a nasty situation. He's exactly the kind of guy you want with you when you're hunting down a baddie.

Unless taking a test is the only way to nab your suspect.

It was the weirdest manifestation of a fear of failure I'd ever seen, and if I'd been a psychologist, it would have been a terrific topic for study. In practice and in training situations, he did fine. He could tackle the most rapid-fire series of spells and hexes like someone who'd been whipping up magic his whole life. But when it came to exam questions and quandaries, Tobey choked. His brain simply took the knowledge stored within it and sent it off on holiday.

So, during any written tests, I'd helped him by rearranging the ink molecules on Tobey's test sheet to fix any wrong answers.

Which had been most of them.

Tobey quickly caught on to what I was doing. Like I said, he's not stupid, and it'd be hard for even the worst detective to miss his answer of '1922' for the year the Vampire Tolerance Act was enacted suddenly changing to '1964'.

It was all going so well. Tobey and I were nearly four weeks into our time at the Academy. But even though I was scoring at the top of the class and was eager to prove myself, Inspector Oberlin refused to let go of his boulder-sized grudge against me.

Which made no sense, whatsoever.

After all, Tobey and I had put in the same amount of work with Mr T prior to joining the Academy. We'd both — thanks to pressure from HQ — been squeezed into a cohort that was already well into their curriculum. And Tobey and I both had nearly the same amount of magical experience. In fact, since I'd taught Tobey his first spells, I had the slight advantage when it came to magical expertise.

But whereas Tobey quickly became teacher's pet, I became the one who the Inspector took a disliking to.

Out of nowhere, he'd snidely bring up my failed test at HQ, and I'd bite my tongue to refrain from asking him how he'd fare in a fight against the most powerful of Magics. If I tripped over an untied shoelace, he'd be sure to mention my other mishaps from when I'd first arrived in MagicLand (my once melting a student was his favorite). If I raised my hand to answer a question, he'd say I was showing off. But when I didn't raise my hand, he'd imply I didn't know my stuff and had only gotten in because Mr T had pulled strings with HQ. Which, in a way, was true, so fair point.

It was all ridiculous. I'd gone toe-to-toe with the evilest of evil wizards. I'd found my parents when no other Magic could. I'd helped expose a spy within HQ's very walls. And all that within only a few weeks of discovering I had magical powers lurking in my lanky bones. I deserved to be in the Academy far more than most.

And I know this comes as a surprise, but I had made every effort to rein in the attitude whenever Oberlin threw his unconstructive criticism and snarky comments my way. By the end of each day's classes, my jaw would ache from holding back all the retorts I wanted to shout at him.

But sometimes a verbal volcano's just gotta blow. And blow it did.

In my defense, and as proof of how far I've come with controlling my magic impulses, I could have vented my frustration by remaining silent and hitting him with a Stunning Spell. Which would have been appropriate since he'd lectured us on the Stunning Spell nearly every day I'd been at the Academy.

Granted, the Stunning Spell is an important tool in an officer's magical belt, but it's also a pretty basic spell that, unless you're severely cross-eyed, takes only a few tries to learn how to work and aim properly. I mean, we're not talking about something complex like a BrainSweeping Charm or a Mirage Hex.

And I know I'm prone to exaggerating at times, but I'm not kidding about that time frame. For nearly four weeks, at some point during our class time with him, Inspector Oberlin had spent at least a couple hours droning on about how to focus our minds, how to position our hands, how to direct the spell, how to deflect the spell, and on and on.

If not for guest lecturers filling in while Oberlin tended to his policing duties, I and the rest of my information-starved cohort would have completely missed out on important stuff like magic forensics, evidence gathering, suspect profiling and questioning, and all of the other stuff needed to get a proper detective's education.

So, when I showed up for class one day and Oberlin handed out a forty-page booklet he'd written about the theories and origins of the Stunning Spell... well, I kind of lost it.

My mouth running on autopilot, in front of the entire class, I told him he looked like a pregnant walrus suffering from heatstroke.

And that the walrus would make a better teacher.

I then leapt right from enormous sea mammals to the realms of astrophysics by telling him he could stick his booklet in the nearest black hole.

Insults alone weren't grounds for dismissal. Oh, don't get me wrong, I was reprimanded to within an inch of my life. But no matter how much he'd have liked to, Oberlin couldn't boot me out for speaking my mind.

Cheating, though, that was grounds for instant dismissal, and two days after the walrus incident, the Inspector handed out that fateful pop quiz that I was stupid enough to help Tobey with.

So, I was kicked out. As Inspector Oberlin ruled the roost at the Academy, his word was final. Even Olivia at HQ couldn't persuade him to let me stay, which is saying quite a lot.

And because the universe loves to waggle its flabby hind end at me, the day after I packed my proverbial bags, Tobey had texted me Oberlin's study schedule for the following week. Each day was filled with lectures on magic forensics, evidence gathering, and suspect profiling and questioning.

The whole thing left me bitter. I could have told Oberlin the truth, but what would have been gained by that? Tobey and I would have both been on the chopping block for cheating. And I knew that, even as a little kid who had no magic in his veins, Tobey had dreamt of following in his grandfather's footsteps by moving up the ranks to serve at Magic HQ. I couldn't rip that rug out from under his feet.

"You really don't mind if I stay quiet?" Tobey pulled a piece of paper from my stack. "I mean, I'm willing to—"

"You'd be kicked out and you know it."

Tobey shrugged a shoulder as if in defeated acceptance and began plucking at the edges of the paper.

"Exams are coming up," he said, not looking up from the tattered sheet.

Ah yes, the Exams. To graduate from the Academy and become a badge-carrying member of the Magic Detective Squad, you had to pass the Academy's final Exams. They were tough, they were rigorous, they put you through your paces. And you were only allowed three tries. After that…

"You'll do fine," I said with a broad, encouraging smile. Or at least my best attempt at one. Without me there to nudge those ink molecules, I didn't know how Tobey would manage.

"Sauron's snot-balls," Tobey barked a tension-breaking laugh, "you are the worst liar." He then returned his attention to picking nervously at the paper in front of him. With a grimace, he muttered, "I really don't know if I'm going to make it through them."

"Of course you'll make it. You're a Tenpenny."

"My name is not going to help me pass the Exams."

"Has the walrus given you any tests since I left?"

Tobey shook his head. "Says there's no point. That we know our stuff and the Exams are merely going to be a formality. Tobey kept his eyes focused on the pile of picked-apart paper he was creating. *I suppose if worse came to worst, I could employ him as a paper shredder. Although Pablo had already proven himself capable of that job. And he didn't complain about being paid in Kitty Crunch Cat Treats.* "I was wondering if you might help me." Shifting uncomfortably in his seat, Tobey muttered, "With the Exams, I mean."

"Oberlin's not going to allow me anywhere near the Academy during test time," I said scornfully. "I wouldn't be surprised if he set up a Cassie Blocking Charm for a five-mile radius around the building."

"Not help like that. You know, quiz me, go over things with me, maybe work with me on some of the trickier stuff. That sort of thing. Like how you taught me magic."

I did help teach him magic, and I tried not to feel too smug about it. See, Tobey Tenpenny, although the grandson of Mr Tenpenny and a whole line of super-powered Magics, was an Untrained, meaning someone born without magic who should have been. But thanks to me, he got himself full of magic that Rafi and I taught him how to use.

Unfortunately, practice wasn't what Tobey needed. Like I said, he knew everything inside and out, from hexes to habeas corpus. What he needed was to banish his test anxiety, and I didn't know what, besides months of therapy, could do that.

"I'll try, but—"

"Great!" Tobey said, enthusiastically ignoring my hesitation. "How about tomorrow? I've got a two-hour lunch break." Before I could say anything, the words "Help Tobey @ 12pm to 2pm" appeared on my calendar.

"Sure," I agreed, mainly because I was unsure if I could erase an appointment once it was noted. "It's not like I'll be doing much else."

"Thanks, Cass." No longer needing to take out his nerves on my office supplies, Tobey swept his paper bits into my recycle bin. "I swear, I'll pay you back somehow."

"For the paper?"

"No, for helping me. You're the best. Really." I was about to ask who was this and what had he done with the real Tobey, when his watch beeped. "Gotta go. Lunch break's over."

"Have fun, then. Give Oberlin my love."

CHAPTER ELEVEN
VACATION PLANS

After Tobey left, I dared to move the chair back. It seemed to be behaving, so why not. My ability to forgive was rewarded when I lowered my backside — very slowly, mind you — into the seat and ended up sitting like a normal person whose chair isn't out to get them.

I was just waking my computer up when an alarm started blaring from my calendar. Still unaccustomed to the volume and enthusiasm of enchanted calendars, I startled so hard the chair skittered out from under me like a panicked moose on roller skates.

The alarm stopped, but the calendar didn't and switched over to repeatedly shouting at me how rude it was to be late. I reached up and slapped my hand on the thing to shut it up, wondering if I could exchange the calendar for a less nagging version and my chair for one with a less Vaudevillian sense of humor.

I closed up the office and, with the calendar's insistent voice ringing in my head, zigzagged the couple of blocks between the agency and my appointment.

As I usually did, once I reached Runa's I couldn't help but check out her front window arrangement. Some of the historical medical implements on display looked so downright frightening, even the Head of Torment at a medieval torture chamber might hesitate to use them.

One newly added item caught my eye. A small saw whose label noted that it had once been used to hack off fingers. It would have been gruesome if not for a striking row of jewels running along the midline of its wooden handle. Nothing like being dazzled by sparkly things while your fingers are being slowly sawn off, am I right?

Inside, the waiting room was empty and Runa was nowhere in sight. I was just perusing the greeting card rack when the exam room door clicked open.

"Keep the stitches clean and you'll probably be healed up by morning," Runa was saying to a young man with pale skin. Well, it would have been pale if his left cheekbone hadn't been colored with a wide, purple bruise and at least a dozen blue stitches. "You're sure you don't want me to report—"

"No, it's fine," said Runa's patient. "Just a scuffle. Like you say, I'll be good as new by tomorrow." When he caught sight of me, he said, "Heard you defeated Fred. You deserve a medal."

He nearly chuckled, but then grimaced when the movement pulled at his stitches. I then realized why he was familiar. He worked the overnight shift at Spellbound, getting all the croissants, baguettes, and other breads through their final kneading and shaping so they could be risen and baked as soon as Gwendolyn arrived in the morning.

"I'd rather have a *pain au chocolat*."

"I'll have one waiting for you when you come in next."

With a strained smile, he bid us goodbye, tugged a broad-billed baseball cap over his dark hair, and headed out.

"In here, Black," Runa ordered.

"I didn't do anything," I said, her gruffer than usual tone putting me instantly on the defense.

"It's not you," she grumbled as she shut the exam room's door

I glanced down to her feet. She was wearing the same shoes that had been bothering her a couple weeks ago, but I was pretty sure they looked like they'd been enchanted to at least a size larger than they had been.

"Then what is it?"

"Just— Where to begin? Perhaps this." She slapped a copy of Monday's afternoon edition of the *Herald* down on the exam table beside me. "You're featured in the opinion section. Again. You've even managed to take up more newsprint than that journalist's idiotic thoughts on the RetroHex Vaccine."

"I've almost gotten used to them," I said.

"Well, your parents haven't."

"My parents? They brush these things off even more quickly than I do." Or did they? Were they simply pretending the articles didn't affect them?

"Well, of course they don't believe any of it. They think the sun rises and sets around you." She shook her head at such a ridiculous notion. "But they've been facing… I don't know what you call it. Bullying? Getting picked on? Harassment? Whatever term you want to use, some people in town are causing them trouble and they don't need that. They need to be kept in a calm and happy state for the transfusions to effectively take hold."

"Is that why they're having the slippage? Because of some opinionated idiots who'll believe anything they read in the *Herald*?" I contemplated if I could cast a Wart Hex on the *Herald's* entire staff. Perhaps if I sent it through the building's ventilation ducts—

"I can't see what else it would be. They've been coming in regularly, and Merlin knows they've been pumping a steady stream of sugar into their systems. They even seem happy to be reunited with you, which boggles the mind. The only thing they seem bothered by are the articles. Even if they play it off with you, I can see firsthand it's eating at them." I was about to suggest my Wart Hex idea, but Runa went on, sounding exasperated with everything. "It really is imperative they have as little stress in their lives as possible. Although, with you for a daughter, I don't see that happening." She gave a weak smile to show she was only teasing.

"Can you talk to the *Herald*? Tell them their words are harming your patients?"

"Tried that. The editor, that Leo Flourish guy, went on about freedom of the press, how they weren't forcing anyone to read their papers, and that they weren't responsible for readers' reactions to their articles." She paused, a mischievous grin on her lips. "I hope he enjoys the Leftie-Rightie Curse I put on him."

"What's that?"

"Makes all your shoes fit the wrong foot. Try to put the left one on, it only fits the right. Try to put that same shoe on your right foot, it suddenly becomes the left again. People under it either resort to wearing slippers everywhere or force their feet into the shoes and end up with some really painful blisters."

"Remind me never to get on your bad side."

Runa made a dismissive sound. "You've already been there and survived just fine."

Which made me wonder what hexes I might have had put on me that I'd just taken to be my bad luck or lack of coordination.

"Anyway," she said, "I know there's nothing you can do about the articles, but getting your business up and running would help. People put a weird amount of store in having a purpose in this community. Prove yourself, and you should have an easier time. Your parents as well."

"Prove myself?" I said, full of indignation. "Hello? The evil wizard thing? Does that count for nothing?"

"Cassie, I moved to this community more than thirty years ago, and I still haven't fully sorted out their mindset. That last patient— Never mind. Just do whatever you can to prove the *Herald* wrong as soon as possible, okay?"

Feeling like a heel that my parents were facing flack over my own inability to function in society, I told her I'd try. When I changed the subject to when I should come in next, I noticed the words "Trip with Olivia" on Runa's calendar had been crossed out.

"What happened to your vacation plans?"

Runa got up from her stool, the padded leather seat refilling with air like an inflatable mushroom.

"We had to cancel," Runa replied as she busied herself with the vials she used to collect my samples. "Something's come up and Olivia can't leave."

"Something? What kind of something?" Because, trust me, the way Dr D said *something* didn't make it sound like Olivia had merely forgotten about a family wedding or a magic school reunion she couldn't get out of.

"It's just— It's nothing to worry about."

"That sounds exactly like something to worry about."

Runa turned around with a small vial in one hand and a very large syringe with an even larger needle in the other.

"We can do this the Magic way," she lifted the vial, "or we can do this the Norm way," she said and shoved the syringe toward me. Why had I ever told her I hated needles?

"Magic way. Definitely the Magic way."

The Magic way involved placing a small vial on your skin. Enchanted with a Vampire Charm, the vial then quickly and painlessly withdraws a blood sample without any of that barbaric jabbing and stabbing with pointy implements of torture.

"Then no more questions about what Olivia's working on."

Which only made me want to ask more questions. Until my gaze wandered over to the syringe Runa had placed on the counter. The needle alone had to be at least six inches long. I had a sneaking suspicion it wasn't a real medical tool. Not a modern one, anyway. It was likely just something borrowed from her window display, but best not to test my luck.

"Aren't you upset about the vacation, though?" I asked as Runa continued to put more vials on my arm to stock up for my parents' next transfusion. "You were looking forward to it." After having enjoyed their first visit so much, Runa and Olivia had a goal to visit all the Harry Potter theme parks over the next year.

"Comes with dating someone from HQ, I suppose. It's fine really, it'll give me a chance to get the RetroHex Vaccine clinic up and running a few days early. All done." She removed the final vial from my forearm. "As long as you stay away from any evil objects, everything should stay stable, but knowing your luck…"

I was about to protest that the only evil thing in my life right now was my office chair, when Runa distracted me with a lollipop, ushered me out of the exam room, and called in her next patient who turned out to be a deeply tanned man, taller than me, with a painful number of blistering pustules around his mouth. Still, I don't think those were the reason for the sneer he fixed on me as he shouldered past me.

"Mr Cortez," Runa greeted him curtly as he stepped into the exam room. "Let me guess. Mrs Kawasara confused stinging nettles for lettuce?"

There was a muffled assent, then the door clicked closed and the Silencing Spell Runa put on the exam room for patient confidentiality sealed off any other sound. I was on my way to pick up a bottle of hand lotion when, on one of the waiting area's chairs, I saw a copy of the *Herald*. Possibly left behind by Mr Cortez, it was open to the opinion section.

I was going to ignore it. I have stacks of books at home, and there were all those mysteries lining the shelves back at the agency. I didn't need more reading material, especially not material full of the *Herald's* slander.

But then I saw the picture.

CHAPTER TWELVE
THAT COLOR SUITS YOU

The picture took up more than a quarter of the page and was of me sprawled like an upside-down crab on the floor of the agency. Alastair was just barely in the shot, so it had to be the one taken the day my parents had given me the agency.

The paper was well over a week old, but somehow I'd missed this article — sorry, 'opinion piece' — which was titled: *Would You Trust Your Cases to This Basket Case?*

I wanted to brush it off, telling myself that people would have gotten a laugh out of it. Typical clumsy Cassie, right?

But then I started reading. And I'll just say it wasn't a glowing endorsement of my charm and skills.

There's no need to fully quote it here, but let me just sum up the waste of ink by saying it warned everyone in Rosaria to stay away from the No Name Agency (which had a nice ring to it, if I'm being honest) unless they wanted their cases to be handled by the most incompetent Magic who ever lived.

Which seemed a bit harsh, since I was only incompetent at mixing potions. And at sitting in chairs.

As usual, there was no byline. A wise choice since part of my brain was coming up with some rather vindictive hexes that would shock the beards off the members of the Council on Magic Morality.

The article wrapped up by telling the residents of Rosaria that, if they ever considered using my services, to simply look at the photo. "After all, if she can't even figure out how to use a chair, how will she figure out your most troubling cases?"

This was ridiculous. Opinion piece or not, this was slander that could damage my business.

I glanced again at the date. This had been sent out to all of Rosaria two days after the agency had opened, which meant it probably already *had* damaged my business. I grabbed the paper so Pablo could rip it to shreds, then stormed out of the clinic.

I wasn't exactly sure where the offices of the *Herald* were located, but I'd seen a directory amongst the agency's books when I'd been rearranging them by color. Then by size. I planned to find the address, then march over there and file a formal cease-and-desist complaint. If that didn't work, well... I don't know. I'm sure Olivia or Busby could do something about it, but I didn't want to run to them every time I had a problem or needed a favor.

On my way to Runa's, I'd taken the backstreet shortcut from the agency to the clinic. But I was so flustered by the article, my feet — trained to believe a trip to the doctor was followed up by a trip to Spellbound — turned directly onto Main Street.

Big mistake.

I don't know — and it's probably best I didn't know — what was in the *Herald's* latest edition that had left Runa so furious, but apparently the paper had a large readership.

Because if I thought Mr Cortez's sneer had been bad, it was nothing compared to a whole mid-morning stream of scowling glances, threateningly narrowed eyes, and aggressively thrusting chins from people who had recently been content with completely ignoring me.

"Go back to where you came from," a man grumbled. The

coward must have been using a Ventriloquist Spell to throw his voice, because the only people near me were three women pushing strollers.

"Cheat," came another voice, a feminine one this time.

"Waste of magic."

"Sucking absorber."

It was like the stones in the buildings themselves were hurling insults at me. I dashed down a narrow side street as insults, which were growing increasingly foul, bounced off the shop fronts.

Was this what my parents had been putting up with? Surely they would have had said something to me. Or would they? They already felt guilty for everything I'd endured over the past couple decades of my life, and I could imagine them not wanting to burden me with any other troubles. They wanted my life from here on out to be a land of sunshine, rainbows, and baskets of flying kittens.

A prickling sensation along my neck made me throw a glance over my shoulder. Lumbering toward me was a burly man whose forearms would have made Popeye jealous. Instantly going on the defense, a Stunning Spell hummed with painful intensity at the tips of my fingers.

As I turned to face the guy, I raised my hands, magic buzzing and just waiting to be unleashed. The man stopped, apparently not expecting his prey to fight back. Then, as if to show he wasn't going to back down, he lurched three steps forward to narrow the gap between us.

"We don't like cheats in Rosaria," he said with a threateningly deep voice that rumbled into my belly.

My fingers screamed at me to throw the Stunning Spell.

"I'm no cheat." I shifted to better aim the spell. Or, rather, to aim worse. Take the natural strength of my magic, add some fear and frustration to the fire, and any direct hit risked putting him in a coma.

"A liar too, then? We especially don't like liars." He moved forward, closing in. "Strange you taking up business in this shop. Heard the Mauvais ran this place. Kind of proof you two were in cahoots the whole time."

"If you're going to threaten me, at least get your facts straight. And don't use the word *cahoots*. It makes you sound stupider than you look."

While his barely connected neurons were busy working out what insults to hurl at me next, I extended my hands to deliver the Stunning Spell. He did the same.

Just then, his gaze flicked over my shoulder. A ruse to get me to look? I wasn't sure, but his distraction was my best chance to attack. Suddenly, he dropped his brutish expression, jammed his hands into the pockets of his jeans, and began slouching back the way he'd come.

I'd like to say I halted the spell and would never shoot a man in the back, but when you conjure magic under duress, sometimes you can't contain it. As such, even though my wannabe assailant had turned tail as if pretending he'd just wandered down the wrong street, my spell went flying.

Luckily, like I said, I'd changed my aim so it wouldn't be a direct hit. But I never took trigonometry, so how was I to calculate that he'd be right under that lamppost the very second I unleashed my spell?

The lamppost's hanging basket of geraniums took the brunt of my magical attack. The basket's wire broke off its hook, gravity did its thing, and the potted plant fell straight down. Onto the thug's head. It knocked him out cold, but the scarlet red of the geraniums really was a good color on him.

I didn't need to turn around to know what had sent my friend packing. The cumin scent of her magic had already filled the block. A clear sign Lola LeMieux had been readying her own defensive spell to protect me.

When I did turn, Lola wore a concerned but amused look on her round face. The instant she stepped forward, her special breed of power washed away most of my adrenaline surge and filled me with a sense of warmth, calm, and nostalgia.

It also had me, an evangelist for the non-hugging lifestyle, striding over and sinking into the embrace she'd opened her arms for. I still don't understand how she manages to get me to do that.

"Friend of yours?" Lola asked, tilting her chin toward the thug.

"Oh, yeah, we go way back. Silly game we play where I try to Stun him and he tries to dodge it. We're still crafting the rules, but we think it'd be a great addition to the Magical Sports lineup. Although, he was getting a bit cranky, so maybe a nap will do him good. Here for a social call?" I asked hopefully.

"I've got an appointment at Runa's, but I thought I'd come by to see how the new business is going. Please tell me this isn't how you're luring in customers." She gestured toward my snoring friend.

"Business is… well, it's still open," I said, trying and failing to put any amount of cheer into my words. Lola had taken the edge off my low mood, but she wasn't a miracle worker. "You haven't happened to recommend me to anyone, have you?"

"I most certainly have." Even the most hard-of-hearing person could hear the *but* lingering at the end of that sentence.

"But…" I prompted.

"Well, you know Rosaria. It's so… um, crime-free?" she said, as if grasping for any phrase other than *entirely against you*. "So it's been a little hard to drum up detective work for you. Still, I do know a few people in the Eugene community I could try. I don't think they get the *Herald* there." Just then, something in Lola's purse chimed. "I better get to my appointment. You hang in there, child. I'm sure I'll pop across the right person for you any minute now."

As Lola walked away, she snapped her fingers over Mr Burly, who then began stirring from his geranium reverie. With Lola's magic waking him, he'd likely be in a more tolerant mood, but I wasn't about to linger on the sidewalk to find out.

At the agency, I didn't bother with keys, and instead magicked my lock open. Once inside, I pulled the blind down over the door and shuffled to the kitchenette to drown my sorrows in a box of cookies.

Of course, the box was empty. As was the box of Divination Donuts my dad had brought. Apparently, even the junk food of Rosaria was against me. I leaned against the counter in the kitchenette at a complete loss of what to do next.

CHAPTER THIRTEEN
THE COTSWOLDS

I know it's usually much farther into my stories before I get all whiny and morose, but you try facing vicious newspaper articles, scowling Magics, dangerous thugs, and vengeful chairs, all while watching your desire to prove yourself getting hosed down every time it tries to rise up, then contact me and let me know how rose-tinted your sunglasses still are.

Somehow, I'd worn out my welcome in Rosaria without even trying. I could shrug it off, but I couldn't bear it causing my parents strife that might ruin their chances of fully regaining their magical and physical health.

I wasn't under any delusions and fully realized what I was up against. Thanks to the *Herald*, unless my mom kept 'losing' pencils, there'd be no one hiring me. Which meant I had no chance of getting a detective license. And since I'd burnt my bridges at the Academy, that license was now my only chance of working for HQ.

I couldn't ignore Reality when she was slapping me so brutally in the face. Detecting, while a nice dream, wasn't in the cards for me. But what else was I to do?

As I waited for a cup of English Breakfast to steep, I scrolled through my phone. I'm not exactly one for deleting anything — again, Tidy is not my middle name, even with electronic files. As such, I still had hundreds of old texts. The ones from Lola from my time at the Tower of London brought a grin. Hard not to be cheered up when looking at pictures of your cat in various costumes, from Carmen Miranda to the Easter Bunny.

Once I'd reached the end of those, I switched over to Mr Wood's texts from that same time period. This was when he was learning to crochet and also learning just how high you could stack a bacon, lettuce, and tomato sandwich.

I'd sifted through all his pictures — the last one being a pile of yarn that, I think, was meant to be a strip of bacon — when I saw something that gave me a flicker of hope: A text reminding me I always had a job waiting at Wood's Funeral Home.

I had to force down the gulp of tea I'd taken, a sudden burst of emotion getting in the way of fancy things like swallowing.

I didn't need Magics. I didn't need to put up with ridiculous license requirements, slanderous opinion pieces, or psychotic sourdough. I could go back to Mr Wood's where I was always welcome. I could spend my working days in Real Portland, where I could walk down the street and the only dirty looks I'd get would be when I tripped over someone's dog leash (which happens on a weirdly frequent basis).

Perhaps if I spent less time in MagicLand and stopped trying to run a business here, the unwanted attention would die down, the articles would stop, and my parents could get moving a bit more quickly on their road to recovery.

And I can't say this was the first time the thought of going back to Mr Wood's had occurred to me. The very evening I'd gotten kicked out of the Academy, I'd printed off the application to return to school to finish up my mortuary degree.

Wanting to make the application sound as professional as possible, I'd taken a couple days filling it out. I'd then put it in an envelope, expecting to drop it off at the post office Monday morning. But that had been the day my mom and dad had shown up with their little surprise. With their confidence in me and a sense of needing to show Inspector Walrus Face a thing or two, I hadn't mailed the application.

But I also hadn't thrown it out. The envelope was still on a side table at home, waiting to be sent off.

I shut off the lights and closed up the agency, wondering if it would be for the last time.

* * *

Taking only side streets to avoid my fellow Rosarians, Pablo and I made our way to the portal to my apartment — a door in a nondescript building next to Fiona's house. I stepped through, feeling the slight squeeze of passing from MagicLand into Real Portland. Although, my apartment, the whole building really, now felt more within the boundaries of MagicLand than the Norm side of the city, especially with the recent remodeling and expansion Morelli, Alastair, and I had done.

Expanded only on the inside, that is. From the outside, to Norm eyes, Morelli's building still appeared to be the squat, two-story dump I'd moved into a few years ago.

Pablo dashed ahead of me through the closet's portal and expertly leapt over a pair of Alastair's running shoes. Me, not so much. I managed to step on a lace with one foot, trip over the taut lace with my other foot, and smack my forehead into the closet's doorjamb.

After dabbing my brow with an ice pack, I grabbed the envelope from my pile of paperwork. Then, leaving Pablo slurping down a fresh dish of food, I slipped out the door of Morelli's building into Real Portland.

The Unusual Mayor Marheart

* * *

This is where I'm sure you're expecting me to say how refreshing it was to be back on the non-Magic side of the world, how I felt like I was stepping back into the place where I belonged, how birds were chirping and butterflies were sipping nectar from rainbows.

It wasn't like that.

For one thing, even though I'm still unclear on what realm or spectral plane MagicLand is, I do know we don't have cars there. I mean, that's what portals are for, right? As such, the air is super clean. Plus, since all Magics carry a scent that ranges from juniper berry to ginger, that clean air smells like a high-end candle shop. The near constant output of fresh-baked bread from Spellbound also adds to the olfactory bliss.

The air of Real Portland, however, carries the full-array of human body odors, and the streets are choked with motorcycles, diesel trucks, and minivans that were currently clogging the air with exhaust in the midday traffic. Also, it just happened to be garbage day in the neighborhood, so the sidewalks were lined with bins that smelled fouler than a cursed troll.

As for feeling like I belonged, it felt more like being anonymous. Or invisible. No one looked at me, which was a relief since it meant no one was scowling at me, but neither was anyone tipping their hat and saying hello. The closest I got to someone showing any sign that I existed was when a guy forced me to take a flyer advertising a church service.

Flyer Guy then insisted if I didn't attend, I would be damned to hell. I wanted to ask if there was less traffic in hell, but since he wasn't sneering at me — although, he did look very concerned for my immortal soul — I counted that as a win after the way my day had been going, so I chose not to antagonize him.

And butterflies and rainbows? Well, I spotted a butterfly-shaped rainbow decal on one of the cars stuck in traffic. I guess that's something.

Once to Mr Wood's, though, I did feel like I was coming home. The door gave off its gentle chime, the entry room was still its comforting shade of light blue, and a fresh bouquet of lilies gave off their spicy yet calming scent.

It was all very welcoming. Until a chipper-as-a-cheerleader voice trilled, "Oh my gosh! Hello, Cassie!"

And suddenly the owner of the voice was hugging me like we were besties.

I grunted a hello to Daisy, Tobey's girlfriend and stealer of my job at the funeral home. It's not that I'd forgotten she worked for Mr Wood. I'd just been hoping she'd be out on an errand or up to her elbows in dead bodies.

Daisy had taken over my duties when I'd been called off to face a few potentially deadly tests at HQ. I knew she hadn't quit. In fact, Tobey had told me numerous times how great she and Mr Wood were getting along and how she couldn't imagine working anywhere else. But right then, I couldn't imagine working anywhere else either. And I didn't think there were enough corpses for the two of us.

Which is a sentence I might want to rethink.

I endured the embrace with my arms pinned to my sides. When Daisy finally released my board-stiff body, I smiled. It was the only way to stop from hissing at her like a territorial tomcat. I then asked how business was. After all, if it was doing well, maybe there would be enough corpses for everyone.

"Booming. I was just talking to Nino—" that would be Mr Wood to you and me "—about ordering a new case of foundation. You know, the one that has a selection of shades? But he said to hold off on any purchases."

You could almost hear my lips curling into a grin as wicked as the Grinch's when he concocted his diabolical plan to thwart those overly perky Whos down in Whoville.

"I actually came to see Mr Wood," I told her, in a tone that implied, *And not you*. "Is he in with anyone?"

"Nope, he's all yours. Nino, you've got a guest," she called out.

"Daisy, my dear," said Mr Wood, his voice approaching the door to his office that was located just off the lobby. "I've told you time and again not to shout." His head poked out, then he exclaimed, "Oh my golly, it's Cassie."

My heart grew two sizes that day when I heard the honest joy in Mr Wood's voice and saw the glow of delight on his round face.

And yes, he did say, *Oh my golly*, because Mr Wood doesn't curse. Ever. His worst expletive is *Shucks*. I've yet to figure out how he manages it. Especially when he's seen dead clients wandering around and trying to eat all his bacon.

"Come in, come in. Unless you two have more catching up to do?"

"Well, I was—" began Daisy.

"We're done," I said and slipped past Mr Wood's rotund belly and into his office.

Once he'd joined me, I fought off the urge to drop to my knees in supplication and beg for my job back. I do have some dignity.

"How are you doing?" I asked as he gestured me to take a seat. "Dead people still behaving themselves?"

"I have to admit, they're playing their parts much better lately."

Ugh, why did I bring up the dead rising? That was the whole reason someone else was doing my job. If I hadn't started waking the dead — accidentally, mind you, I would never start the Zombie Apocalypse on purpose — I wouldn't have had to leave Mr Wood in the lurch, and he wouldn't have had to bring in Daisy to help put cosmetics on corpses. (Mr Wood once tried doing the dead's makeup himself. He told me he still has nightmares about the clownish results.)

So, of course, what do I do within seconds of what might have been a joyful reunion and new job opportunity? I remind him of exactly how I nearly destroyed his family business.

"As for me," Mr Wood continued, "I can't believe how good I feel, and I can even still…" He waggled his fingers and a pencil lifted a couple centimeters from his desk blotter.

This was more than a little surprising. Morelli had given Mr Wood repeated hits of magic to speed up the healing of his broken leg. It's not unusual to give Norms a little healing power, but since they're unable to retain magic in their cells, the magic doesn't stick and usually dissipates within a couple hours. It had been over three months since Morelli gave Mr Wood a dose of magic medicine, and although I couldn't figure out why it had stuck, it would explain why Mr Wood was now feeling so spectacular.

"But how are you?" he asked. "I heard you're a private detective now. That sounds exciting."

"It's not." A flash of my organized paperclips came to mind. "And that's actually what I came here to talk to you about."

"I didn't do it." He threw up his hands then started laughing at his own joke. At least he was in a good mood for this awkward request. "Sorry, I'm being silly. You were saying…?"

"I was wondering if I might be able to have my old job back?" Mr Wood started to say something, but I pulled out the envelope. "Look, I'm even preparing to get my license. You wouldn't have to worry about pretending I was just your office assistant."

Mr Wood slid open his desk drawer, and I knew from the apologetic look behind his round-framed glasses that he wasn't going to whip out a hiring contract.

"Sorry," I muttered. "I shouldn't have put you on the spot. I just… well, Daisy said business was doing well, so I thought you might need some more help?" The statement rose into a pleading question by the time I reached the end.

"Business has been good. Really good. So good I've been able to sock away quite a bit of cash."

He then slid a brochure he'd pulled from his drawer toward me. On the front was a white woman in her mid-sixties holding a pair of trekking poles. Behind her was a village street dotted with cottages that were at risk of exceeding the legal limit of cute.

Inside, the brochure detailed the highlights and amenities of a stroll through the Cotswolds, promising that anyone of any fitness level could manage the journey, and that each day would begin with a full English breakfast (read: lots of pork products) and be followed up by dinner in a traditional English pub (where even more pork products would be on the menu. In other words, Mr Wood's dream holiday).

"You're going on vacation?" I asked, hope sneaking back into my voice. Perhaps he didn't need me to swish eyeshadow on the dead. Perhaps he needed me to manage the funeral home while he was away. I then cringed at the thought of dealing with and being sympathetic to grieving people, but at least they wouldn't be scowling at me. Not at first, anyway.

"No, I'm retiring." He then leaned forward and whispered. "I haven't told Daisy yet. She's so enthusiastic about the work, I hate to burst her bubble."

I barely refrained from shouting, *I'd be glad to do it!* Instead, I said, "Retiring? But you just said you were feeling good."

"Exactly. I want to live life while I'm healthy. My father stayed in this office until he could barely move. Two weeks after his retirement, he died. I love my work, Cassie, you know I do, but I've done a lot of thinking since the attack—" that would be a vicious attack on him that was entirely my fault "—and I want to get out there and do things while I'm still relatively young and healthy. I've got my retirement fund, I've got social security kicking in, and I've got an itch to travel."

"Could be a rash. Better get that looked at before you go." I gave him a weak smile. I was happy for him, but this wasn't the news I wanted to hear.

"If it's any consolation, I would have hired you in an instant if I wasn't retiring."

"Thanks, Mr Wood," I said, my voice wavering. But I wasn't about to give up just yet. "Wait, you wouldn't want me to come along? Personal assistant, perhaps? Someone to carry your bags, hold the map?"

"No, no," he chuckled. "The tour will take care of all that. They meet you at Heathrow, your bags are whisked off to each night's stop, and you're under their care every step of the way."

"Sounds nice. And you haven't told Daisy?"

"Suppose I should. You wouldn't mind helping me with that, would you?"

"I'd be delighted." After all, I needed something to boost my mood.

CHAPTER FOURTEEN
GARY THE GOLDFISH

Daisy wasn't upset by the news. Instead, she immediately launched into an ecstatic flurry of planning Mr Wood's retirement party.

"You do realize you'll be out of a job," I reminded her.

"Oh, it's no big deal. Everyone's always offering me positions in their offices, shops, restaurants, and whathaveyous. They say my smile alone would lure in business like nothing else could."

I fought the urge to bang my head against the nearest wall.

* * *

With the casket lid now firmly closed on what I had thought would be a sure career option, I grudgingly accepted I'd need to make a go of this whole detective agency thing. If only I knew how.

On the walk home, I considered drumming up business by stealing objects from a few people, then showing up and offering my sleuthing services to them. Problem was, I think the Little Rascals had already beat me to that ruse. And I suppose it'd be considered illegal and immoral. Details details.

After dodging a few scruffy kids playing kickball in the lot in front of Morelli's building, I slumped up the stairs and into the kitchen, wanting nothing more than to drown my sorrows in carbs and hoppy beverages.

I pulled out some leftovers from the night before and tossed them in the microwave. The buttons beeped as I pressed them, but nothing happened when I pushed the start button. I pressed harder, as you do, opened the door, closed it again, then pressed start once more. Nothing. Then I noticed the clock on the stove was out and recalled the refrigerator light hadn't come on when I'd gone rooting around for my grub.

I shook my head. I wanted to take it as yet another sign the universe was against me, but this had been happening a lot lately. Despite my pestering, Morelli swore the building's electrical system was up-to-date, had passed inspection, and should be shielded from the double dose of magical creativity happening in the workroom below.

I removed the box of leftover drunken noodles from the microwave, zapped it with a Heating Spell, and started eating the thick, four-star spicy noodles as I headed downstairs. I would have rather flopped into an armchair and moped, but it was already turning dusk, I didn't fancy moping in the dark, and I also had no energy to conjure a Solas Charm. Pablo, not wanting to miss out on any noodle handouts, followed after me.

Rosencrantz (or perhaps Guildenstern) was still on duty at the entrance to the workroom. I nodded a greeting. He immediately stood to attention. Even his hat stood straighter.

"Alert! Alert!" he shouted, his Broad Yorkshire accent trilling out as he pounded on the door. He then gave me an apologetic shrug. "Sorry, mum. Orders."

"Orders for what?"

"S'pposed to make sure I alert them if you're coming, aren't I?"

"Because?"

"Can't say, mum. Haven't been privy to that information, have I? Secret stuff, I'd imagine."

I didn't like the sound of this. The electricity was already wonky enough without anyone crafting secret (read: *hazardous*) projects. Then again, maybe I was jumping to conclusions. Maybe the door was being closely guarded because Morelli was knitting himself a full-length tank top and had to keep undressing to try it on for size. The sight of Morelli in his skivvies? I couldn't thank the gnome enough if he was saving me from that.

There came an answering *thump* from the other side of the door.

"Safe to go in, then."

The gnome swept off his pointed hat, snapped his fingers to unlock the door, then ushered me in with a bow.

"Cassie!" Alastair said with delight. Sometimes he reminded me of a puppy who gets crazily excited to see his human, even when that human's barely been gone an hour. And it made me smile every time. Alastair's attention went instantly from me to the orange ball of fur darting across the workroom. "No, Pablo," Alastair scolded, but kindly, like someone reprimanding a baby. "You know you're not allowed in here."

Pablo ignored him and leapt onto Alastair's table, sat in the one spot that was free of metal bits and bobs, and meowed.

"Yes, you're very cute, but no touching anything this time." Alastair scratched Pablo under the chin, then strode over and gave me a peck on the lips.

"Disgusting." The grumbled comment came from Morelli's side of the workroom.

"Sorry, we can't all be satisfied with kissing our pillows," I retorted. "Unless, of course, your pillow has dumped you for something that smells better. Like Pablo's cat box."

"All the chances I had to kick you out. All the chances. Why didn't I take them?" Morelli complained as he set down his crochet needle to sprinkle some flakes into the goldfish bowl on his worktable.

"Because there are desperate raccoons who would have declined to live here before the renovations."

Morelli was about to say something when Alastair cut in, "What are you doing home?"

"Long day. Thankfully, it's nearly over." I pointed to the wall clock as I took a bite of noodles.

"It can't be—" Alastair shot a look at the time, then groaned. "I haven't even gotten to the research HQ needs me to do tonight. Sorry, Cass, I'm probably going to be down here half the night."

"It's fine."

It so wasn't. Even though I didn't think I'd be good company, I could have used someone besides Pablo to vent to.

"Oh, and what's with the guard gnome barring my entrance?" I asked. "Oberlin might disagree, but I'm not a criminal."

"Pablo is," Alastair said. "Stole a cardinal timer I was nearly done with. I just don't know how he keeps getting in."

"Then why keep the gnome twins if they're not doing their job?"

"Because," Morelli said gruffly, "we have projects that we want to protect from your clumsy limbs."

Which was a fair point. I mean, as the *Herald* correctly noted, I couldn't even sit in a chair without causing harm.

My gaze drifted to Morelli's worktable. There were no troll-sized dresses in the works, but I did notice the dragon he'd been working on a couple weeks ago. Fully assembled now, the doe-eyed creature held a red heart between its front paws, and its wings had been treated with a Sparkle Charm.

Morelli saw me looking and moved to stand in front of it. Curious. I'd assumed it was a commission, but could this be a love token to someone? I wondered who the unlucky lady was. Or fellow. I'd never delved into Morelli's love life. And I preferred to keep it that way. Lady or fellow, there are just some images you don't want stuck in your head.

"Well, whatever you're doing," I said, "it's knocked out the upstairs power again."

"I fixed that," Morelli protested.

"No, you did a patchwork job of troll magic on the old fuse box. Which is why it keeps going out every time you two enchant your projects at the same time."

"Goes out when we run the dryer and the stereo at the same time, too," Alastair said with an apologetic grin. "I can fix it, you know. I'm pretty sure a Buffering Spell would do the trick."

"Yeah, but this building is in Real Portland," said Morelli. "There's certain codes that need to be met. I know *some* people in this building don't care about rules and all that, but I gotta keep my nose clean."

So said the guy who, after his 'repair' job, had used a Voice Modulation Charm to convince the county inspector to look past how *not* up-to-code the fuse box was.

"Well, at least one part of you would be clean," I said, unable to resist such low-hanging fruit.

In truth, Morelli really had spruced himself up. Instead of his former threadbare tank tops that were so dingy a mechanic would refuse to use them as clean-up rags, he now wore clean t-shirts with silly sayings or cartoons on them. And there was only that one time he smelled, but that hadn't been his fault. Curses, I'd learned, caused trolls, even half-trolls like Morelli, to emit an odor akin to a fish market's garbage bin during a summer heat wave.

"Look," Alastair said before Morelli and I could continue our verbal game, "I can put together an electrical panel that can handle the magic taking place in here. There's an Insulation Charm Rafi and I have been working on, so the panel won't show any sign of magical tampering."

"You got time for that? Thought you were busy with some commission," Morelli said as Pablo jumped down from the worktable and began nosing around Alastair's supply cabinet.

"I am, but there's a part I can't find."

"A missing part? Need me to locate it for you?" I volunteered. A bit pathetically, if I'm being honest.

"You that desperate for clients, Black?"

"Business could be better, yes," I grumbled before cramming a forkful of noodles into my mouth. Suddenly, thoughts of my day came flooding in. Frustration reddened my nose and prickled at my eyes. I was *not* going to cry in front of Morelli. I'd never hear the end of it.

"Cass, what's up?" asked Alastair. The concern in his voice and his expression made my throat catch.

"Nothing. Just got a chunk of chili pepper," I said, but he quirked his mouth in that way he did when he knew I was lying.

With his eyes goading me to spill the beans, I told him about what Runa had said, about the articles, about my little back alley buddy, and then, since I was on a roll, I whined a little about the license application. Not wanting him to think I was a quitter, I didn't tell him about going to Mr Wood.

"You're supposed to know about magic law and all that civics stuff," I said to Alastair, hating the accusatory note in my voice. "Why didn't you know I needed a license for the agency?"

"It was stupid of me not to have looked into it. I should have the minute Simon and Chloe mentioned their little surprise for you. But the idea came together so quickly after Oberlin kicked you out, then HQ dumped their research request on me, some commissions came in, I still had to finish my current orders, and, well... I sort of figured your parents had taken care of arranging everything you needed to set up shop.

"It's no excuse, but in my defense, you might be the first person in Rosaria to become a detective who hasn't already been a member of the Academy's police force. As for the *Herald*—"

"Circe's stinking cesspit," grunted Morelli, "I don't know how anyone reads that rag." He dipped his finger into the fishbowl to tickle Gary the goldfish's scaly head. "Can't tell you how many times I wanted to throw a Flaming Arrow Curse at their offices lately. The things they said about— Ow!" Morelli yanked his hand away from the bowl and nearly stuck his finger in his mouth before possibly realizing how disgusting sucking a fishwater soaked digit would be. "What the hell, Gary?"

I wasn't aware goldfish had teeth that could pierce troll flesh, but Gary had indeed drawn blood. Morelli grabbed a strip of fabric from his worktable and hastily wrapped it around the injury while shooting a quick glance at the workroom's clock. He then whipped around, scowling at me like I'd missed some hint I was meant to take.

"What?" I asked because Morelli kept staring at me. And rent wasn't even due for another two weeks, two days, and sixteen hours.

"You've upset Gary with your complaints and bad news. Shouldn't you go back upstairs now?"

Before I could respond, there came a knock at the workroom's door. Sorry, let me clarify. The workroom's *other* door. Not the one I'd just come through, but the one that served as a portal to MagicLand.

Pablo trotted over to the door, ready to greet any guest who might have treats in hand. He then stopped, the fur standing up along his spine momentarily before he shook it off and loped back over to me.

Morelli's face, however, had filled with a look of such anticipation that it reminded me of Pablo when I pulled the lid off a can of the fancy cat food (how he knows the difference between that and the cheap stuff is one of the world's unsolved mysteries). My landlord began brushing down his t-shirt (which featured a picture of a smiling, cartoon-style Gary) and smoothing his closely shorn black hair as he strode over to the portal.

"Expecting someone?" I teased.

Before Morelli reached for the doorknob, he shot me a warning glare. I toasted him with my fork, then took a mouthful of noodles.

This time, however, the bite was indeed nothing but one large chunk of chili pepper. Tears sprang to my eyes, my cheeks flared, and I gasped to cool my tongue as Morelli opened the door.

CHAPTER FIFTEEN
A GENIE IN THE WORKROOM

Our guest hesitated at first, until Morelli said, "Come in, Matilda," and stepped aside to usher her in. Even through my chili-induced tears I could see the blush heating up his cheeks. I'd have been laughing if I wasn't about to die from a capsaicin overdose.

I wafted a Cooling Spell over my mouth, paying careful attention not to overdo it and give myself frostbite. A mistake you only make once. Trust me.

Being escorted by Morelli as if she might get lost if he didn't stick close by her side, was Matilda Marheart, Rosaria's newly elected mayor who'd won by a slim margin after a heated campaign.

I hadn't particularly liked her as a candidate. She came off as too cool, too overly confident, like she couldn't be touched. But her opposition, Inspector Oberlin himself, hadn't appealed to me either. And that was before I knew he'd kick me out of the Academy for a little creative test taking.

Oberlin had run a vicious race against Matilda, spreading all kinds of nasty rumors about her background, about what she really stood for, about how far she could be trusted, about how her promise to protect the people of Rosaria was merely a ruse for her to forward her own agenda. What that agenda was, he never did clarify.

Matilda, for her part, had remained aloof and didn't react to the slander, but stories suddenly began popping up around MagicLand about Oberlin having ties to some unsavory characters.

Matilda had been very careful to distance herself from being the source of these tales or promoting their spread. She insisted on running a clean campaign which did indeed center on keeping Rosaria safe from whatever trouble might arise. A pleasantly vague campaign promise that, given the worst threat to MagicLand had been taken care of by me and Tobey, would be easy to keep. But it was a strong enough platform to get her the votes she needed.

The mayor was an attractive woman. Too attractive to be dating Morelli — or whatever was going on there. Taller than the average woman and supermodel slim, she had dark hair cropped into an elegant pixie cut that highlighted her sharp features. Although I'd guess her to be in her early forties, she must have had a high-priced beauty routine because her porcelain skin showed no signs of aging except for some fine lines around her eyes that, rather than age her, merely softened what could have been a stony face.

"Is it done, Genie?" she asked, pulling her phone out of the pocket of her navy blue slacks.

Genie? I mouthed to Alastair, who grinned while giving me an admonishing, don't-tease-the-troll look. Still, I filed away this cutesy twist on Morelli's first name for future mocking.

And in case you've forgotten, trolls, even half-trolls like Eugene Morelli, are named for their hometown. This is handy for the times they get lost and someone needs to point them home. That's not to say trolls are stupid; they simply find themselves geographically challenged if they stray too far beyond their home turf, which is why there are no annals of any great troll explorers on the shelves of your local library.

It was only as Matilda started toward Morelli's worktable that she noticed she had an audience.

"Why, Alastair, I didn't realize you'd be here." Her tone was full of practiced charm, like Alastair's presence made her visit so much better. "And you must be Cassie Black." She strode toward me, arm outstretched, her elegant, long-fingered hand ready to offer up a politician's handshake. "Matilda Marheart, so good to meet you."

"You too," I said, then had no idea what to say or do next. Did you bow to a mayor? Curtsey? Really, I just wanted to finish my noodles while being entertained by the Morelli & Matilda Show.

"Eugene has made me one of his crochet creations. Or, at least, I think he has," she teased, giving him a wink. I snorted a laugh and Alastair pinched my arm.

Morelli stammered out that he had and gestured to the pink dragon on his worktable.

"Oh, it's perfect. He's the spitting image of Caliban," enthused Matilda as she slipped her way over to the worktable, then crouched down to snap what sounded like a hundred photos of the dragon from various angles. When she stood up, she smiled indulgently at me and Alastair. "A little hobby of mine. Although," she raised her phone, "this is a far cry from my usual equipment. Still, it does the trick in a pinch."

"Speaking of," Morelli said, his throat sounding rather parched. He pulled something from a file on his table. "Here's your photo back."

Matilda retrieved the picture and held it up next to Morelli's creation. Now, I know I give my landlord a lot of flack, but he is a dab hand with the crochet needle, and the dragon he'd made really was cute; its too large head and big eyes giving it a puppy-like appearance.

However, the dragon in the photo — with its enormous fangs, lots of teeth, and spiky things protruding from various places — would have made an alligator seem cuddly in comparison. Plus, he was shooting a fireball from his mouth. Oh, and did I mention he had what looked like a mammalian heart clutched in one of his blood-drenched forepaws?

"Caliban?" I asked stupidly. And yes, I was trying to wrap my head around dragons actually being somewhere out there in the world.

"My pet dragon," explained Matilda. "Staying with a foster family until I can find a place for him here. I miss him terribly. He's such a dear. Of course, in this photo, he looks fierce, but he was just playing around, lighting the coals for the grill."

"And the heart?"

"Cally simply can't get enough of cow hearts, so the local butcher always saves them for him. He'd just gotten this one and refused to let go of it even to light the barbecue."

Matilda gushed some more about how perfect the crochet Caliban was, causing Morelli's cheeks to burn almost as brightly as the dragon's flame.

I had just taken a mouthful of noodles (chili-free this time), when Mayor Matilda turned to me. "This is actually very convenient. I was going to stop by your office, but you were closed up for the day."

This time, the five-alarm chili spice had nothing to do with me choking on my noodles.

"You were?" I sputtered.

"Shall we?"

She gestured to the far side of the workroom. For the briefest moment I hoped she might be wanting to hire me. But then her face dropped the glee she'd shown over the dragon and had gone worryingly serious. It was a look that was like a sledgehammer to the knees of my optimism. I mean, how stupid could I be? This was a government representative. She could only want to talk to me about one thing.

"If this is about the detective's license—" I began.

"Oh, fiddlesticks with the license. I've heard of the little mixup. And I know that, while you can't take *official*—" she made air quotes around the word "—cases, you can still take personal ones. Am I right?"

I nodded, and inside my head a veritable Fourth of July fireworks show of delight was going off. Sure, she was only the mayor of a small Magic community, but hers could still be counted as a high-profile case. A chance at publicity. A boon to my burgeoning business. I almost wanted to take her hand and kiss her ring.

Then I realized that not only would kissing some stranger's hand jewelry be weird, unsanitary, and socially unacceptable in this day and age, but she may have only been asking about personal cases in general. Plus, me groveling in gratitude would be like gasoline for Morelli's bonfire of insults.

"Yes, I heard you find things for people," said Matilda.

"I do? I mean, yes, I do." That pounding? That was my heart daring to hope. Or it could have been palpitations from all the chilis.

"That's what a friend of mine told me. Said you were very easy to work with. So, I wonder, might you be able to locate a family heirloom? Just to warn you, it has been missing for some time."

"That's exactly what the, uh—" I faltered, hunting for a name for my business since the Black Magic Detective Agency wasn't winning any opinion polls "—what my agency is all about. If you have time to chat tomorrow, I can get the details."

Because even though the shock that I might actually have a client was settling over me, I wasn't going to repeat the mistake of taking her case without first filling out HQ's damn form.

"That would be fabulous," said Matilda. "How about first thing tomorrow morning?"

"Sounds great." I told her what time I'd be in. Despite the early hour, she agreed to show up soon after. She then went back to collect her dragon. When she tried to pay Morelli for his work, I could have sworn, despite how quietly he tried to whisper the words, that he said she could repay him by going out to dinner with him sometime.

"I'll let you know when I'm free, Genie," Matilda told him.

At this point, even Alastair was having trouble holding back the giggles.

While Morelli escorted the mayor out, Alastair asked, "So, good conversation with Matilda?"

"*Very* good. I think Lola has finally convinced someone to give me a chance. It's only a matter of time before others fall into line, right? This detecting thing might really work. Stupid police don't know what they lost out on."

"A smart-mouthed trainee?" Morelli quipped, as he started arranging skeins for a new project.

"A smart-mouthed trainee who's going to put them out of business."

"I don't think that's how the police work," Alastair said.

"Is Morelli dating the mayor?" I whispered to Alastair when Morelli went over to the cabinet where he kept his knitting supplies.

"I think it's meant to be a secret."

"I might have to question her mental state. I mean, if she's making choices like that, should I be worrying about her competence to sign contracts?"

"Morelli's not that bad, and you know it."

I did know it, I thought as I watched him flicking yarn with practiced speed over his crochet hook. And I owed him more than I'd like to admit. Actually, more than I would ever admit, because he'd lord it over me until the end of time.

"We should celebrate," I said. And while I was craving one of the IPAs in the fridge, I also wanted to air my unease about this case to Alastair. A family heirloom that hadn't been seen in who knows how long? I needed to hear Alastair tell me my fears were unfounded. And maybe for him to reveal he knew exactly where the Marhearts kept all their family goodies. A girl can dream, right?

"Can't. Sorry, but I've got to get the electricity sorted, I need to get this last batch of timers done for Tremaine, then," he added with a put-upon sigh, "the research awaits."

"It can keep waiting, can't it? Does Olivia really need all of what Banna had in her head restored tonight?"

"She's pressing Fiona, Rafi, and me to get to it. She won't say why exactly, but I think something's come across her desk she needs to verify. We'll celebrate when you solve the case, okay?"

At the door, Alastair kissed the tip of my nose. With Pablo in my arms, I trudged up the steps, unable to stop, *"But what if I can't solve it?"* from racing through my mind.

CHAPTER SIXTEEN
A MAYORAL CASE

I was fast asleep by the time Alastair came to bed, and he was still out cold when I woke early the next morning, again denying me the chance for a much needed pep talk.

Still, I was keyed up. I had a client. I had a case. I was going to be a success.

Assuming, of course, that I could solve the case in only a few days, get the contract signed off and the application filled out, and make it through the week without anyone threatening or attacking me. Which reminded me that I needed to talk to my parents about what people had been saying or doing to them.

I glopped some wet food into Pablo's bowl, and he immediately tucked in, making strange murmuring sounds of delight as he gobbled up the saucy slop. The electricity had kicked back in some time during the night, so I hurriedly ate some yogurt and toast. Apparently ready for a day at the office, Pablo was waiting by the closet door before I'd finished putting on my shoes.

"Just don't expect me to put you on the payroll," I told him.

Wanting to get there before the streets were swarmed with grumpy Magics, Pablo and I practically jogged to the agency. Thankfully, the only people out and about were the hungry ones lining up at Spellbound's yet-to-open doors. I didn't see my parents in the queue, but I wouldn't be surprised if my dad knew to the minute when the morning rush died down and wouldn't bother showing up a moment sooner.

Glad to have managed the trip without any sneers, snarls, or sniping remarks, my first chore of the day was to move the desk chair from hell off to a far corner and to replace it with one of the guest chairs. I was firmly resolved to stay off the floor today. A good goal for any day, really.

I'd barely had time to make a cup of tea, and the sun still loitered on the horizon when there was a knock at the agency's door. I thought I'd unlocked it, but perhaps in my well-founded worry that Mr Thug would return for round two, I'd re-latched it.

Through the window, Matilda Marheart waved at me. I went to the door, found it unlocked, and figured I better get it looked at if it was sticking. Once I'd invited the mayor in and she'd taken a seat in front of my desk, Pablo, ever the meeter-and-greeter, strode up to her.

"Aren't you a handsome fellow?" she cooed at him.

Pablo crouched and wiggled his butt, preparing to leap onto the desk, but he halted in mid-wiggle when Matilda pulled a box from her bag. Since he seemed curious, she showed it to him. A low rumble came from deep in his throat. It was a sound I'd never heard from him before. More lion's warning than house cat curiosity.

Pablo turned his nose up, flicked his tail, then marched over toward the bookshelves where an empty shoebox waited for him. He leapt inside and curled up, but stayed alert, chin propped on the edge of his makeshift bed, watching us with focused intensity.

"Sorry, he's usually friendly." I pointed to Matilda's box. "So, is that the family heirloom you're looking for?"

Which was a stupid question even for me, since detective

work usually doesn't involve clients bringing in the very objects they're looking for."

"This is part of it."

What she'd pulled out was only the box's base, inside of which were five small compartments, each section divided from the other with a thin vertical piece of dark wood. The object was about as big as my hand, maybe three inches deep, and made of ebony that still held a mirror-like finish despite its age.

"How old is it?" I asked.

"I believe it was made in the late-1500s. I've looked into the family stories, and from what I understand, the craftsman only made a handful of these boxes. He died soon after, you see. Killed by the king," she said with an amused gleam in her eye. "According to family legend, that is. Who knows how many of those old tales are true, but I think the craftsman — the name Boncoeur keeps popping up, if that helps — came from somewhere along the Danube." Which was a bit vague, but after nearly five hundred years, I suppose you had to expect some details to fall by the wayside. "But this," Matilda said, pulling something else from her bag, "is the real treasure, and why I've come to you."

Using both hands, she settled a perfectly fitted lid over the base. And this really was a treasure. Most of the surface was covered in seed pearls, tinier than grains of rice, with the sheen of opals. At each corner, a trio of sapphires were arranged in a shape that reminded me of the fleur-de-lis. At the center, the white seed pearls had been swapped for black ones. These outlined an empty, heart-shaped depression.

"Is something missing here?" I pointed to the shallow depression on the lid.

"You really are a detective," Matilda said with a cheeky wink. "A garnet goes there, held by a wire cage that must have broken off long ago. Or maybe it's a ruby. Either way, that jewel is what I'd like you to find, if you're willing to take my case."

Last night, I'd had a bear of a time falling to sleep because I couldn't stop thinking about what working for Mayor Marheart could mean. Not only would I get HQ's form completed, but if she liked my work, Matilda could pull some very influential strings.

Problem was, I'd been picturing a slightly easier job. Maybe not Mom's Missing Pencil easy, but something along the lines of Lola's stolen vacuum.

But this? This was an impossibly challenging case. I'd love to crack it, but — since Matilda seemed rather uncertain about it herself — just nailing down the box's history could take several days of solid work. And uncovering some long-missing jewel? How was I to manage that before Mr Tenpenny's deadline? I needed a quick-and-easy case, not one this complex. But I also knew I'd be an idiot to turn Matilda down.

Biding my time, I pictured the dragon Morelli — sorry, 'Genie' — had made for her.

"You have a thing for hearts?" I asked.

She smiled wistfully. "A family symbol. The name, you know. Goes back ages. It's now Marheart, but you can also find plenty of Hardhearts, Goodhearts, and Newharts in my ancestry."

An image of Bob Newhart (look him up) in a witch's hat hovered in my head as I considered my own family. My parents' last name was Starling. I hadn't taken it because I simply couldn't get used to it, and because I was too lazy to do all the paperwork for a name change. But like Matilda's hearts, there were black birds sitting all over our family tree, including Tobey's middle name of Raven, which I still teased him about.

"Have you had any luck with your own research on the jewel?" I asked.

"I've looked through a few antique shops and museum collections, even a pawnshop or two, but no luck." The permanently neutral smile of a politician dropped for the first time since she'd walked in. "It seems very daunting now that I think about it. I'd understand if you didn't want to take this. I'm sure you have other cases to focus on."

It was daunting. I hadn't even taken the job and I already felt overwhelmed by the complexity of it. Other than doing an eBay search, which could cough up miles of results, I had absolutely no idea how I would go about finding this thing. And that's assuming the jewel still existed and hadn't been, say, chucked into a river during some lover's quarrel.

But if I turned the case down, what then? Lola may have convinced the mayor to give me a chance, but she hadn't seemed very hopeful when I spoke to her yesterday about sending more work my way. Dithering over what to do, I couldn't think of what to say to the person sitting across from me.

Perhaps interpreting my silence as a bargaining ploy, Matilda said, "I'm prepared to pay twenty percent of the item's value. That would have to be determined by an appraiser once it's found, of course, but I imagine the jewel is worth quite a bit. Does that sound fair? And for any incidentals, I could pay you an advance of five hundred up front. Yours to keep even if you fail. Which I'm sure you won't."

She then added, in a way that seemed worryingly desperate, "I can't tell you how important it is for this jewel to be found."

Five hundred dollars? *Plus* twenty percent? Judging by the space for it in the lid, this ancient gem was at least the size of a golf ball. It'd be worth… Well, I had no idea. A lot, that was for sure. Definitely enough to repay my parents a good chunk of what they'd invested to remodel Vivian's Boutique into a detective agency.

A niggling little beaver gnawed at my gut, insisting I had no idea how to tackle this. This wasn't a vacuum, this wasn't even something that had ever been in MagicLand, as far as I knew. But the possibility and potential was too tempting, and I'd be damned if I was going to let a case like this slip through my fingers.

"I'll see what I can do," I told her. "If I get no hits in the next couple of weeks, I'll return your deposit and maybe you could keep quiet about my not being able to finish the job? Publicity, you know."

"I am well aware of how important the public-facing façade can be, Miss Black. And I understand completely how a failure this soon could hurt your future prospects. Especially after the whole debacle with the Academy."

Again, hesitation struck me. If word got around that I screwed up this investigation, it could permanently cement my reputation as Cassie the Flake. But if I succeeded...

Using one of the forms from Mr Tenpenny's file folder, Matilda and I filled out a contract, we dotted our Ts and crossed our Is, and I had five hundred dollars cash in my pocket before most Rosarians' days had even begun.

And that was just the start.

CHAPTER SEVENTEEN
MISSING MARBLES

Once Matilda left, I gave myself time to think about how to go about her case. Which is another way of saying, I procrastinated to avoid facing up to the fact that I had no idea how to go about her case.

After brewing another cup of tea and making a second breakfast of the bag of Lola's coconut-almond cookies I still had hidden in my desk drawer, I tidied the kitchenette even though it was already cleaner than my own kitchen had ever been prior to Alastair moving in.

As I did so, another name for the agency came to me. This one really had a ring to it, so I magicked a few cards just in case any clients started streaming through my door. Charged up by this moment of business creativity, I sat down to my computer, ready to dive headfirst into Matilda's case.

Search results on eBay for *heart-shaped jewel* yielded thirty pages of items ranging from cheap art supplies to costume jewelry for dogs to sparkly stickers to decorate your cell phone case.

Trying a more exact search for *antique heart-shaped ruby* yielded — I'm not kidding — a rubberized, Dorothy-from-Oz costume complete with ruby-studded shoes that "had only been worn once to a screening of the Rocky Horror Picture Show."

Clearly, this was going to require legwork, not simply hiding behind the computer. But I didn't know who to question or what to ask even if I did.

I closed the laptop with a grunt of annoyance and caught sight of my calendar. I only had five more days to get a beyond-my-level-of-expertise case done, a form signed, and an application submitted if I hoped to keep the agency open. The planet-sized impossibility of it all blocked any forward momentum. I glanced at the bookcase and considered rearranging the books by publication date.

Then, as if Gandalf himself were smiling down upon me, the door's entry bell chirped. A client! My head jerked toward the sound, immediately causing a protesting crick in my neck.

My shoulders then sagged in disappointment, because standing in the door's threshold and looking none-to-sure he was where he needed to be, was an elderly man I recognized from the Wandering Wizard Pub.

"Can I help you?" I asked.

Wait. Should I get a receptionist? No, I suppose in a one-room open office, it'd look like a whole pile of jack-assery to have someone sitting at one desk, pretending he or she wasn't sure if I was in, looking over his or her shoulder, then asking the client to wait a few moments while I finished alphabetizing my paperclips.

And no, I hadn't alphabetized my paperclips. They were only in order by size. And color.

"Yes, I'm Clive Coppersmith," he said, his voice full of doubt, "and I've lost my marbles."

Oh boy.

Like I said, I'd seen this fellow at the Wandering Wizard nearly every time I'd been in there. He always sat on the same stool and always had half a pint of ale in front of him. Granted, he never seemed to be swaying in his seat, but he'd be there from the time I'd show up to the time I'd leave. That spoke of someone dedicated to drink and might explain his current predicament.

"I think Dr Dunwiddle would be more helpful than I could be. I can walk you over there, if—"

"Not those marbles," he snapped. "*Marbles*, girl. Little glass balls. What kind of fool do you take me for?"

Because I'm not completely ignorant of the concept of customer service, I did not say, "Drunken fool." And to be fair, the guy didn't seem drunk or like a drunkard biding his time until the bars opened. His suit, while not as nice as Mr Tenpenny's Saville Row splendor, was spotless and freshly pressed with a pale blue button-down worn underneath. There was no scent of stale alcohol wafting from his pores, his salt-and-pepper hair was neatly combed, and he was cleanly shaven.

He was also standing soberly tall as he stared at me like I was the one who'd had a few too many.

"Sorry, my mistake. Have a seat and tell me about losing your marbles."

I nearly protested when he rolled the evil desk chair over, since I could only imagine what the *Herald* would make of someone leaving my office on a stretcher. But, just as Tobey had done, Clive somehow managed to place his behind in the seat without it trying to scurry away from him. Were there such things as chair whisperers?

Despite his appearance and chair-taming ways, I still expected Mr Coppersmith to ramble on incoherently about fading memories, jumbled thoughts, and unwanted hallucinations. Instead, he told me of a set of marbles he'd gotten when he'd first started his training. That would be magic training. Which did not commence with a letter from Hogwarts.

So disappointing.

The missing marbles, he explained, were family heirlooms. As was standard with marbles, they were made of glass, but the majority of his had been infused with a tiny amount of the ashes of his ancestors. Which was both creepy and kind of cool. As such, the marbles had a touch of magic to them.

"Never lost a game," he said with a wink.

"That's hardly fair, is it?" I asked, even though I didn't know a thing about playing marbles.

"The other kids' marbles were enchanted too, so it was all fair and square. Mine just happened to be more enchanted. Shouldn't have let them out of my sight, really." He shook his head in admonishment, causing a lock of his hair to slip forward. "I wouldn't mind if someone wanted to borrow them, but there is one in particular I wouldn't want to lose."

"Did they all go missing at the same time?"

"Yep. Kept 'em in a velvet sack. When I brought up my predicament to a friend, they recommended this place." Thank you, Lola. It had taken a bit, but she really was coming through. And finding marbles that were likely somewhere in MagicLand couldn't be that hard, could it? I saw another eBay search in my near future. This time to find a frame for my detective's license. "My friend told me you could help me with such things."

I couldn't blame him for the dubious glance he gave the agency after he said that last sentence. The office was far too tidy. It screamed of someone without enough to do. Especially since a few days ago, I'd arranged the books on the shelves behind me by color, then by size. It might have created an attractive Instagram-worthy effect, but it wasn't what someone suffering under a groaning caseload would have time for.

Okay, forget the frame hunting. As soon as Mr Coppersmith left, I swore to pull some books down from the shelves and scatter them across my desk. And I'd toss a clipboard onto the pile too. Busy people always had clipboards, right?

"I can help you," I assured him. "Straight away, in fact. We just have a quick bit of paperwork to do first." I pulled out another of the contracts from the HQ file and we filled in a few details.

"So, when did you last have all your marbles?" I asked.

Mr Coppersmith, rather than answer the question, leaned forward, squinting his dark brown eyes at me.

"You're Starling's kid, aren't you? Simon Starling?" He eased back, a grin warming his wrinkled face. "I nearly lost my metaphorical marbles having him in class."

"You were his teacher?" Even though I'd spent hours flipping through family photo albums with my parents over the past several weeks, I still couldn't fathom the pair of them in classes learning about spells and potions and Magic history and all that. "What did you teach?"

"Potion mixing. He was terrible at it. I lost count of how many times his recipes exploded. And the colors his mice would end up were, well, impressive, I suppose." He shook his head, but had a nostalgic glint in his eyes. "Poor Gwendolyn Morgan kept partnering up with him. Can't imagine why. Felt sorry for him, I guess. Must have had the teaching bug in her even back then. She was a natural, but she claims her talent is all thanks to me. I'm not going to argue with her, though." He pulled a crumpled napkin from his jacket pocket and gave me a mischievous smile as he showed me the Spellbound logo on it. "To this day, she insists on giving me free scones whenever I pass by."

I let him wander down Memory Lane a little longer, then brought things back around to the case. I repeated my question of when he'd last seen his marbles.

"Must have been last week. I'd taken them to Rosaria's Magical Articles & Collectibles Expo."

"What's that?"

"Antiques, unique collections, memorabilia, that sort of thing. Really, it's just a way for old Magics to get together, show off our stuff, and have a few drinks."

"Speaking of drinks," I asked, mainly because I worried about Mr Coppersmith being considered 'in his right mind' enough to sign the agency contract. "Is it rude of me to ask why you're always at the Wandering Wizard?"

"It is," he said curtly, then chuckled. He had good teeth. I wondered if they were false or if this was what Magic dentistry could do for your chompers. "But I'll answer. I like beer and I get lonely. Since my wife died six years ago, I've lived alone, above the Wizard, in fact. The pub, call it an old man's fancy, but I like to think of it as my living room, and I like to pretend it's me everyone's come to see when I'm down there."

I didn't know what to say to that. Before Alastair moved in, I lived alone. Well, except for the sound of Morelli's game shows and classic TV reruns emanating from the floor below. For the most part, since I don't like most humans, I enjoyed the solitude. But now I could see how, once you got used to being around someone, you might come to crave company when they were no longer there.

"I don't drink much," Clive said defensively, perhaps taking my silence for continued doubt. "I learned long ago how to make a pint last. It's why the proprietor at the Burning Wand told me to stop coming in. They're more about quantity than quality, if you know what I mean."

I told him I did. The Burning Wand was a rough and tumble place that most of the people I was close to in MagicLand avoided.

"So, did anyone at this expo seem unusually interested in your marbles?"

"Everyone admired them, sure, but can't say anyone acted strange about them, eyed them up suspiciously, or anything like that."

Once I asked a few more questions, Mr Coppersmith gave me a picture of the marbles, which I didn't think would be terribly helpful. He also offered a fifty-dollar deposit for my services, but I declined, saying he could pay in full when I'd recovered his glassy treasure. As he stood to leave, I handed him one of the business cards with the amazing new business name I'd come up with before he arrived.

"Sleuths R' Us?" he said critically. "That really what you're calling this place?"

"It's, um… I'm still working on it," I said. "You know, A/B testing. But the number will stay the same, so call if you think of anything that might help."

After Mr Coppersmith left, I dared to approach the chair.

"So, are you choosing to behave today?" I asked, then shook my head. I was talking to office furniture. I'm sure my admirer at the *Herald* would love an exclusive on that one.

Since the chair wasn't giving off any evil vibes, and since it was more ergonomic than the guest chairs, I dared to move it back behind my desk. My ability to forgive was rewarded when I lowered my backside — very slowly, mind you — into the seat and ended up sitting like a normal person.

Then, in one of those pressing-your-luck moments, I couldn't help but give the chair a twirl of delight. In one morning I had gotten two clients. I had two cases. Better yet, I had two contracts and only needed one of them signed off to get my license. I spun around again at this double dose of chances to actually pull this off.

As the rotating chair came to a slow stop, I caught sight of who was right outside my window. My uncharacteristic light-hearted glee crumbled to ash faster than a chain-smoker's first cigarette of the day.

CHAPTER EIGHTEEN
ONE-UPPING THE WALRUS

Mrs Oberlin had been walking with a newspaper tucked under her arm and a determination in her step. I'd hoped she might keep on walking without noticing whose business she was passing by. But then, just as she got to the section of my window where my business name was waiting to be added, she slowed her stride.

Still, she hadn't yet peered inside. I might just be able to avoid her.

I tried to fling myself from the chair to duck under my desk, but it wouldn't budge. Of all the times for the damn thing to decide it wanted me in it. Something had locked up, which meant the rubber wheels wouldn't scoot against the wood floor. As such, when Mrs Oberlin entered the agency, her first impression was of me straining against the desk, trying to force the chair to move.

She eyed me curiously, but I was the queen of playing off foolish behavior. I released the desktop, stretched my arms over my head then out to my sides.

"Desk exercises," I explained. "Helps keep you limber."

"Very wise." She quickly took in the office's tidy interior and gave a nod of approval. "I have to admit, I was a little worried you'd be out on a case. Thing is," she fidgeted with her purse strap, "you're just the person I need right now."

Confusion hit me. This, in case you didn't figure it out from her last name, was Winnifred Oberlin. As in the wife of Inspector Oberlin, finalist for the Best Walrus Impersonator of the Year Award. And her words hadn't been delivered in a mocking way, nor was she speaking to me scornfully.

I didn't know how to reply. I just sat there, showing off my social skills by gaping at her with my mouth hanging open.

Winnifred was an attractive woman in her mid-fifties with an unlined, apple-cheeked face. Although she was about my same height, which is pretty tall for a woman, she was much broader and sturdier than me. In the wrong clothes, you might think she was fat, but despite looking very put together in her linen slacks and jacket, you couldn't miss the strength in her bulky frame. If she decided to ditch her life with Inspector Oberlin, she could probably make a great career on the body-building circuit.

"May I?" she said, and gestured toward the guest chairs.

Coming to my senses, I stood (of course *now* the chair let me loose) and invited her to sit. As she stepped closer, I caught a whiff of her magic's tropical, hibiscus scent.

She set her newspaper (I was relieved to see it was *The Preternatural Times*) on the spare chair, then loosened the floral-patterned silk scarf she had expertly arranged around her neck. I long ago admitted defeat in the Art of the Scarf and still marvel that anyone can get those lengths of fabric to behave.

Once seated, Mrs Oberlin held out a hand that, despite its princess pink-lacquered nails, looked like it could crush walnuts. I shook it with the lightest of grips.

"What can I help you with, Mrs Oberlin?"

"Winnifred, please. A friend told me you were some sort of detective, despite not… Well, not receiving the official training."

"You mean despite your husband kicking me out of the Academy?"

"Wesley can be a bit rash at times. I'm sure he overreacted, because when I brought up the little problem I had to my acquaintance, they couldn't recommend you enough." Thank you again, Lola. "I assume the recommendation is well deserved?"

"I have proven myself in the past. And just because I haven't completed the Academy's training, doesn't mean I don't know how to proceed on a case." I tried to keep my tone reasonable, but the picture of Oberlin scolding me, of the thrill in his eyes when he booted me out that day, brought a bitterness to my words.

"No need to get defensive. I'm on your side." She smiled conspiratorially. "Sometimes self-education is the best kind."

"Yes, well, if only self-licensing was the same."

"You're still not licensed?" she asked, but then waved her question away. "No, don't worry about answering that. I know you have a certain grace period during which you can conduct cases before making things official. And I would like you to conduct a case for me."

"Really?" I didn't mean to sound so pathetically eager, but even though Mr T had granted me an extra few days to finish my application, that due date would be here before I knew it, and I didn't know which case might be the one that'd get me the signature I needed. Plus, this was Inspector Oberlin's wife, someone just as high up the social ranks as Mayor Marheart. If I could solve her case, it could only lead to good things for the agency.

Plus, beyond good exposure, beyond getting my application completed, bills still had to be paid in MagicLand, and more clients meant more chances to start making up for my lack of income over the past few weeks. It was either take as many cases as possible, or rob a bank. And don't think I hadn't considered the latter. I mean a non-Magic teller against my BrainSweeping Charm? It'd be like stealing hundred-dollar bills from a baby.

"Really," Mrs Oberlin confirmed with a wry smile.

"Then, how may I help?" I asked, flipping open the notebook I'd picked up from the Dollar Store. With its black cover, it looked very detective-y.

"I've lost something. A rooster brooch." She lifted her hand to an empty space on her cream-colored blouse. "It's a family treasure, but it's gone missing. I'd do anything to get it back."

"You've come to the right place." I clicked my pen, ready to fill the page with notes that would have me cracking this case in no time.

"Terrific," Mrs Oberlin enthused. She sat up a bit straighter, then glanced back to the window. "What is this place called, anyway?"

I could have told the truth. I could have said I hadn't come up with a name yet. I could have probably earned a bit more respect from my client if I hadn't blurted out the answer I thought she'd want to hear.

"Find-It-Fast Detective Service?" I said doubtfully, then hurriedly magicked another dozen cards. One of which I handed to her.

Winnifred glanced at it skeptically, then said, "No offense, but the name doesn't ring with... How should I say?" She twirled a meaty hand as if stirring up a polite way to answer her question. "*Quality* work?"

"The marketing division is still workshopping the name. But I will do good work. Quality work."

"Yes, that's what I was told."

I reminded myself to stop by and thank Lola as soon as I got a chance. I then had Mrs Oberlin fill out another contract from

Mr Tenpenny's file. It seemed a new one appeared every time I took one out. Magic is handy like that.

"So," I said, once the case and client details were noted, "two questions: When was the last time you saw this brooch, and do you have a picture of it?"

"I know I wore it for Wesley's last graduation ceremony. I'm sure I have a picture from that event somewhere that shows the brooch, but I didn't think to bring it with me. It's no problem if you want me to drop it off later." I told her that would be great and offered to pick it up if she needed. "And the last time I saw it was two weeks ago when I wore it to a dinner party. On the Friday, to be precise. Or would it be Saturday?"

I wrote the possible dates on my notepad. "Did you still have it on when you got home?"

"I think I must have."

"You think, but you're not sure?"

"If I didn't, I would have gotten in touch with the dinner host, wouldn't I?"

Great goblins, the woman couldn't remember her own actions? And here I'd been worried about Mr Coppersmith being scatterbrained.

"Could it have fallen off at the party?" I tried, feeling this supposedly easy case growing more difficult with every second that passed.

Winnifred glanced down guiltily at her purse. "There was a lot of champagne. That's why I say 'I think'." I tried to keep any dubious expressions from crossing my face. As I said, this woman was big. I couldn't imagine a few glasses of champagne, hell, a few *bottles* of the stuff, rendering her too foggy to remember things. But maybe she had a low tolerance level. "However, I do have a fuzzy memory of taking it off when I got home."

The first, and the easiest, course of action would have been to go to her home and check the place over to see if this brooch had merely been misplaced. Stuck in a pocket, lost in a vanity drawer, left in the medicine cabinet when she'd pulled out the aspirin bottle the next morning. But lunchtime was approaching and I knew Oberlin often went home for his midday meal. Not being in the mood for a walrus encounter, I decided to skip the easy route for now.

"I think the best thing would be for me to go back over the streets you would have taken home. Do you remember which way you went to this party?"

"Oh, well, that *is* an excellent idea, but I didn't walk home. I took a portal."

I nearly tore up the contract then and there.

"Where exactly was this dinner party?"

"It was a sort of policeman's ball." She then added almost apologetically, "With the Canberra community."

"Canberra? As in Australia?"

She nodded, and I fought down the urge to bang my head on the desk as punishment for allowing any amount of hope or optimism into my life.

If she'd taken a long-distance portal that far, the bauble could have popped off on a side branch that went to India, Italy, or Indiana. My throat went dry with dismay. This wasn't quite as bad as Matilda's gem, but nearly so.

Still, I told myself, I had a client in my office. A client sitting in the chair that had stood empty for two weeks. I wouldn't let her slip through my fingers. And the best way to keep my grip on her was to stall until I could figure out how to tackle her case. Or until reality slapped me in the face and told me this, like Matilda's jewel, was a fool's errand.

"I'd be glad to help," I said, "but I really can't start on anything until I know exactly what I'm looking for. Once you get me the photo, then we'll get things rolling."

"You'll really take the case? Even though Wesley—"

"Yes, even though Wesley." And maybe a little because of him. After all, how foolish would Oberlin look if people knew his own wife went elsewhere for her sleuthing needs. "Speaking of the Inspector, why aren't you having him work on this?"

"Honestly?" she asked. I raised my eyebrows, inviting her to spill the beans. "The brooch has been handed down in his family for ages, since—" she fluttered a hand with uncertainty "—oh, I don't know. The way he goes on about it, you'd think Henry VIII himself gave it to them. But I swear I've seen the same thing in a 1950s Sears catalog.

"Anyway, it was a wedding gift to me from his mother. We never got along, and, well, you know how he is. If he knew I lost it, he'd go off on a rant about how I did it on purpose just to spite his dearest Mom-Mom." I bit my lip to fight back a smirk. "If I can recover it without his knowing, it would avoid a great deal of strife. Which is why I'm so very glad you're willing to work with me."

I smiled indulgently and took a few more notes about the brooch. With an international portal added into the equation, hers could be a tough case, but certainly an easier one than Matilda's. Once I saw her out, I sighed with relief. Another client. Another chance at the license. Plus, the possibility of one-upping Inspector Oberlin? Winnifred's might prove to be my favorite case yet.

CHAPTER NINETEEN
CHOCOLATE ATTACK

I needed to think about how to approach these cases, but I also felt I deserved a little reward after nabbing three clients, three *amazing* opportunities to get my license, all in the space of a single morning. I had no doubt I could think and eat a pear tart at the same time, and I had an hour before Tobey was supposed to stop by, so I closed up shop and headed to Spellbound Patisserie.

As I approached the familiar façade, the scent of cinnamon scones, sourdough loaves, and apple strudel wafted from the ovens, and my belly let out a growl.

Of course, with so many people under the *Herald's* influence, I was risking angry words and steely stares. But I also knew the morning rush would be over, the people who streamed in for their lunchtime boost wouldn't have started lining up yet, and anyone who was already at Spellbound would hopefully be so lost in sugary bliss, they wouldn't bother hurling insults at me.

Just as I pulled open the door to step in (after a deep inhale of carb-filled deliciousness), my dad came rushing out. He had crumbs on his shirt and a large Spellbound box in his hand.

"Fancy meeting you here," he said as he hooked his arm in mine and pulled me away from the door. You know, away from the sugar, and the butter, and the... Were those one-dollar grab bags of yesterday's leftovers?

I may have whimpered at this point, made speechless at the very idea of getting so close to a chocolatine or a peanut butter cookie, or maybe both.

"Don't worry. I've got supplies." He held up the box.

"But—" My protest died off into a strangled sound of defeat as my eyes lingered on a hunk of blackberry cobbler on display.

"Your mom— She's got—" The sense of fretful urgency in his fumbled words snapped me to attention.

Had my mom had a relapse? Runa had just taken samples from me yesterday. Did she lose them? Had the donations gone bad? My stomach lurched. My mom had been looking a little tired lately. I told her I could help with the housekeeping (stop laughing, I can magic a mop when I have to). Worse yet, what if she'd overexerted herself trying to set up her flake of a daughter in her new business?

"Is something wrong with Mom?" I asked as my dad tugged me by the arm over to a table like a misbehaving toddler.

This tidal wave of fretting was made worse when I recalled what Runa had told me about people harassing my parents. Was that what had put my mom in a coma?

Okay, maybe I was catastrophizing a bit.

"No, no," my dad said dismissively. "Chloe's fine. She's meeting us here."

I then wondered if there'd been some trouble at the house. Had my dad, distracted by donuts, forgotten about the electric kettle and let it go dry? Had one of them left the iron on next to a can of gasoline? Had a ravenous crocodile come crawling out of the toilet? Despite several cups of morning tea coursing through my system, I suddenly felt wiped out. Having family to worry about was so exhausting.

"What's going on?" I asked impatiently.

"In a minute. Really, your mom ought to be the one to tell you."

"Dad, seriously, you can't do this to me."

"I got you a triple chocolate cupcake," he said, as if that both fixed and explained everything. "You like those, don't you?"

"Dad, I'm not talking about treats." Although, I was a junkie for those chocolate bombs. "What are you hiding?"

Before he could answer, my mom was bending down, kissing him, then me, on the cheek, and slipping into one of the wrought-iron bistro chairs. Her cheeks were flushed, but not like she was feverish, only like she'd been in a rush to meet up with us.

"All sorted?" he asked her. She shook her head, darted a glance at me, then gave him a meaningful look that screamed, *Not in front of you-know-who*.

"Would someone please tell me what's going on? I'm about to see if slapping one's parents has any potential as a heart attack prevention measure."

"Have a chocolate attack instead," my dad said and whipped a cupcake out of the box like a magician pulling a rabbit out of a hat. "And stop worrying. We just have a job for you. We were going to meet you at the agency, but then you came to us. You should advertise that service."

I took the cupcake, licked half the frosting off with one swipe of my tongue, then resisted popping the entire thing in my mouth as I stared witheringly at Simon and Chloe Starling.

"Really, you guys? I have clients. I don't need your pity jobs. I mean, what was it going to be this time? Mom can't find her pink handkerchief?" Because my mom had a pink handkerchief tied around the band holding her ponytail.

"No, this is a real case," my mom said as my dad placed an apple chausson on a napkin in front of her. "You know how I've been going through things, trying to get our world back in order?"

I did know this. After being gone both mentally and physically for over twenty years, my parents were trying to regain a sense of their lives. Plus, after returning to a house that hadn't been cleaned in a couple decades, they also had plenty of housework to do. In addition to clearing away years of dust, my parents were also regaining a sense of themselves by sifting through their dressers, drawers, and files. Lucky for them, many of the clothes they had from when they disappeared were now back in fashion. And, thanks to their Mauvais-sponsored diet camp, the clothes fit even more loosely than they had back when they were new.

Although, if my dad kept making thrice daily trips to Spellbound, he wasn't going to fit into those retro-stylish clothes much longer. I gestured for my mom to continue as I nibbled at the cupcake, being careful not to bite into the gooey chocolate center. You had to eat around that, saving it for last when you'd pop the whole molten mass into your mouth. Okay, maybe I spent too much time at Spellbound myself.

"Well," my mom continued, "I discovered something's gone missing."

"Mom, it's been twenty years. Are you sure you have an accurate mental inventory of everything that should be amongst your stuff?"

"Not everything, but I do know when the necklace your grandmother's pendant was on isn't in the place I always kept it."

Grandmother. That was so weird. I mean, as a kid, I knew I hadn't been hatched — although as out of place as I felt, I wouldn't have been surprised — and I knew I had some sort of parents out there somewhere. At the time, when I knew nothing of why I'd been thrown into the foster system, I wanted them to be dead because that was an easier pill to swallow than thinking they'd just tossed me aside, leaving me to be raised by the vilest families Portland could muster.

But to imagine an extended family? I mean, I was still struggling to wrap my head around having parents, a cousin, and an uncle of some degree or other. That already was a whole lotta family for someone who'd never had any sort of kin. But grandparents? Great-grandparents? A whole string of ancestors? Crazy.

"Grandmother's pendant," I said stupidly. I shook my head to clear it. If my mom wasn't making things up, if the pendant wasn't dangling under her shirt, I guess this really might be a case. "You're sure you didn't move it somewhere else, or maybe you were wearing it when…? Well, you know."

"No, I wasn't wearing it the night we went after the Mauvais. I hadn't even taken it with me to London. I only wore it for very special occasions."

Oh no. She was getting that wistful, teary look in her eyes that meant she was recalling something that involved me. I paid special attention to the crumbs in my cupcake wrapper.

"You wore it to Cassie's first birthday party, didn't you?" My mom nodded in answer to my dad's question.

"That's why I went looking for it. I found a picture from the party." She pulled out a photo from her shirt pocket. This was from back in the day when you had to take film to a shop to have it developed. Odd, since you'd think Magics would have some more, well, *magical* way of developing pictures.

The back of the photo had the shop's name across it in faint print: Phenomenal Photo. On the front was me, black hair, scrawny limbs, and pale skin even then. No third-hand Doc Martins, though. Instead, I had on itty bitty, bright pink Converse high tops, which I had to admit were pretty cute.

My mom was sitting behind me. Her legs in a diamond shape, acting like a baby corral. At her neck was a thin chain from which hung a filigree, heart-shaped pendant in silver. From somewhere off camera, someone was handing me a present, but I was too intent on making a disaster of a length of wrapping paper from some previous gift. Which just goes to show I've never been much for tidiness.

"And you're sure it's not in some drawer you haven't gone through yet?"

"No, I always kept it in the box it came in. I think it's the same box from when my grandmother gave it to my mother. It should be yours now. We always handed it down on the eighteenth birthday. That's what I was telling you when that picture was taken. Do you remember?" she said with a nostalgic smile.

There were a lot of these nostalgic smiles, and it continued to make me uncomfortable. My parents had gone missing when I was four. I had absolutely nothing but the vaguest of memories of them. Nothing concrete, neither happy, miserable, or even neutral. Lola LeMieux, my occasional babysitter from back then, stirred up more in me, but they tell me that's just because the power of her magic is so enduring, like the Super Glue of magic.

Whenever my parents talked about our time together in the past, it was like they wanted me to remember something, and I felt guilty that I simply couldn't. I steered the conversation back to the present, pulling my notebook out of my back pocket to show her it was time for business, not chitchat.

"And this box was normally kept where?"

"My jewelry case."

"Nothing else is missing from it?"

"Well," my dad said, then swallowed the bite of cheddar scone he'd taken, "I'm having trouble finding my cufflinks."

I dropped my pencil and leaned back in my chair. Crossing my arms over my chest, I eyed them both.

"Guys, is this serious? Because I have real cases I could be working on."

"No, it's serious. Okay, your dad probably did misplace his cufflinks. He was always fidgeting with them." We both looked at my dad, who, even then, was plucking at the cuff of his sleeve. He darted his hand under his leg with a guilty look on his face. "But my... well, *your* necklace is truly missing from my jewelry case."

"And by missing, you mean actually missing. Not like you've placed this pendant in a box of tea back at the agency, knowing I'll find it so you can sign off on one of Mr T's forms and let HQ know all about my sleuthing prowess?"

"Are we that clever, darling?" my dad asked my mom.

"We are, but that's not what we're doing." She met my stern gaze, honesty oozing from her expression. "This item really is missing. We really would like to hire you to find it. And we really will force ourselves to only pay the going rate for your services. Although we would gladly pay you a very large deposit, if you'd take it." I started to protest, but she spoke over me. "Which we know you won't, so we won't even try. Now, will you take us on as clients?"

"And do we get a buy-one-get-one-free discount? You know, just in case I can't find the cufflinks?" my dad asked.

Once I'd agreed, my dad handed me a miniature pear tart and my mom pulled out one of the forms from HQ. When I gave her a questioning look, she said, "Stole one from your file when we were in yesterday. Just in case." Which did nothing to quell my suspicion that they'd made up this whole missing-pendant scenario to move my career along.

We filled in the paperwork, then chatted about nothing in

particular and ate our treats until they had to leave for their appointment with Dr Dunwiddle.

As they walked away, I hit them with an Amplify Charm to see if there were any whispered comments along the lines of, *'I can't believe she bought it.'* But I only heard my dad wondering what might be in the grab bags at Spellbound and asking if they shouldn't go back and see if any were left.

Despite the sugar racing through me, I slumped down in my bistro chair. (Not advisable, by the way. Those stiff iron backs are murder on your spine.)

Sure, I had clients. I even had loads of forms waiting for signatures. But where did I start? Matilda's would be high-profile, which would be good for future business prospects. My parents and Mr Coppersmith's would be easy, but not terribly brag-worthy. Then there was Winnifred. If I solved her case, it would annoy Oberlin, which had both its good and bad merits. So, did I work in order of how easy they would be? By the amount I'd get paid? Or should I just write the cases on slips of paper, draw one from a hat, and let fate decide?

Of course, that was assuming I'd be able to solve any of them.

I'd been encouraged by Mr Tenpenny to become a detective because of my work at uncovering the Mauvais. But that wasn't the same as true investigative work, was it? I mean, the Mauvais had been looking for me, not me him, which probably made the whole affair a lot easier.

So to think I could be a detective because I'd blundered onto a few clues, ones that the evil wizard wanted me to find…? That wasn't real detecting. That was just dumb luck.

The more I thought about it, the more I doubted I could do this. The pastries in my gut knotted and twisted into all new shapes as I pictured my embarrassment when I failed at this entire endeavor.

Luckily, my phone, which had somehow gotten linked up to my calendar, started screaming in a high-pitched, siren-like wail, "Appointment! Arriving in two minutes! Appointment!"

Like they say, there's nothing like hearing damage to take your mind off making tough decisions.

CHAPTER TWENTY
THE ADVISOR

When I returned to the agency and reached for the door's handle, a charge raced along my fingers. I'd experienced this before when sensing magic on something, but sorting out what it meant wasn't an exact science. It could be something good, such as Alastair having dropped by, or it could be a warning. Given my recent experiences with the residents of Rosaria, my inner pessimist barged her way forward and put me on the alert.

I peered through the front window, but saw no one moving about inside. Not for the first time did flashes of my fight with the Mauvais snap into my head and send prickles along my legs. The interior was completely different now, but some memories can't be wiped away with new furniture and a paint job.

When I tried the latch, it was unlocked. My mental sirens started blaring. My body tensed as my magic geared up for a fight. My legs, possibly the smartest part of my body, were ready to run the other way, but I forced them to step into the agency.

My intruder emerged from the kitchenette. I pinned my hands to my sides, barely holding back the attack hex I'd been prepared to throw.

"Just because you can undo my locks doesn't mean you should," I complained. "Even magic police need warrants, don't they?"

I took a seat and gestured Tobey to do the same. As an almost detective, he didn't have to wear the uniform of a police officer, but he did have to wear a suit, tie optional. The outfit looked terribly formal on someone who, up until a few weeks ago, I'd only ever seen in blue jeans and a t-shirt. Still, the dipping sauce from his chicken nuggets that was smeared across his lips threw a more casual spin on the whole ensemble.

"Inspector Oberlin says if you have probable cause or suspect a Magic's life is in danger, that entering without any official paperwork is allowed."

"You know, once you make it onto the force, no one is going to be able to tell you and Oberlin apart if you keep quoting him so perfectly."

"That's assuming I make it onto the force."

"Oh, please, if I knew this was going to be a Pity Party, I would have picked up some Whiny Pie from Spellbound. Come on," I said, getting up and taking a stance in the open area between the front door and my desk, "Stunning Spell. Hit me."

Tobey gave a heavy sigh and didn't get up. "You know I do fine on the practical stuff. I need help with the book stuff."

"It'll loosen you up. Come on," I taunted, "you know you want to."

As if being dragged through mud, Tobey moved into position and lobbed a Stunning Spell at my shoulder. Using skills Alastair had taught me when we weren't supposed to be anywhere near each other, I conjured a Shield Spell. I then called out various spells and hexes that would be needed in any police situation, and Tobey had no trouble keeping up.

When we switched roles, it was Tobey's turn to maintain the correct variation of a Shield Spell while I walloped him with whatever fighting spells I could think of. If nothing else, it was great for stress relief. After twenty minutes, I called it quits and went to the kitchenette to grab a box of cookies.

"Okay," I said, handing him a couple gingersnaps from the box, "quiz time?"

Tobey agreed, and I racked my brain, trying to recall some of what had been on our last few tests at the Academy. He breezily barreled through fifteen questions without a single wrong answer.

"Quit asking me easy things," Tobey complained after he replied with the name of the Magics' fingerprint database before I'd even finished asking the question. "Something more in-depth. More legal history. I think that's where I get stuck the most."

I should point out here that, in class, he'd gotten stuck on every single one of the problems he'd just answered correctly. It wasn't the subject matter. It was him.

I thought back to when I'd first taught Tobey magic. At least then I'd had help as Rafi guided me on how to show Tenpenny the Younger quite a few of the magical ropes. Rafi, as Olivia's assistant, had all manner of knowledge about the rules and regulations and historical background for the Magical Moral Code that most police procedure was based on.

I suddenly missed Rafi. I missed London. I'd been in business for two weeks. Surely I deserved some vacation time, right?

"Rafi's better at this sort of thing," I said. "Maybe we should go see if he'll help you."

"He's got work going on with the trolls. Some increased security thing. And no, I didn't ask him first. I sort of heard Grandpa talking to Fiona about it."

"Eavesdropping? Sneakily gathering intel?" I teased. "See? You're already proving yourself more than qualified to be a detective." Tobey didn't even give a hint of a smile at this. "Look, you did great today, but I need a little time to come up with some tougher questions for you. Plus," I said, a sense of impatience creeping along my spine, "I've got my own work to do."

"Okay, but if I fail my test, we're going to have to become partners. We could call the place Tenpenny and Black."

"One, that sounds like a fancy brand of chocolate. Two, I don't work well with others." Tobey nodded his agreement a bit too readily. "And three, like I said, you have to pass. I need a man on the inside."

"So, how is business?" Tobey asked, a straining-to-be-casual tone to his voice. "I heard you got some cases."

"How did you hear about that?"

"These are Magics, Cassie. They spread gossip faster than photons carry a beam of light."

"True. Well, after languishing in utter boredom, I've suddenly got five clients. Although two are my parents, so I don't know if that counts."

"They still trying to do that?"

"Yeah, but I think this time it's legit." I told him about the pendant.

"I could check the Academy's lost and found."

"See, told you I needed you on the inside."

"Still, four cases is kind of a lot. Inspector Oberlin advises us that we can really only give our full attention to three cases at any one time, and that's only after—"

"Years of experience. Yes, Tobey, I do remember the lecture." Because it had been Oberlin's only lecture *not* about the Stunning Spell. "Besides, it's only finding some lost doodads. I'm not trying to solve a murder or anything complicated like that."

In response to Tobey's curious expression, I told him about the other cases.

"Which ones are you going to focus on first?"

"My parents' case would be easiest since the necklace is probably in their house somewhere, but I'm not keen on jumping on that one. I mean, 'Found my mom's necklace' isn't exactly impressive if other clients ask for references about my sleuthing skills. The mayor's case is the highest profile," I continued. "And it's the highest paying, which is appealing, but it's also the toughest."

"I'm sure you'll have some snide comment about this, but Mayor Marheart's case is a crapshoot, and if you waste time on that without solving any others, you're screwed for getting your license. I'd suggest tackling Mr Coppersmith's marbles, and then if you have time, the Oberlin brooch. I doubt if either would take much digging since they were both last seen in Rosaria, or so the owners think. Quick solutions, non-parental clients, and some detecting feathers in your cap? Kind of a no-brainer. Plus, solving two cases for your application would look really good. You only need one, of course, but you do know they give points for how many completed cases you can submit?"

I actually didn't know this, but I wasn't about to admit that to my cousin who had a tendency to gloat when he knew things that I didn't.

"You seem awfully keen on this," I said suspiciously. "Why?"

"Like I said, it'd be good to keep this place running in case I need somewhere to work if I don't make the force. And think about it. The mayor's jewel could literally be anywhere. The marbles and the brooch are likely somewhere within Rosaria. And that means you'd be around for our next study session."

"Oh, I guess I'm helping you again. Good to know."

"No problem," Tobey said, completely missing my sarcasm. "I figure my best bet is to cram as much stuff into my head right before my exam."

"Which is…?"

"In two days, one p.m. sharp." Tobey's voice sounded like his throat had suddenly gone dry.

"That soon?" There'd still been well over a month of training left when I'd been booted out of the Academy, and I assumed the tests would be given then.

Tobey nodded. "Oberlin is offering it to those of us who feel we're ready to take it."

"And you feel you're ready?" I asked, my tone overflowing with skepticism.

"No, but Oberlin really wants me to. If I don't do it, he'll be disappointed in me."

Personally, I'd have loved to see Inspector Walrus hit so hard with disappointment that his face wound up on the back of his head. But I knew Tobey — as the first Untrained to be... well, *trained* in recent history — felt the need to prove himself. We didn't have a lot in common, but we did have that.

Plus, like me, he'd gotten into the Academy on Mr T's word. If he didn't pass, it would show that he hadn't been qualified in the first place, that only strings being pulled had gotten him there. Tobey needed to show he had the skills and the merit to succeed.

But so did I, and I barely knew how to help myself.

I thought of the cases. Four cases. At least one of which I had to solve to complete my license application. I really didn't have time to play tutor to Tobey. And I know that sounds selfish and awful, but he already knew this stuff. Study time with me wasn't going to make it stick in his head. He needed a psychiatrist, not lunchtime quiz sessions.

"That's a pretty tight turn around, Tobey. And if I'm tackling these cases, how am I going to have time to work with you? Getting this agency on its feet is my only chance to prove myself." Tobey slumped in his seat. A real guilt-inducing, pitiful slump. For someone who had such good posture, he could sure muster some manipulative slumping. "But," I said after letting out a very long sigh of defeat, "I'll try to fit you in."

Tobey perked up. "Seriously?"

"Yes, seriously." We agreed to ten a.m. the day after next — time enough just before the test to, hopefully, cram as much into his head as possible. The calendar automatically filled in the appointment. "But if I end up not having time to solve a case or two for my license, I'm coming at you with a BedHead Charm so severe it'll be decades before you can manage that perfect coif you've got going on."

"Fair enough. So where have you gotten on the cases?"

I didn't know why he was asking, but it felt good to vent about the failed eBay search. I then told him about my encounter with the thug and my frustration with where to begin on Mr Coppersmith's and Mrs Oberlin's cases. Searching their homes from top to bottom was the only strategy I could think of.

"Well, you could put in the legwork and ask around town," Tobey suggested.

"Considering how everyone on the streets has been treating me, that might not be a good idea."

"Then think of what you would have done before you came to MagicLand. If you needed to research something, where would you go?"

"The library. But MagicLand has no library." Something which really needed remedied, in my opinion.

"No, but we do have a certain schoolteacher who has quite the collection of books. She might be able to steer you toward something that would help."

"See, this is why, even though you annoy me on a regular basis, I keep you around."

"Well, Inspector Oberlin does say that failing to research a case is failing the case altogether."

I sighed. "And we were getting along so well there for a moment."

Thankfully, before he could shed any more Oberlin wisdom all over my desk, Tobey said he needed to get back to class.

"Don't forget. The marbles and the brooch. They're your best bets."

Once he left, I gathered up a pen and notepad. Then, even though it had come from Tobey, I took his advice and headed over to Fiona's. It wasn't much, but at least it was somewhere to start.

CHAPTER TWENTY-ONE
CHEZ FIONA

I wasn't entirely sure when Fiona's classes let out for the day, so I bided my time by trying to learn more about the Marheart family. Perhaps figuring out where they'd come from might clue me into where Matilda's jewel had been.

I began by looking up the various Heart-related family names Matilda had mentioned. The staggering number of results this produced pretty much crushed my motivation and I ended up down a very deep rabbit hole of cat videos.

When I finally climbed my way back out of felines falling off tables and flicking fancy collectibles off shelves, I ended up on a Norm news website. The big headline was a possible home invasion that had left two people dead, murdered in what the article vaguely referred to as a "disturbing manner." Kind of a redundant statement, since I imagine finding yourself being murdered is rather disturbing no matter how gently your killer goes about it.

Realizing I'd gotten desperately sidetracked, I refocused my attempts at research. Specifically on Matilda's jewel box.

And that's when I nearly squealed with joy. The pattern on the jewel box did indeed match up with a popular Tudor style. Combining the search terms *jewel box* and *Queen Elizabeth* then adding Matilda's family names, one by one, produced nothing until I tried *Boncoeur*. My heart gave a little leap at the results.

Queen Elizabeth had patronized a jewelry designer with the name of William Boncoeur. There was no outright statement of him crafting a jewel box, but Queen Elizabeth had given William a knighthood for his work and she kept him in her service until the end of her very long reign. I couldn't find much else about Old William, so, my hand shaking with excitement, I made a note to ask Matilda about him.

Closing the notebook, I caught sight of the time. It was well past three o'clock. Fiona should be done with classes, and I needed to catch her before she got too wrapped up in her after-school activities.

Call me cowardly, but before I left, I gobbled down an entire village of gingerbread men. Not because gluttony is my favorite deadly sin, but because I needed the extra energy to work a Mirage Hex on myself. I didn't plan to disguise myself as anyone in particular, I just wanted to give my face enough of a fuzzy filter that, unless the people on the streets stared me down, I'd be nothing more than another random, forgettable face in the crowd.

The spell worked, and I was able to stroll down Main Street without a single rude comment. Still, the Mirage Hex is a tough one, so my belly was growling by the time I reached Fiona's wrap-around porch. Her front door was open, so I stepped in.

Classes were still going, and Fiona stood lecturing at the head of the classroom that took up most of the ground floor of her home. She then caught sight of me and bustled over right when I'd crammed a few more ill-fated gingerbread chaps into my mouth.

"I've got a class right now," she told me, stating the obvious since I could see twelve students seated at their desks, a few of them were making hand movements near their ears as if trying to eavesdrop with an Amplify Charm. "I should be done in about twenty minutes if you want to wait upstairs. But maybe," she added, giving my shirt a critical glance, "dust yourself off first."

I looked down at my t-shirt. It was covered in the final remains of Family Gingerbread. I ducked outside, brushed down my front, then went upstairs to Fiona's living quarters.

I spent the next twenty minutes scouring the spines of Fiona's book collection. Or at least every spine I could see. I wouldn't be surprised if the walls of bookshelves weren't enchanted to hide a dozen more rows of books. Still, nothing on the first couple of shelves sparked any amazing insights. Instead, my attention was drawn to a large notebook open on a side table.

I'd barely absorbed the words *Fiona, is this evidence of an uprising...???* written in Alastair's handwriting, when the room's door creaked open. I guiltily scurried back over to the bookshelf.

"Did you need something, Cassie?" Fiona asked. Her strawberry-blonde hair, which is normally smooth and tidy, had frazzled bits sticking up. I held off the temptation to smooth them down as she strolled by the desk and flipped the notebook shut. "Only, I don't have much time. My next class starts in a few minutes. Sophomores," she said with an uncharacteristic grumble in her tone.

"You don't like them?"

"I don't like to speak ill of anyone, but sophomores, in my experience, are a nightmare. They've lost the timidity of being freshmen, they don't have the calm air of juniors who are excited about only having a year to go, and they aren't distracted by future plans like the seniors. They don't seem to know where they fit in, so they can either be too needy, overly meek, or attention-seeking pests. Don't think I haven't considered adding a shot of rum to my coffee before their classes. But you didn't come here to hear me gripe."

"I was wondering if you had a book on jewelry? Or marbles? Or dinner parties in Australia?" Ugh, I really was terrible at this. "Oh, and do you know the name William Boncoeur?"

Seeming unfazed by the odd string of questions, Fiona asked, "Is this a general curiosity, or is there a specific reason for these queries?"

As quickly as I could, I explained about my cases, including what I'd just discovered online. Fiona tilted her head as if tuning in to an inner voice.

"I'm afraid I don't know any William Boncoeur off the top of my head. If you want genealogy information, I believe Alastair might be able to help. If not, Professor Dodding is your best bet. I honestly don't know a thing about marbles, but Winnifred's brooch..." She paused, then nodded. "I've seen that brooch. Garnet, perhaps a ruby, for the cockscomb, emeralds for the wings, and diamonds along the body. But somehow it doesn't look gaudy, if you can believe that. It's excellent work. I'm not sure I know anything about Mayor Marheart's jewel, but..."

She trailed off, and I couldn't tell if it was because she didn't know much about the jewel, or because she couldn't tell me what she did know. Eventually, she said, "I've been doing some research for HQ."

"The Banna stuff?"

"What? Oh, yes, that too. But gemstones have come up several times in some troubling—"

Just then, a crash came from below, followed by a hoot of male laughter. Fiona's cheeks flared red, and I swear the frazzled bits of her hair frazzled even further. She jabbed her arm downward, palm flat. The classroom went silent.

"Freezing Spell," she said, with a don't-tell-anyone grin. "It'll only last a minute, so I better get down there. Feel free to look around. Books on gemstones are there," she pointed to the fourth shelf over, then hurried to the door as fast as the permanent limp in her leg could carry her.

"Thanks, Fiona," I said as she was crossing the threshold. "I owe you one."

Fiona turned around abruptly, looking like she was about to say something. I worried she was going to tell me to leave, or to at least not magically hurl any books through the wall. Not that that's ever happened. More than once.

Suddenly, the peals of laughter started up again, like a movie resuming mid-scene after pausing it. "That cannot be good. We'll chat later, okay?"

She dashed down the stairs, her uneven footfalls echoing on the wooden stairs. I could tell the instant she stepped into the classroom. All the rowdy noises stopped. I don't know if she'd Stunned them, or if these students knew not to mess with her, but whatever it was, it worked. I leafed through a few books on gemstones, and while I was intrigued by the pictures (which were enchanted to sparkle when the light hit them), I didn't find any information on rooster brooches or red, heart-shaped rocks that fit into jewel boxes.

As I did whenever I was at her home, I eventually found myself drawn to Fiona's photos. Her walls were filled with pictures of every class Fiona had taught, each one with the students in rows with the tallest kids in the back.

In one photo, I recognized Mr Coppersmith. Not as a student — Fiona was at least a couple decades younger than him — but as a teacher in a snapshot that showed him with a bunch of other teachers.

I then noticed there were a few of these teacher-only photos scattered amongst the class ones. They bore labels such as *The*

42nd Annual Teachers in Magic Education Meeting or *The Magic Instructors of the Year Gala*. Each time I found Mr Coppersmith, he was standing beside a tall man of about his same age. I recognized him as Penley Tremaine, the very same Tremaine who ran the toy shop in MagicLand.

Coppersmith and Tremaine posed side by side in all the photos except for one — the most recent one, which, from the date, I'd guess had been taken soon before Mr C retired to spend his days at the Wandering Wizard. In that shot, the two stood at opposite sides of the group photo. The glares they were giving each other made my recent encounters on the streets of Rosaria seem friendly in comparison.

Unsure if it would have the answer I was after or not, I went back over to the bookshelves and pulled down a massive book I'd recently become familiar with: *An Enchanted History of the Portland Community*. Nearly every event within Rosaria was recorded in this book, going all the way back to the founding of the magic community over hundred and fifty years ago and continuing on through today. As there were no blank pages, I wasn't sure how the book worked, how room was made for new events. Perhaps, like the forms in my application file, new pages magically appeared as needed.

I set the book on Fiona's desk, and as I flipped open the cover, a strange sensation tugged at my belly. This was the book that had given me my first glimpse of my parents. It was also the book that had started me down the road of uncovering who the Mauvais really was. Or who he was pretending to be.

It was a long shot that anyone would record the meeting of a marble club. But, as luck would have it, Magics loved their record keeping almost as much as they loved their gossip. The conference was indeed considered newsworthy, and the book had a list of attendees. There was even a picture of Mr

Coppersmith proudly showing off his marbles. And can you guess who was in the background? Mr Tremaine, eyeing the collection with naked scorn.

A clue? Who knew? But this guy was giving off all kinds of suspicious vibes. Who was I to argue with that?

I closed the book, and I swear I really wasn't trying to snoop, but when the heavy thing shut, it sent a puff of air that fluttered and shifted the papers on Fiona's desk. Written at the top of one sheet, in Fiona's cursive, was a question: *Can non-Magics use magic to end magic?* It sounded like some sort of philosophically rhetorical riddle, perhaps a writing assignment for the seniors to tackle.

I started to tease the sheet out to read more, but before I could reveal much, I heard the front door downstairs shut, then dress shoes clicking up the stairs. I clumsily shuffled the papers to cover over what I'd read, and was hefting the massive tome back into its spot when Mr T entered.

"Good day, Cassie. Making some additions to that?" He tipped his head to the book.

"No, just some research. Clue hunting," I added.

"And does this clue hunting mean you'll have a case solved in time?" He asked this lightly, conversationally, but his face showed worry. "It would be good if you filed the application before the deadline."

"Well, you could just give me a license and let me do the form later."

Despite the gravity in his eyes, the corner of Mr T's lips quirked up at that. In a knowing tone, he said, "You wouldn't accept it even if I could."

Wait, was this a possibility? Could I just *ask* for a license, even a probationary one, then take my time with these cases?

"Try me," I said.

"Unless you're planning on staying for tea, I'd rather you try to work on your case. A tough one?"

"Nearly solved."

Mr T's flicker of a grin revealed his relief. "Good to hear. Now, I've got to get a snack ready for Fiona. She always needs a little pick-me-up after the sophomores."

I said my goodbyes, and on my way out, I passed by Fiona's classroom. The students sat at their desks with their postures rigid, their eyes fixed on the front of the room, and their mouths glued shut. I wondered what the Norm's Board of Education would have to say about discipline in the Magic classroom.

At the head of the class, her back to a blackboard where a piece of white chalk made notes, was Fiona. I was impressed by her magic prowess. Not only was she casting a spell on the chalk to jot down key points as she spoke, but she was also maintaining a hex over a class of a dozen Magics. That's pretty next-level, if you ask me.

"And what do spells like this require?" Fiona was asking her pupils. Several students raised their hands. She nodded to one and made a flicking motion with her hand. "Cicero, go ahead."

The spell temporarily released, Cicero's body relaxed. He stretched his jaw before saying, "They require magical items to make them work."

"I'll leave the Behave Hex off of you for the rest of the class if you can tell me why."

Cicero perked up at this and glanced to the ceiling in the way people do when searching for an answer. I could almost feel Fiona ready to cast the Behave Hex back over him when his eyes brightened and he said in a rush, "Because the words alone aren't enough. You have to speak them over something to make what you want to happen actually happen."

"That's very good, Cicero. Now, we call these Assist Spells and they first originated…"

I kind of wanted to stick around to learn more about this aspect of magic history, but I had clues to uncover and suspects to question.

Since it was my only lead, and a pretty good lead at that, I was nearly giddy with optimism as I headed south from Fiona's house, then zigzagged along a few side streets to Tremaine's Toy Emporium. Where I came face to face with Penley Tremaine's hand-lettered *'Closed for the Day'* sign.

Optimism is so stupid.

CHAPTER TWENTY-TWO
TREMAINE'S TOY SHOP

The following morning, having double-checked Tremaine's business hours, I made a beeline for the toy shop. Strangely enough, I was rather looking forward to this encounter. Mainly because the first time I'd been there, I'd discovered Tremaine's had bins upon bins of miniature chocolate bars, gummy bear packets, and assorted other candies for only ten cents each.

What? Sometimes a girl needs a break from pastries. Or a snack to tide her over until the scones are ready.

Anyway, that first trip had been when Penley Tremaine had grudgingly agreed to sell some of Alastair's more whimsical mechanical timers on commission, all the while grumbling that something like timers would never be as popular as the new puzzles he'd just gotten in. These were the latest iteration of a recent craze in the magical gaming world: puzzles that were made especially challenging by the image on them shifting as you worked.

Trouble was, a few Magics got so obsessed with solving the impossible things, they ended up hitting a mental breaking point. The only way for them to recover was to be taken to a secluded retreat with minimal stimulation.

This actually drove up sales for a while, as if people saw *not* going mentally unstable as part of the challenge. But then someone discovered a variation of the Freezing Hex that could halt the ever-changing images, and the puzzles instantly dropped in popularity.

The new-and-improved version of the puzzles that Tremaine thought would outshine Alastair's timers had been enchanted to resist the Freezing Hex. But the fad had already passed. So, since toy lovers are always after the latest craze, the walking penguins and trundling tortoises Alastair crafted began selling out within days of Tremaine putting them on display.

Soon after this, Alastair had received some business advice from Morelli, who had some of his own crochet creations in the shop. I know… Morelli advising on business matters? Who'd have believed it, right? I mean, I could understand if it was tips on which season of *The Jeffersons* was the best, but business advice? Not in a million years.

Anyway, Morelli told Alastair that the key to keeping customers coming was to keep his stock fresh.

Which is why, currently on display in Tremaine's window, were a few of Alastair's timers from the previous week alongside a placard announcing next week's release. This was going to be a new product line Alastair had come up with: circus-themed timers that cartwheeled, summersaulted, or twirled until time ran out.

He'd made a collection of ten of them. I knew one was a dragon named Duncan, and another was a unicorn called Fergus, but I was uncertain what the others were. A centaur couple, maybe? Regardless, he planned to release one each week over the next ten weeks, and Tremaine had told him interest was already skyrocketing.

Inside, the shop carried your standard-issue, non-magical board games, plush bears and bunnies, and building block sets of which castles and dragons seemed to be the most popular choices.

Dusting off a display of card games was Tremaine himself. He had a ring of grey hair around a shiny head, and a long face with cheekbones that looked sharp enough to slice ham.

"How may I help you?" he asked in a cheery voice that you wouldn't expect from such a severe face. Recognition sparked in his eyes. "You're Alastair's little friend, aren't you?"

Bristling at this, I pulled out one of my altered business cards.

"I'm Cassie Black from the—" Damn it, which card had I grabbed? I gave it a quick glance. "The Black Magic Detective Agency."

"Might want to give that a rethink. What can I help you with? Looking for a toy magnifying glass, perhaps?"

Reminding myself that subjecting suspects to a Strangulation Hex would go against the detective's code of conduct, I forced myself to speak calmly as I said, "I'm investigating something for Mr Coppersmith. I believe you know him."

"I do," Tremaine said in a tone that implied he wished he didn't.

"Have you had a falling out?"

"Wait." The shopkeeper's face, already pale, lost even more color, to the point I feared he might pass out. "Detective, you say? He hasn't been murdered, has he? I would never—"

"No, no, nothing like that," I reassured him while also thinking what a strange conclusion to immediately jump to. "So, you and Mr Coppersmith? What's your relationship?"

"We were friends." Tremaine practically snorted the word *friends* as if it were a curse. He resumed dusting his shelf. "But friends don't cheat friends."

"He cheated you?" I asked conversationally. "What was that about?"

"He knows what he did. If he'd only 'fess up to it, I'd forgive him. Wouldn't even care all that much if he'd just admit things.

But that stubborn old goat acts like he's in the right."

"Is this to do with marbles?" I asked, recalling Mr Coppersmith talking about his little balls being enchanted. He'd played it off like all Magic marble games involved a bit of trickery, but maybe Tremaine hadn't gotten the message.

"Damn right it is. Sure, we all have our hexes and charms on our collections. Some marbles have the magic ingrained in them. But to outright cheat? That's just bad sportsmanship. Then you know what he does?" I said I didn't, my head already reeling at how much passion marbles could stir up. "He has the nerve to show up to the Magical Articles & Collectibles Expo with *my* marble."

"You're a member of the Marble Society?" I asked to confirm what I'd seen at Fiona's. I mean, he might have just been at the expo as an observer. A marble stalker? Marble groupie?

"Of good standing. Unlike some people," Tremaine said through tight lips. He straightened a few packs of cards, stood back, and gave his work a nod of approval.

"Did you hear Mr Coppersmith's marbles have gone missing?"

It was only a momentary reaction, barely half a second, but Tremaine's gaze flicked toward the ten-cent candy bins. At first I thought he was hinting I should buy something if I was going to take up his time, but then I remembered a scene from a Sherlock Holmes story in which Irene Adler gave away the location of a hidden safe with an involuntary glance at a painting.

"Mr Tremaine, is there something you want to tell me?"

"No," he said petulantly.

"Okay, is there anything you think you should tell me given my cousin is a member of the police?" Granted, Tobey was only a student, but still, you gotta use your connections when you can.

"Fine." Mr Tremaine folded his lanky frame onto a step stool and let out a heavy sigh. "Some years ago, when we were both still teachers, before I had this shop, we started playing a weekly game. We'd capture one another's marbles, as you do, but at the end of the game we'd return each other's marbles to keep our collections intact.

"It was supposed to be a friendly competition of a game that few people play these days. Then one day, after a game he'd won, I get home and notice he hasn't returned one of my marbles. My favorite one. He swore up, down, and sideways that he hadn't taken it, that I must have lost it. I knew as well as I know my own name that I didn't lose it."

"When did this happen?"

"Dunno, maybe three years ago."

Because when they weren't busy making up convoluted pieces of bureaucracy and spreading gossip with the speed of a bullet, Magics practiced the fine art of holding a grudge.

"And so what happened at the expo?"

"He had his marbles on display. It's a good collection, I'll give him that. Some fine specimens, one opaque dating from Elizabethan times, or so he claims, but he's got others that were definitely made by the best Venetian Magics. Top glassmakers, they were. But the fool messed up, didn't he? Or maybe he just forgot he'd stolen mine, because there it was, amongst the bunch: my marble."

"And how'd you recognize it?"

"A man knows his balls when he sees them." A statement I'd laugh over later, but right now I had to maintain a tiny bit of professionalism.

"It's a sulphide," he continued. "Know what those are?" It sounded like a type of medicine, but I merely shook my head. "German-made with a figure inside. Mine had a black cat. Very distinctive."

"I have to ask this, but did you steal Mr Coppersmith's marbles?"

"One of them's mine. And who knows how many others in his collection are pilfered."

"That doesn't exactly answer the question."

When he started digging in one of the candy bins — some sort of banana-flavored taffy that was brimming full — I thought he was avoiding answering me. His hand went nearly to the bottom before he pulled it back out. In his grasp was a small, black velvet bag whose contents clacked together with the distinctive sound of glass hitting glass.

"You kept them in the candy bins?" I asked incredulously.

"No one ever buys the banana ones," Tremaine said with a shrug. He passed me the bag.

"Are they all here?"

"I've only removed the one that's mine."

"Why not just take yours and return the rest to Mr Coppersmith?"

With a smile that was both guilty and pleased with himself, Tremaine said, "Wanted to make him sweat a bit, didn't I?"

I wasn't sure what to say to that, but Mr Coppersmith had hired me to find his marbles, and technically, I had. If he was going to complain about one missing, I'd just have to sit these two down for the same chat about friendship and sharing my kindergarten teacher had given me when I'd once hoarded all of the classroom's crayons.

"I'll have to have him verify everything's in order, but I'm sure he'll be glad to have these back. He was pretty upset over having lost them."

"Guy lost his marbles long before I took those," mumbled Tremaine. "You doing any shopping today?" he asked, pointing to the candy bins.

Taking the hint, I filled a small paper sack with a variety of mini chocolate bars, jelly bean packets, licorice strips, and out of pity, a few banana taffies. It ended up setting me back two dollars and sixty cents. And yes, I did plan to claim it as a business expense.

CHAPTER TWENTY-THREE
CONNECTING DOTS

I wouldn't exactly say I skipped back to the agency. After all, I'm not a skipping kind of gal. Especially not when I'm enjoying a lime-flavored lollipop that could cause serious internal damage if I tripped and fell with it in my mouth. But I was filled with a skip-worthy wonder over how ridiculously easy detecting was.

Think about it. I see one picture, I walk a few blocks, I ask one or two questions, and I had my culprit. Sleuthing was a piece of six-layer cake with cream cheese frosting.

And people thought I needed to pass some silly course from the Academy. Pshaw! Oberlin could jam my lollipop stick up his nose, because I was well on my way to getting my license and becoming the greatest detective in MagicLand.

I was in such an uncharacteristically good mood that, on passing a newsstand, I picked up a copy of the *Herald*. Who knows, I might want to write my own opinion piece about my now-proven investigative talents. Or perhaps I could propose a weekly column about the life of a detective extraordinaire.

And why was I heading back to the agency? Because even though Tremaine's wasn't far from Mr Coppersmith's place, I wasn't so giddy with triumph that I'd forgotten about my license application.

I didn't know the exact rules, but I wasn't about to risk there being some sort of fine print that would render the contract invalid if I returned Mr Coppersmith's marbles before having him sign his form.

Once at the office, I took a peek inside the velvet bag. I didn't know marbles from anything, and I'd never known anyone who played with them. To me, they'd always been nothing more than novelty items people with too much money poured into the bottom of overpriced vases.

I had to admit, though, the ones in the bag were intriguing. There were some with twists of green or blue. Others had spirals of silver throughout the orb. Some resembled agates. A few had gold flecks floating inside the glass. And one was a pure deep red — possibly the opaque Tremaine had mentioned.

I closed the bag and tossed it onto my desk, then chewed my way through two packets of black licorice while sifting through the piles of paper that seemed to have grown on the desk's surface since yesterday morning. I'd finally found Mr Coppersmith's file and his number when Pablo pawed at my leg and let out an attention-seeking meow.

"Where did you come from?" I asked as he leapt onto the desk. Or tried to. Although he'd executed a perfectly effortless cat jump, he landed on a few pens I'd left out. He scrambled, sending them scattering, then slid right onto the floor, dragging with him my calendar, the newspaper, and the bag of marbles, which landed with a glassy *clank* next to him.

Pablo's back arched and he hissed at the velvet sack. Sort of like the feline equivalent of when you trip while walking down the street, then glare accusingly back at the sidewalk as if your clumsiness was the pavement's fault.

Perhaps deciding he'd told the marbles a thing or two and they'd never do anything to offend him again, Pablo sauntered over to an empty cardboard box, jumped inside, and curled up for a nap.

As I was squatting down to find the sheet of paper Mr C's number had been on, my phone rang. I stretched up and answered it without checking the caller ID.

"Have you gotten anywhere on my case?" a woman asked. She sounded rather serious, but there was a chuckle lurking behind the stern tone.

"It was next on my to-do list," I lied.

"Good. We'd hate to have to fire you." My mom then burst out laughing, and in the background I could hear my dad's laugh rumbling up like thunder from his slim torso.

"Very funny, guys. Is this really a legit case? I need to know, because I do have other clients. *Real* clients."

"We are real clients, but there really is no rush. We know you'll get to it when you can."

I told them of solving Mr Coppersmith's case, which launched them into a round of congratulations and knew-you-could-do-its. It was all very awkward. I didn't think I'd ever get used to their praise over my successes or sympathy over my failures.

"We better let you go, so you can call Clive. I'm sure he'll be thrilled." Or vengeful when he discovered Tremaine kept one of the marbles, but I'd jump over that hobby horse when I got to it. "You should also call Busby. He's very keen on you getting that form done sooner rather than later. And it looks like you'll have it to him sooner," my mom said, gushing with pride.

I promised her I would, and once we'd said our goodbyes, I called Mr T and told him I'd have the form ready by lunchtime.

"So soon?"

"Don't sound so surprised."

"I'm not. It's just— Well, it's a relief."

"You thought I couldn't manage it?" I teased.

"No, not relief in that sense. We simply have work you could assist with." Before I could tell him HQ was being a stable of stubborn mules, and that I could obviously work on cases without any sort of license in hand, Mr T hurriedly added, "Lunchtime, you said? Shall I come by at noon, then?"

"Better make it one. Just in case. The form's not exactly signed off," I added reluctantly.

"Cassie," he said, putting six metric tons of warning behind the single word.

"Look, if I get all your silly bits of paperwork done early, I'll call you. Okay?"

Once Mr T had tepidly agreed, I hung up and dialed Mr Coppersmith's number. As it rang, I muttered to myself, practicing what I'd say about my discovery, about arranging when to meet, about reminding him to sign his contract, about— I then realized my rehearsal had gotten quite lengthy and that the line was still ringing. I hung up and dialed again. Again, no answer and no voicemail.

I shrugged it off and decided to try again in a bit. Who knows, maybe he was out running a marble-related errand.

Not wanting to lose track of time by delving into any research (read: cat videos), I picked up the *Herald*.

I'd like to say I resisted, but the first page I turned to when I opened the newspaper was the opinion section. A smile lifted my lips when I saw there were no articles about me. This really was turning out to be a good day.

One piece did catch my eye, however. A short editorial that had my detective senses tingling.

IS ANYONE CONNECTING THE MISSING DOTS?

Over the past few weeks, if you follow national and international Magic news, you may have noticed a smattering of reports about missing Magics, even Magics found dead in their homes.

And you may have ignored these reports.

After all, they didn't happen to you or your loved ones, so what's to make you sit up and take notice?

I admit, I would probably be the same if I weren't in the news business. If I didn't have a background in investigative journalism.

But I am and I do. These reports, the increasing frequency of them, leaves me concerned. And sometimes I feel I'm the only one who is. HQ hasn't sent up any type of alert, and neither are the police warning the public to be on their guard.

But perhaps they should be. Perhaps they need to connect the dots between these cases. Because witches and wizards are disappearing from their communities at a rate we haven't seen since the early days of the Mauvais.

And we have seen this pattern before. Not with the Mauvais, of course, but with another, far more sinister group.

Those of you who know your history will recall a string of missing Magics when the vampires thought they could take over our communities. Personally, I believe we never should have allowed them to integrate with us. Which, for the most part, they haven't.

So ask yourselves, why do they stay in their own enclaves? Why don't they mix with us? Perhaps it's because they need privacy to plot against us once more?

Or are we to think what's happening is completely innocent? Magics simply in need of a break and escaping for a time. Perhaps all these missing practitioners are *sneaking off on a cruise together. I know damn well that the* Herald's *readers aren't so gullible. You are smart. I am smart. And we must connect the dots if the authorities won't.*

Here is my promise to you, dear reader: I will dig further into what might link all these disappearances together. I will uncover the truth.

I wondered if this was simply the *Herald* being hyperbolic to sell papers, or if it was part of the problem HQ wanted my help with. With my parents, I'd proven I could find people from only the tiniest of clues. If Magics were being kidnapped, surely I should be part of solving what was behind it all. And if HQ wasn't going to bring me onto the case, maybe the editor and I could collaborate on—

I stopped my dreams of detecting fame right there. This was the same editor who regularly printed anti-Cassie articles in his paper. He wasn't about to call me up as a partner in fighting crime and figuring out who was behind all these disappearances.

No, if he even bothered to delve further, the editor would go to Oberlin's team. The team I'd failed to make because of stupid Tobey Tenpenny. Oberlin would be the one out there sorting through the real mysteries, the compelling mysteries, while I was left to find missing marbles and other trinkets.

Luckily, I was pulled from my morose thoughts when the phone rang. The number was familiar, but I couldn't place who it might be. I took the call, but before I could say anything, the caller blurted, "Cassie, this is Winnifred Oberlin."

My stomach dropped. She was firing me. I knew it. She'd come to her senses and wanted Inspector Walrus to handle her case. That was okay, I tried to tell myself. I didn't need her. I had the marbles, after all. Still, a little cushion, a few extra kudos for my application would be nice.

"Hello, Mrs Oberlin," I said, hiding my worry behind an excessively bright tone. "Can I help you?"

"Oh, yes, I've found that photo of the brooch, but I'm up to my ears with things today. Wesley's got some big student thing he's hosting at the Academy— Oh, sorry, I didn't mean to bring up a sore subject—"

"It's not a big deal. I'm over it."

"Oh good. Very professional of you. But like I said, very busy, so could you do me a favor and come by this morning to pick up the picture? Say, around ten? And don't worry, Wesley will be out, so you don't have to worry about running into him."

It's like the woman was telepathic because that had been the exact worry that had sprung to mind.

"Sounds great. I'll pop by then."

Mrs Oberlin, sounding quite giddy, thanked me and wished me a good day. Before I'd even ended the call, my calendar had added our meeting in pink ink in a flourishing script right above the formal handwriting of Mr T's appointment.

* * *

Deciding there was nothing wrong with killing two birds with one stone so long as the birds are only metaphorical ones, I figured I'd work on tracking down Mr Coppersmith on my way to Winnifred's.

Since they do a full English breakfast, the Wandering Wizard was open even though it was only half-past nine in the morning. The proprietor said Mr Coppersmith hadn't been in since the night before. He then told me if I wanted to try his apartment, it was just up the outside stairs. As I took the exterior walkway to the further back of the two upper-story apartments, the neighbor's curtains twitched, but my knock on Clive's door yielded no response.

Fueled up with Tremaine's candy, I worked a Mirage Hex over my face for the journey down Main Street to Winnifred's house. When I reached Spellbound, I recalled Mr Coppersmith's napkin. I dropped my magical disguise and asked the clerk at the register if anyone had seen him that morning.

"Nope, no Coppersmith sightings," she told me after returning from the kitchen to ask around. She then passed me a cranberry-orange scone. Even though I prefer the lemon poppyseed ones, I pulled out some money to pay, but the clerk pushed the money back toward me. "For what you did to Fred," she whispered. "Gwendolyn's begun a new sourdough, and this one's so much better behaved. Although, when they're young, you never can tell how they'll be later in life. But Ned's an absolute darling so far."

She then told me she'd give me a shout if Mr Coppersmith came by. I thanked her, reinstated the Mirage Hex, and continued on my way to the Oberlin house.

Once there, Winnifred handed me the photo in an envelope, then asked if I wanted to come in for tea, saying she had just bought a chocolate cake. Tempting as dessert-for-second-breakfast sounded, I declined, knowing I needed to hunt down Mr Coppersmith. Besides, I'd be too worried about a walrus sighting to enjoy the treat.

Once I was off the Oberlins' block, I tried Clive's number again. And again, he didn't answer. I wanted to hurl his stupid marbles to the ground. Instead, I pounded the pavement trying to find him. I even returned to the toy shop in case the two marble enthusiasts had suddenly made amends. Tremaine only scowled when I asked about Mr Coppersmith.

I realized there was no way around it. I was not getting that form signed off before lunch. I called Mr Tenpenny and told him I'd have to reschedule.

"Until…?" he asked.

"Later?" I replied without conviction. "I can't seem to get ahold of Mr Coppersmith. But his case really is solved," I rushed to say. "Isn't that good enough?"

"You know it's not. I'll keep my eye out for him when I run a few errands today, but do try to track him down as soon as possible."

As if I hadn't been doing just that. I'd keep at it, but for now, I needed a quick break.

Back at the agency. I locked Mr C's marbles in my safe, which until then, had mainly been used to store cookies and cupcakes. After all, if I left any sweets in the kitchenette, my dad would eat them before I ever got a taste.

I'd barely sat down with a much-needed sandwich when the agency's phone rang. Drawing a blank over which business name I was using, I merely answered with, "Detective Agency. How may I help you?"

"Black? Inspector Oberlin here." I did not like the smug tone in his voice. "I'm calling to issue you with a formal warning."

"For what?" And I really did start racking my brain for something I might have done. I had jaywalked a few times this morning. Was I in trouble for using a Mirage Hex? You weren't supposed to use it to impersonate people — which I hadn't, I'd merely used it to blur my features — but maybe there was some arcane spell-casting law I didn't know about.

"For going on private property without permission. Seems you were loitering around Clive Coppersmith's place. Neighbor didn't like the looks of you, and I knew exactly who she was talking about when she described you."

"I didn't—"

"She's got a photo of you hammering on Coppersmith's door."

"But I—"

"And then later you go and harass my wife? My own home, Black? You think I don't have cameras on my door? I'm tempted to give you more than a warning, but Winnifred tells me you weren't bothering her. Still, I know your skills with a BrainSweeping Charm, so I'm not sure she's remembering correctly." I gave up defending myself at this point and remained silent. He was being ridiculous and there's no arguing with people who lack space in their tiny brains for reason. "Again, it's just a warning, but you are on my radar. Especially after reading today's *Herald*. Another incident, and I'll have to pull you in. Understand?"

My jaw so tense I could barely speak, I told him I did and hung up before he could harangue me any further.

Of all the nerve. And what was he talking about in the *Herald*? Today had been a blissfully Cassie-free day for the paper, hadn't it? I brushed my sandwich crumbs off the newspaper and flicked through from the front to the opinion section, where I'd read the missing Magics article earlier. He was insane. There was nothing about me.

Nothing that is, until I turned the page.

CHAPTER TWENTY-FOUR
THE FACTS OF LIFE

CASSIE BLACK HASN'T GOT A CLUE

Cassie Black, kicked out of the Academy for cheating and for disrespecting an honorable and highly respected member of the Rosaria community, is either delusional or has a very strange sense of humor, because she is still trying to lure people into her detective agency.

Of course, the one client she has been able to bring into her agency is none other than Mayor Matilda Marheart.

Should we be surprised that this woman who ran a corrupt campaign and who this author believes is part of a group that has no good intentions for Rosaria, should be associating with someone like Cassie Black so readily?

No, we shouldn't.

A thought having stuck me, I stopped reading. Inspector Oberlin had run against Matilda. And he'd been a very sore loser with all the usual rhetoric of campaign corruption and voter fraud.

Oberlin was no friend of Matilda. Oberlin was no friend of

mine. Could he be the one behind all these articles? He'd certainly have enough influence in Rosaria to push the *Herald* into what was nearing slander territory. I filed the theory away to consider later, then scanned the rest of the piece.

> *What's worse? I've just learned that Miss Black hasn't even obtained her detective's license. She pulled this trick at her previous job in the Norm world, and now she thinks she can pull the magical wool over our eyes?*
>
> *Hardly.*
>
> *Thankfully, most residents of Rosaria are smart enough to stay away. And why would they want her services, anyway? Ms Black has no experience in sifting through clues, working with clients, or showing any sort of common courtesy. Any person who trusts her with their cases would have to be either drunk or under the influence of a Confounding Spell. Which I wouldn't put past someone like her.*
>
> *Don't stand for it, folks. Don't trust her with your cases or your personal lives. Remember, Inspector Oberlin wouldn't have dismissed her without good cause. Again, I urge you to avoid her agency at all costs.*

I hurled the paper into the recycle bin. Then decided recycling wasn't good enough for it (nuclear weapon test subject would do). I plucked it out of the bin and was just heading over to the paper shredder when my calendar started squawking at me that it was time to get a move on, that productivity came first, and that my coffee break was over.

This was apparently a standard feature of this model of calendar, a way to keep employees from lingering too long in the break room. I ignored it and, while it wasn't as satisfying as an earth-shattering mushroom cloud, I did enjoy a malicious thrill as the *Herald* ground through the hungry teeth of the shredder.

After taking a moment to catch its breath, the calendar started in again, informing me of my deadlines, reminding me how management didn't reward slackers, chastising me for not being more of a go-getter.

I threw a Silencing Spell on it. Surprisingly, it worked.

Seated in a guest chair at my desk, I got out the photo Winnifred had given me and used a magnifying glass to take a good look at the brooch. Fiona was right. The thing bordered on the Land of Gaudy, but the delicate craftsmanship gave it a refined delicacy.

I then texted Runa to ask where the portal to Canberra could be found in MagicLand. My plan was, the next time I was out, to retrace Mrs Oberlin's steps on the night she last remembered wearing the brooch. Handily, the portal was down a side alley from the Wandering Wizard.

Since three in the afternoon was the earliest I'd ever recalled seeing Mr Coppersmith at the Wizard, I spent the next couple of hours trying to find information on the Boncoeur family, on Tudor-era jewelry, on folklore tied to garnets, and then once again on losing myself down a cat video rabbit hole. If there's any doubt cats rule the Internet, the fact that you can't be online for more than an hour without getting suckered into one cat-related GIF, meme, or compilation should make it very clear they do.

As three o'clock approached, I texted Alastair, asking if he wanted to meet at the Wizard for a late lunch. He quickly responded, saying he was too busy and we'd catch up over dinner. I let out a heavy sigh, pulled the marbles out of the safe, and with Pablo sticking close to my heels, headed for the Wizard on my own, hoping like mad that Mr Coppersmith was there.

Not only to get the case completed, but because, like him, I could really use some company.

The meandering route I took to the Wizard covered all the ground (and then some) Mrs Oberlin would have logically taken to return to her home from the Canberra portal. All except for the final block to the Oberlin house, since I was in no mood for Inspector Oberlin to accuse me of casing their street.

I found no bejeweled roosters. And at the Wandering Wizard, I found no Mr Coppersmith.

* * *

Pablo and I loitered at the pub for over two hours, me nursing a pint just like my nowhere-to-be-found client, and Pablo lapping up several saucers of cream. By six p.m. I was fed up with wasting my time. And with pretty much everything else, if I'm being honest.

I left a note with the Wizard's proprietor to have Mr C call me straight away if he showed up. Then, too worn down and too hungry to muster a Mirage Hex, I zigzagged along side streets, hoping to avoid the Anti-Cassie League on my way home. And also hoping Alastair had whipped up something for dinner.

Unfortunately, once Pablo leapt and I tripped through my closet, there were no scents of home cooking wafting through the apartment. Despite all the cream, Pablo's first order of business was to run to his dish, sit beside it, and give a chirruping meow as he stared at me expectantly.

"Alastair?" I called as I plopped a scoop of wet food into the bowl. No one was in the apartment, so I went downstairs to see if I might be allowed into the man cave/workroom.

Big mistake.

Just like old times, Morelli must have heard me on the steps. Looking like he was ready to tell me off for some minor infraction, he poked his head out of his apartment door. From inside blared the theme song to *The Facts of Life*, and I just knew that was going to be stuck in my head for the rest of the week.

"You getting anywhere with Matilda's case?" he barked.

"It hasn't even been two days."

"Thirty-four hours and eighteen minutes," he corrected. "Is that your way of saying you haven't? It's important she finds that jewel."

"She's not my only client, you know. Then again, I understand it's difficult for you to relate to having more than one person who wants to do business with you."

"Very funny, Black. I just— Look, not as though you care, but there's things—" He visibly bit back his words.

"Things?"

"Never mind. It'd just mean a lot if you made her case a priority."

It certainly would be since hers was the highest paying job I had. But unless clues about a garnet that had been missing for a few hundred years started falling into my lap, Matilda's case remained as impossible to solve as it had been when I'd stupidly accepted it.

"I'll see what I can do." This vague statement seemed to appease Morelli, so I pointed to the workroom door and asked, "No gnomes… does that mean it's safe to go in?"

"Yeah, you might want to check on him. It's been awful quiet in there. Why you in such a funk, anyway?"

Was my mood really so low that even Morelli could sense it?

"Bad day at the office. Well, good day, then bad day, then total crap day. I kind of need a shoulder to scream on."

"You can always talk to me, you know."

The instant he made this offer, we both shrank back with looks of horror on our faces.

"That would be weird," I said. "Too weird."

"Right, sorry." Morelli shook his head as if trying to rid his ears of mites. "Just an automatic response."

"Right. I'm going now," I said warily. "You enjoy Mrs Garrett and the girls."

Morelli gave a sharp nod, then hurriedly shut the door.

CHAPTER TWENTY-FIVE
BOILING CHARMS

Inside the workroom, it was eerily quiet. No metal clanking against metal, no needles clacking away, not even any music. Most of Alastair's worktable was covered in tidy piles of gears in various sizes, animal parts (metallic ones, not real ones, just to be clear), and lengths of wire. But one area was covered under a floral-patterned sheet. Was this the secret commission? The reason for the gnome guards?

I couldn't resist. I stepped over, and my fingers were mere inches from the edge of the sheet when I looked up to see Alastair sitting at the next table over. He had three massive books opened before him and was busily scribbling notes onto a pad. I jerked my hand back, but he hadn't even noticed me.

"Alastair. Earth to Alastair," I said, realizing I could have taken a peek and probably walked off with the mystery project and he'd have been none the wiser.

"Cass, hey." The puppy dog excitement was nowhere to be seen behind his research-glazed eyes. "Is it dinnertime already?"

"Yeah, but no big deal. I just came by to talk."

"That's nice," he said, distractedly jotting down something. "Look, Rafi came by with some more files for me, and I'm up to my eyebrows in this."

"Rafi was here?"

"Yeah, had to drop some things off for me and Fiona from Olivia. Oh, and he brought a hamper from Fortnum's." Without taking his eyes off his paperwork, he pointed to a carry-on size wicker basket that looked unopened, judging by the big pale blue ribbon still tied around the handle. He then looked up, his eyes clearing, almost as if just realizing I was there. "How was today? At the agency?"

"Okay. Solved a case, but can't get ahold of the client, and then Oberlin—"

"Great! That's great. Another case solved." He gave me a glancing kiss on the cheek. "Look, we'll celebrate later, but I've really got to get to this."

"Maybe I can help. What is this?" I reached for a file, but Alastair snatched it and moved it under his pile of notes.

"The research HQ's pressing me to get done. Do you know anything about the history leading up to the Vampire Revolt, in enchantments they specialize in, or methods they use to increase their power?"

"You know, I think I skimmed over that during my training. Is this all part of replacing what history Banna had in her head?"

"Yeah, I guess. And HQ's really eager for it, so maybe we can meet up later for whatever dessert's in there." He indicated the basket with his pen. "I'll come up when I get a break, okay?"

"Sure," I said, trying to not slump my shoulders in disappointment.

I grabbed the Fortnum's basket as Alastair, his attention already fixed firmly on a book to his left, mumbled something that might have been, "See you in a bit." I was starting to feel like I spent more time with him before we lived together. Still, if you were going to have to eat dinner alone, eating it from a five-hundred-dollar picnic basket wasn't a bad way to go about it.

* * *

The next morning, I prepared a balanced — and solitary — breakfast of Fortnum scones, jam, and tea.

Or tried to.

I filled the kettle with water, but, feeling too impatient to get my day underway, I aimed a Boiling Charm at the pot rather than waiting for electricity to do the job. The water rumbled a bit and induction bubbles churned up with a delightful dance of Brownian motion. I was just about to grab the handle to pour the hot-enough water over my bag of Irish Breakfast when the entire contents of the pot froze solid.

Curious, I hit it with a Boiling Charm again. The ice melted, which seemed like a good start. Then, in the very next second, steam billowed out of the spout like Old Faithful showing its stuff. Pablo wandered in, gave a curious meow, then watched in wonder as a cloud of steam formed.

Not knowing what might happen next — a lightning storm in the kitchen was my first thought — I pinned my arms to my sides until the kettle went dry.

Worried about what my magic was up to, I refilled the kettle and flicked the switch to heat the water like a normal person. Realizing I ought to bring up this little mishap during my afternoon appointment with Dr Dunwiddle, I could already picture the what-have-you-done-now look on her face.

At a quarter to seven, Pablo and I headed out. We'd made it a whole two steps past the portal before I had to turn on my heels and return to the apartment. In my desire to call it quits last night, rather than trudge back to the agency, I'd taken Mr Coppersmith's marbles home with me and had forgotten to grab them on the way out.

Marbles now in hand, I sidetracked to the apartments above

the Wandering Wizard and tried Mr Coppersmith's door again on the off chance I might catch him before he could sneak away for the day. But, other than the neighbor's curtain twitching, there was no sign of life.

From the Wizard, I had just stepped onto a blissfully quiet Magical Main Street when Mayor Marheart came hurrying from the opposite direction. Her red pumps clacked hard against the pavement, and her elegant, normally pale face was tight and reddened with fury.

Paranoid that her anger might be with me — what can I say, I was a little gun-shy with all the grumpy Magics I'd been dealing with lately — I scanned my surroundings for a shopfront's entryway to tuck myself into, but it was too late.

"Cassie. Morning." This grunted greeting called to mind the dead I'd brought back to life a few months ago. The Queen's English hadn't been one of their top skills when they'd first woken up.

"Mayor Marheart."

She shook some tension out of her shoulders. I then noticed her right hand was wrapped in a bandage. "Call me Matilda, please. How's the case proceeding? I— Look, some things have come to my attention. If I added more to your fee, do you think you could rush things along? Prioritize my case?"

If I hadn't already solved Mr Coppersmith's case, if I wasn't one signature away from getting my detective license, I'd have made up a string of excuses to hide the fact that, whenever I tried to work on her case, I got distracted by cat videos.

Once I'd completed the tiny task of tracking down Mr C — which I intended to do that morning — the pressure of the license application would be gone, and I'd be able to devote more time to Matilda's case. Still, as I couldn't see how to proceed with locating the missing jewel, I wasn't ready to make any promises.

"Everything okay?" I asked, avoiding committing to her offer. "You seem a little—?"

"Pissed off?"

"That would cover it, yeah."

"It's the *Herald*. Did you see the editorial yesterday? I have half a mind to—" Seeming to remember she was a politician, she cut off her words and instead forced a pleasant smile that didn't reach her eyes. "It's slander."

"I'm familiar with how the *Herald* tests the limits of free speech."

"Ah, yes, you are, aren't you? Which is why it's even more important we find that jewel."

"Because…?" I prodded, not seeing the connection between finding an heirloom and stopping libelous prose.

"Well," Matilda began, hesitating as if she'd already said too much and was searching for the best way out of the verbal corner she'd backed herself into. "It would show what a great detective you are and how wrong that idiot Oberlin was to kick you out. It would also prove that I know how to assemble a good team to get done what I intend to accomplish."

I had to admit, the lady could think on her feet.

"So the case?" she asked insistently.

"Like I said, give me a little more time to see if I can get anywhere with it. Then we can talk." Because she wasn't the only one who knew their way around a vague answer.

"The sooner the better," she stated curtly before saying a brusque goodbye and marching off.

I barely had time to process the odd nature of the brief conversation when my phone rang. For a heart-leaping moment I thought it was Mr Coppersmith calling. But the caller ID brought me back down to earth.

"Hey, Dr D," I answered.

"Cassie, can you come in early for your appointment? It's—" There was a noise in the background that sounded like the tinkle of broken glass. "No, over there," she snapped at someone. "Sorry, Cassie, I've got to see to this, but can you come in now instead of later?"

"Sure, but what's up?"

"You can't place those next to each other, they'll—" A loud pop made me pull the phone away from my ear. "Just come by as soon as you can, okay? I've apparently been given the most incompetent clean-up crew in all of Rosaria."

The phone went silent.

CHAPTER TWENTY-SIX
INVISIBILITY OINTMENT

If I thought my encounter with Matilda was going to be the oddest part of my day, it was nothing compared to what greeted me when I approached Runa's clinic.

You remember her front window, right? Where she shows off an array of historical medical tools that either prove how far magical medicine has come, or are meant to frighten off less stouthearted patients? Well, the glass of the window had been shattered, and the artfully arranged display now looked like a pair of monkeys had been let loose in it to find a well-hidden banana.

Several workers were sweeping up the glass without touching their brooms or dustpans, reminding me of Mickey in *The Sorcerer's Apprentice*. Which, as I recall, didn't turn out so well for him in the end.

Other workers were magically gluing back together all of Runa's RetroHex Vaccine placards, placing Runa's historical objects into boxes, and discussing what thickness of glass to replace the broken pane with. While I went in, Pablo remained outside, watching it all with intense interest.

Inside the clinic itself, a quartet of early morning customers were speculatively, and loudly, gossiping by the counter. When I entered, they stopped chatting and swiveled their heads like owls to look at me. As one, they narrowed their eyes, then turned back to each other and began whispering cattily. I tucked my chin and shuffled over to the chair farthest from them. Really, where was an invisibility cloak when you needed one?

The gossiping customers soon left, giving me one more nasty glance over their shoulders as they exited. Just as that door closed, another opened (because some sayings are true). This was the door to Runa's exam room, and from it stepped Morelli. Dr Dunwiddle followed close behind, reciting instructions on wound care.

"What are you doing here?" I asked. This wasn't me being rude, it was true curiosity. See, trolls, even half-trolls like Morelli, have a healing power within their magic. It's what set Mr Wood speeding along the road to recovery after he'd been left for dead, and also why I'd spent very little time in a cast over the past few months despite having my hand broken into a billion pieces twice within only a couple weeks. "Shouldn't you be able to heal yourself?"

"Don't be an idiot, Black. Trolls can't heal themselves." As he said this, Morelli kept his hands behind his back.

"What happened? Nasty crochet accident?"

Even Dr Dunwiddle snorted a laugh at that. She then hurriedly slipped the slim box that contained, I assumed, Morelli's file into its slot.

"Gary bit me again." Morelli held up his right hand. The index finger was wrapped in gauze. He eyed me levelly. "It's almost like someone enchanted him with a Piranha Hex."

"I didn't even know such a hex existed, so don't look at me."

"Alright, Eugene," said Runa as she placed a small tube on the counter. "Apply this tonight, change the bandage, and it should be healed by morning. And maybe keep your fingers out of the fishbowl from now on."

"But he likes his head scratched."

"So use a toothbrush, a teaspoon, anything but your fingers. They're apparently quite tasty," she said with a barely suppressed grin.

"Matilda's case?" Morelli asked me after paying for his ointment.

"Working on it," I lied as a worker knocked a remaining chunk of glass from the front window.

A flash of Matilda's injured hand came to mind. It was possible she also had a misbehaving goldfish, but what if—

Before I could complete the thought, Runa barked out, "Cassie, come through."

"Gotta go, Genie."

"We're talking later, Black."

"Looking forward to it," I said before dashing into the relative safety of the exam room.

Suddenly feeling self-conscious about my little magic problem, I didn't immediately bring up the kettle incident to Runa. I mean, that could have been caused by anything, right? Bad mood. Low blood sugar. Vile newspaper articles.

"What happened to the window?" I asked, not afraid to use a delaying tactic when needed.

"Someone broke it," Runa said as she pulled out my file and prepared the collection vials.

"Clearly. But why? I mean, couldn't someone have just magicked your door to break in?"

"Suppose they could, which is why Oberlin wrote it off as a few anti-RetroHex Vaccine vandals trying to make some sort of point. I told him I was pretty sure there was more to it, but he wouldn't listen." With a weak grin, she added, "I almost called him a pig-headed walrus."

"So what did happen?"

"They broke the glass, came into the pharmacy, took a few

things, then ransacked the display. Not thrilled about it, either. Olivia told me I ought to put more protective spells on that window, but this is Rosaria. I just didn't expect it here."

"Stolen items? You want me to search for them?" I asked, all but waggling my eyebrows with the hint.

"Sure, why not?" Runa said dismissively, as if she had no hope whatsoever that her stuff could be recovered.

"So, what was taken?"

"Amongst a few of my more expensive lotions, they grabbed the bone saw from my window display. Thing was a gift from one of my first clients," she complained, quirking her lips in irritation. "And, for whatever reason, they swiped the entire stock of your vials. Don't know what in the world the idiots think they're going to do with them, but that's why I needed you to come in. Your parents are due for an infusion this afternoon, and I'm now out of Cassie Juice." Runa's eyeglasses flew over and scrutinized the bag of marbles I'd set next to me. Runa herself raised a questioning eyebrow.

"They're Mr Coppersmith's," I answered. "Solved his case, but couldn't get ahold of him yesterday. Or this morning."

"Congratulations." Although she was clearly having a rough morning, Runa did seem genuinely pleased. She began prepping a few vials for my donation. "And how's the magic been?"

"Mostly okay." Diverting the conversation again, I said, "So, about this break-in—"

"What's 'mostly okay' mean?" Runa demanded, her face full of perturbed concern. "It's all okay or it's not."

After an eye roll to indicate this really wasn't a good use of her time, I told her about the kettle, then rushed to add, "I'm sure it's nothing."

"It's not nothing. I've been checking your magic levels with each donation. Your magic hasn't wavered a fraction for weeks.

This can happen to some witches when they become—"

"I'm not pregnant," I blurted.

"I was going to say when they become worried about their sugar intake. You're not dieting, are you?"

I glanced down at my bony frame. "And where exactly would I lose weight from? I mean, my feet are a little big, but I don't think dropping toe fat is really a thing, is it?"

"Fine. Not a diet thing, but it is concerning. Arm." I held out my arm and she placed a dozen collection vials on it. "I'll run labs on a couple of these. If all looks good, I can give the others to your parents."

"And if it doesn't look good?"

"I'll have Busby and Tobey come in. It won't do much good for your dad since they're only related by marriage, and obviously the tie between them and your mom isn't as strong as yours is, but it'll keep their levels from dropping too much until we get this sorted."

"But what if my parents—"

"They're doing fine." Dr Dunwiddle sat on her rollie stool with a pensive look on her round face. "I'm more concerned about you. You haven't been around any evil objects, have you? Strange watches? Anything like that?"

"I won't even allow Alastair to have a Dollar Store digital watch." I then recalled something. "Pablo did hiss at Mr Coppersmith's marbles."

"Let's see them."

I handed her the bag, but Runa refused to take it and instead pointed to her countertop. Never touching the velvet, she waved her hands over the sack as her glasses shifted back and forth as if scanning the contents. Runa then asked the marbles if they had any wicked intentions, if anyone had cursed them, if they were in any way bad marbles.

While I was curious to see if they'd reply, it was also really hard not to laugh at this. I pictured the marbles as a pack of misbehaved Pomeranians hanging their heads in shame for displeasing their master.

"They seem to be in order," she declared as her glasses zipped back into her breast pocket. "But you say Pablo hissed at them?"

"Yep, a good ol' cat fight hiss. Then again, they had fallen off my desk and nearly landed on him."

"Always trust the cat. Still, the marbles seem fine. Maybe Pablo just doesn't like something about the smell of Mr Coppersmith. But that's really not important. What is important is this fluctuating magic you've got going on."

"It was only the once. Is it really that big of a deal?"

Dr D looked at me in that way that told me there really are stupid questions. "It is very much a big deal. It means your magic is unreliable. If you go to cast a spell, say something like the Match Charm, it might produce a bonfire, or it might only generate a weak spark."

I didn't like the worried expression on Runa's face. This was someone who normally radiated confidence and determination to uncover the solution to any magical medical problem. She wasn't someone to wear the look of being lost in an impossible-to-solve puzzle like she was doing now.

"Okay, I get that this is bad, but why is it happening and what can I do about it? Is there something like hormone replacement therapy for my magic levels?"

"Why it's happening, I don't know. That's the most concerning part. Sometimes kids have a bit of fluctuation as they're settling into their magic, but not to the extreme you've described. You haven't been doing any experimenting? Magic capsules? You need to be honest with me."

I knew exactly what she was hinting at. As a way to earn

extra credit, Oberlin had set up a few lecturers from the police department for students to attend. Desperate for any information that wasn't a Stunning Spell, I went to all of them, including a presentation from the Drugs, Potions, and Poisons Unit, who scared the bejesus out of us with all the ways Magics illegally messed with their power.

The worst was magic meth. This sent your magic levels soaring, which was just the thing if you were cramming for a magic exam or were about to face a life-or-death magic battle. Problem was, once the high was over, your power plummeted back to earth and crashed hard when it landed. It could be days before your magic levels were back to normal. And the more you were on it, the less effect it had, leading to higher doses and deeper crashes.

"I didn't even know magic drugs existed until a few weeks ago," I replied. "And since I learned about them from a very scary police lecture, I've no desire to try them out. Which brings us back to what's causing this. Have you seen it before?"

"Obviously not, otherwise I'd be able to give you more concrete answers. I need to research this, see if I can find information about previous cases, but for now, testing those," she pointed to the vials, "is our first step. In the meantime, go easy on the magic."

"Not long ago you were mad at me for *not* embracing my magic. Now you're telling me to *avoid* using it?" I teased.

"I'm not telling you to avoid it, you pest of a girl. I'm just saying, maybe don't aim it at any living creatures. Or valuable objects. And until I can check your samples, I'm wary about giving any of your donated magic to your parents. They've got enough to contend with." I was about to protest that it had just been a Boiling Charm on a bad morning, but Runa held up a hand to stop me. "I'll take another sample tomorrow and the day after to see if you stabilize. Today could just be a fluke brought on by stress. Now, any other problems to work on?"

"Not unless you have an ointment that doubles as an invisibility cloak."

"Best I can do is one that hides bruises until they go away. Are you trying to hide from someone?" I told her about the articles, the thug, and the grumpy ladies when I entered the clinic. "Wait, could all that be affecting my magic?"

Because magic, as I'd learned, required some degree of self-assurance. If you were browbeat, if you were made to feel bad about yourself, your magic struggled to exist.

"It's a good theory, and we'll look into it, but those articles should never be printed in the first place. If it helps, just remember that you've got people on your side complaining to the editor about them. And, trust me, you'll survive a few dirty looks. I certainly had my fair share back in the day."

"What day was this?"

"Not long after I set up my first practice. People avoided it like the Poltergeist Plague. On the street, they gave me dirty looks, called me names."

"Why?"

"I was one of the few practitioners who were willing to treat vampires. I'd been raised to think they were just like us, that they wanted to be a part of magic society," she said in the tone of someone drifting off to other thoughts. "It's how I developed those." She gestured to the sample vials.

"*You* invented those?"

"With help, yes. I've always enjoyed research. My point is, you're tough. You'll get through it. Just hang in there."

While I appreciated her confidence, I still considered asking for a gallon-sized jar of the bruise-covering ointment. If I could spread it all over my body…

***

Once back at the agency, Pablo sat beside my desk. I patted my lap, which normally has him leaping up without hesitation. But he hesitated, his tail flicking as if annoyed about something. I looked at the bag of marbles I'd tossed onto my desk. Could it be? I chided myself for the ridiculous thought, but that didn't stop me from putting Mr Coppersmith's marbles in the safe.

"Now?" I asked Pablo and patted my thighs again. This time, he launched into my lap. Curiouser and curiouser, right?

Even though it was still a bit early in the day for phone calls, I tried Mr Coppersmith's number. No answer. Snoopy neighbor or not, if I didn't get ahold of him by ten, I was going to camp outside his door until he either left for the Wizard or returned from whatever marble adventures he was on. Not really looking forward to the prospect of sitting on his welcome mat all day, I tried the number again. My growl of frustration as it rang on and on woke Pablo, who crawled off my lap and spread out across my desktop.

Clearly, I needed a pick-me-up. Plus, despite doctor's orders, I was curious to test out the Boiling Charm again. Don't worry. I made sure the fire extinguisher was at hand before performing the spell. Which worked this time without a hitch.

Brushing off what I deemed to be a glitch in the magic matrix, I carried my steaming mug back to my desk and was just about to sit down when the bell above the door chimed.

Pablo's usual greeting choked off mid-meow. He then scurried off the desk and hopped into the deepest cardboard box he could find.

CHAPTER TWENTY-SEVEN
A SQUIDGY CLIENT

I couldn't help but jerk at the sight of who had entered. My elbow knocked into my mug, splashing half-brewed tea all across my desk. I tried to clean up the puddles with a Drying Spell, and maybe it was the shock I'd just had, but the spell only managed to whisk up half the liquid. Still, half was better than none. My calendar would need to be air dried, but at least I hadn't sent my entire desk up in a puff of smoke.

And let's also blame the shock of seeing my visitor outside of his natural habitat for what came out of my mouth next.

"What are you doing here?" I said, mentally kicking myself very hard in the backside. Despite the sudden boon in business, I still needed clients. No matter how detestable.

My guest sniffed haughtily and looked ready to head right back out the door. He then muttered to himself something that sounded like, "Remember the shelf space," took a deep sigh of resignation, and wriggled back around to face me.

I wish he hadn't. I'd only met the Bookworm once, but that had been enough. The lumpy body, the squat frame, the snidely superior look over the wire-rimmed glasses. That I could handle with a hefty dose of Cassie-ness.

What I couldn't handle, though, was watching him move. Which he was doing now. Extending a few segments, gripping the ground, retracting the segments, then starting all over again. It was disconcerting, and the squidgy sound his body made as those segments contracted and expanded sent spiders with icy-cold feet crawling along my spine.

Watching me over the rim of his glasses, he snorted some sort of general disapproval as he sidled up to the Evil Chair — still in place where the guest chair should be since I could only handle so many pratfalls in a week.

And I know it's terrible to admit, but I kind of wanted the chair to misbehave and plop him onto the ground. I realize this gives the impression that I go around judging people based on their weird bodies, but the Bookworm, well, he just gets under your skin. Like a larva that will later hatch and consume your living flesh.

But apparently Evil Chair was less judge-y than me, and it didn't move a millimeter as the Bookworm slithered into its ergonomically cushioned seat. I might have been scowling at this point, but I swear it was at the chair, not my guest.

"Is this how you greet all your customers?" he asked, tucking a satchel beside him. "No wonder you're having such difficulties."

"Difficulties?" I said, crossing my arms over my chest. "What difficulties would those be? Just this week, I've been hired for four new cases." I shook my head. "Why am I defending myself to you?" I took a seat. Warily, of course, just in case all chairs had it in for me. "But really, why *are* you here? And don't try to pin any fines on me, because I never checked anything out from the library."

That would be the Magics' Library in the Tower of London, of which the Bookworm was head librarian.

"No, of course, not. You wouldn't have been allowed to, because although you've been part of a Magic community for— How long now?"

"Four months."

"Four months," he repeated scornfully. "And you have yet to get a library card."

"I have a library card," I said defensively. Given that I had a fairly sizable book addiction, and, until recently, had barely had enough money to feed myself, the only way I could get my fix was my library card. I considered it my most valuable possession.

"Only for the Norm library system," he said with utter disdain for such a banal institution. "Not for the MILC."

"Milk?"

"The Magics' International Library Consortium. You have no card. You've not even applied for one." From his tone, I guessed that, in his opinion, this was the worst atrocity a Magic could commit. I wanted to tell him that his was the only Magic library I'd ever visited, and that it hadn't exactly been a welcoming place. But considering the welcome I'd just given him, I hardly had room to talk.

"So you're here on a public relations mission for magical libraries?" I asked.

"Hardly."

He glanced around the space. I wished it looked like it did two days ago. But in that time, I'd somehow Cassie-fied the interior, beginning with the scattered printer paper, followed by my inability to put a pen away after using it, moving on to the various cardboard boxes for Pablo to nap in and scratch up, and then proceeding to today's sodden, tea-stained desktop. What can I say? I've got a talent for mess making. A highly underrated skill, if you ask me.

"What is it you've called the place?"

"I—" Gandalf's gonads, none of the names I'd picked so far had given my clients much confidence. I opened my mouth, not knowing what name-buffoonery would come out. "The Bureau of Found Objects."

Hey, that wasn't too bad.

"Really?" he asked, seeming somewhat more keen to speak with me.

"Yep, business cards and everything." I reached down and was relieved to see my magic had recuperated from its shock and allowed me to shift a few ink molecules on a business card. Name Number Four (or was I on five?) replaced the words *Wood's Funeral Home* without a glitch. I handed the card over.

"What's the lily have to do with anything?" he asked, pointing at the symbol on the card's left-hand side.

Damn it. That should have changed into a fingerprint under a magnifying glass. Instead, it had remained the symbol of tranquility of the old cards. So much for hoping my magic had suddenly recovered.

"It's to, um, represent the calmness you'll feel when I'm on the case. Because you'll know I'll get the job done?" I added, my voice rising to a question by the end of the sentence. Although, as a sales pitch, it wasn't too shabby. Before the Bookworm could question me any further about my business choices, I asked, "Is there something I can do for you?"

Then, very grudgingly, like the words were barbed wire being pulled from between his fleshy lips, my guest said, "I need help finding a book. One has gone missing from the collection."

"But you—"

"I was at a conference," he said sharply. "The books I took for demonstration were supposed to be sent back by courier, but upon my return, I discovered one title missing from the container."

"And you've checked the library? All of it?"

The dubious tone in my voice was fair. The Magic library in the Tower of London was hidden in a secret alcove in the same building where the crown jewels are on display. As such, while it didn't have the largest footprint, it did soar upwards to, from what I could recall, at least ten stories, with every inch of wall space crammed full of books. It would take days, if not weeks, to inventory every shelf. The spider tiptoed along my spine again as I recalled the Bookworm slithering and sliding up and down the stacks when I'd gone there to do some research.

"I don't need to check the library shelves like some amateur," he scoffed. "I can *sense* when one of my tomes has gone missing. I'd hardly expect you to understand."

I understood. I mean, without stepping one foot inside, I could tell when a fresh Sacher Torte was coming out of Spellbound's kitchen just by the quality and intensity of chocolate and apricot in the air. But I doubted the Bookworm would see this as being on the same level as his bookish super powers.

"It's only the one that's missing?" My guest nodded. "Do you know which one?"

Why did I ask? Of course he knew which one. And of course he chided me with an eye roll for asking such a stupid question. Could I charge clients extra for an overabundance of attitude?

"*The British Witch's and Wizard's Guide to Magical Creatures, Untoward Spells, and Enchanted Objects of the Tudor and Stuart Eras.*"

So the book was probably not off accepting its Catchiest Title of the Decade award.

"And you're sure someone didn't check it out?"

"Very sure. Is this something your little," he sneered at the dirty Spellbound napkins on my desk, "detective agency can do?"

"It can. I'm just— Well, frankly, I'm surprised you're asking me to work a case this important."

"I didn't want to."

"So why—?"

"Olivia bribed me. She said if I brought this to you, I could have three more floors of shelf space."

Well, at least Olivia had confidence in me even if my client didn't.

Olivia, I thought with a groan. The stupid HQ rules.

Feeling a mix of disappointment at having to turn down such a big case and relief over not having to work with the Bookworm, I told him, "I'm not allowed to work cases for HQ yet."

"This is not for HQ, young lady. The library is its own entity. Entirely separate from all that snooping and filing and busy work. Which means this is a personal case that you can indeed take."

"Right," I said, drawing out the word.

"That said, Olivia is providing me the budget for this endeavor as she knows it is important for the welfare of the London community." She probably also wanted to keep him out of her hair. "Therefore, the fee will be substantial since the book, considering there are only a few copies in existence, is quite valuable."

"How substantial?"

"As it's important the collection not be compromised, I am willing to accept one of the other copies if you can find any. I do not know where they are located, so don't bother asking me. For one of those, I will pay six hundred of your U.S. dollars. However, I would prefer the library's original copy. So, if that one is found, I will pay an additional six hundred dollars. I'm told it's called a bonus."

Twelve hundred dollars? That dripping sound you hear would be the greedy drool falling from my mouth.

"That's very generous," I stammered.

The Bookworm sniffed. "It's a very valuable book. Keep in mind, regardless of which copy you bring me, it must be intact. I will not have any damaged books in my collection."

Although I'd solved Mr Coppersmith's case and tried to reassure myself that I'd be getting his signature for my application in the next few hours, doubts about that were prickling along my skin.

Which is why, in an effort to make sure all my application bases were fully covered, I pulled another of the forms from HQ's file and took down the Bookworm's information, feeling stupidly surprised to learn he actually had a name.

I was not surprised, however, when Wordsworth declared the basic HQ form wasn't thorough enough and insisted I transcribe onto the back of the sheet the very detailed hiring contract he dictated to me.

Once we'd both signed our agreement to abide every word of each of the clauses, I asked, "So, could you describe the book?"

"I can do better than that."

He grinned as he reached into his satchel. I really would have preferred he stick to his usual disdainful scowl, as the awkward smile revealed a disturbing number of tiny teeth.

He pulled out a paper. It was a copy of the *Herald* that had been folded open to show a color photo of Wordsworth standing proudly next to a book that would make the *Oxford English Dictionary* look slim. It had a dark green cover that appeared to be some type of leather, with the lengthy title tooled onto the front in cream-colored letters.

"Why is this in the *Herald*?" I asked.

"Because the conference was held here in Rosaria," he said, then unfolded the paper to reveal the article that went along with the photo. "It was also the last place I saw the book. I watched it get packed into the courier box, sealed with a few book-protecting enchantments, and then loaded onto the courier's trolley."

"Corrigan's Courier?"

"The very same. I don't know how they could have done it, but when the box arrived at the library, the enchantments were broken, and only the one book was missing."

Interesting. And I have to say my toes started tingling with the possibilities this presented. I still wasn't sure what those possibilities were, but the conference taking place in MagicLand did seem like a clue, or at least a place to start doing some detecting.

"Can I keep this?" I pointed to the paper. "It might help."

"Of course. I have several of my own copies. Now, do you think this matter can be resolved in a timely manner?"

"That's what the Bureau of Found Objects is all about," I said, with an uncharacteristic amount of salesgirl enthusiasm.

Wordsworth, an eyebrow raised skeptically, didn't seem to find this statement impressive or convincing. "Yes, well, I must be going. I've done my part in this deal with Olivia, which means my new shelves should be in by now."

Like a pool of sentient goo, Wordsworth oozed from the chair, then stretched and squished his way out the door.

CHAPTER TWENTY-EIGHT
THE BURNING WAND

Begging Lady Luck to finally smile down upon me, once I'd put away Wordsworth's contract I dialed Mr Coppersmith's number. The phone was on its third ring when the agency's door twittered open.

"Just wanted to say hello and drop off some supplies," said my mom, holding up the shopping bag in her hand. When she saw the phone at my ear, she mouthed an apology, then whispered. "I won't get in your hair."

I let the line ring seven more times before stabbing at my phone to end the call, and, since my mom was within earshot, grunting a curse even Mr Wood would approve of.

"Trouble, dear?" my mom asked from the kitchen.

"I can't get ahold of Mr Coppersmith. I found his marbles."

"That's wonderful. It's always troubling when old men lose their marbles. Tea?"

With the application deadline approaching like a bullet train, I knew I couldn't sit around the agency sipping tea all day.

"I've got to track down Clive," I said after declining my mom's offer. "But maybe later today I can come by and look around your place to see if I can't find that pendant?"

"Won't that be fun," she said a bit too enthusiastically.

"Mom, this is a real case, isn't it?"

"I've told you already; it is a real case. That pendant means a lot to me, and I'm worried I might not see it again. I tricked you before with my silly games, but this time something truly has gone missing."

She said this in a pleasant yet no-nonsense tone that had the effect of making me feel like an utter heel who wasn't taking her seriously.

Just then, my calendar went off. The soaking of tea the previous day must have damaged something, because its wail had lost some of its ear-piercing volume. Also, when I checked it, there was no appointment listed. I tried to slap it into silence, but the stack of papers mounded over it stifled my attempts. The calendar's unrelenting criticism started in, reminding me of my responsibilities, informing me that punctuality was a virtue, and criticizing me for not already being out the door.

My mom stepped forward and snapped her fingers, instantly silencing the calendar. I was relieved to see her magic levels were still doing well.

"By Merlin, I hate those things," she grumbled.

"Speaking of hate, Dr Dunwiddle told me you guys have been getting some flack because of me."

"Oh, pishposh. Runa exaggerates things sometimes. She asked us if anything might have affected our magic levels since our last transfusion. It's a routine question, and I told her that a few people had made some rude comments. I also told her how your dad had hit them with a textbook-perfect Itching Powder Hex, then reminded them that he still had the authority of HQ to keep the hex on them until they apologized. Which they did. Rather quickly, I might add."

"And that's it?" I asked, because I knew very well that Dr Dunwiddle was not one for exaggerations when it came to her patients.

"Well, the Itching Powder Hex wore off far sooner than it should have, but I'm sure it's only because Simon's out of practice. It's nothing we can't handle." Then, before I could get more out of her, she handed me my satchel and said, "Now, off you go to get your signature. You come by our place when you can, and I'll lock up here when I go."

I bid my mom and Pablo goodbye, slipped Mr C's velvet sack into my bag, then headed off to hunt down what I hoped would be the last marble enthusiast I'd ever have to deal with.

* * *

From the agency, I made a quick jog south, then over a few blocks to the Burning Wand Saloon.

Yes, the Burning Wand. And no, I hadn't forgotten where Mr Coppersmith lived, but trips to the Wandering Wizard were getting me nowhere, and Clive had mentioned frequenting the Burning Wand in the past. But maybe he wasn't telling the whole truth.

What if Clive Coppersmith only nursed a single beer during his evenings at the Wizard because he'd already downed several pints elsewhere earlier in the day? He could very well be an equal opportunity barfly who'd happily alight on any barstool that would have him.

It was barely after ten in the morning, but the Burning Wand served the type of people who considered lager a breakfast drink. I pushed my way through the wooden, batwing doors and wondered how they kept the place warm in the winter. I then remembered that this was MagicLand, and a simple Warming Charm would solve the problem of exorbitant heating bills.

Once inside, it took me a moment to adjust to the dimly lit

interior. Morning sunlight had long ago lost its struggle to get through the filthy front windows, and the three flickering incandescent lightbulbs behind the bar made only the slightest dent in the murky gloom.

"Help you?" the owner asked. He had a thick, grey mustache that hid his upper lip. A real soup strainer, and I couldn't help but shudder at what might be crusted into that thing.

"I was wondering if Clive Coppersmith has been in here recently?"

"Who wants to know?"

"I do. I've found his marbles."

"Didn't know he'd lost 'em. Always seemed right in the head to me."

"Not those— Never mind. So, you do know him?"

"Yeah, he used to come in here. But now he prefers the short commute to the Wizard. Said it was nicer to drink without bar fights going on. Sounds boring to me. But I see him passing by sometimes." He lifted his chin to indicate the view of the street from where he stood.

"Thanks, then."

"Hold on, there. Answers don't come for free around here."

A stupid statement. After all, if he was going to extract cash in exchange for information, shouldn't he have gotten it before answering my questions? But instead of giving him lessons on coercion, I bought a packet of peanuts. Although coated in dust, they looked to be the most sanitary item in the place.

Outside, after squinting and blinking away the sudden burst of daylight, I checked the wrapper to discover the nuts were past their expiration date. Like a decade past.

I tried Mr C's number, and yet again got nothing but ringing. That was it. Even if I had to walk twenty miles, I was going to track him down.

But first, since energy would be needed for the legwork ahead of me, and since the idea of peanuts had stirred my appetite, I zigzagged over a few blocks for a refueling stop.

* * *

When I entered Spellbound, I instantly recognized the strawberry blonde hair of the customer at the counter.

"I know they're the best for this sort of thing," Fiona was saying as Gwendolyn filled a bag with various flavors of scones, "but I simply don't have time for it today. This research Olivia has me doing, she's in such a rush to get it I've barely got time to breathe. And Busby's so busy going back and forth to HQ… I think there's something going on— Oh hello, Cassie," she said when I stepped up to the counter.

Too focused both on what Fiona had been saying and on the seven-layer carrot cake in the display case, I walked straight into a thick book that was tied together with twine and hovering obediently beside Fiona.

"Cassie!" Fiona's eyes went wide with delight. Mine had too, but that was because I'd just caught sight of some miniature fruit tartlets lined up next to the cake. "Remember how you said you owed me one? This book is in need of repair." I was about to tell her I had nothing to do with it, but since I might have, I stayed silent. "Would you happen to have time to take it in for me…?"

I wanted to protest that I was busy, but seeing how frazzled Fiona looked, I figured my business wasn't going to suffer if my errands were delayed for an hour, so I agreed to help.

"What a relief. It's this one." She pointed to the book which caused it to zip over, practically throwing itself into my arms like an overexcited mastiff. The weight of it staggered me momentarily. Seeing my discomfort, Fiona apologized and put a Lighten the Load Spell on the book, making it feel as light as a hunk of balsa wood. "That should last until you get it to Bookman's Bookshop. You know where that is?"

"Bookman's? In Real Portland?" It was rare for Magics to do business with Norm sources, so I was surprised she used a bookshop that, back when I worked for Mr Wood, I'd often wander into during my lunch break.

"Exactly. Just drop this off. They're already expecting it. I'd be glad to pay you for your time."

"Thanks, but maybe you could pay me with some information?" I asked. After all, I'd had luck solving Mr Coppersmith's case after talking to Fiona. Perhaps she was my lucky witch. "If you have time."

"A few minutes."

"I wondered if you knew anything about a book called *The British Wizard's Guide to Magical Creatures, Untoward Spells, and Enchanted Objects of the Tudor and Stuart Eras*?"

"I assume this isn't for a little light reading."

"No, it's missing. Wordsworth hired me to find it."

After a quick look of impressed surprise, Fiona explained, "It's mainly a reference book, but it's also, as you'd guess from the title, a book of spells. Old spells that really aren't practical in the modern world. In fact, some of them are outright banned."

"Wait. Banned? Are they evil spells?" My stomach tightened. If I didn't locate this book and it somehow led to, oh say, the destruction of the world, I just knew I'd get the blame for it. I could already imagine the *Herald's* opinion piece on that one.

"No, not that I recall. More nuisance than evil."

"Do you have a copy of the book in your collection?" I asked, figuring it was worth a shot.

"No. There are a few copies, not more than five, likely less, but I can't recall off the top of my head where they're located. Still, you've got one thing going for you: wherever the copies are, they won't be hidden. Magic books want to be owned, they want to be part of a collection. They're a bit needy in that regard."

"Thanks, that's actually helpful. And encouraging."

"Thank you, Gwendolyn," Fiona said as Gwendolyn handed her a now-sagging bag of goodies. "And whatever Cassie wants, add it to my tab."

Wait? Tabs? You could start tabs at Spellbound? Oh, the debts I could rack up.

"Are you sure about that?" Gwendolyn asked. "She manages to fit a lot into that skinny frame."

"I'm sure she'll be sensible."

I was. I only ordered three of the tartlets.

Well, and then two chocolate panini, but only because Gwendolyn the Temptress told me she'd ordered top-notch chocolate from Belgium especially for the batch.

And, okay, I also added a slice of the carrot cake to my order, but it had carrots. It was practically health food.

CHAPTER TWENTY-NINE
BOOKMAN'S BOOKSHOP

Bookman's Bookshop was only a handful of blocks from the non-Magic side of Morelli's building. When I entered, a bell jingled my arrival, and a slim, dark-haired clerk glanced up from behind the cash register.

I nearly dropped Fiona's book.

Not because of his thickly lashed, mischievous eyes, but because he carried the scent of magic on him: a familiar aroma of ink and paper and books, like the smell of an old library.

And, before you ask, no, it wasn't the bookshop itself, which carried no smell other than wood polish. His bookish scent clearly held the signature of magic, but didn't have the same 'feel' as that of the other Magics I'd met. It struck me as a new flavor of magic. And really, after gnomes, trolls, elves, and pixies, I thought I'd gotten a whiff of most magical beings.

Standing at the counter and chatting with the clerk was another slim, black-haired man. Even without seeing his face, I recognized him by the sandalwood scent of his magic. When the clerk lifted his eyes to meet mine, his customer turned and leaned an elbow casually on the counter.

"If it isn't Cassie Black," said Rafi, a devilish twinkle in his dark eyes. He arched an eyebrow sardonically when he caught sight of the tattered book in my hand. "Another of your victims?"

"Unicorns, Rafi. Just remember the unicorns."

Because I'd learned the hard way that elves, like Rafi, are highly allergic to unicorns. In fact, I'd nearly killed him once when I accidentally conjured one during one of our lessons. Obviously he'd recovered, but threatening him with another unicorn attack, even if only in jest, proved to be a great way to stop his teasing.

Rafi strode over, then hooked his arm in mine as he guided me to the cashier's desk. "Sebastian, meet Cassie Black. Cassie, meet Sebastian. He works here."

"I kind of gathered that already," I said as I shook the clerk's hand. A tingle of magic drifted from his fingers to mine.

I glanced questioningly to Rafi.

"Not what you're thinking, but close. Sebastian's— What are you calling yourself these days?" he asked the clerk.

"I'm the guardian spirit of this bookshop. Fae," he told me, "but not exactly of the human variety. More of the demi-god variety."

This was a whole new concept for me. Like I said, I'd met trolls, gnomes, elves, and even ghosts, but not a guardian-deity thing.

Then, with a sparkle in his eyes, he added, "There's no need to bow. Did away with that ages ago. Now, what can I help you with? I assume it's that?"

"Fiona said you'd know what to do with this," I said, hefting the book onto the counter. Fiona's spell had been slowly dissipating and, by now, my biceps were aching.

Sebastian's eyes lit up.

"Oh, you're *that* Cassie Black," he enthused. "Yes, I've heard of you. You're the one who broke the *Enchanted History of the Portland Community*, aren't you? That was some damage you did to it, but I enjoyed the challenge of getting it back together. It's always tricky with that sort of book." Before I could ask what sort of book he meant, he gave a cursory glance at what I'd brought in. "Let's get a better peek at this fellow, then." Sebastian untied the twine and examined the spine, then the interior.

"Not enough damage to be your work," Rafi said, being oh-so very helpful.

Sebastian scolded Rafi with a glance, then smiled at me in a way that made me feel like I'd done everything right. "Shouldn't be a problem. It'll probably be ready in, say, a couple days?" I told him that'd be great. "Anything else?" He glanced between both of us. His eyes lingering a little longer on Rafi than me, and I worried I might have interrupted something when I'd shown up.

I grabbed a newspaper. A good old *Oregonian*. Thin, overpriced, and mostly ads these days, but at least it wouldn't have any nasty articles about me in it. At least, I hoped it wouldn't.

"Just this." Then, because I can be a little slow on the uptake at times, I realized I was in a bookshop. A bookshop manned by a magical clerk. "Well, maybe one other thing." Sebastian arched an eyebrow, inviting me to speak. "A book's gone missing, and I was wondering if you might have come across it, or heard about it, or I dunno... something."

That's me, Cassie Black: Super Sleuth and Smooth Talker.

"I'd need a title," said Sebastian.

"Right." I pulled out my notebook, flipped to the right page, and read, "*The British Wizard's Guide to Magical Creatures, Untoward Spells, and Enchanted Objects of the Tudor and Stuart Eras.*" If only I could charge clients by the word.

Sebastian let out a puff of air that was in no way encouraging. "That's a rare one."

"Wordsworth came to see you, then?" Rafi asked me.

"You knew he was coming and didn't warn me?"

"Honestly? I didn't think he'd take the recommendation, but I suppose he'll do anything for more shelf space. Any clues for our detective here, Sebastian?"

"There's three copies. I know that. One's at the Tower, or should be, and the others..." Sebastian mused while tapping his finger on his temple. After several seconds, he shook his head. "No, can't come up with it. I can do a bit of research, though, and let you know what I find when you pick this up."

"If it helps," I said, "this copy, the one I'm looking for, was in Portland recently. Stolen from a book conference Wordsworth recently attended. So, if you happen to uncover anything..." I trailed off, coming to grips with what a long shot this could be.

"Who knows? We get all kinds of surprises here at Bookman's," Sebastian said encouragingly. "Maybe it'll just wander in." Bookman's might specialize in used books people traded in or donated, but I highly doubted my luck could ever be that good.

Rather than leave one of the various-named business cards I had in my pocket, I wrote my name and number on a slip of scrap paper from a stack sitting next to the register.

"I'll call when the book's ready for you," Sebastian said, pocketing the note. He then indicated the newspaper. "And that's on the house."

I thanked him and was about to head out the door when Rafi offered to join me, telling Sebastian he'd see him later.

Once outside, I hesitated, torn between needing to get back to MagicLand to hunt down Mr Coppersmith and wanting to stop in to say hello to Mr Wood.

"So," said Rafi, "what are we up to?"

"We?"

"I've got a few hours before I need to be back."

"What are you doing here, anyway?"

"Had to take some files to Alastair, clarify some stuff he had questions about, and get an update on where he's at since Olivia's getting fidgety for his summary."

"Fidgety?" I asked. "Olivia doesn't strike me as the fidgety sort."

"I'm not supposed to say anything until you've— Ooh, a coffee shop!"

I knew the place well. Being both cheap and only a block away from Morelli's building, it had occasionally supplied my sugar and caffeine needs before I'd discovered Spellbound Patisserie.

"Rafi, this is Portland. There's a city statute that requires we have at least three coffee shops per block."

"But this one has donuts." His eyes had grown nearly as large as the glazed dough rings in the window. "The pixies at the Tower are very talented with their meal choices, but they simply can't do donuts like you Americans."

"We do know our fried food."

After practically dragging me into the coffee shop, Rafi ordered a dozen donuts, then, in all seriousness, asked if I wanted anything. I opted for nothing but a black tea, which raised the eyebrows of both the barista and Rafi.

"I just had something from Spellbound."

"And?" Rafi said, bewildered that I wasn't willing to cram more carbs into my gut. He had a point, so I ordered a buttermilk bar.

We took a table, and Rafi ate, or rather inhaled, donut after donut, barely coming up for air except to make noises of blissful satisfaction while I flipped through my newspaper. It really was thin on news, but as I'd hoped, also absent of any negative Cassie articles.

Finally, Rafi's donut devouring slowed. Then again, he had worked his way through seven of them by this point (much to the shock of the shop's other customers who had been staring ever since he'd wolfed down the third one).

"Need a breather," he said.

"Good, now finish what you were saying. What aren't you supposed to tell me?"

"Quite a lot of things, come to think of it. But you mean about the research?" I nodded and picked some sprinkles off one of his remaining donuts. "Olivia's just worried something's going on with the vampires. To be fair, she's not sure who's causing the trouble, but vampires keep popping up in the research and rumors, so they've climbed to the top of her list. And that's all I'm saying."

"But isn't there an accord with the vampires?"

Vampires were one magical being I hadn't met. There weren't any in MagicLand that I knew of, nor had I met any during my time at IIQ, but vampires were supposed to now live and work amongst the other magically inclined beings as part of the Vampire Tolerance Act of 1964.

I'm a little rusty on the full scope of the Act since I skipped over my history lessons in my attempts to quickly tame my overdose of magic, but vampires these days were supposed to have equal rights as Magics, with no discrimination in employment or housing or trade. In return, all they had to do was not drain us of our blood (blood banks had been set up like coffee shops for them).

"There is," said Rafi, "but it wouldn't be the first time an agreement has been broken in the magic world. I want to argue against Olivia's line of reasoning, but it's hard to ignore these disappearances. It all feels too familiar."

"Disappearances? So this has something to do with the

articles about missing Magics I've been seeing?"

Rafi shrugged. "It's not unheard of for Magics to want to disappear into the Norm world when life throws them for a loop, but it's happening far too often for Olivia's comfort. That's why HQ wants you to get your license as soon as possible."

"They do know I can detect without a license, right?"

"And you'd probably blunder your way right into this mess if you had more details, but since I refuse to tell you anything else about it..." He took a large bite of a chocolate twist. Then, perhaps to appease my impatient glare, he pushed the now-denuded-of-sprinkles donut my way. I set the newspaper down to pick at the sweet treat as he continued. "Believe me, I find the rules ridiculous as well, but we must maintain tradition. Also, I don't think anyone knows how to undo the license requirement enchantment."

"You should work on that," I said, since Rafi had a flair for creative spell-crafting. "Still, Mr Tenpenny's my case manager. Couldn't he pull some strings if they needed my help?"

"Busby?" Rafi laugh-snorted. "He's the worst stickler for the rules of the bunch."

"You'd think he'd be more lenient. I did bring him back from the dead. Twice."

"And he repaid you for that by giving you your magic back."

"Returned a borrowed item," I corrected, since that was the official line about how I'd gotten my power restored after I was supposed to have been fully drained of it.

"Either way, when it comes to forms and protocol, he won't budge, so I hope you're on the verge of getting your first case done and dusted. Speaking of done and dusted..." He popped half of a powdered donut in his mouth and swooned appreciatively.

"Done, yes. Dusted, not so much." I told him of my cases, and of how I couldn't get ahold of Mr Coppersmith after finding his marbles.

"Well, you can thank your friend Rafi for the Wordsworth case. And for negotiating the fee he'll pay you."

"That was you? I thought Olivia—"

"She gave the final go ahead, but I recommended your agency to him the instant I found out about the missing book."

"Thanks. I think. The fee is nice, but it's not exactly an open-and-shut case. Plus, him as a client...?"

"I'm sure it'll be worth it in the end, and Sebastian will do all he can to help. Now," he said, swiping the coating off a maple bar, "tell me more about this brooch thing. That sounds like it might be your next best bet since this Coppersmith cad isn't playing nicely."

I described to him Mrs Oberlin's brooch and what I knew about it.

"Did it look anything like this?" he asked, tapping the newspaper with a maple-sticky finger. I'd left it open to one of the back pages where the ads started getting cheaper. And shadier. Tucked amongst postings for questionable legal firms and puppy mill pets was one for a pawnshop. "I believe that is what you detective types call a clue, yes?"

CHAPTER THIRTY
THE PAWNSHOP

"You've got to be kidding," I blurted.

The ad, tucked into a corner on page fifteen, was for a pawnshop only a few blocks away. It touted their "stupendous selection for discerning shoppers" and made clear how glad they'd be to take all that pesky gold, silver, and jewelry off your hands.

Next to this Pulitzer-worthy copywriting was a photo of a pile of watches, necklaces, and rings. And just off to the side, nearly cropped out of the image, was a jeweled rooster that, even in the black-and-white photo, was an exact match for the one I'd seen in Mrs Oberlin's photo.

I couldn't find the words to express my disbelief.

"You didn't…?" I waggled my fingers over the ad. Wonderful coincidences didn't happen like this, not in my experience, anyway. It had to be magic. Or a practical joke. Maybe both.

"You've had your training. What do you think?"

I'd only had a few hours of training with Morelli on detecting magically forged documents, but that's not why I hesitated.

"You should do it. My magic's being weird." I briefly explained to him Runa's concerns over my Boiling Charm incident.

"Won't affect this," Rafi tapped the paper. "It uses different… let's call it, *areas* of your magic than casting spells.

I'd explain, but I've got donuts to finish. Besides, you're the detective here."

I wasn't sure if it would work, but as Morelli had taught me, I sniffed the paper and held my hands over it, checking for any magic influence. I didn't, however, resort to asking it if it was up to any dirty tricks since we were already drawing more than our share of strange glances. Even so, I could detect no magical chicanery having been done to it.

I looked up at Rafi. He'd just finished the last donut, and his eyes were as glazed as the dough bombs he'd eaten. Still, he raised his eyebrows encouragingly.

"If you're wondering what to do," Rafi said, "you could either buy it now and add it to her fee, or you could bring her to the pawnshop so she can claim it herself. It's your call."

I didn't know what to do. If I brought Winnifred in, I was pretty sure we'd also have to bring the police, and I doubted Inspector Oberlin would be willing to help me out on a case he should have been asked to solve.

I could bring in the Portland Police, but that could end up being a lengthy process of Mrs Oberlin having to prove provenance and all that. Plus, if I waited, someone else might buy it in the meantime. Assuming, of course, that the brooch hadn't been snatched up since the photo had been taken.

"I think we'll have to buy it," I decided, then recalled my cash-strapped status. "Do you have any money?"

"I just bought you a donut," he complained, but under my withering stare, he gave in and pulled out a billfold from his trousers' pocket. He opened the wallet, then twisted his lips. "Nothing but pounds left. I'd suggest you try a Confounding Charm on whoever's working at the shop, but Runa's right about not using your magic. We don't want to lobotomize any sales clerks, do we?"

"Maybe not as a first tactic." My thrill over the lucky coincidence collapsed. Why did my magic have to choose today of all days to go wacky? With a defeated sigh, I said, "I suppose I should go get Mrs Oberlin."

"Not just yet," Rafi said. "I do have my special skills."

Like Lola, Rafi was an elf. Also like Lola, he had a calming air to his magic. But rather than a soothing effect like Lola's, Rafi's, when applied with a certain spin to it, could be almost as powerful as a BrainSweeping Charm to get people to do what he wanted.

"Are you allowed to use those special skills on Norms?"

"It's not like I'd be persuading this person to walk down Main Street naked while doing the chicken dance." Which did make me wonder what Rafi might use his powers for if left to his own devices. "We'd simply suggest to the shop's proprietor that he overvalued it, and that it's only worth ten dollars. You do have ten dollars, don't you?"

I honestly didn't know.

When I'd quit Mr Wood's to join the Academy, he'd insisted on giving me a severance package. A very generous severance package. I'd been careful with it, placing most of it in savings while using my stipend from the Academy to pay the rent. But by now, it had been weeks since I'd drawn a paycheck and who knows when, or if, I'd start seeing a steady flow of money again. As such, to avoid the temptation of spending money, I'd gotten out of the habit of carrying much cash around.

And the retainer Mayor Marheart had paid me? With the impossibility of her case nagging at my pessimistic nature, I'd set it aside for the day when she realized her mistake in hiring me and demanded I return it to her.

I dug into my pocket and pulled out an old gum wrapper, a dime I'd found on the sidewalk the week before, and two crumpled bills: a ten and a five.

Rafi gave a nod of approval when I showed him the tenner.

"It's time for some shopping," he announced.

* * *

A ten-minute walk delivered us to our destination. Like any pawnshop in this area of town, this one had bars on the window and numerous neon signs flashing "Gold! Coins! Silver! BUY OR SELL!" You know, just in case you didn't know what a pawnshop was all about.

Inside, the shop was so disorganized it made my closet look like the homepage image for a minimalist-living website. Rafi and I went straight to a row of glass-fronted display cases where jewelry glittered under intensely bright lights.

"Help you?" asked a wiry-framed, heavily bearded clerk.

"Just looking for a treat for my honey pie," said Rafi in a painfully bad East Coast accent. He then threw his arm over my shoulder and nearly knocked me over when he pulled me closer to him. He could have at least warned me this was the angle we were going to play. "You like this one, sweetie?" he asked, pointing to a garish piece of costume jewelry.

I leaned closer, inspecting the price tag. "That's all I'm worth?"

The clerk's pale eyes lit up. "The little lady's got taste. You'll want that display there, darling."

Rafi gripped me tightly when I started to lunge for the condescending clerk. The guy pointed to a case nearer to the cash register. Security cameras dotted every corner of the shop, but two were aimed directly at this particular display. I hurried over and scanned the sparklies like a greedy gold digger eagerly searching for the most expensive item.

And there it was, resting on a piece of black velvet: Mrs Oberlin's brooch.

I suppose at this point I should have been concerned about how easy finding these lost items was. But at the time, all I could see was getting another chance to complete my license application, and moving another step closer to not being the flake Oberlin and the rest of Rosaria thought me to be.

"Ooh, this one. Can I have this one, babe? I want this one," I added with an insistent whine.

"Sweetheart, I told you not to act so excited. Now this fine gentleman is going to know we'll pay top dollar for it." Somehow, Rafi's accent, which had started out with a hint of Robert deNiro, had morphed into Val Kilmer's version of Doc Holladay. I half expected him to say something about being the clerk's huckleberry when he gave the man a what-can-you-do smile.

The clerk showed up behind the counter and pulled out the brooch. A scent of sandalwood hit my nose as Rafi asked, "And how much would this be?"

"Five hundred."

"Gosh, that's an awful lot. Are you willing to bargain?"

"What were you thinking?"

The warm, woody scent increased, and the clerk's shrewd gaze turned to something far more amenable, far more open to suggestion.

"Oh, maybe ten dollars?" Rafi suggested offhandedly.

"That sounds reasonable," the clerk said, nodding his head.

"Great." Rafi handed him my ten-dollar bill. "She'll just wear it out. No need to wrap it up."

Before the clerk could come out of his stupor, I plucked the rooster off his perch and we double-timed it for the door.

"Hold on a minute," the clerk mumbled. My fingers twitched,

like I'd gone all Bonnie and Clyde and was ready to Stun if needed to pull off this heist. Rafi put his hand on mine and shook his head.

"What is it, kind sir?" And yes, Rafi had abandoned Doc Holladay for a prim and proper English butler.

"Your receipt. You gotta take a receipt in case the cops come nosing around."

With Rafi's sandalwood-scented magic hanging in the air, the guy sifted through a card file, pulled out a quarter-sheet of paper, then said he needed to see ID to complete the sale. I handed over my driver's license, and the clerk jotted my name and address on the bottom of the receipt. He then pulled the top sheet off and gave us the copy underneath. We thanked him and hurried out.

The receipt, I noted, included a portion of the original record of intake for the brooch at the top, with the sale to us noted at the bottom. The brooch had been brought in ten days ago by one Charlie Brown, who lived at what I was pretty sure was Homer Simpsons's address. It also showed the brooch had been sold to the pawnshop for five dollars.

So really, I didn't need to feel bad. After all, the guy had just doubled his money.

CHAPTER THIRTY-ONE
NO ESCAPE

Despite popular opinion, I'm no idiot, and the contents of the receipt did strike me as fishy. But excitement over another solved case washed away that fishy suspicion better than a lemon-soaked scrub brush.

As soon as Rafi and I were off the pawnshop's noisy street, I pulled out my phone and hastily dialed Mrs Oberlin's number. Given my experience with Mr Coppersmith, I expected the call to do nothing but ring. Which is why, when Mrs O did answer, Rafi had to catch me from falling on my face when I tripped over my own feet.

"I can't tell you how relieved I am," she enthused when I told her I'd found her treasure. "Wesley found out about it going missing and he was furious that I didn't file a police report immediately." Sounds of clothes rustling and keys jangling came across the line as she spoke. From the tinny, far-away quality of her voice, I would have bet she was on speakerphone. "Went on about doing things by the book. So, to shut him up, I filled in his silly report form thingie. Look, I've got to take off soon. I'm rushed off my feet, but if you can come by now, we can wrap everything up." I told her I was on my way. "That's great, and if we miss each other, I'll just pop by the agency sometime tomorrow."

Before I could tell her a good time to drop by, she hung up.

Back at the apartment building, sounds of metal clinking against metal rang out from the workroom.

"Is he still working on that commission?" asked Rafi.

"Wouldn't know," I said, bristling that he was privilege to knowledge of the mysterious creation. "Alastair won't tell me."

"That could be scary."

"I've thought the same thing. Come on, let's get this to Mrs Oberlin."

"Nope, sorry. This is where we part ways. The research." He tilted his head toward the workroom door. "Now, hurry up and get that signature. And, Cassie," he said when I was nearly to the top of the stairs, "now that you've had your practice, do get cracking on Wordsworth's case."

I assured him I would.

My mom had brought Pablo home for me, but I was in such a rush not to miss Mrs Oberlin that, despite his pathetic meows and pleading eyes, I didn't pause to give him any Kitty Crunch treats.

I did, however, have the sense to drop by the agency to get Winnifred's paperwork. A note was stuck on the agency door. I assumed it was nothing more than insults or advertisements, so I snatched it off the window and crammed it into my pocket.

Inside, I rummaged through my desk drawers to find the file I needed, then grabbed Mr Coppersmith's marbles from the safe. After all, while I was out delivering lost items and collecting signatures like some sort of paid petitioner, I might as well see if luck was on my side with the Coppersmith case.

I was just leaving the agency when I saw someone approaching. In the shadow of the buildings, I couldn't make out who it was, but they were super slim, tall, and carrying a camera.

Now, my legs can tangle themselves together at the best of times, but when I'm in a hurry, my limbs take 'clumsy' to all new levels. Which meant, right then, my Make a Fool of Yourself chances were at an absolute high. Not wanting to provide the *Herald's* photographer with any hilarious shots, I started to dash off in the opposite direction.

"Cassie! Cassie, please, could I have a moment?"

My feet halted. Okay, they halted after I tripped over a crack in the sidewalk. The sound of heels *click-clacked* toward me at a quick pace.

"Mayor Marheart?" I said with relief, then looked questionably at the camera.

"It's not the best time of day for photography, but some of the shadows make an interesting chiaroscuro effect. That's not what I came by for, though. I wanted to explain why I need—"

"I'm really sorry, and I know this seems rude, but can we make an appointment? I just— It's kind of an emergency." Because after catching sight of my calendar just now, I'd realized how little time I had left to get a contract signed and the application submitted. "Tomorrow morning, perhaps?"

"I do feel this matter—"

"I promise. Tomorrow morning. Undivided attention."

"Fine," she said tersely. "But if you aren't here, I will come looking for you."

This was said in a joking tone, but the hardness of her eyes told me she was serious. Guess the woman really wanted her jewel found. I gave a quick smile and hoped Mrs Oberlin hadn't taken off yet.

* * *

I had just passed the Sorcerer's Skein and was only a block away from the Oberlins' street when Inspector Oberlin and Tobey Tenpenny came strolling along from the opposite direction.

"Always good to get some fresh air while you wait," Oberlin was saying. Tobey, his face etched with what looked like nausea, simply nodded.

Now, I'd been wise enough to brush off Matilda. I should have been sensible enough to do the same with Tobey and the Walrus. I should have just continued on to my destination. But the two looked so annoyingly chummy, and I was riding on such a so-close-to-success high that reason took a holiday and I stopped right in their path.

And then stood there, unable to think of anything clever to say.

While Tobey glowered at me like I'd just insulted his favorite socks, Inspector Oberlin let out an exasperated sigh. "I don't have time to haul you in for obstructing a public way, Black. So, either say what you have to say or get moving."

"Just thought I'd let you know I've solved two cases in less than forty-eight hours. You know, me, the person you said would never become a detective. Well, I have… um…" damn it, I was really horrible at gloating "…detected!"

Tobey visibly winced.

"Yeah?" sniped Oberlin. "And how's that license coming along for ya? 'Coz as far as I've heard, you're still working illegally, and if you don't get that license, I'm coming in on the due date and closing you down myself."

Oberlin's jab knocked me off my stride harder than a horseman galloping into a low-hanging branch.

"I'm— I'm working on it. Nearly there."

"It does seem kind of convenient you 'solving' these cases so quickly. I might almost think you had some sort of knowledge about them."

"Well, yeah. The clients told me about them when I asked."

"You sure you didn't steal the items in question and then maybe work a Confounding Spell on these unsuspecting people?"

I was about to tell him that, with the state of my magic, my Confounding Spell might turn my clients into catatonics, but I knew better than to give Oberlin anything further to use against me.

"Inspector," Tobey said uncomfortably, which earned him a sharp look from Oberlin.

"No, I think this needs clarified. You doing anything like that, Black?"

"For your information, I've proof the item in my most recent case was pawned by someone."

I showed him the receipt from the pawnshop.

Oberlin scrutinized it, then showed it to Tobey, pointing at something toward the top. Too late, I remembered the name on the intake portion.

"Tenpenny, what do we call that?"

"False identity. Or at least questionable, per Code 14 A, Section two."

See, told you Tobey knew his stuff. Something struck me just then. Something I was supposed to have remembered.

"Which means," said Oberlin, eyeing me, "that this place clearly doesn't require ID, and that you could have stolen the item, sold it to the pawnshop, then 'retrieved' it."

But, I recalled, the pawnshop *had* required ID. Even under Rafi's influence, the clerk hadn't forgotten his paperwork requirements. Which meant he might have been under a Confounding Spell when he accepted the brooch. Which meant a Magic, possibly someone from MagicLand, had brought that brooch to the pawnshop to get rid of it.

"Now, if you don't mind," Walrus Face stuck out his hand, palm up, "I'll take that brooch back to my wife. And from now on, I'd prefer you keep your distance from her."

I hesitated. I needed Winnifred's signature, but I was too taken aback by Oberlin's hostile tone to come up with a reason not to hand over the brooch. I was reaching into my pocket to give him the item when Tobey stepped forward.

"Sir, I don't think that's allowed."

"What are you talking about, Tenpenny? It's technically my property."

"Not once your mother gave it to Mrs Oberlin. And," Tobey went on, rather boldly I might add, "since Mrs Oberlin hired Cassie and signed a magically binding contract, it can't be broken unless the parties involved agree. As such, since Cassie has found the brooch per the contract, it must be returned by her to Mrs Oberlin." Almost as an afterthought, Tobey added, "It's a clause in Code 42, Section C."

Oberlin's mustache fluffed up as he blustered some nonsensical sounds before finally blurting, "Very good, Tenpenny. Another little test to keep you on your toes. Flying colors, of course. Wouldn't expect anything less. As for you," the Inspector turned to me, "seems you only paid ten dollars to get the brooch back."

"Yeah, and…?"

"Isn't your fee a percentage of what the found item is worth? So, let me see, that means, since my wife says she agreed to pay you twenty percent of the item's value, you'll earn a whole two dollars from this one. Try not to spend it all in one place."

Inspector Oberlin guffawed in such a hearty way that anyone who wanted to learn how to guffaw properly would have done well to watch him and take careful notes.

Angry with myself for wasting time with my idiotic decision to show off, I snatched back the receipt and was about to march off with very heavy steps indeed, when Oberlin ordered me to stop. His years of police work meant his commands instinctively included a touch of Voice Modulation Charm, so my feet stopped moving before my brain could tell them not to.

"What?" I asked. "More wit you want to subject me to?"

"Since that might have been a stolen object, you gotta register finding it with the police just in case charges need to be made in the future. You'd know that if you'd paid any attention in my classes instead of just relying on others for the answers."

Damn it. I did know that, but in my flustered haste I'd forgotten there was no escaping bureaucracy. Especially not in MagicLand.

CHAPTER THIRTY-TWO
POLICE HUMOR

Like a child being led off to a dental cleaning, I traipsed after Tobey and the Inspector to the Academy where I filled in forms, dotted Is, and crossed Ts instead of delivering the brooch to Mrs Oberlin, getting her signature, then stopping off at Spellbound for a celebratory cupcake.

Okay, maybe a cupcake platter.

Once the paperwork was complete, I was finally given permission to get on with my day. Not wanting to waste any time, I remained at the police desk, swiped past all my phone's missed message alerts, and immediately called Mrs Oberlin.

There was no answer.

I groaned, cursing myself under my breath.

If I hadn't stopped to gloat to Oberlin, I'd have caught Winnifred before she left. If I'd just kept my mouth shut, I'd have a case wrapped up and my application ready for sending off to HQ.

Stupid stupid stupid Cassie.

It was at this point I forcefully introduced my forehead to the hard surface of the police desk one, two, three times. But the effect was diminished after the first hit. Apparently, police paperwork often leads to frustration, so the desktop had been enchanted. The first strike immediately triggered a

Marshmallow Charm, making the blows as effective as, well, hitting myself with a marshmallow.

I was poking curiously at the squishy surface when I caught the grating sound of arrogant laughter, a boorish kind of laugh that speaks nothing of good humor, only of too much ego and malice.

I swiveled in the chair to see Tobey, Oberlin, and two other detectives braying like donkeys and pointing. In my direction. I scowled, thinking of Tobey's advice, his odd tone when he'd insisted I should focus on the brooch and the marbles over anything else.

The realization of what an idiot I'd been hit like an asteroid taking out a family of stegosaurs.

Now, I'm not proud of what's about to happen over the rest of this chapter, but I was angry with myself, feeling more foolish than normal, and had been denied the opportunity to take my frustration out on my own forehead. Although, I doubt blaming a Marshmallow-Charmed desk for my bad behavior makes it any better.

I marched over to the men, my legs shaking with fury. I had to clench my hands into fists to avoid launching any stray Stunning Spells. The two detectives, seeing a woman on the warpath, chummily slapped Tobey on the shoulder and ambled off, still grinning and shaking their heads as if the joke's hilarity just wouldn't end.

"What's so funny?" I snapped.

"Nothing," said Tobey, still chuckling. "Inside joke."

I bristled at this. And then noticed Inspector Oberlin smirking at me with far too much amusement in his eyes.

"Are you making fun of me?"

"What?" Tobey asked. "No, the—"

"The clients. The cases I should 'devote my attention to'? It was just some practical joke, wasn't it? Some sort of initiation rite for you? I mean, surely it'd be the pinnacle of police comedy to fool the flunky."

"That's so stupidly far-fetched," said Tobey, which later I'd admit it was, but at the time it seemed perfectly logical.

"Is it? Because you," I said, stabbing Tobey in the chest with a finger that might go off at any minute, "could have stood up for me when—" I bit back my comment, but just barely. I was annoyed with everything to do with the Academy, and I was pretty sure Tobey — possibly with Oberlin's encouragement — had set me up for a career-dooming prank. But even with all that, I couldn't expose his test-taking secret. My jaw tight with restraint, I said, "When I got kicked out."

Oberlin's head jerked from me, to Tobey, then back to me, his brow furrowed and his mustache bristled. "Defend a cheat like you?" he barked incredulously. "How dare you try to involve him in your conniving tricks. I should have you arrested for speaking to a future officer in this manner."

"Future officer," I scoffed. "Not without—" Again, I swallowed back the words. My tongue and brain were having the cage match of the century as they fought against bringing up how Tobey was going to need my help to even get his name right on his Exams.

The Exams? Why did that suddenly seem significant?

Seeing my hesitation, Oberlin went on, "I might also have to bring you in for questioning regarding your interactions with Mayor Marheart. There's certain things about her that don't add up. A collusion charge would be just the thing to put you in your place."

Torn between wanting to ask Oberlin what he knew about Matilda and wanting to get as far from him as possible, I snarled, "You're getting pretty desperate there, Wesley. Now, if you don't mind, I have cases to solve."

"You're going to fail, Black, so I don't even know why you bother to try."

"I am not going to fail." And at that moment, I was damned well determined to show this walrus who held the harpoon in this town.

"Just because you repeat it, doesn't make it true," quipped Oberlin. "I guarantee it. You will fail. I see it all the time, and I get tired of you amateurs who can't hack it in the Academy sticking your noses where it doesn't belong. Tenpenny, we've got a call-out, and I'd like you to personally assist me. Black, why don't you move along with your little cases? Missing marbles," he snorted derisively. "That's certainly keeping crime off the streets of Rosaria."

"You told him about my cases?" I asked Tobey. "Of course you did. He probably put you up to the whole gag." I clapped my hands in unenthusiastic applause. "Our police force at work. I'm sure we'll all sleep better at night knowing fine gentlemen like you are on the job."

"Tenpenny, see her out of here."

Tobey made to grab my arm to execute a proper policeman's walk of shame, but I stepped ahead of him before his fingers could touch me. Still, he followed me out, blocking my path when I tried to put some distance between us.

"You missed our study session," he said once we'd gotten to the front door. "I left a note. You could have at least called to let me know you weren't going to make it."

I pulled the paper I'd found on the agency's door from my pocket and flattened it out. I glared at Tobey before reading: *Cassie, Sorry I missed you. Big case? Give me a call.*

Then, scribbled below this was: *Where are you? I really need your help.*

And in different colored ink below that: *Okay, if you get this, wish me luck, off to the Exams.*

The calendar. It had been reminding me of an appointment, but the spilled tea must have erased the note about Tobey's study session. And Tobey's exam. That's what had been niggling at my brain. He must have just finished it before I bumped into him and Oberlin. It also must be what the Inspector had meant about getting some air while they waited.

This is when I should have asked him how long until the results came in, but, like I said, I was on my worst behavior.

"So you took the Exams, even though you're clearly not ready?" I asked critically.

"I couldn't back out. You know I have as much to prove as you do."

"Yeah, well, at least you get to prove yourself without pranks being pulled on you."

"Do you seriously think—?"

"You were laughing at me with your cop buddies."

"They weren't laughing at you. They were ribbing me, trying to get me to relax while I wait for the test sheets to be scored. Never mind. I don't know why I printed this out for you." He slipped a folded sheet of paper from his breast pocket. "I was going to give it to you when we met up to study. It might help you with finding—"

"I don't need your help, Tobey. Besides, it's probably just some wild goose chase you're sending me on. Thanks, but no thanks."

I then flicked my fingers, intending to do a quick Spark Spell that would briefly electrify the paper and make Tobey drop it, a sort of magical joy buzzer. But I forgot my magic wasn't behaving, and with irritation churning through my veins, that misbehaving magic sent the spell into overdrive.

The paper sparked. Then it caught on fire, going up in cold flames with such speed that, if you blinked, you would have missed it. Luckily, the spark in this spell is cool, so Tobey didn't feel a thing other than a little chill along his fingertips.

"What the hell, Cassie?" Tobey complained as he inspected his fingers. "That's it. I'm glad you didn't help me. I probably never needed your help, but you couldn't resist being a know-it-all, could you? And the test went well. Thanks for asking. Not a hitch, so I'm sure I passed. I'm going to advance to Detective Inspector rank while you're floundering to keep your stupid little business afloat."

Like magnets repelling each other, Tobey spun on his heel to go back into the Academy at the same time I spun on my heel to get away from the place as quickly as possible.

CHAPTER THIRTY-THREE
THE SORCERER'S SKEIN

Brooch in hand, I marched my way over to the Oberlin house. It may have been my determined gait. It may have been my muttering Tobey-centric obscenities. Or it may have been the curse-the-world look on my face, but no one dared insult me or block my way. I'd have to try this ferocious tactic more often.

Even if Coppersmith's and Winnifred's cases were a joke, Tobey was right. They had both agreed to magically binding contracts. If I completed the jobs to their satisfaction, they had to sign their paperwork. All I needed to do was get the brooch or the marbles into their owners' hands, get their signatures, and my application could be in the magical mail by dinnertime. I wasn't kidding when I told Oberlin I wasn't going to fail. And his bitter attitude toward me only made me more determined to succeed.

Of course, by the time I got to Mrs Oberlin's home, she'd already left. Probably while I was filling in police paperwork.

Part of me knew that we'd just missed each other. And that it had been entirely my fault. But part of me couldn't stop the negative thoughts, and had me imagining the Inspector phoning up his wife and telling her not to answer the door if I came around.

I aimlessly slumped my way along side streets as guilt over how I'd treated Tobey started crawling all over me. He had saved me from having to forfeit the brooch to Oberlin. Would he have done that if he was trying to make a joke of me? And I was the jerk who had completely forgotten our appointment when he really needed help, but yet he had still come to my defense when Oberlin had chastised me.

Of all the things I didn't want to do, it was to apologize to Tobey Tenpenny. But I supposed I should. And I should also ask if he still had that information he wanted to give me. Could he really have found something that might help? And, if so, which case would it help with?

Swallowing painful lumps of pride, I made my way back to the Academy.

"Black!" a familiar voice shouted before I'd climbed the entry steps' first riser.

I groaned. Of all the people I didn't want to meet right now.

"I paid the rent," I told him. Wait. Hadn't I? It had been a wild few days.

"It's not about the rent," said Morelli, who then gave the Academy a wary look as if the building might try to get him. "Come on, let's get out of here. I don't like this place."

"Stir up too many bad memories?"

It was only intended as a joke, but under his breath Morelli muttered, "Something like that."

We moved down the block and turned onto Main Street. I then noticed the paper shopping bag he was carrying. "What's in the sack? Or is it to cover your face?"

"It *is* to cover my face," he said, like he was praising a five-year-old who'd just figured out what one plus one equals. "And I'm not poking eyeholes in it. That way, I won't have to look at you." I grinned at the comeback, which seemed to please Morelli.

"It's yarn, if you must know. The Sorcerer's Skein was having a sale. Got some Shimmer Sheep wool for half price," he said excitedly.

"Shimmer Sheep?"

He held the bag open for me to peer inside. Seven skeins of yarn glimmered with an almost metallic sheen.

"It's a special English breed. Few centuries ago, a shepherd fell in love with a fairy, then she worked some magic on his flock to give their wool a little sparkle. Turned out the ewes could pass it down to their lambs. Wouldn't mind getting a breeding pair for myself. I think if you could somehow cross them with a Glitter Goat, you'd be a hit in the knitting world. I could probably expand the garden to fit them in," he mused.

"Well, Dr Moreau, this is fascinating, but I've got business to tend to."

Actually, at this point I just wanted to go home and sulk, but Morelli stood there, twisting the sack's handle in his big hands.

"Look, can I have a word?"

"Prestidigitation," I said. "That's a word."

"Gee, I don't know, Black, I think you might want to reconsider the whole detective thing to become a comedian. Now, a word? Please?" he said insistently.

"It's not about that mark in the stairwell, is it? Because that wasn't me."

"It's not about the damned rent, the building, or the grounds, you pest of a human."

Besides that, television reruns, and crocheting, I didn't know Morelli had any other topics of conversation.

"What's up, Genie?"

"Well, that, to be precise."

"Your pet name? Because telling me you don't like it will only make me want to use it more."

"As if I'm not well aware of that. It's more about the person who came up with that name."

"Matilda Marheart?" I cooed.

"Look, I really like her. It was me who recommended you to her—"

"Seriously?"

"Yes, seriously. You're annoying, but I was part of special ops with M.A.G.E.—" that would be the Magical Armed Guard Elite "—so I can recognize someone who knows her investigative stuff. Clues and making connections, you're a good detective. Maybe you just stumble into some things, but you stumble well."

"Comes from a lifetime of being clumsy."

"Regardless, I recommended you to her and," he hesitated, "well, I don't want to get into it, but I think there's something more to this jewel than it just being some family heirloom."

"Something like what?"

"Like I'm not sure yet. Information keeps drifting my way. I don't know what to make of it, but the jewel is important. Or will be."

Okay, I was a little curious, but my first instinct was to assume Morelli was simply so gaga for Matilda he would believe anything she did or said or wanted was of vital importance. I understood. I've had a few gaga moments in my life. Still, I wondered how this tied into what Oberlin had just said about certain things not adding up with Mayor Marheart.

"Besides," Morelli continued, "solving her case, getting her recommendation, that'd be quite the testimonial, wouldn't it?"

"Sure, but I've also got a missing book Wordsworth wants found. Matilda's case is high-profile, but his might be even more high-profile since he works with HQ. Plus, his book was last seen fairly recently. Did Matilda happen to tell you how long it's been since her jewel's been seen?"

"Well, no, not exactly."

"Hundreds of years. And there's only one jewel. I don't have an exact number, but I do know there are other copies of Wordsworth's book. Which means the odds are way higher that I'll come across one. Even through your love-tinted glasses, you have to see Wordsworth's case is more likely to be solved than Matilda's."

I felt I was making a good point, but after Morelli's glowing, and downright shocking, praise still echoing in my ears, I hated to admit to him I was afraid I'd bitten off more than I could chew with Matilda's case. I also didn't want to admit that if I couldn't get a contract signed soon, I was going to cave in and take the easy way out by solving my parents' missing pendant problem.

"Look, Black, I don't know why I'm telling you this since you'll only tease me about it, but Matilda's a great gal, and I haven't met a lot of great gals lately."

"It would help if you actually left the building other than to go buy sparkly yarn."

"Well, for the past few years I've been kind of busy making sure you stayed alive, haven't I? Now, any normal person would think, 'Hmm, this guy kept me safe from evil wizards for years and years. Maybe I ought to help him with a favor when he asks.' But you aren't normal, so I'm not sure why I bothered asking," he said, sounding defeated.

Morelli turned away and started walking off. I'd never seen him like this. Eugene Morelli was always gruff, tough, and ready to put me in line. It was disconcerting. And pitiful.

"Okay, okay." I jogged up to and fell into step with him. "I give in."

"You'll focus on her case? Black, I can't tell you what that means. I'll, I'll—" Morelli's arms started to lift.

"If you hug me, I will knee you in the groin."

Morelli's arms dropped back to his sides, but the gleeful grin was still lighting up his entire face. "I owe you big time, okay?"

"Hold on. Don't get too excited there. I will work on her case. But, one, I'm not going to abandon Wordsworth's case; and two, I don't know how successful I'll be with hers. What she's looking for is insanely rare."

"I could help," Morelli offered.

"What? Like partners? Cagney and Lacey? Holmes and Watson?" Morelli shrugged as if that had been exactly what he'd been thinking. "You know I don't play well with others."

"We don't have to work side by side. I could dig into things. Remember, I've got contacts you don't."

"Underworld contacts?"

Because Morelli, I'd learned not long ago, had had quite the past. When he was part of M.A.G.E., he served as a sort of army nurse due to his innate healing abilities. But he'd also gained knowledge about detecting forgeries by working alongside the forgers themselves and about how to build illegal portals (temporary portals that didn't get registered with HQ, which was very much against the rules). He was the kind of guy who kept one foot on the up and up, while dipping the other into the shallow end of the criminal pool.

"All I'm saying is I might be able to ask around where you can't. So, what do you say? We going to help each other?" I hesitated just long enough for Morelli to narrow his eyes at me. "Come on, Black, don't do your stubborn thing."

"No, I'm not being stubborn. It's just that I *have* solved two cases."

"Great, then you're ready to solve more."

"No, I solved them, but I haven't wrapped them up. Can't get ahold of the clients. And time's running out for the application to be sent in for my license. I will work on Matilda's case, but hers and Wordsworth's are both going to take far longer than the two days I have left."

"Okay, then let's get those other two wrapped up. Where to first?"

I wasn't sure I could handle this new, gung-ho Morelli.

"Well, I just struck out with Mrs Oberlin. If I could find Mr Coppersmith and get his damn marbles back to him, I could focus on—"

"I know right where he'll be."

Morelli hooked his arm in mine and tugged me forward. I tried to protest when he started dragging me toward the Wandering Wizard, but Morelli insisted that on his way to the Sorcerer's Skein, he'd seen Clive going up to his apartment.

Despite the ungainly gait I was being forced into, I couldn't help but hope.

*　*　*

When we reached the Wandering Wizard, Morelli directed me toward the far side of the building where we climbed the stairs to a pair of apartments, situated side by side. As I knew from my previous attempts, Mr Coppersmith's was the one toward the back.

I wasn't the least bit surprised when no one answered my knocking. Morelli swore he'd just seen Clive, but maybe the guy had only come back to collect a suitcase for a long-awaited trip to the Marble Universe Competition.

"Help you?" snapped an elderly Korean woman with grey-streaked black hair pulled up into a bun that wiggled as she spoke. Although clutching a cane, she maintained a defiant stance.

"Are you Mr Coppersmith's neighbor?" I asked. Under his breath, Morelli mumbled something about my unprecedented skills of deduction.

"I am," the woman said.

"Have you seen him today?"

"Nope."

Real talker, this one.

Then Morelli, with perfect fluency — to my ears, anyway — rattled off something to the woman. Her face lit up, even as her eyes continued to flick warily to me. She responded, and Morelli translated for me.

"She says she last saw him late this morning, coming back from the shop with his paper. She hasn't seen him since."

I recalled the curtain flicking when I'd come by before. She was definitely the sort of woman who watched the comings and goings of her neighbors. No wonder she and Morelli hit it off so quickly.

The woman barely let Morelli finish before she continued prattling on. My landlord, showing an amazing talent for this sort of thing, translated as quickly as she spoke.

"She also says she heard some noise about an hour ago. Yelling, but it died down pretty quick. She hadn't heard anyone come up and wanted to check if Mr Coppersmith was talking to himself, which she wouldn't put past him, but she was in the bathroom. And," Morelli went on with a grimace, "she stayed in there a long time since her belly hasn't been doing so well lately and she'd taken a handful of prunes—"

"I get the picture. Maybe we could skip that bit, ma'am?" I said. Again, I got the stink eye, and now that she had a captive audience, she wasn't about to miss out on the chance to describe her stomach ailment and its miraculous cure. In detail.

Once done sharing exactly what brand of prunes works best if we ever found ourselves in her situation, the woman's eyes narrowed on me before continuing.

"She says she saw someone tall, thin, and dark-haired leaving Clive's this afternoon. Not that she's a snoop, she just happens to have a direct line of sight to his doorstep."

I glanced toward Mr Coppersmith's door, then hers. There was no way she would have been able to see anything but his doormat without having eyeballs that came out on stalks like some sort of alien insect. Guessing from the way she was sizing me up, she clearly identified me as this thin, dark-haired person. I hadn't been by since early morning, but it's always possible Morelli had mistranslated her quick-fire words, or she had the time wrong. I thanked her in a tone that hinted she could go back to whatever she was doing. She didn't take it.

With her watching my every move, I went past Mr Coppersmith's door to peer in the window. There was a sheer curtain pulled over the glass, but it hadn't been fully closed, leaving a two-inch gap through which I could see a couch so saggy and threadbare it was either secondhand or Mr C was its original owner. I could also just make out a boxy, older model television and a well-worn circular rug.

My stomach lurched. Not at the tattered state of the rug, but at what was on the rug.

CHAPTER THIRTY-FOUR
MAKING AMENDS

At the rug's edge, a corded phone rested on its side, off the hook and beeping as if in protest. Next to it was a pair of slippered feet, splayed out and not moving.

I didn't think twice about my magic levels. I zapped the door's lock — much to the nosy neighbor's protests. Luckily, my magic was behaving just then, and the lock unlatched without me blowing up the entire neighborhood.

I rushed in while Morelli shouted something about tenants' rights and what in the world was I doing. I urged him to stay back and to keep the neighbor away. I was hoping Mr Coppersmith was only passed out, but if there'd been yelling earlier, this could be a crime scene and I couldn't have anyone messing up the forensics, magical or otherwise.

I touched my fingers to Mr C's neck. The disturbingly cold skin told me all I needed, but I still followed procedure to locate the pulse. There was none. I gave Morelli Tobey's number and told him to call it in.

As I backed carefully out of the room, I glanced around, hoping to find some clue as to what had happened. The only thing that caught my attention was a framed photo on the mantle. It showed Mr Coppersmith accepting some sort of prize ribbon from Mayor Marheart. Above them was the banner for the conference where Clive had lost his marbles.

My gaze lingered on the tall, slim, dark-haired woman until Morelli barked me out of my reverie, telling me to get the hell out of there.

* * *

Tobey and Inspector Oberlin arrived in little time. Using their fancy Rosaria-funded equipment, they went over the room and found minute traces of magic having been used. But even with their high-quality tech, they couldn't identify whose magic it was.

"You probably let the scent of the magic out when you rushed in," Oberlin snapped accusingly. The neighbor, who wasn't missing a thing, stood beside him and nodded in full agreement.

"In a potential emergency situation, she was obliged to go in to see if she could help," said Morelli. "If you'd just open your eyes and look around, there's no obvious sign of a struggle that would tip anyone off to this being a crime scene."

"And," I added, "there was no scent when I entered." Other than the scent of a home occupied by a lonely old man, which is a very distinctive aroma indeed.

"Fine, fine. For now, I'll agree with that assessment," Oberlin said to Morelli while completely ignoring me. "It doesn't appear there was any sort of struggle, so what should be our next obvious step?" he asked Tobey pointedly.

Tobey was already looking unwell. I'd never taken him for someone who was squeamish around dead bodies, but after working at a funeral home, I recognized the signs.

I also recognized what a jumping-to-ridiculous-conclusions jerk I'd been. I mean, I highly doubted even the most devoted prankster would go so far as to kill someone to beef up their practical joke.

I had to make amends, even if only a little. So, since Oberlin was still ignoring me, I mouthed 'trace' at Tobey, then did the Exploding Heart Charm gesture over my chest.

Giving me a weak smile of thanks, Tobey answered, "If any killing magic was done, it should leave a trace. We'd need to check for that."

"Exactly." Oberlin looked at Tobey like a parent whose child has just won the National Spelling Bee. "Hard to believe you failed your Exam." My stomach dropped. No wonder Tobey had looked so unsettled. Oberlin fixed his gaze on me. "I wonder whose fault that might be?"

"What do I have to do with him failing his test?" Other than eating donuts and chasing down brooches when I was supposed to be helping Tobey study.

"Distraction Hex, cursed pencils, Perplexing Potion. I'd really rather not think about all the things you might do to sabotage him. Let's just be glad Tenpenny has two more tries. Tobey, you might want to consider practicing your protection spells. Now, I should question the neighbor—"

And here, the nosy neighbor took her cue, and without a single question being asked, began explaining to the Inspector — in perfect English, mind you — everything she had seen. I left him to it at the very first mention of the prunes.

I signaled for Tobey to step aside. Morelli, apparently not wanting to hear about the wonders prunes can work on one's bowels again, joined us.

"Thanks for that thing with the trace. I'm probably supposed to question you further," he said flatly.

"Clive was murdered," I said with equal flatness.

I couldn't have explained why or how I knew, but I knew Mr Coppersmith's death was somehow tied to his missing marbles. I then pictured myself moving from what started as a simple case of a lost treasure to cracking a murder case. I'd be instantly catapulted to the Detecting Hall of Fame. If there was one, that is.

And with the neighbor's description of the person she'd seen, I had to wonder if Matilda was involved, but I wasn't ready to tread into that murky water just yet.

"I know he was murdered, Cass. I'm not as dumb as you—"

"No, he was *murdered*," I emphasized. "What I mean is, this case wasn't a practical joke, was it?"

"Of course it wasn't a joke. I told Clive to contact you. Winnifred too."

And that's when blazing hot fireballs of surprise exploded from my head.

"Wait, I thought they came because of Lola. It was *you* recommending me to them?"

Tobey crammed his hands into his pockets and nodded. "I figured they'd be two relatively easy cases. It should have cinched you fulfilling your license requirements. That's why I pushed you to work them, not for some elaborate joke."

"But how?" I asked, still in shocked disbelief.

"Winnifred and I got to chatting at a dinner party Oberlin invited me to. She mentioned the brooch and how she wouldn't dare ask Wesley to look into it. And I know, sorry, *knew* Clive from the Wizard. He was tutoring me on potions that were often used in crimes. Somehow we got talking about his marbles going missing, so I suggested he go to you. I thought you'd appreciate the work."

I mumbled an apology.

"What was that, Black?" said Morelli, cupping a hand over his ear. "I didn't catch it."

"I'm sorry, okay? I'm sorry I accused you of being a jerk, and I'm sorry I missed our study session. You still have those two other chances, right?"

Tobey nodded. "Next one's—" He turned a worrying shade of

green. "Soon. Too soon."

"I'll help you this time, I swear. I'll work with you as much as I can," I added, since completing my license application was still my main priority.

"Why were you here, anyway?" asked Tobey.

"He was my client," I said in a very *well-duh* way.

"No, I mean, were you coming to get more information about his marbles?"

"No, dimwit, I was trying to *bring* him his marbles. I solved his case."

"Really?" Tobey gaped. "That fast? And Winnifred's too?"

I brushed down the lapels I wasn't wearing, then haughtily examined my fingernails. "Some of us are just naturally talented at this."

"Too bad you aren't naturally talented at keeping your clients alive," quipped Morelli. "And here we all thought he'd drink himself to death at the Wizard."

Not wanting his memory sullied, I told them what Clive had told me about nursing his single pint each night.

"Wait. Do you think someone from the pub could have done it?" I asked. I mean, the Wandering Wizard's clientele were a much gentler crowd than that of the Burning Wand, but they had once turned on me pretty darn quickly. It was only thanks to Alastair getting me out in time that I wasn't attacked.

"Why would they?" asked Tobey. "He was quiet, kept to himself, and people generally liked him. Also, he didn't have much, so robbery couldn't be a motive. Why would anyone want to hurt him? I don't like to think it was just random, but what if it was?"

"Well, there's a happy thought," Morelli grumbled.

"Where'd you find the marbles, anyway?"

"Tremaine's. Mr Coppersmith apparently took one of Penley's precious marbles. Tremaine wanted it back, so he swiped the whole bag at some marble conference. But," I continued when Tobey got that look in his eyes like he'd just had an insightful breakthrough, "I let him keep his marble, so he wouldn't have had any excuse to come here looking for it."

"Revenge killing?" suggested Tobey.

"For taking a marble? Although, these guys do seem to take their little balls pretty seriously." A comment which made us all giggle, proving maturity wasn't winning over just yet.

"I'll have to talk to Tremaine. Just to make sure everything's on the up and up there," said Tobey. He then added, with genuine feeling, "Sorry about the client, Cass."

"Sorry about the test."

"This better not turn into some sappy hugging session," Morelli groaned.

Just then I noticed Oberlin waddling our way, giving me the stink eye.

"Come with me, Black," he grumbled.

"I didn't do anything."

"No, but you're going to have to give us a statement. So, we can either record your side of things here and now, or I can drag you back down to the Academy."

I nearly mentioned I'd be happier to make a statement over an IPA in the pub just down the steps, but knew Oberlin would stick me with the tab if I did. So, standing on Mr Coppersmith's stoop as Oberlin's notepad magically dictated my words, I gave my statement about why I'd been there, what had led to me solving Clive's case, my numerous attempts to track him down, and the discovery of Mr C's body.

"I'll have to confirm all this checks out. In the meantime," Oberlin snarled as he snapped his notepad shut, "I suggest you not leave town. Tenpenny, come on, I want to confirm a few things with this Tremaine guy."

CHAPTER THIRTY-FIVE
BRAINS!

"Heading home?" Morelli asked, his tone suggesting that's exactly what I should do. "I've got a couple imperial ales in the fridge."

Well, if he was going to twist my arm…

I told myself I should go back to the agency, that I should try Mrs Oberlin again, that the deadline for my application was avalanching toward me, but I'd had enough for the day, so I trailed after Morelli. He kept blissfully silent on the way back to a portal that led, not to my closet, but to the apartment's ground floor.

"Rosencrantz," said Morelli, giving a little salute of greeting.

"Captain Morelli," the gnome replied. Captain? Of what? All I could picture was a listing, broken-down tugboat.

When Rosencrantz (I tried to take note of any features that distinguished him from his twin, but couldn't find any) caught sight of me, he smoothed his red, conical cap, snapped to attention, and held out a cream-colored envelope.

"For you, ma'am."

Now, you've seen garden gnomes. A large one might measure two feet tall. Rosencrantz and Guildenstern are not of the large variety and only stand a foot high. The building's mailbox, I should note, is way up at chest level.

"How did you reach the mailbox?" I asked, wondering if he'd performed a Floating Charm on himself.

"Didn't have to." His cheeks turned crimson and his accent grew heavier. "It were hand-delivered."

I flipped the card over. The front bore no address, just my name, but I easily recognized Mr Wood's loop-filled handwriting.

"Wait, did Mr Wood drop this off?" And if so, what did he make of a living garden gnome serving as butler and security guard for my apartment building?

"No, ma'am. That one lass…" He scrunched up one side of his mouth, trying to recall a name. "Blonde, goes around with the Tenpenny bloke."

"Daisy."

"That's it," he said dreamily as he began twirling his beard with his index finger. "Real nice girl. You two friends?" He asked this like he hoped I might put in a good word for him.

"Hardly." The twirling stopped and the tip of his cap sagged slightly. "Alastair in there?" I asked, tilting my chin toward the door.

"Can't answer that, ma'am."

I was in no mood to figure out the covert mindset of security gnomes or what it would take to gain access to the workroom, so I followed Morelli into his apartment. As he cracked the caps off two bottles of beer, I opened the envelope. Inside was an invitation to Mr Wood's retirement party. In only three days. My throat tightened with emotion. Talk about a door to my past being slammed shut and surrounded by concrete barricades.

Still, the idea of Daisy soon being out of job helped counteract at least eighty percent of any gloomy feelings.

Morelli and I chatted about nothing in particular. I didn't want to speak about work, and he was wise enough not to bring it up. He was just explaining, after lecturing me about my skills of observation, how to tell the difference between the two guard gnomes when I heard the click of the workroom's door opening.

"It's alive!" Morelli said, then nudged me with his elbow. "Better get him while you can."

I thanked Morelli for the beer, then dashed out of the apartment. Alastair was halfway up the stairs. His eyes looked bleary, but warmed when he caught sight of me. Which is always good for one's ego.

"Time for dinner?" I asked, catching up to him and trying to remember when we'd last had a proper meal together.

"Sure, that'd—" Alastair cut himself off as he opened the apartment door. "Hey, can you keep Pablo out of the workroom?"

"I didn't let him in."

"Well, Houdini keeps finding his way in."

"I think Houdini was known for finding his way *out* of things."

"Fair point, but he's got a bad habit of thinking everything on my worktable is a toy."

"Houdini?"

Alastair looked at me levelly, then grinned. "No, not Houdini. Pasta?"

"Oh, Alastair," I said with mock worry, "you really have been working too hard. His name's Pablo. Say it with me. *Pahhh-blow.*"

"Just for that, you're cooking."

"Alright, but you asked for it."

* * *

Alastair and I tucked into our plates of spaghetti with marinara — the only meal besides cereal I could reliably make without risk of food poisoning. Pointing to the invite I'd tossed onto the table, he asked, "Mr Wood's retiring?"

"Yep. Morelli magicked him so well, he now has the energy to retire."

"The magic stuck?" Alastair asked in surprise. "But that was months ago. It should have completely dissipated within a week."

"Maybe the repeated doses made it stick," I suggested, since after magically treating Mr Wood's broken bones, Morelli had continued to pump Mr Wood with additional hits of magic when he discovered just how many sandwiches my former boss could eat in a single day. I then made a mental note to bring this stickiness thing up with Runa in case it might help with replenishing my parents' magic. "Or maybe there was some strange magical reaction from all the bacon he ate while staying with Morelli."

"Interesting. I wonder if Runa— Ow!" Alastair jerked back the hand that had been reaching down to pet Pablo. "What the hell, Pablo?"

Pablo dashed over to my side, making a weird little growling noise. Alastair twisted his arm to look at the edge of his hand. There were four shallow puncture wounds but no blood.

"Maybe he wanted some spaghetti," I said. "You know how he likes noodles."

I got up and dropped some pasta into Pablo's dish, but he ignored it and continued to watch Alastair.

"Are you sure he's really alive? Not a zombie?" Alastair teased. Pablo, in trying to keep me from getting beaten to death, had lost his life. But only for a little while. A grin on his face, Alastair peered past my chair. "Look, Cassie, he's eyeing up my head. He wants my brains."

"Biting your hand is hardly zombie behavior," I ridiculed. "It's vampires who bite. Speaking of vampires, are you really helping HQ with researching them? Do they have anything to do with the missing Magics?"

"I'm not supposed to tell you about any of that. You have a bad track record of running off on your own with information."

"I'm way too busy with these cases to go chasing after the undead. So come on, do you really think it's vampires behind these disappearances?"

"First off, I'm only gathering background information for Olivia, not trying to solve anything. That's HQ's job. Second, if I'm being honest, I think she's barking up the wrong tree with the vampires."

Now this was interesting. Olivia seemed like the sort of lady who had good intuitions. But then again, she had completely missed the baddie who'd been right under her nose at the Tower.

"So who do you think is behind it?" I asked as Pablo began weaving in and out of the chair legs, butting his head against my shins as he went.

"That's the problem. Everything really does point to the vampires, and I can't exactly tell Olivia to back off because I've got a hunch they aren't responsible for the missing Magics. I just feel what's going on is far too similar to what the vampires did when they got into trouble before."

"Doesn't that point to them more strongly?"

"No, that's the thing: It's too similar. Vampires are intelligent, clever. Clever enough to come up with another tactic if they were trying to rise up against Magics again. Think about it; why would they use the same methods that didn't work before?"

"Maybe they've honed them, worked out the kinks, and are giving it another go?"

"Could be. I keep coming across things that seem like good leads, but nothing quite fits together. Or it might be that I'm not getting the full picture. I'm really only doing some side research. Fiona's been bearing the brunt of the work, but she feels the same way. Like she's close, like she has hunches, but can't quite get to a solid conclusion. Sort of like having a word on the tip of your tongue."

Just then, Pablo, who'd been standing patiently by his dish, meowed loudly. I took the hint and gave him a fresh clump of spaghetti. This time, he gobbled it up like he'd never eaten before.

"See, he thinks they're brains." Alastair whispered theatrically, as if Pablo might hear.

"He's not a zombie."

"Say what you like, but I'm not letting him anywhere near my pillow tonight."

CHAPTER THIRTY-SIX
CALLS AND EMAILS

The next day I woke up determined to sort out some clues, get Mrs Oberlin's signature, and file my application. With Pablo at my side and with the streets of MagicLand only just lightening with the dawn, I slipped as quickly as I could down side streets to the agency. Apparently, angry mobs aren't made up of early risers, because I made it in without incident.

My tea barely had time to steep before the phone rang. And yes, the sudden noise in the silence of the agency shocked me. And yes, I did spill half a mug of tea all over my desk. Again. You'd think I'd learn, right?

Not trusting my Drying Spell, I answered the phone while jogging to the kitchenette for a towel.

"Cassie, this is Matilda Marheart. *Mayor* Matilda Marheart," she emphasized, just in case I didn't know which of all the world's Matilda Marhearts was calling. "I'm wondering how you're proceeding with my case."

"I've been working hard and have some pretty good leads." Okay, so maybe that work and those leads weren't for her, but still…

"That's such a relief to hear. So, maybe you don't need the information I have?"

I threw aside the towel and fumbled for a pen and something

dry to write on. Pen poised and ready for clue gathering, I told her, "No, any additional information would only make the search go that much more quickly."

"Fabulous. And don't think because I'm assisting you that I'll want to reduce our agreed upon fee." Which hadn't even crossed my mind, but now that it had, I reminded myself to check first when someone offered to help out with their own case. "Apparently, for a time the jewel box was at the Tower of London. We think that Queen Elizabeth, because she was a bit passive-aggressive, had given it to Mary Queen of Scots as a token of friendship when she was imprisoned there. It reportedly left the Tower sometime after Mary departed the place a little shorter than when she arrived, but the jewel may not have."

I tossed down my pen and pushed my notes away.

"Matilda, the Tower is HQ territory. I can't go swiping things from there."

"No?" Matilda said innocently, like she really did expect me to go to any lengths to get this jewel for her.

"Well, I mean, if push came to shove. But do you have any hints as to when the jewel came off, or any places it might have been seen after it was at the Tower? You know, places that aren't going to get Olivia Whalen on my bad side?"

"No, that's it. Now, I know you have other cases, but I would like to see action on this as soon as possible. It's getting— Well, as I said yesterday morning, it's very important."

"Got it," I said, a bit dismissively. Did she expect this jewel just to appear out of the ether after being missing for several centuries?

"I hope you do," she said, all playfulness gone from her voice. "Because it's quite vital — quite pressing, in fact — that this jewel be returned to me. Soon."

Which sounded rather ominous, but Matilda hung up before I could ask her what the hurry was.

I took a few deep breaths. It was nice to have a client who was actually staying in touch, but pressuring me to work her case wasn't going to make finding the jewel any less of a challenge.

Despite being twice drenched in tea, Mr T's due date hadn't vanished from the calendar like Tobey's study session had. In fact, the red note seemed to glow even more brightly than it had before. If I didn't get a signature today… Well, let's just hope that due date was for tomorrow at midnight, not first thing tomorrow morning.

Thinking it was far too early to call Mrs Oberlin, I checked my email. My heart nearly leapt out of my chest when I saw Sebastian from Bookman's had sent a document he'd uncovered. It confirmed there were indeed three copies of *The British Wizard's Guide to Magical Creatures, Untoward Spells, and Enchanted Objects of the Tudor and Stuart Eras*.

"And if I never have to type that again, I will be a very happy demi-god," he added. "Trouble is, even though we know one copy is, or *was,* at the Tower, the document gives no clues as to the whereabouts of the other copies. But look on the bright side, that might mean no one else knows where they are. Sorry, maybe not the brightest of bright sides, but I am quite enjoying this bit of sleuthing and plan to keep digging. For my own curiosity, if nothing else."

I opened the document. It had little information on current, or even past, locations of the three existing copies, but a note under copy number three caught my eye. It had once been owned by Queen Anne. She was one of the rare royals who were Magic, but none of her children survived to carry on her magical lineage. A shame really, because I think a Sparkle Spell or a

Paparazzi Potion (which makes those vile hounds report only good gossip) might have worked wonders for the British monarchy in recent years.

I replied to Sebastian, thanking him for the information and all but begging him to keep fanning those flames of curiosity.

Although interesting, Sebastian's intel wasn't going to deliver Wordsworth's book to my desperate hands anytime soon. I stared at my phone. Early hour or not, I had a client whose case I had solved, and she was damn well going to sign off on a job done. I rang Mrs Oberlin.

Who, of course, failed to answer her phone.

I slumped back in one of the guest chairs and scanned the paperwork on my desk. A photo peered out from one of the files. It showed a one-year-old me playing with wrapping paper while being corralled by my mom's legs. I let out a heavy sigh. It wasn't an impressive job, it wasn't a case I'd be boasting about, but it was a case that could probably be solved by lunchtime. And I had no doubt the clients would be enthusiastic to sign off on my paperwork.

I guzzled the rest of my tea and left for my parents' place.

CHAPTER THIRTY-SEVEN
SPARKS AND SPARKLIES

The route to my parents' house took me past the Academy. I could have avoided it, but I had a feeling today was going to involve a lot of walking, so rather than make the fifteen-minute diversion to bypass it, I stayed on the opposite side of the street, tucking myself under the awnings of the shops that faced the police building.

I tried to keep my head down, but I couldn't help but watch as a pair of officers steered a vociferously complaining Penley Tremaine toward the front staircase. Before they turned to march him up the steps, Tremaine somehow caught sight of me. And let's just say the look on his face was not of someone having a good morning and that I was the reason for every bad morning he'd ever had. I moved deeper into the shadow of the awnings and hurried down the block.

The stroll up the walkway to my parents' door was a riot of color and fragrance. They'd put in a garden (hopefully not with Mrs Kawasara's help), and the entire front area was bursting with lavender, fuchsias, daisy-type things, and well, other sensationally scented, colorful plants that my brown thumb could probably kill just by looking at them the wrong way.

My parents weren't home — probably out making their first trip to Spellbound for the day — but I knew they wouldn't mind me breaking and entering (okay, just entering, as the door wasn't locked) and sifting through their things.

I started in the living room, searching under furniture and checking books for any hidden compartments. I even caught myself saying "*Accio* pendant" a few times because you just never know. After all, Rowling had learned a thing or two about magic from Mr Tenpenny, and I was convinced that one day I'd discover one of her fictional spells actually worked.

The living room didn't have many hiding places, so after about twenty minutes, I moved the search upstairs. I didn't know where to begin, but since most of my own 'lost' items ended up under my bed, I figured digging around under theirs was the best place to begin.

Dropping down to my belly, I found three long cardboard storage boxes. I pulled each of them out, then quickly scanned under the bed. Other than a single pink slipper, I didn't find anything.

Curious, I opened the first box to find it full of winter clothes: gloves, scarves, and knit hats in the same color of yarn I'd seen on some of Morelli's older couch cushions.

The second box also seemed dedicated to winter wear, with heavy Nordic-style sweaters and ski pants. Did my parents ski? Had they ever taken me? Had I been any good at it? With my long limbs that had a mind of their own, I could only imagine myself ending up as a snow-covered pretzel in need of immediate medical attention if I ever dared to strap skis onto my feet. Ski resorts would probably have to ban me from the slopes because having the ambulance arrive every time I showed up would be bad for business.

The third box looked promising. It was packed full of Christmas decorations, and wasn't it just possible for a pendant to get lost amongst all the shiny bits and baubles?

After pushing aside several boxes of your basic, store-bought balls, I pulled out a smaller container about the size of a shoe box. Inside were what looked like homemade ornaments and a few antique blown-glass snowmen and Santas.

I didn't find any rogue pendants, but I did find a piece of heavy paper decorated with a crudely drawn cat in a Santa hat and gold glitter messily glued around the edges. When I turned it over, that little squeeze in my throat that comes when I get emotional really gripped on tight. On the back, in my dad's handwriting, was *Cassie, 3 years old.*

Well, I certainly wasn't much of an artist, but at least it showed my love of cats went way back. I put it away carefully and continued digging further into the box. Some items had been wrapped in newspaper to cushion them. Around a disturbingly busty angel tree topper was a sheet from an old copy of the *Preternatural Times of London.* It immediately snared my attention.

The headline read: *Renowned Jewel Box Donated to British Museum.* The article, although some parts had been ripped, possibly by the angel's torpedo-like boobs, went on to say the box dated from the Elizabethan era (at least I was getting plenty of confirmation on that end of things) and had been found amongst a collection of donated items passed on from—

The rest of the article had been torn away, but to the side of what remained was part of a photo. The picture was in black and white, and not of good quality, so it was tough to make out the details. But what was there showed the edge of a box that looked like Matilda's, with the depression in the center for the heart-shaped jewel. In what was left of the caption were the words: *workmanship of William Boncoeur.*

Since Matilda had shown me this very box, I knew it was no longer at the British Museum, but could the jewel still be there? Popped off during all the shuffling around, then rolled under a cabinet, perhaps? I was suddenly very keen to take a trip to London.

Okay, even if my magic had been behaving, I couldn't exactly steal something from the British Museum. But if I could show that the item actually belonged to my client due to her relation to the box's creator... I mean, the British Museum was already having enough issues with provenance and finders-keepers complaints, so maybe they'd just let it go to keep any more fuss from being raised. I made a mental note to look into it. But for now, the pendant.

Feeling awkward doing so, I did a quick search through my parents' bureau. When I entered the bedroom's adjoining bathroom, I shook my head. My parents, having gone missing right when cell phones started becoming a thing, weren't physically attached to their shared phone like most people are these days. As such, they often left it at home when they went out. Which they had done again despite my constant reminders that they should take it in case they had a magical meltdown or there was a flash sale at Spellbound.

After pushing the phone to the side of the counter, I poked around the bathroom drawers and cabinets with no luck. I was about to head downstairs when that nagging voice told me I'd forgotten to check *under* the bureau.

Back in the bedroom, I dropped down to my belly once more.

Something sparkled.

Unfortunately, the something had wedged itself into the shag piling (my parents hadn't gotten around to re-decorating).

My skinny arms and long fingers had no trouble reaching what was under there, but it had hooked itself deep into the carpet's pile. With my power all wacky, a spell to free the item risked destroying it. And possibly the whole house. I also worried tugging the thing free would damage something. And no, I don't mean the purple and orange carpet that would give modern interior decorators nightmares.

In my parents' bathroom, I found a small pair of nail scissors. I used these to cut around the treasure. The carpet would have a bald spot, but that was the least of its hideous problems.

Gripping tightly to the sparkly thing, I sat back up. When I opened my hand, my palm was a mess of purple and orange fuzz, but underneath, a pendant glinted. A pendant that exactly matched the one in my mom's photo.

With a wild sense of success surging through me, I was just about to put the scissors back when I heard a noise downstairs. A door clicking open. Soft footsteps. Items being shifted.

"Mom?" No answer. "Dad?" I inhaled deeply, but couldn't detect any scent of magic coming from below. "Guys?" I called, my voice now sounding shaky to my own ears.

Tiny scissors at the ready as if they'd be helpful in a fight, I peered over the stairwell's railing. The long shadow of someone tall and lean shifted, and I picked up the sound of drawers sliding out, of contents being dumped. Defensive magic surged into my fingers, and I jutted out my hand, shooting a Glacier Charm in the direction of the shadow.

Stupid move. With my magic on the fritz, instead of halting the person in his or her tracks, the spell coated the staircase in a sheet of ice. Unless I wanted to give that skiing idea a practice run, I was stuck.

Even though any form of heating or warming charm might incinerate the place, a Drying Spell was my safest bet. I hit the staircase hard and, thankfully, the ice evaporated into a steaming cloud. Blinded by the fog I'd created, I raced down the stairs.

And yes, I know. Running with scissors, dangerous. Don't try this at home, kids.

I had a Shoving Charm ready to go. I would have set up for a Stunning Spell, but I was already pressing my luck with my magic and I didn't need to deal with an accidental murder charge right now.

But before I could throw it, the room lit up, blinding me and knocking me back. A Spark Spell combined with a Shoving Charm, I guessed.

A Spark Spell is meant to generate cool light with no heat, but my cheeks suddenly felt like I'd spent the whole day in Death Valley staring at the sun. My head swam, and perhaps I passed out momentarily, but the next thing I remember was taking a whiff, trying to scent whose magic might be floating in the air. Trouble was, with the floral aroma of the garden streaming through the wide-open front door, I couldn't tease out any one scent.

And then I cursed myself for bothering to sort out smells and spells when I was sprawled out blind as a cave fish with footsteps approaching me.

My eyes still not focusing, I jerked my hands out and threw the Shoving Charm blindly. The electrical feel of a Shield Spell buzzed around me as someone grabbed my arms.

I squirmed and jerked and yelled. The hands let go and, still unable to see properly, I jabbed the scissors forward.

"I don't know whether to feel threatened or amused."

"Mayor Marheart?" I squinted. The blindness was clearing, but I could only make out a blurred, vaguely feminine shape.

"Please, call me Matilda. What happened? This place is a mess."

"I didn't do that. Someone—"

"Someone did quite a number on your face. Come on." She hoisted me to my feet, nearly adding *dislocated shoulder* to my list of injuries. "Let's get you to Runa."

"She's busy," I said, because for some reason my addled brain remembered that today was the start of the RetroHex Vaccine clinic.

"She'll make time. Especially for someone who looks as terrible as you do."

"I'd like to say you should see the other guy, but I don't think I did much damage."

"Next time, maybe consider a bigger pair of scissors," the mayor said as she guided me out the door, closing it behind us. I still couldn't see well, but felt her bend down at some point like someone adjusting their shoe.

"Did you see him? Her? Whoever? You came in right after they hit me with whatever that spell was. Or," I hesitated, my sense of time as fuzzy as a moldy orange, "I think you did."

"You were knocked out on the staircase when I came in. You don't remember?"

"No," I said nervously. "I could have sworn the spell hit and then I was stabbing at you. Sorry about that."

"If I ever write up a testimonial for your agency, I'll be sure to leave it out."

"Your case! I found a clue," I blurted as Matilda tugged on my arm and guided me around a corner. By now I was feeling pretty punchy and may have been babbling incoherently, but I think this is what I told her, "I might have to break into the British Museum. Morelli, he could help with that. Build an illegal portal for me or something."

"We'll talk about that later."

A door clicked open, and I caught the familiar sound of the entry bell of Runa's clinic. I may have mimicked it. A dozen times or so. My eyes had mostly cleared by then, which meant I got a full view of the crowd of people inside smirking at my musical impersonation.

"Saruman's stinking beard," Morelli cursed. "What have you done to yourself now? Emergency," he bellowed. "Step aside!"

Everyone moved out of our way, and no one gave me a single dirty look.

Sometimes it's good to have a half-troll on your side.

CHAPTER THIRTY-EIGHT
MAGIC SUSPENSION

Peering out from behind a screened-off area of the pharmacy area of the clinic, Runa took one look at me and gave an exasperated shake of her head, while also seeming oddly relieved to see me. Even her glasses zipped over to me as if seeking safety.

"Get her started," Runa told Morelli, "and I'll look her over when I finish jabbing this one."

"Will do, boss."

Boss? I knew I was out of sorts from the attack, but had my hearing been affected as well? Before I could ask anything, though, Morelli put his hands to my face. They were big enough to cover my cheeks, nose, chin, and forehead. The soothing effect was immediate, and I let out a grateful sigh of relief. When he removed his hands, I opened my eyes. Spots still floated in my vision, but I could see clearly again. Even my head was feeling less fuzzy.

When Runa's victim-patient — a tween beanpole of a boy — darted out from behind the screen, Morelli explained to her what he'd done in very technical terms (who knew the laying on of troll hands was so *medical*). She then handed him a clipboard and said, in an unnecessarily clear voice, as if making sure everyone crowding the pharmacy/waiting area heard, "Oh, good.

Just in time for your appointment. Come on back. This could take a while. *Quite* a while."

"But aren't you busy?" I asked once we'd squeezed through the masses toward the exam room.

"Rushed off my feet," she muttered, "but you're giving me the perfect excuse for a break." Once in the exam room, Runa pulled a mug from her lab coat (Magics' pockets are remarkably handy for concealing bulky objects), then drew her finger along it. The room filled with the scent of richly roasted coffee. She took a sip, sighed deeply, then dropped down onto her rollie stool with a huff of relief.

"I know it's necessary, but I hate RetroHex vaccine time. I spend all year sticking to schedule, trying to run a well-organized medical office, and it all gets blown to dragon turds by the damn vaccine clinic." She took a few more sips of her coffee, then stood and used a penlight to check my eyes. "I keep telling parents they can get the vaccines done at any of the pop-up clinics around town, but they all insist on coming here."

With a nod of satisfaction, Runa turned off the penlight and began examining my face.

"Damn it," she blurted. My gut dropped. How bad was it? My face still tingled from whatever Morelli had done, but what damage was the soothing effect hiding? I suddenly wanted a mirror, but at the same time didn't think I could bear to look.

"Am I hideous?"

"What? No, I just have to go out there to get something. Best to get it over with. Sit tight and," she slapped my hand away from my cheek, "don't pick at it."

Runa stepped out, but she didn't fully close the door, and I heard her telling a few insistent customers that she was with a patient and they'd just have to wait their turn. When she returned, and after putting a Barrier Hex on the door, she opened the jar of cream she'd grabbed from the pharmacy and dabbed it on my cheeks. She then instructed me to apply it twice a day to keep the skin from peeling.

"Now, while Morelli's keeping everyone in line out there, we've got time for this," Runa said as she pulled a full-size manilla file from a slim box that looked barely big enough to contain a wand.

"Your sample results from yesterday came in this morning, probably while you were out getting your face cooked." I didn't like the way she or her glasses were scrutinizing the paperwork. "They're not normal."

"That shouldn't surprise you."

"True. You've always been odd. Still, in most Magics this kind of testing would show a slight fluctuation from day to day, but the variation might be, at the most, ten percent. Yours from the past week, however, are all over the place. One time, your magic levels are nearly off the charts. The next day, you're almost as low as a Norm."

"So what should I do?" And yes, I was thinking of a medically approved reason for parking myself at Spellbound for the rest of the day.

"That's the problem. I don't know. I've never come across a case like this."

My heart sank. Runa wasn't old, late forties at a guess, but she'd had plenty of experience in practicing medicine, researching magic healing techniques, and was even the first person Olivia had called in to tackle the tough case of healing my parents after they'd been found. She was one of those doctors you think has seen it all. Until I became her patient, that is. I guess I've always had a tendency to defy expectations. Just never in a good way.

"I'm hoping to find a pattern," Runa continued. "Maybe

something to do with the weather, solar flares, something you're eating? I just can't nail it down. Sometimes women have fluctuating magic levels when they're pregnant, but not to this degree. You're really sure you're not pregnant?" she asked in a way that spoke of someone hoping for an easy answer. I shook my head and didn't like the defeated look on Runa's face. "I'm going to have to bring this up to Olivia."

"Do you have to?" I was afraid if Olivia knew about my on-again-off-again magic levels, she'd never let me work with HQ, license or not. She might even consider pulling me off Wordsworth's case. I didn't like him — I doubted anyone did — but even though I'm not normally Annie Optimist, I had a weird certainty that I could find his book, that a copy was just within my reach and would prove to everyone I wasn't the flake the *Herald* claimed me to be.

If I was pulled off his case, though, it would again make me look like a failure, like someone who couldn't be trusted to complete a job.

"I'm not doing it to tattle on you," said Runa. "But as head of HQ, she's seen far more than I have, and she's got access to more records than I do. She might be able to direct me to someone who can help, or at least to someone who can explain these fluctuations. Unless you want to go around with off-kilter magic for the rest of your life?"

"No, but couldn't you wait until I figure out this case with Wordsworth?" Reluctantly, I explained my reasoning.

"I don't like hiding things from her."

"You hide the fact that you don't like the chocolates she brings you each time you two have a date. You going to divulge that as well?"

In truth, I hoped Runa did keep this to herself because, with the excuse that we needed to keep our sugar levels up, she usually gave the boxes of chocolates to me or my parents. Which is why I now kept a very close eye on their dating schedule. What can I say? I like chocolate. And I especially like free chocolate.

"That's between you and me, Black. But this is a little bigger than not liking some candy. Ask your parents about how dangerous detecting work can be. You've just seen yourself how even the simplest case can lead to trouble. If your magic isn't up to speed, well, I don't like to think about it."

"Aw, I didn't know you cared."

"You're my patient. I'm required by law to care for you." She then paid careful attention to the contents of her mug. "And part of that care means I have to report this to Olivia." That certainly didn't sound good, but not as terrible as Runa's tone was implying. "And when a Magic is being investigated by HQ—"

"Investigated? Wait. Am I a suspect or something?"

"No, not that kind of investigation. More of a look into what's happening with your magic. It's odd, to say the least, but like I said, with Olivia's resources, we should be able to dig up a cause and, hopefully, a solution. In the meantime, I'm afraid I need to insist you not use any magic except in an emergency. And no," she said, cutting off my comment, "needing to charm a broom to do the cleaning up is not an emergency."

Damn it, how did she know cleaning day was tomorrow?

"So I'm on magical suspension?"

"Basically, but I'm sure it won't—"

"That's so unfair. None of my spells have hurt anyone." Okay, there was the Spark Charm on Tobey that went a little awry, and my parents' stairwell might end up with dry rot, but no one had gotten hurt.

"Not yet. We can't know what might come out of you until we sort this out. Until then, every spell you cast will be traced, and any harm that comes to someone you've been around could be blamed on you. So, until this is fixed, you need to resist doing any magic."

"And donating to my parents? What about that?"

"Like I said, we can use Busby's and Tobey's magic to keep your parents steady. Who knows, maybe that's all this is. You donating too much. Even for a strong Magic, such as yourself, I have been taking a lot from you these past weeks. A rest from donating might be all you need. Speaking of your parents—"

"What? Is their magic going wacky too?" I then recalled my mom's perfectly executed Silencing Spell and told myself that had to be a good sign, didn't it? Then, because my mind was racing all over the place, I blurted, "Your robbery. I've completely forgotten to look into it."

"Forget the break in. I mean, don't forget it entirely. If you uncover anything, I'd appreciate it, but can we get back to your parents?" I nodded, gripping the edge of the exam table. At least it was keeping me from picking at my cheeks, which were starting to itch. "They cancelled their appointment yesterday, so if you could pester them into getting their butts in here today, you'd be doing my schedule a huge favor."

"Why'd they cancel?" It wasn't like they had a jumping social calendar. Dropping by to pick up the bargain grab bags at Spellbound was the highlight of most of their days.

"Dunno, something about needing to meet with someone. They seemed to be looking forward to it," she added, possibly in response to the worry on my face. "As for the break in, I had Oberlin go over the place again, and he still thinks it was just some kids pulling a prank. Pretty stupid prank, if you ask me."

I thought of what I'd learned about Alastair's research and asked, "You don't think it was vampires, do you? Needing blood to gain strength?" Even as it came out of my mouth, I realized how stupid it sounded. Well, that and the fact that Runa was looking at me like I was an idiot.

"I only had a dozen of those little vials on hand. So that's what? Maybe sixty milliliters of blood? How long do you think that's going to keep a vampire going?" Runa sipped her coffee pensively. "I don't like this line of inquiry Olivia's on, but at least she's keeping it mostly quiet. You weren't around when the vampires were being persecuted last time, but I was. It was ridiculous and cruel and not a good representation of the magic community as a whole. A lot of hateful targeting. A lot of unjustified killing. I just hope Olivia considers all angles before she announces anything."

Runa dragged her finger upward along her mug to refill it. "So," she asked like someone killing as much time as they could before returning to a tedious task, "where are you with Wordsworth's case?"

"Are you asking out of personal curiosity or to report back to Olivia?"

"Why can't it be both?"

I told her what little I'd learned about the other copies, then added, "Wordsworth would prefer getting his copy back, but I'm not sure where to begin searching for it. I'm certainly not going to be able to go through the bookshelves of the homes of every Magic from Portland to Paris."

"True, but it's a magic book. It has a signature."

"Like a scent?"

"Close, but not exactly. Obviously Fiona could explain this stuff better, but magic books give off a signal of sorts. It can be detected, so no Magic would be stupid enough to keep a stolen one in their home. Whoever took it would likely get what they wanted from it, then discard it as quickly as possible."

I thought of Winnifred's brooch. Someone had taken it and

then sold it to a pawnshop. And not for a profit. Was there a connection between the book and the brooch?

Just then, someone pounded on the exam room door. A man bellowed something about how much longer they'd have to wait, and I didn't catch the rest because Runa threw a Silencing Spell on the door. Or on the man outside of it. She rolled her eyes and sighed. "I suppose I should get back out there. I'll let you know as soon as I find anything. In the meantime, get your parents in here and don't do any magic."

Although the waiting area was crammed full of people, most of them were eager to catch Dr Dunwiddle's attention, which meant by keeping my head down, I was able to slip through the tangle of people with the only complaints coming when I stepped on a few toes as I made a beeline for the door.

It was only when I got outside that I realized my mom's pendant was nowhere on me. Not in my hand, not in my pockets.

First missing clients, now missing found objects. Was there such a thing as Anti-Detecting? Because I had apparently cornered the market.

CHAPTER THIRTY-NINE
ALCHEMIST ALMONDS

Paying zero attention to where my legs were taking me, I kept checking my pockets, my sleeves... hell, I even darted a hand under my shirt to check my bra for the pendant.

Completely dumbfounded that I could lose something I'd literally just found, I walked straight into Fiona as she stepped out from the Sugar Charms Candy Shoppe which sits at the corner of Main Street. With her hair smoothed back and her cheeks having lost their stress-induced splotches of color, she looked far less agitated than she had the last time I'd seen her.

At least that made one of us.

Snapping out of my dazed stupor, or possibly just instinctively honing in on sucrose, my eyes were drawn straight to the large pink-and-white-striped paper sack Fiona was carrying. On its side, the name Sugar Charms was boldly written in dark-pink letters.

"Is that your lunch?" I asked.

"Bribes for students. You wouldn't believe how readily they volunteer to answer questions when they think they'll get a Crafty Caramel or Batty Butterscotch. Also, I picked up a Chocolate Wand for Tobey. Figured he could use some cheering up."

I shifted awkwardly on my feet. Maybe if I'd been there for

Tobey's cram session— But no, that was silly. Quizzes and flashcards wouldn't have suddenly cured his test phobia. I could feel bad for him, but I had enough issues with making a go of my own things without feeling responsible for Tobey Tenpenny.

"How are the cases going?" Fiona asked after what I only then realized had been a lengthy silence.

"Sebastian at Bookman's is keeping an eye out for Wordsworth's book. He even sent me some clues about the other copies this morning." Not very helpful clues, but it was progress of a sort. "I did solve a couple cases—" Fiona began to congratulate me, but I continued, "Trouble is, one client got himself killed, and the other has a social calendar I'm having trouble finding a gap in. I really didn't think returning people's belongings to them would be the difficult part of detecting."

"I certainly wouldn't either. But you have other cases?"

"The mayor's still pestering me to find her jewel, Runa said I could work on finding the stuff stolen from her clinic, and then there's my mom's pendant."

"Your mother's pendant?" There was a clear note of criticism in the question.

"I know. I wasn't going to work on it, but with two tough cases and two clients who won't or can't wrap up their cases, I needed to solve something that would be quick and easy. And it was easy, because I found it—" again, Fiona looked about to congratulate me "—but then I lost it or someone took it or… I don't know. I should probably retrace my steps, see if I dropped it…" Realizing I was babbling, I pinched my lips shut. I then pulled out the photo my mom had given me from the notepad in my pocket. "Haven't seen this anywhere, have you?"

"I have," she said.

"Really? Where? Take me there. Or tell me. Or just—"

"No, sorry. I didn't mean recently."

You know when you see hot air balloons, all colorful and vibrant, suddenly deflate into a pool of tangled up cords and fabric? That was me right then.

"That pendant," explained Fiona, "was something HQ used to give to recruits who excelled at their training. A top-of-the-class bit of bling, as the kids say. And by top of the class, I mean *top*. Strong magic."

"But that seems a little unfair. Isn't magic ability genetic?"

"Having magic is genetic, but not the strength of it. Two strong Magics don't necessarily make someone with super powers, and two weaker Magics won't produce a magic imbecile. If that were true, by now we'd have a sharp divide in magic abilities. You know how we used to be a little segregationist in our magic mating."

"Good point."

It wasn't that long ago that a giver, that's someone like Fiona who easily donates magic, could only marry a giver. If they wed an absorber — a Magic who, like me, pulls magic from others — people might think that the absorber was only in the relationship to exploit the giver for a regular magic boost. I'm sure, given human nature, this would have been true in some cases, but it also kept people apart. Which is why, even though they'd been gaga for each other for years, it was only recently that Mr Tenpenny and Fiona finally tied the knot.

So, yes, I could easily see how a division between strong Magics and weak Magics might have formed, with only the most rebellious of lovers daring to cross the line.

"Anyway," Fiona continued, "it's no longer the case now, hasn't been for at least a hundred years, but back in the day, the pendants were given as a symbol that these Magics were qualified for the top tier of Magic protection."

"Top tier?"

"They guarded royalty."

Something tickled at the back of my brain. "And when did all this begin?" I asked, although I was pretty sure I knew the answer.

"Tudor era." See, told you I knew the answer. "Elizabeth I loved handing out rewards to her most loyal advisors and courtiers, as long as no one messed with her right to rule."

"And this passed down through my family, because my ancestors were part of the royal entourage?"

"Exactly. You'd have to ask your parents about the lineage. I can't keep every tidbit of history in my head, but you'd be surprised how many Magics in Rosaria are descended from people who were very close to the English monarchy. Not me, of course. My Irish ancestors at that time were probably more apt to curse the queen than safeguard her."

"The mayor's jewel box dates from the same time period. Do you think they're related?"

"Not that I'm aware. But good sleuthing there, Cassie. Would you like me to look into it?"

"No, you're busy, but if you happen to stumble across anything in your research… By the way, what are you finding out with that?" I asked, but Fiona hardened her eyes in a way that told me I'd get nowhere with my clumsy line of questioning.

"Speaking of Matilda's jewel," she said, deftly avoiding the question, "you know we have our contact at the Historical Society, don't you?"

I did, and I recalled delivering a package to the Oregon Historical Society on my first day as a bike courier for Corrine Corrigan. Corrine had practically grabbed me off the street and, because her usual courier was out sick, insisted I do a job for her. I knew nothing about who she was or what sort of operation she was running, and my pessimistic mind was convinced I was transporting illegal goods. Or a bomb. Which meant every pothole I hit and every bumpy railroad track I crossed had me gritting my teeth.

"You might want to pop in there sometime to see if he has any information on it," Fiona advised.

I thanked her for the lead, and she told me who to ask for. Before we went our separate ways, she gave me an Alchemist's Almond — a candy-coated treat that changes flavors three times before melting away to reveal the nut inside.

* * *

I spent the next couple of hours searching for the dropped pendant, starting with repeatedly retracing my steps from Runa's to my parents' place. Even though I'd been in a hex-befuddled daze when Matilda had guided me to the clinic, I assumed she would have taken the most direct route, so I scoured one side of the street, then the other along that route. I even made several passes down the middle of the street, begging the blazing summer sun to glint on something shiny.

No luck.

I also had no luck reaching Mrs Oberlin, calling her every time I reached the end of my route before turning around to go over it yet again.

I then checked my parents' walkway, pushing aside the foliage and flowers of their garden with ever diminishing hope. Inside, I sifted through and even tidied up the disaster zone the intruder had made of their kitchen, examined every inch of the stairway, and looked under the bureau again because you never know with magic items. Maybe, just maybe, the pendant had a homing instinct.

It didn't.

Wondering if perhaps I'd dropped the pendant inside the clinic, I returned to Runa's. The crowd of people waiting for their jabs did not appreciate me asking them to move aside so I could make sure they weren't crushing underfoot the only thing that might prevent me from failing miserably.

Caving in under about seventy tons of despair, I was heading for the door when my phone buzzed in my pocket. The unexpected sensation gave me a start, and I knocked my elbow into one of the card racks flanking the doorway. Several *Witching You the Best*, *Sorry for Hexing You*, and *Hope You're Better in a Spell* cards tumbled from their wire holders. I scrambled to pick them up to return them to the rack while several of Runa's patients snorted with cruel laughter.

The phone had stopped buzzing during this uncomfortable clean-up session, but once outside, I scrambled to check the number, praying to the gods of cell service that it was Mrs Oberlin wanting to collect her damn brooch. No such luck. Since at this point Winnifred Oberlin was the only person I wanted to speak to, I shoved the phone back into my pocket.

I probably should have just turned around, gone to Spellbound, and drowned myself in cake, cookies, and crumpets. But I've never been good at following the 'should do' route. Instead, I made the mistake of heading back toward the agency.

I say 'mistake' because along the way I passed a news box, glanced in, and saw '*Latest Con from Cassie Black, Special Report*!' emblazoned across the front page.

Who knows why I did it. Maybe I felt the need to feed my foul mood. Maybe my curiosity overrides any of my common sense. Either way, I dropped in a coin, pulled open the box, and grabbed a copy.

CHAPTER FORTY
WHERE JOURNALISM MEANS INTEGRITY

Unlike newspapers on the Norm side of Portland, in MagicLand, the *Herald* still puts out both a morning and afternoon edition. What I had in my hands was the day's afternoon edition, still warm from the presses.

Even the *Herald* didn't print opinion pieces as front-page news, but the announcement telling people to look inside was so large it took up more space than the feature article about another missing Magic.

And if you need further proof that someone at the *Herald* had it in for me, the front page should have been devoted entirely to that feature article since the missing Magic this time was one of Rosaria's own. A retiree named Mel Faegan. I scanned the article, then flipped to the opinion section.

THE MOST DESPICABLE CON YET

Cassie Black, as my fellow citizens of Rosaria might know, is still running her little detective agency. And although this writer doesn't believe in miracles, it does strike me as miraculous that she's lured in a few clients.

It's just too bad those clients were obtained using some very underhanded methods.

It's almost too ridiculous to believe, like something from a farce. But this isn't a farce. And it's despicable, to say the least.

According to a trusted informant, Miss Black has in fact been stealing objects from around Rosaria. Small objects, mind you. No one's accusing her of being a criminal mastermind. That'd be giving her too much intellectual credit.

She steals these items, then hires herself out to unsuspecting clients to "find" their lost treasures.

And before you go around thinking I'm making this up, my informant saw her this very morning engaging in this activity at her parents' home.

Now, I could go on for several paragraphs about how pathetic it is that she has to resort to stealing from her own parents. But to con Simon and Chloe Starling? Two of our most respected Magics, who I might remind you are still recovering from their heroic ordeal?

Only someone like Miss Black would cause them duress to further her own aims.

This is still breaking news, but according to my witness, she was seen fleeing the scene after ransacking the Starlings' home. Will she now coerce her parents into hiring her to find what was supposedly stolen? I wouldn't put it past her.

My dear friends and readers, updates on this heinous activity will come as soon as I have them. In the meantime, I beg you not to do business with this underhanded scoundrel.

I crammed the paper into a street-side recycling bin, then used the last coin in my pocket to unlatch the news box again. My plan was to take all the papers and get rid of them before more people could read this ludicrously inaccurate tripe.

I mean, if you're going to badmouth me, at least be factual about it. My parents had hired me well before I went to their house to poke around. And ransacked? That hadn't been me. Why hadn't this witness seen the person who'd attacked me? And I hadn't fled. I'd been led out by Matilda Marheart—

A sneaking suspicion tried to creep over me, but I was distracted from my theorizing when I tried to yank the rest of the papers — a dozen or so — from the news box. They wouldn't budge.

"Only one, please. Only one, please. Only one, please," a scolding school-marm voice squawked repeatedly from somewhere inside the box. I should have known the damn thing would be enchanted to only allow one paper per coin.

I considered hurling a Flaming Arrow Charm at the contents, but since my magic could now be traced, and since Oberlin would probably love to haul me in on a public nuisance charge, I slammed the box's door shut.

The voice then trilled, "Please respect the property of *The Herald*, where journalism means integrity."

I was just debating if an Exploding Heart Charm would work on news boxes when my phone pinged a message. It was Fiona telling me her book was ready, asking if I had time to pick it up today, and if I did, to stop by her place before I went to Bookman's so she could give me the money to pay for the repair. Since I really needed some time away from MagicLand, I told her I'd be right over.

* * *

When I arrived, rather than invite me in as she would normally have done, Fiona stepped out onto the covered porch and closed the door behind her, leaving it just slightly ajar

"You got here quickly," Fiona said, speaking softly. She darted a glance upstairs, then fished a fifty out of her billfold. "That should do. And keep any extra for the legwork."

Unlike her usual calm cadence, she spoke quickly, as if needing to get back to something. From inside, I heard the rhythmic *click* of dress shoes coming down the wooden staircase. Fiona pushed the money into my hand and was just telling me not to rush back when a familiar, posher-than-the-King voice called, "Fiona?"

Fiona, already naturally pale, turned the color of chalk. With a harried look in her green eyes, she whispered, "You really ought to go. Sebastian might want to—"

Fiona's words were cut off by Mr Tenpenny peering out the door. "Who's—?" When he caught sight of me, Mr T's face soured like a cat who's just caught sight of a rival feline. Through tight lips, he grumbled, "I'll be upstairs."

Mr T turned on his highly polished heels, but before he could fully close the door, Fiona, sounding every bit the schoolteacher she was, said sharply, "Busby, get back here this instant. You'll not go skulking back upstairs to stew in your own juices."

Dutifully, Mr T opened the door once again. He refused to meet my eye. Although, he didn't seem able to meet Fiona's eye either. In fact, the doorjamb seemed to hold special fascination for him.

"Out with it," she insisted.

"Tobey failed his test," he told me curtly. "Are you happy?"

"Why would I be happy about that? And why are you mad at me?"

"He said you refused to help him."

"I missed our study session. I was on a case. That's a far cry from refusing to help. Besides, Tobey knows his stuff. I can't do anything about his inability to take a test."

"Your help might have given him a little confidence, a little fortitude to face the examination."

I highly doubted this, but didn't feel like arguing the point.

"He's got two more tries," I said, trying to sound reasonable even if Mr T had forgotten the meaning of the word. "It's not that big of a deal."

"It is when an Untrained has, for the first time, been allowed into the Academy. He needs to prove himself."

As do I, I didn't say, because I could see what this was about. Mr T needed someone to blame, so why shouldn't it be me?

"I've offered to help him study for the next test, okay?"

"We'll see," Mr Tenpenny huffed dismissively. After a heartbeat of painful silence, he turned his back on me and headed upstairs.

"He's just upset," Fiona told me. "He thought Tobey would pass with a perfect score on his first try."

"He should have. I wasn't kidding when I said he knows his stuff. He can, and does, quote nearly every rule, procedure, and statute by heart. He's just got this block in his head when it comes to taking tests. Then again, Tobey has always been a blockhead. Does he," I directed my eyes to the upper floor, "really blame me for it?"

"I think it's more that his family pride has been hurt. And just a warning, he did say he planned to come by to speak to you later today."

"About the test?"

"About your license."

"When he's already peeved with me?" That could not be good. In fact, it was probably going to be pretty dreadful. I wondered if now would be a good time to crawl under the porch and hide for the next month or so. Who knows? Maybe a family of raccoons living under there might want to adopt me.

"I'll try to make him see sense, but he can be stubborn." Fiona lifted her eyebrows and gave me a knowing grin. "Must be a family trait."

Before I could reply, Rafi jogged up the steps to join us. Fiona's teasing demeanor fell, and she now looked like one of her students who's forgotten to do their homework.

After we exchanged a few pleasantries, Rafi asked, "Fiona, did you have the files ready? Olivia sent me here to collect what you've got so far."

"Sorry, I don't," replied Fiona. "Nearly there, but it got a bit more complicated than I expected, and I need to compile the report in an order that makes sense to someone other than me. If she can just wait a bit longer, I'm sure I can have it ready by this evening if I really push it. I just—"

"Don't worry about rushing things. It's already late in the day in London, and even Olivia needs to sleep once in a while."

"I do need to make a trip to London tomorrow to pick up a few things. Do you think it would be alright if I drop it off with her then?"

"Should be fine. I'm sure she's got more than enough reading material until you pop by. That pile of documents and files she's got stacked on her desk is already defying at least a dozen health and safety codes, as well as a few laws of physics. So," he said, turning to me with a cheeky grin, "what are you up to, Cassie?"

"Going to Bookman's," I said with an equally cheeky grin. "Want to go with me?"

Rafi pretended to think it over for all of about three seconds.

"I suppose I could spare a few minutes. Just to make sure you don't get lost."

"You're as transparent as an invisibility cloak," said Fiona.

Wait, there really were invisibility cloaks? More importantly, could I order one online? You know, as a backup in case the family of raccoons rejects me?

CHAPTER FORTY-ONE
CHRISTMAS SWEATERS

When we entered Bookman's, Sebastian was assisting a turbaned man dressed in — strangely enough, given it was late August — a Christmas sweater, blue with a snow globe scene on the back.

The clerk lifted his eyebrows to acknowledge us. His cheeks warmed at the sight of Rafi, then he returned to ringing up his customer's books. As he did so, I stood gaping like a trout as the paperbacks, whose covers looked like a particularly hungry rabbit had gotten to them, changed to appear brand new just before Sebastian slipped them into a cloth satchel.

"Part of his work, his talent," Rafi whispered to me, tipping his head to indicate the altered books. "They gain a new life when a new reader discovers them."

"There you go, Mr Nazzar," said Sebastian as he handed the man his shopping bag that now sagged under the weight of his purchases. "Enjoy those."

The man turned, nodded a greeting to us, and I noticed his sweater had the front scene of the snow globe on it. He saw me admiring his fashion piece. "Gift from Mr Bookman," he said proudly before leaving the shop through a door over which hung a sign stating *Books are magic*. I wondered how many customers knew how true that really was.

"Hello again," Sebastian said as we stepped up to the counter. I didn't miss the sparkle in his eye when he greeted Rafi before turning to me. "Tell me, Cassie, are you psychic?"

I scrunched my brow in confusion. "Pretty sure that's not in my skill set. I'm just here to collect Fiona's book. Why?"

"Because I was just about to call you before Mr Nazzar came in. It seems something you were after has turned up."

"Wait. You have information on Wordsworth's book?"

"Better than that," Sebastian said as he bent over and hoisted a thick book with a green leather cover from a shelf underneath the register to the countertop. Cream-colored letters confirmed this was the book, but I still blinked several times to make sure I wasn't seeing things. "If you think that's impressive, you might want to peek inside."

Sebastian flicked open the front cover with his index finger, and an invisible donkey kicked me right in the heart. The front page bore the lengthy title in a faded, playbill script; and to the left, pasted into the inner cover, was a bookplate that read: *Property of the Library of Magical HeadQuarters, Tower of London. Return immediately if found. And don't you dare spill anything on this precious item when it is in your undeserving hands.*

If Wordsworth weren't so off-putting, I'd think we were kindred spirits.

"When did it come in?"

"About an hour ago, give or take. I left the till to help a few customers. When I was on my way back, I saw someone leaving it by the cash register. They started for the door, and I asked if they wanted store credit or cash for the book, but they just shook their head, mumbling something about how they picked it up by accident and that maybe I might know someone who'd be interested in it."

It didn't take Sherlock Holmes's level of deduction to think the story sounded fishy. I mean, this wasn't exactly the kind of book you picked up by accident. Unless you happened to be part forklift.

"The someone, what did they look like?" I checked the ceiling, but saw no security cameras.

Sebastian rubbed the back of his neck, then said sheepishly, "I'm not sure."

"Is temporary blindness common in your kind?" Rafi joked.

"No, I should have recognized it at the time. I should have been able to Shield against it, but I think they must have been doing a Confounding Charm. Or perhaps a Morphing Spell. Maybe both. I couldn't even say if it was a man or a woman, but they were tall, slim, and definitely some sort of Magic. Strong magic too, if they were able to hit me so easily."

"Did you catch their scent?" I asked. "Sorry, do your kind do scents?"

"Do my kind do scents?" Sebastian chuckled. "That's cute. We actually clued your lot into the whole scent thing. Before that, you thought Witchy Aunt Gertrude just happened to always smell like gingersnaps."

"So, the scent...?" This was a long shot. Every Magic had a scent, but it was perceived differently by the person doing the smelling. Even if Sebastian had detected, say, citrus on the person, that same person might smell like pine to me. But it would at least be something. Too bad Sebastian was again looking sheepishly apologetic.

"They were wearing perfume. Or cologne. I'm not sure. It was one of those unisex ones that work on men and women. Like I said, that should have sent up alarm bells, but this person had some serious magic going on. It sort of wiped any concerns away."

"Not much of a guardian spirit," Rafi teased.

"We all have our bad days."

I thanked Sebastian, then left him and Rafi to chat while I resisted the book addict's desire to browse the shelves. Instead, I stepped outside and phoned Wordsworth, unable to resist telling him the good news. And unable to believe I might actually wrap up my license application before tomorrow's due date.

Since my clients seemed to forget how to use their phones once I'd solved their cases, and since London was now creeping toward the wee hours of the night, I didn't expect the Bookworm to answer. Which is why I nearly fell into the gutter with shock when my call was picked up.

Wordsworth whispered a greeting, then promptly shushed himself.

"Wordsworth? It's Cassie Black." For some reason, I'd also gone into whisper mode. "I've found your book."

There was a gurgled little yelp of glee, another shushing sound, then he asked, "You're sure? Rafi told me you had no leads on my case."

Through the bookshop's glass door, I scowled at Rafi, but he was too busy flirting with Sebastian.

"Just his little joke, I think. I have it with me right now. Can you come by to pick it up?" And please please *please* sign my paperwork, I very nearly begged.

"I won't be able to leave my library unattended until tomorrow afternoon, early morning your time. Will that do?"

It would. Barely.

Again, trying to maintain a tiny bit of professionalism, I did not launch into a round of groveling, overly needy thanks. But I did do a rather embarrassing happy dance that caught Sebastian's and Rafi's attention. They were gasping with laughter when I told Wordsworth, "That will be perfect. I'll have your paperwork in order when you arrive."

After saying our goodbyes, I let out a squeal of triumph.

"Shhhhh!" came from my phone, because apparently in my hasty excitement, my finger had missed the end-call button.

* * *

Since my magic ran the risk of things blowing up, disappearing, or turning into fluffy bunnies, I left it to Rafi to work a Lighten the Load Spell on both books so we could haul them back to MagicLand without either of us popping a hernia.

Rafi was telling me about the Tower's pixies' failed attempts at making donuts when we entered Morelli's building. A fair deal of clanging and cursing was coming from the workroom. Even Guildenstern was looking worried. Or was this Rosencrantz? For the life of me, I couldn't remember what Morelli said was the trick to telling them apart.

"Alastair?" I asked the gnome.

"Not having the best day, ma'am," he replied, the troubled look on his face made me wonder if he'd already felt the brunt of Alastair's frustration.

"I need to see him, but maybe it can wait?" Rafi said, as if asking himself. Something heavy clattered to the floor followed by swear words I didn't even know existed. "Yes, best wait. After all, you need help with these books, don't you?"

I replied that I most certainly did, then we hurried upstairs, as Guildenstern-possibly-Rosencrantz pleaded for us to take him with us. I was opening the door to my closet when Pablo marched over and hissed at the books hovering next to Rafi.

"Well, if you don't like heavy objects floating over your head, get out from under them," I told him.

Stepping into the closet, it finally hit me. I'd done it. I was mere hours away from becoming a card-carrying magic detective. If there wasn't the danger of tripping over a tangle of shoes and breaking my neck, I would have skipped like a giddy schoolgirl through my back-of-the-closet portal.

* * *

Fiona was pleased with the repair job when we dropped off her book, but warned me that Busby had already headed over to the agency to speak with me. Which really put a damper on the good mood I'd finally found.

She wasn't wrong. Waiting outside my office door was Mr Tenpenny. I realize I should have been on cloud nine. I had found Wordsworth's book. He was coming by in just under sixteen hours. But after my previous two 'solved' cases, until I had a signature in hand, I feared it might all fall through.

Plus, from the look on Mr T's face, I was pretty sure he was still misguidedly grumpy with me over Tobey's failed exam.

I took a deep breath and dreaded the upcoming lecture. And, because he'd worn his crispest shirt and his pocket square couldn't have been more precisely placed without involving a survey crew, I knew this was going to be a lecture, not an avuncular checking in to see how things were going.

I busied myself with unlocking the door while he chatted pleasantly with Rafi.

"Let me guess, you're here about my license application?" I asked, trying to head him off at the pass as I made a beeline for my desk and gently nudged the calendar over my still-blank application form.

"I am," he replied in a tone full of patience that has run its limit. I'm not exaggerating when I say that, at that moment, the room was vibrating with more tension than the cables of a suspension bridge at rush hour. I wanted to clear the air about

Tobey, about how it wasn't my fault he'd failed his exam, but Mr T's sharp tone put me at a loss for words. "You are aware that your license application is due tomorrow?"

"Hard to forget," I said and pointed to the tea-stained calendar where *License Due* was now flashing like a warning light.

"And you are aware of how few hours you have until tomorrow? Because it appears you haven't even begun filling out the form." To emphasize his point, he tapped the corner of my application that had managed to sneak out from under the desk calendar. Who knew paperwork could be traitorous?

"You never did tell me exactly what time it was due," I said, both ignoring his comment and clarifying things. Because right about then, eight a.m. versus eight p.m. was going to make all the difference.

"Noon."

"Plenty of time. As you can see," I said breezily as I thumped Wordsworth's book, which Rafi had parked at the edge of my desk, "another case has been solved. I'll have the required contract signed off as soon as Wordsworth gets here tomorrow morning."

"Why must you leave these things to the last minute?"

"Cheap thrills?"

Rafi snorted a laugh at this. Mr T didn't.

"You're sure he's arriving? He's been rather occupied with—" Busby caught himself, then cleared his throat. "With retrieving requested research items."

"He doesn't strike me as the kind of guy who's late for things."

"True. His punctuality makes Runa look like a procrastinator." He glanced critically at my desk once more, then straightened his already straight jacket.

As soon as Mr Tenpenny was out the door, I swear the entire agency breathed a sigh of relief. After helping me cram Wordsworth's book into my safe, Rafi said he needed to get going, but reassured me he'd be back before Wordsworth arrived the next morning.

"For moral support?" I asked.

"That, and, well, call me chicken, but I don't think it's going to put Alastair in any better of a mood if I pester him for paperwork today, do you? Tomorrow. That'll be safer, right?"

I shrugged. I honestly didn't know. Alastair had a cool head and things didn't rattle him for any length of time, but I'd never heard him as angry as he'd just been.

"I'll catch you tomorrow, then." A broad smile lighting up his face, Rafi held out his hand. "Excellent work, Detective Black."

I smiled and shook his hand, but his using that title with me didn't sit right. Almost like he'd just jinxed me with his positivity.

CHAPTER FORTY-TWO
BITTER SACHER TORTE

I felt fidgety after Rafi left. I needed to distract myself, and work seemed like the most productive option. Absent-mindedly nibbling on some leftovers from Spellbound, I searched for information about Matilda's jewel box.

My heart skipped a few beats when I discovered a handful of images of ones similar to the mayor's on two higher-end auction sites. Similar but for one difference: Instead of the heart-shaped depression Matilda's box had, the lids on these simply had a flat surface with a heart shape crafted from what looked like tiny garnet chips.

Still, it was too good of a clue to dismiss for a small difference in design.

The two boxes had already been sold, but I jotted down the names of the auction houses to see if they might be able to tell me who had bought the items or where they had come from. With one house being in Europe and the other on the East Coast, they were now closed for the day, so my questions would have to wait. But I made a note to remind myself to ask if any of the boxes might have had jewels in them at some point. Which I thought was a good bit of detective work.

I then called a few of Real Portland's classier jewelry shops to see if they knew anything about heart-shaped jewels from the

Elizabethan era, but they each told me that wasn't their speciality.

On a whim, I even tried the phoning up the pawnshop Rafi and I had visited. I mean, lightning sometimes strikes twice, right? Not in this case.

Finally, there was the Oregon Historical Society contact Fiona had mentioned. The museum would be closing up soon, and the receptionist didn't sound happy to be answering calls so close to quitting time. When I asked for the name Fiona had given me, she told me he was out for the day, and would be back Monday if I'd like to try again then. She hung up without bothering to ask if I'd like to leave him a message.

I ended up staying at the agency far longer than I'd intended, and the sun was already setting before I closed the computer, double-checked the safe was locked, and headed home.

In hindsight, I should have just kept working.

When I waded through the closet and into the apartment, Alastair was sitting at the dining table with a Sacher torte, two bottles of IPA, and a pair of lit candles. The Sacher torte, I noted, hadn't been touched, but both bottles of beer were empty. I also noticed Pablo had tucked himself into a corner as far from Alastair as he could get without being too far from the kitchen.

After flicking me a glance filled with bitter disappointment, Alastair waved a hand to switch on the lights and extinguish the candles — magic candles that would only ever burn halfway down and, rather than dripping, channeled their wax back into the candle itself. Needless to say, candle making isn't a lucrative profession in MagicLand.

"I forgot something, didn't I?" I said, proving I'm not as imperceptive as some people might believe.

"Our anniversary." Annoyance ground through his words. "Five months, Cassie. Five months since we shared that first Sacher torte."

Alastair was the love of my life. Now that we were together, I couldn't imagine not being with him. But I couldn't possibly live up to all these little anniversaries. This first date Alastair was referencing (which only happened because I was trying to avoid one of my magic classes). The first time he held my hand. Our first kiss. The day I rescued him from the Mauvais. The day we moved in together. It was terribly romantic and kind of cute, but I honestly couldn't keep up.

And I know that sounds terrible, but it was a non-stop calendar of celebrations, and I was losing track of what he considered an anniversary and what he didn't. It was like being Catholic and having to throw a big to-do for every single saints' day.

"I'm sorry," I said sincerely. I didn't want to argue. I wanted to ask him what he knew about magic books, about jewel boxes, about royal courtiers, about all the various little things that were bouncing around my skull.

I also wanted some of that torte.

I reached for a plate, but Alastair stood, slapped the cake box shut, and practically threw it onto the kitchen counter.

Then, because someone was in the kitchen and that's where glorious things like cans of gloopy food and bags of crunchy treats are kept, Pablo trotted in and let out a very demanding meow. Alastair glared at him like someone who wished they could shoot lasers from their eyes.

"Is this about more than me being a little late?" I asked, truly curious.

"He," Alastair seethed, jutting a finger at Pablo, "needs to stay out of the workroom. I've told you a dozen times I don't want him in there."

"You know very well I don't let him in. It's not like I'd even be allowed to with the guard gnomes on duty twenty-four, seven."

"He's messed up the commission. Again."

"So magic it back to how it was."

"It doesn't work like that. It's— Never mind," he snapped. Alastair then brushed past me and jerked open the front door. "I'm going back to the workroom."

What was going on with us? Not only had I apologized, but it was his own Barrier Charm protecting the workroom. If Pablo was getting in there, how was that my fault? I didn't have the relationship skills to know what to say or do, so I figured the best thing would be a little time-out before either of us said something we'd regret.

"Can I still have the torte?" I shouted as he stormed down the stairs.

"Knock yourself out."

I heard Rosencrantz (or Guildenstern) tentatively greet Alastair. Alastair gave no response other than to slam the workroom door behind him.

Not having had any true parental units in my life until recently, I wasn't in the habit of sharing my relationship woes with my mom. But right now, I needed to vent, I needed someone to reassure me I wasn't in the wrong, I needed to hear someone else say, "Gosh, that Alastair Zeller sure is being a right wanker."

My parents' phone rang. And rang. And rang. When their silly co-narrated voicemail picked up, I ended the call. They must have gone out again without their phone. Still, it struck me as odd that they hadn't come by or called me about the break-in at their place. Okay, more than odd. More like seriously concerning to the point of distraction, as evidenced by the fact that I hadn't touched a single slice of the Sacher Torte yet.

With my ability to create fully formed worst-case scenarios, I knew I'd get no sleep unless I checked on them, so I grabbed my satchel, told Pablo to come along, and went through my closet portal. When I got to my parents' house, though, all the lights were out.

I honestly had no idea what time my mom and dad went to bed, but with their recovery still in full swing, early nights might be just what the doctor ordered. As Pablo sprawled out on their doorstep, I eased my way into a flower bed and peered in the kitchen window. A wash of relief flushed over me when I saw that things looked as though they'd been tidied, proving the Starlings hadn't been snatched off Magical Main Street, sucked through a manhole into another dimension, or trampled by an angry hippopotamus.

What? I told you I'm a whiz as worst-case scenarios; I didn't say those scenarios were based in reality.

After untangling myself from a rosebush that had been doing its best to give me a round of agricultural acupuncture, I whispered to Pablo to come along and we headed home.

Tomorrow, though, Simon and Chloe Starling were getting a talking to about staying in touch.

CHAPTER FORTY-THREE
CONTRACT NEGOTIATIONS

The next morning, Rafi was true to his word and met me at the agency. Not the apartment, I noted, wondering if elves could detect the odor of a foul mood hanging over a place, since Alastair was still barely speaking to me — something I was determined to sort out as soon as I finished up with Wordsworth and rushed my application over to Mr Tenpenny.

In the agency's kitchenette, Rafi had just poured us a couple mugs of tea, and I was dumping the crumbs from a box of oatmeal cookies into my mouth when the bell above the agency's door chirped. My whole body tensed and I nearly spit oat-y bits all over the counter as my glass-is-half-empty mind conjured all manner of ghastly scenarios.

It would be an accountant from HQ coming to say they wouldn't pay for a book they already owned.

It would be Sebastian coming to say the book was a fake.

It would be Olivia coming to break the news that Wordsworth had been eaten by a giant blue jay.

Rafi shoved me unceremoniously out of the kitchenette, and I found myself standing face to snout with the Bookworm. While I wouldn't say I was pleased at the sight of his strange face and haughty demeanor, I was relieved to see him.

He stretched and slithered his way to a guest chair and

climbed into it without a word of hello.

"So you've found the book," he said flatly, like a poker player giving nothing away.

"Pretty sure I have," I replied. I brushed cookie crumbs from my hands before lugging his book from the safe and gingerly taking a seat in the office chair from hell. "And," I added, flipping open the cover to reveal the bookplate inside, "I'm pretty sure it's the copy from your collection."

Wordsworth leaned in. Placing his nostrils barely a centimeter from the title page, he sucked in a deep breath, then sat up as straight as his lumpy body could manage. The stoic façade had loosened, and he was even giving what might pass for a smile.

"It is indeed my copy."

Rafi had seated himself in the chair next to the Bookworm. Using some sort of telekinetic power I'd be curious to learn more about, he gave me a congratulatory pat on the back without ever moving his arms.

Wordsworth pulled out a fountain pen. From where he pulled it, I don't know because it wasn't like he wore clothes except for a chain to hold his glasses. Did he have folds of skin that served as pockets? A disgusting notion if I thought about it for too long, but right then I didn't care. That pen and the signature he was about to make with it were going to save my butt and turn me into a worthy member of this community.

With his pen poised expectantly, I scrambled in my desk drawer for Wordsworth's file. Some tea must have seeped into the drawer because the top page of the contract was stained, but the signature sheet was still clean. I pulled only that out and placed it in front of him, mentally urging him to lower his pen to the line and sign it.

"I believe our agreed upon fee was twelve hundred for

finding my own copy," he droned.

"It was. Did you want to see the entire contract?"

"No, I have a very good memory." He lowered his pen to the signature line. My heart began thudding with frightening intensity. "I know exactly what is owed, but I will need a—"

I was just opening the desk's middle drawer where I kept a receipt booklet when the Bookworm halted. His attention shifted back to the book, and he narrowed his eyes at it.

"Where was this found, exactly?"

I explained to him about Bookman's Bookshop and Sebastian's strange customer.

Wordsworth placed his empty hand on the book's cover. After a moment, he jerked his hand away, his face scrunched up with disgust. There was a literal pain in my gut as Wordsworth recapped his pen and tucked it back into his gelatinous flesh.

"I'm sorry, but this is unacceptable," he huffed. "The book is damaged. Pages are missing."

My mind raced. Had there been a clause in the contract about finding the book in any condition? Could he really deny the job was complete if some pages were missing?

Unfortunately, I also have a good memory, and I knew he could. He'd been very thorough in each and every stipulation of the contract. And one of those stipulations was to find a copy in the same condition as his had been when it had left the Tower's library.

"Could those pages have been missing when you took it to the conference?" I suggested.

"I should think not." And the way he said this, you'd have thought I'd asked him if he liked licking poison ivy in his spare time.

Rafi, possibly seeing the rumbling warning signs of a Cassie Volcano, tapped the book and said, "Just to verify, could you show us which pages are missing?"

The Bookworm let out a *harrumph*, but scoot forward in his seat. With disproportionately strong arms that reminded me of Popeye's, Wordsworth opened the cover. He then slid a knobby finger along the gilt-edged pages, stopping about two-thirds of the way through. He flicked a finger, and the book fell open without him touching it. Wordsworth then pointed to the center, to the inner margin where the pages met the binding, and indicated the remaining tattered edges where pages had once been.

I glanced at what was open before me, noting the numbers at the bottom margins and also noting something familiar in the flourishing script on one of the facing pages.

"As you can see, I could not possibly sign off on this job as complete."

Wordsworth was right. Unless this ancient tome used some arcane page-numbering system, two sheets had been removed. A meager two-sheet gap in a thousand-page book. Two damn pieces of, at a guess, vellum were all that separated me from a signature for my license application.

The Cassie Volcano fizzled out with dismay.

"But you hired Cassie to find a copy of the book," said Rafi, coming to my professional rescue. "She not only found a copy, but your exact copy."

"As I stated, I have a very good memory, and I know for a fact that the contract says I will only give up my signature for an intact copy of the book. This," he swished his finger, and the book shut, "is not an intact copy. It would not do to have it in my collection. What would people think?"

They probably wouldn't know the difference, to tell the truth. But I didn't have the heart for smart retorts.

"Like you say," I began, forcing my voice to remain reasonable and to give no indication of how much I wanted to wring his squidgy neck, "you have a good memory. You probably know the contents of most of your books."

"A good portion, yes," Wordsworth stated.

"Very impressive," I said, feigning my awe as I fell into butt-kissing mode. "With a mind like that, surely you could copy the contents of the missing pages from memory and put them in as an addendum."

This was the wrong thing to say. Wordsworth looked at me like I'd just suggested he take up the new and exciting hobby of poisoning baby hippos.

"First off, this is not a book I have read. The contents are only for advanced Magics, and I would not violate Olivia's trust in my discretion. Second, copying pages and gluing them in is *not* how a library is run."

He'd obviously never been to an under-funded public library. If a damaged or missing page could be photocopied and taped into a book to save a few dollars on a slim budget, it would happen.

"Come on, Wordsworth," said Rafi. "She found the book."

"I'm sorry," he said in a way that carried no hint of apology, "but pages are missing, and this book, while it is mine, does not meet the criteria of our contract. Therefore, I am not contractually obligated to sign or to pay."

"If we find you another copy. An intact copy?" I blurted. And yes, I was visualizing myself suddenly discovering one of the other copies, stealing it like the world's cleverest cat burglar, and racing it to Wordsworth in the next few hours. Sometimes my brain takes a break from reality.

"Then, yes, that would be per our contract."

"And you wouldn't consider signing that contract on faith? I mean, I have proved my capabilities so far."

Hey, it was worth a shot, right?

"No. Our contract says nothing about that. But you have done fast work here." I nearly fell out of my chair at the grudging praise. "I'm sure it won't take you long to find a copy that isn't damaged. For a smaller fee, of course."

"Of course," I muttered.

And with that, Wordsworth slid out of his chair, then waddled, stretched, and slithered his way out the door, leaving his damaged book behind like the ugliest kitten in the litter.

CHAPTER FORTY-FOUR
NO LONGER WELCOME

 I have to give Rafi points for friendship, because for the next hour, he commiserated with me about Wordsworth's unreasonable behavior, about the ridiculousness of the entire license application process, and about the byzantine nature of Magic bureaucracy in general.

 Rafi also got in touch with the Tower's pixies, who were able to whip us up two plates of mushroom-and-gruyere omelets accompanied by a mountain of blueberry pancakes with all the trimmings. In exchange, he promised to bring them back a two hundred-gram bag of gold glitter.

 "Glitter?" I asked through a mouthful of pancake. "They do know that stuff's only a couple dollars, right?"

 "Apparently not. Glitter, especially gold glitter, is a valuable commodity in their circles. There have been wars fought over it. And *with* it, now that I think about it. The mess left behind is legendary."

 Sadly, since my agency was outside the influence of the Tower, once we'd finished our meals, our plates didn't magically refill. That's not to say we didn't watch them for several minutes after we'd eaten the final crumbs. You know, just in case.

 "Well," said Rafi, standing up and stretching like a tawny brown cat, "I should probably attempt to collect Alastair's notes."

"I suppose you're still not allowed to tell me anything about this big research project?"

Rafi shook his head and did the lip-zipping motion, although he did look apologetic about it.

"I don't get it. I mean, I know I'm not the best at paperwork." I pointed to my desk as an example — and to think there was a time only a few days ago when it had been tidier than a computer chip factory's cleanroom. "But HQ knows I'm good at figuring things out from only a little bit of information. If it's so important to act on these reports, then why not bring me into it? It's like they hint at thinking I'd be a big help, but then they throw this stupid you've-got-to-have-your-license thing at me."

"I agree completely, and I have argued the case to bring you in, license or not. In my opinion, we need all the Magic hands on deck as we can get. Is that how that saying goes?" We both tried to untangle the correct phrasing but couldn't come up with anything that sounded right. Finally, Rafi let out a sigh of defeat. "Look, you didn't hear this from me, but Olivia has reliable information about an uprising amongst the—"

Just then, the agency door whipped open, banging against the wall and startling both me and Rafi, who threw up his hands as if ready to cast a defensive spell. I would have been right there ready to fight alongside him, but the sudden noise sent my chair into a panicked retreat, spilling me onto the floor as it bucked away like a gun-shy palomino.

"Alastair," said Rafi, his greeting wary and trying-too-hard-to-be-cheerful.

"Of course *you're* here," Alastair growled. Only as he marched across the agency's floor did I notice his face. Four long scratches stood out on his right cheek. Clutched in his hand was Pablo's carrier.

From inside the carrier, Pablo howled.

I jumped up from the floor and hurried over, kneeling down beside the cage.

"You know he doesn't like this thing," I criticized.

The first time I'd met Pablo, he'd been in this very carrier. His former owner's sister was Cat Hater Number One and had stuck him in it when his owner, Mrs Escobar, had died. Not only stuck him in it, but also left him in the hot sun, waiting for the animal executioners to take him away. Luckily, I'd turned up before they did, but Pablo had detested this piece of kitty luggage ever since.

I made to open it, but Alastair hit the latch with a complicated locking spell.

"He's staying in there. You need to get him to the vet."

"Is that the kettle?" Rafi said, glancing toward the kitchenette like a drowning man who's just caught sight of a dinghy. "I completely forgot about… something."

I mouthed the word *coward* at him as he backed into the kitchenette and pretended to busy himself with arranging boxes of cookies and tea.

"Why are you doing this to him?" I asked Alastair.

"Your cat is a complete psychopath."

Pablo howled again, breaking my heart but clearly having no effect on the stony demon formerly known as Alastair.

"What did he do?" I reached out to touch the scratches on Alastair's cheeks, but he flinched back from my touch.

"I swear he hates me." I gave him a look that implied he was the crazy one if he really believed that. These days, Pablo spent more time curled up with Alastair than he did me. "He may have liked me once, but something's gone wrong in that cat's brain. I don't think we can keep him."

Pablo whined at this, and I knew if I looked into the cage he'd be staring up at me with those big Puss-in-Boots eyes. Although, if he started speaking in Antonio Banderas's voice, that would be pretty cool.

"What happened?" I asked, then darted into the kitchenette. I received a sympathetic look from Rafi as I fetched a damp cloth for Alastair's face. When I brought it to him, he snatched it from my hand, but dabbed at the wounds nonetheless.

"I was in the workroom. I don't know how he got in. The room was completely shut off, doors closed, Barrier Hex in place. But there I am, working on the commission, on the damn tension. It's taken me weeks. Just ask Eugene. I was at my wits' end with it.

"Then, not even forty minutes ago, I finally got it right. So I set it up to put it through a practice run. And what happens? That terror of yours launches an attack. Barrels right into my project, parts go flying, and the main component crashes to the ground. I found one piece, but the minute I picked it up, he swatted and did this." Alastair made a sharp gesture toward his cheek. "Something is not right with him, and I don't want him in the apartment until he's been looked at."

"He's our cat. You can't kick him out. Can't you put stronger Barrier Hexes on the workroom?"

"Apparently they're not working. Cat magic," he spit the words. "I don't want him around. He's probably ruined me. You both have."

I could understand his frustration over the setback, but that seemed a little much.

"We've got nothing—" I clenched my jaw tight to stop myself. "No, I am not having this conversation. Something broke. It can be fixed. You've got the Tremaine orders, so it's not the end of the world if the commission gets delayed. As for Pablo, he's a cat. You can't seriously think he hates you. And, to tell you the truth, if he doesn't like you, I don't think I can blame him right now."

"What are you saying?" Alastair demanded, red flaring into his cheeks.

"I'm saying that if Pablo can't come home, I won't either."

"Well, he's not welcome in the apartment until he's been examined. And if you're going to choose a cat over me, fine."

With that, Alastair stormed out. It was our first real fight. And for some reason, it felt like our last.

Rafi emerged from the kitchen and let out a silent *Wow* of disbelief.

"Tell me about it. What did he mean about cat magic, anyway? Pablo's just Pablo."

"All cats have magic, but it's on a different level than human magic. Part of that difference means the stronger the Barrier Hex, the more keen they are to get around it." Knowing cats as well as I did, this made perfect sense. "I'll go see if I can't talk some sense into him," Rafi said, then squeezed my shoulder companionably before striding to the door and jogging away from the agency, calling Alastair's name.

I sat on the floor in front of the cage. Pablo mewed at me. It was only then I realized Alastair hadn't released whatever locking spell he'd put on the carrier. I considered magicking it open, but I was on magic suspension. And even if I wasn't, I couldn't risk a spell going wrong and making Pablo's head explode, his skin turn inside out, or some other horror movie scenario.

The upper portion of the carrier was attached to the lower portion with a series of sixteen well-spaced wing nuts. The task should have distracted me. Instead, every twist only ratcheted my irritation and frustration and dismay up another notch. My fingers ached and my head was throbbing by the time I unscrewed the last nut.

When I pulled off the top portion (and, okay, hurled it angrily across the room) Pablo looked around as if confused by his newfound liberty. He then nudged my hand, purring deep within his throat.

I was just about to lift him out for some much needed cat cuddles when my phone rang.

I stabbed at my phone's screen to answer the call.

I probably shouldn't have.

CHAPTER FORTY-FIVE
CUSTOMER SERVICE

"Yes?" I snapped.

"Miss Black? Mayor Matilda Marheart here. Where are you with my case?" she asked, her voice cracker crisp. "I ask because, to be perfectly honest, I feel I've been left high and dry. After all, it would seem you had plenty of time to visit with Fiona yesterday, to make a trip to Bookman's Bookshop, and to even stroll around Rosaria for over two hours." Which was so weirdly accurate it made me wonder if this woman had a drone tracking me. "So I would very much like to know if you're giving any attention to my case."

"I'm working on it," I said through tight lips.

"I can't stress how important it is for this jewel to be found, Miss Black. If you feel you aren't up to the job... Well, let's just say I don't normally give credence to what I read in the *Herald*, but in this case, I might just have to believe its most recent claims that you aren't all you're cracked up to be are true."

I was too furious to come up with words to defend myself. She, of all people, should know the *Herald's* opinion section lately was little better than a tabloid.

"...all a little scam," she was saying. "Maybe it's just to get your business afloat, but I have to say, it's quite unethical, and frankly not behavior I would expect from someone Eugene ever spoke highly of."

By now I was in such a rage that if you looked into my eyes, you'd probably see a pair of infernos. I was allowed to call myself a loser as much as I wanted, but for someone else to throw it in my face? Someone who barely knew me…

"I would very much like to know," Matilda continued in her imperious tone, "if you ever plan to make this case a priority. Be honest with me. Have you even bothered to look for the jewel? Done the tiniest iota of research? Need I remind you that I am the mayor?"

I opened my mouth. I shouldn't have. I should have just hung up the phone and called back later with an excuse about a dead battery. But I was already having such a wonderful day, why not make it just a smidge better?

"Just because you're the mayor of some rinky-dink magical community doesn't give you any right to boss people around. Perhaps if you got off your political high horse, you'd see how ridiculous it is to expect me to find, in the blink of an eye, an object that hasn't been seen in over five hundred years. So, if you can't show a little patience, maybe you should take your mayoral sash and stick it up your—"

"That is enough, Miss Black," Matilda stated, the terse words hissing through her teeth. "Apparently, all those articles about you are correct. I will no longer require your services. And I will be sure to let others know what kind of treatment they'll get if they do business with the Black Magic Detective Agency."

"Good. Go ahead," I said flippantly, since I'd likely have a different business name by lunchtime.

The line went silent. Pablo tilted his head at me and let out a questioning meow. I don't know if the question was, "Are you handing out treats now?" or "Are you a complete idiot?"

Pablo's pretty perceptive, so probably the latter.

Suddenly, my stomach lurched and an acrid taste filled my mouth.

What had I done? I'd just told off a much-needed client. One who was actually willing to stay in contact, to help me with my clue gathering, and to pay me while I worked, not just once I'd completed the job.

Of course, she also bore a striking similarity to the person seen at Clive's place before his death, her hand had been bandaged the morning Runa's clinic had been broken into, and she'd conveniently been at my parents' house right after I'd been attacked. Was that simply a whole lot of coincidence, or was there something more I should know about Mayor Marheart?

Then, because the day was already going so splendidly, my calendar began blaring, "Overdue! Overdue! Overdue!"

A blanket of dismay settled over me.

I'd failed.

Despite having a bag of marbles, a rooster brooch, and a giant magic book, I didn't have any officially completed jobs. Those items, while they did prove I could sleuth my way around a problem, didn't do me a lick of good in regards to getting my license.

I didn't want to be in the agency when Mr Tenpenny showed up with his looks and words of disapproval. Also, I couldn't figure out how to get the calendar to shut off. Seriously, whoever out there is selling those things, you need to include instructions.

"Come on, Pablo." I stood, and he leapt off the desk. "Let's go drown our sorrows."

I shut out the lights in the agency, pulled the blinds, and left, unsure if there'd be any point in ever coming back.

CHAPTER FORTY-SIX
SCONE-FILLED WISDOM

Because it was Spellbound's early closing day to prepare dough and chocolate and fillings for the coming week, the morning rush of customers had already stocked up and cleared out.

Gwendolyn would only be open for another twenty minutes, but that would be plenty of time for me to load up on whatever sugary-buttery items were still in the display case.

Pablo, needing no instruction from me, sprawled along the pavement and leaned against the building's façade to bask in the warmth of the late morning summer sun.

Inside, Gwendolyn was at the counter and, perhaps sensing my foul mood, offered, "How about a trio of scones, on the house?"

"I can pay," I protested, then checked the price tag just to be sure.

"Don't be silly. They're just going into one of the bargain grab bags if you don't take them."

Gwendolyn arranged the scones on a silver-edged plate and passed it to me. The pillowy goodies were still oven-warm, so I think she was lying about needing to get rid of them, but I didn't have the energy to argue. Instead, I slipped a five-dollar bill — all I had left of Fiona's change from Bookman's — into the tip jar when Gwendolyn turned around to grab me a cup of hot water into which she 'accidentally' dropped a bag of Spellbound's Special Blend Tea.

Not wanting to put up with passersby stopping to insult me, I slid into one of the indoor seats that was farthest away from any window. Because it was apparently the *Herald's* mission to haunt my every step lately, the seat also included a copy of the paper someone had left behind. Trying to ignore the vile rag, I dialed my parents' number. A surge of irritability rampaged through me when the call went to voicemail.

I broke a piece off from a lavender-and-honey scone as I scanned the discarded *Herald's* front page. Well, I scanned the front page after first checking the opinion section. Shockingly, there hadn't been a single bad word against me.

It was either a slow news day at the *Herald* or Tremaine had paid to be featured on page one, because more than half of the front page was taken up with an article about Tremaine's Toy Emporium, including an eye-catching sidebar highlighting all the new merchandise that would be arriving soon.

After a detailed story of Tremaine setting up the shop after he'd retired from teaching, the article regaled its readers with Tremaine's recent visit to the Marble Convention, his "inconsolable" sadness over the loss of his longtime friend Clive Coppersmith, and the embarrassment of being pulled in for questioning regarding Clive's murder.

The piece concluded with a lengthy quote from Tremaine:

> "All this talk about foul play against my dear friend Clive is a bunch of malarkey. I've seen how that Cassie Black can harass you — she did it to me only a few days ago. And I'd bet you anything that's what did poor Clive in.

"His real cause of death wasn't an Exploding Heart Charm; it was the strain he must have endured from her coercing him into making a case out a few missing marbles.

"Cassie Black tried to imply I was a thief, but I'd only taken the marbles as a little joke. We did such things all the time. Clive would have known he could ask for them back whenever he wanted. We were such close friends, you know. The ache of his loss is breaking my heart.

"The whole thing's put me off of anything to do with Cassie Black. Which is why, the moment Inspector Oberlin apologized for bringing me into the Academy for questioning and fully acknowledged my innocence, I cancelled all my orders and contracts with Alastair Zeller.

"After all, something had to be done to show her how things work here in Rosaria. Just the thought of my customers' money going to someone who associates with that Cassie Black is enough to turn my stomach, and I want your readers to be reassured that, as of today, none of their hard-earned dollars will go to supporting that detestable Cassie Black.

"I agree whole-heartedly with what the Herald has been reporting, and I think a criminal investigation needs to be undertaken against that detective agency."

At least now I knew the real reason why Alastair had been so angry.

Because the orders for Tremaine had become so insanely profitable, Alastair had devoted the majority of his time to filling them. This meant he'd been turning down all other work. All except for this mysterious commission, which it would now appear was his only source of income thanks to Tremaine's misguided vengeance against me.

I shoved the paper away, then looked at my plate. The lavender scone was now little more than a mound of crumbs. I guess in my fury over the ridiculous interview, I'd obliterated the poor thing.

How could Tremaine be such a jerk? How could he fire Alastair for something as simple as the police asking him a few questions? That was weapons-grade harsh. Even Morelli on his worst day hadn't been that mean to me.

Gwendolyn, possibly thinking I was done, had come over to collect my plate. When she saw the disaster I'd made of her lovely scone, she gasped at the crime I'd committed against pastry.

"Was it not good?" she asked, sounding truly worried.

"Sorry. This article," I said, taking a swipe at the paper. "I guess I needed to destroy something."

"Oh dear, I did see that. I should have cleared up the papers when you came in. Half days are always so busy. This is the first lull we've had."

"It's okay. Not your fault. Or the scones'."

To show her all was good in the world of baking, I ate half of the apple-cinnamon scone in one bite. It wasn't the first time I'd drowned my magic sorrows in carbs, and I think Gwendolyn recognized this. She probably saw a lot of it in her shop.

"Don't get yourself down. It's just a stupid article."

"It's not just this one. It's all the opinion pieces before it. Everyone's seeing these things and judging me for them. It wasn't so bad before. At least I knew they were lies. But this one," I indicated the paper, "it's true. I've ruined Alastair's business. It's like my failure is contagious."

I explained to her my argument with Alastair. Well,

arguments. Then I babbled on about the license due date flying by faster than an osprey diving for a trout. Gwendolyn slid her tall frame into the seat across from me.

"That's nonsense. You're not a failure. I was witness to how terrible your magic was when you first came here."

"And you suffered the consequences."

When she found herself unable to teach me anything about mixing potions, Gwendolyn momentarily lost all confidence in her teaching skills. This had been a terrible time for her students, since she worked them three times as hard to prove she really could instruct others in the fine art of a color-changing potion.

"But I got over it, and you improved," she said. "You mess up now and then, but we all do. I still sometimes mix up the baking powder and baking soda in a recipe."

"That's hardly failing. And it's hardly disastrous."

Gwendolyn flashed a look that said I was a culinary idiot who would never comprehend the sanctity of non-yeast leavening.

"You get my point," she said. I didn't, but I let her continue, mainly because my mouth was too full of apple-cinnamon deliciousness. "You missed a deadline. So what? You only need to ask to have it extended."

I swallowed a painful amount of scone all at once.

"Really? Mr T acted so rigid about the timeframe. 'You must submit your application, Cassie, or the world will end as we know it'," I said in a pretty good impersonation of Mr T that had Gwendolyn giggling.

"Busby does act like that, doesn't he? It was the same when I first opened Spellbound and was working toward my business license. My case manager from HQ was all over me about the approaching deadline, but I simply couldn't get my sourdough starter to behave."

"*You* couldn't manage a sourdough starter?" I asked

incredulously as I started in on the lemon-poppyseed scone. Gwendolyn nodded.

"Kept wandering off. They do that if you're not careful. I really did think it was the end of the world with the way my case manager acted. And then I missed my deadline."

"You did?"

"Yep, calendar started screaming at me and everything. But then Rooney, she runs the Sorcerer's Skein, told me it really wasn't the end of the world and what to do. So, I took her advice, mustered up my courage, and went to HQ. Olivia didn't hesitate to grant me an extension. It was only a couple of weeks, and there were miles of stipulations, but it bought me enough time to get things in order and to figure out the right spell to contain the sourdough starter."

"Was this Fred?"

"No, his cousin, Ted. Ended up being such a well-behaved fellow," she said wistfully. I wondered what had happened to dear old Teddy. Fred probably murdered him. Assault and breadery?

"Do you really think it will work? Asking?" I cringed at the word. You know how some people fear a root canal? That's how I felt about asking for help. In addition to an overwhelming desire to prove I could do things on my own, I feared appearing weak. And I feared rejection.

As if reading my mind, Gwendolyn said, "Sometimes you need a little help from your friends to prove you can do things on your own. That doesn't really make sense, but you know what I mean. No one does anything all on their own. There's always a little help along the way."

"And who helped you? With the sourdough starter?"

"Lola. Her calming influence works on yeast just as well as it does on people. So, will you go to HQ?"

"You don't think Mr T will think I'm undermining him?"

"You brought him back from the dead. He can hardly complain if you go over his head to save your business, to get yourself going in the very career he said you'd be perfect for."

She made a fair point.

Gwendolyn and I chatted a little more before I swore to her that I would go to HQ. She even volunteered to watch Pablo until I got back.

It was only after I walked out of Spellbound — with a roasted veggie sandwich boxed up for my lunch, and Pablo curled up next to a still-warm oven — that I realized there was only one problem with my plan.

With my magic on pause, I had no way of getting to HQ.

CHAPTER FORTY-SEVEN
PORTAL PROBLEMS

To get from Rosaria to Magic HeadQuarters in London without the use of an airplane is very simple. You only need to step through a long-distance portal. This employs a similar, but higher level of magic and physics than the short-distance portals such as the ones that can take you through, say, a closet door in Real Portland and drop you off in MagicLand.

To use one of these long-distance portals, you have to either travel with a Magic or have magic yourself. Reliable magic, that is. With my powers in disarray, I hadn't given much thought to using the short-distance portals within MagicLand, since the worst that could happen is I might end up on the wrong street or in the wrong house. Which would be embarrassing, but not exactly lethal.

However, if my magic went wacky halfway through a long-distance journey, I might end up a thousand miles off course, I might be torn in half as one part of me went to London and the other half went to Lisbon, or I might find myself somewhere in space getting sucked over the edge of a black hole.

I could just picture the joy on the face of my admirer at the *Herald* as he typed out the headline: *Great Detective Loses Herself*.

I considered asking Gwendolyn to go with me, but she was in

the midst of coaxing ten balls of dough to knead themselves. Even if she had assistants getting things prepped for the upcoming week, she'd still be too busy delegating tasks to pop off for a quick jaunt across the pond.

Luckily, I knew a witch doctor who I not only had to visit to have my daily sample taken, but who was always looking for an excuse to make a trip to HQ to see a certain someone. I just hoped if I told her it was urgent, she wouldn't have time to change into one of those frilly tops she thinks Olivia likes.

* * *

"It won't take long," I promised, as Runa placed the sample vial into a rack. "I mean, it can't take Olivia more than fifteen minutes to dash my hopes."

"I can't, Cassie," Dr Dunwiddle asserted. "The vaccine clinic ate up so much time, I've had to shift a bunch of appointments. Which means I've got an afternoon of rashes and sprains to look forward to."

"I'll just have to go on my own, then," I goaded.

"Don't you dare try it. With your luck, you'd probably end up somewhere in the middle of the Atlantic."

Which says a lot about how far Runa and I had progressed in the past months. There was a time not long ago when she would have paid to see me drown in a vast body of water. Now, she'd probably be satisfied with a good dunking.

"Have you tried Fiona?" she asked.

"No, you were the first person I came to."

Dr Dunwiddle — the stern, the stalwart, the stringent Dr Dunwiddle — actually stammered at this revelation.

"I— That is— Really?"

I nodded. Runa looked about to embrace me, but just because

she no longer wanted to see me drown, didn't mean our friendship had reached the hugging point. Runa cleared her throat.

"Fine, I'll go with you. It can't take much more than an hour." She waved a hand for me to follow her, so I hopped off the exam table. "I'll see if Morelli can handle some of the patients who only need first aid. But first," she said, halting at the exam room's door so abruptly I nearly crashed into her, "a little advice since you're going to be asking Olivia for a big favor." Ooh, secret HQ tips? I really had earned a spot on Runa's good list, hadn't I? "She's very old-school British, which means she loves it when people mind the niceties. Please, thank you, and all that. Say the magic words and, well, she might still say no, but it could nudge you just that bit closer to getting a yes."

Runa brushed off my oversized dose of gratitude with her usual gruff demeanor and we stepped into the pharmacy area of the clinic. I braced myself for the scrutiny that I'd become so familiar with lately. But instead of a crowd of catty patients, the only person in the waiting area was Fiona. Clutching a folder in one hand, she was looking through the card racks and rearranging a few of the greetings that weren't perfectly straight.

"Just the witch I wanted to see," Runa said. "I know you're my next appointment, but do you mind if I move you to later?"

"You? Not on schedule?" Fiona asked with genuine shock. Runa was a stickler for punctuality. You could set Swiss watches to the timing of her day. I wondered if this was the first time she'd cancelled an appointment on such short notice.

"This one," she jutted her thumb at me, "needs to make an emergency trip to HQ."

"Oh my, you're not injured, are you?"

"Not this time," I said. "I sort of screwed up, but I was told asking nicely might fix it."

They both looked at me like this would be impossible. Me asking nicely, that is. Not me screwing up. I was an All-Star Champion at that.

"If I'm not being a third wheel," said Fiona, "could I tag along? I meant to go earlier, but time got away from me."

"Dropping that off?" Runa asked, glancing down at the folder in Fiona's hand.

"The research," Fiona said by way of a reply "I thought this report would be the end of it, but Olivia sent word that she's got a few more files for me to sift through. When were you planning on going?"

"As soon as I make some calls to get Morelli in here and to swap a few appointments. Ten, fifteen minutes at most."

"That is short notice. But since I now seem to have a small opening in my own schedule, no time like the present, I suppose."

While waiting for Runa to make her calls, Fiona asked me about my cases.

"Touchy subject," I said. "It's why I'm going to HQ. Apparently, groveling to superiors is part of detective work these days."

"But you've had some success, haven't you?"

"Success might be stretching it. I seem to be the go-to gal for hunting down trinkets that have gone missing in MagicLand. Marbles, a brooch, and the pendant I mentioned. Which I found and is now missing again."

"But you have bigger cases as well, yes? High-profile ones? That should feel good. I know you like a challenge."

I shrugged.

"It did feel good. Until it didn't." I told her about my meeting with Wordsworth. "And as for finding the mayor's jewel, well, let's just say that request has been withdrawn."

Perhaps Fiona had already heard about my behavior toward Matilda, because she didn't comment further on this. Instead, she went all pensive for a moment. Then, in a contemplative tone, she said, "So, a pendant, some marbles, and a brooch… And then you have a jewel, a ruby you said?"

"Or a garnet."

"Which is still missing."

"What?" I asked, impatient with possibility. "Do you know where the jewel might be? I'd pay you a consultancy fee."

"No, sorry. I don't know where it is, but there is something that sounds oddly familiar about all this. Or maybe not those exact pieces themselves, but," she hesitated, searching for the word she was after, "a connection perhaps. The jewel within the pendants from HQ was a garnet, I believe. And then there's the cockscomb on the brooch."

"Also a garnet," I said, a tingle of excitement racing along my arms.

Could there really be some sort of link between these items? Or were garnets just easy to come by in the world of Magics, and I was trying to read more into a coincidence than was truly there?

"But Winnifred's brooch also has emeralds and diamonds," said Fiona, bursting my pattern-seeking bubble. "And the marbles, those are made of glass." Fiona smiled in a self-deprecating manner. "Listen to me playing detective. It's all this research. I've been forced to make so many links and ties between tiny scraps of information that my brain seems to be doing it with everything. Just yesterday morning, I thought the pattern on Busby's pocket square was an exact match for some wallpaper I'd seen on a piece of Victorian-era stationery."

"Alright, all settled," Runa said before I could prod Fiona more about a possible relationship between my clients' treasures.

Because although I'd been heavily focused on completing these cases to get my license, I'd also had plenty of time to think. And something in my own head wanted to weave the various missing items together. Obviously, some things like the book and the stolen samples from Runa's clinic were outliers, but if I could just brainstorm with someone else, the puzzle pieces might come together more quickly.

But for now, it was time to focus on the license application.

Which meant it was also time to beg HQ for help.

Ugh.

CHAPTER FORTY-EIGHT
POLITE GROVELING

We made a quick journey through the streets of MagicLand over to the London-Portland portal in Lola's neighborhood, where I quickly discovered Bunny hadn't given up on (or gotten any better at) playing the drums.

As you might remember, we could also have traveled to London through the parcel slot at Corrine Corrigan's courier service, but that was a bruising experience that dumped you onto a conveyor belt in the basement of the British Library, not into HQ itself.

But, thanks to the portal at the end of Lola's street, in mere seconds we were at the Tower of London. No airport security, no missed connections, no lost luggage (usually). Sometimes magic could still make me marvel.

"Hello, Sir Dunwiddle," greeted Chester, the troll who took Tower security very seriously, especially if it was a rodent breeching the historic walls. Chester also had the strange habit of addressing everyone as *Sir* or *Mister*, although Rafi had been trying to train him out of it. "No frills this time?" Runa shook her head. "Too bad. I really like the frills."

He and Runa had to be the only ones.

"We need to see Olivia," Runa told him. "It's important. Is she in her office?"

"I could go check," Chester offered, unabashedly enthused at the chance to do some recon, another task Rafi thought the Tower's trolls might be good at. Although, how he thought a seven-foot, four-hundred-pound person could go unnoticed in a surveillance situation still baffled me.

"No, that's fine. We'll just run up there and hope we catch her."

"Oh, good, because I saw a rat's nest down this hall earlier."

"Best get to it, then."

Chester snapped his heels together smartly and saluted Runa, then trudged off. It wasn't long before a heavy stomp and the cringe-inducing crunch of bones echoed from somewhere down the stone corridor.

"You did let Olivia know we were coming, didn't you?" asked Fiona as we turned onto another hallway.

Runa replied with a wince. After all, Olivia wasn't exactly the kind of person into whose office you simply sauntered for a casual, unplanned natter.

"Not to worry. She was expecting me soon. I'm sure she won't mind a few extra guests," Fiona said, in a way that made it clear she knew Olivia would very much mind. She pulled out her phone and began typing something.

The Tower of London, even with its various walls, towers, and museums, is fairly easy for tourists to navigate. But the White Tower — the central keep within the Tower of London complex — is a different story. This is Magic HeadQuarters. To Norm eyes, it appears only a few stories tall, but if you're Magic, once inside, you discover an impossible number of floors all connected with a jumbled tangle of stairwells and hallways. Many of which all look alike, making it easy to get lost.

Luckily, thanks to her many dates with Olivia, Runa now knew the place as well as her own clinic. So, although on my own I'd have likely ended up on the roof, we made it to Olivia's office without having to backtrack a single time.

When we reached a familiar door, my two companions took a step back.

"Cowards," I whispered as I knocked three times.

"Is that you, Cassie?" Olivia called. "Come in."

Startled by her uncanny knowledge, I pushed open the door — which, for being made of oak planks nearly as thick as the original trees must have been, was surprisingly light — and stepped into Olivia's office.

At some point in the White Tower's history, this impressive room might have been a royal bedchamber. These days, it featured medieval tapestries over the stone walls and a sleek modern desk that somehow worked with the ancient interior. Olivia stood to greet us, her chair shifting aside politely. I wondered if I could send mine here for etiquette lessons.

"How did you know it was me?" I asked, looking for security cameras, then after finding none, imagining some sort of Spy Spell trained on the door.

"Fiona just texted me that you were on your way." Which seemed so mundane.

Glancing over my shoulder, Olivia's cool smile warmed considerably. She strode over to Runa, and the two did that air-kissy thing to each other's cheeks. This seemed rather stiff given how much they'd been seeing of each other, but when I looked down to their hands, their fingers were entwined. And, when Runa stepped out of the embrace, her cheeks were flushing worse than a schoolgirl who's just gotten an autograph from the cutest member of her favorite boy band.

"And Fiona," Olivia said, releasing Runa's hand and reaching for the folder Fiona had brought. She then returned to her desk and tapped a file full of yellowed papers. "These are the documents I thought you might be interested in."

We each took a seat in the three chairs before Olivia's desk. Fiona eased back to look at the contents of the file, but I remained perched on the edge of my seat.

Olivia watched me for several uncomfortable seconds before saying, "Miss Black, it is very late in the day and clairvoyance is not one of my talents, so if you'd care to enlighten me as to why you're here…"

Damn it, I'd been hoping Fiona might have included that in the text. I gripped the edge of my chair, worried that if I didn't, I might just run out of the room.

"I was wondering if there was any possible way I might get an extension for my detective's license application." Then, because I felt Runa's eyes boring into me, I awkwardly added, "Please?"

"But you've had cases. I believe they've been going well, or am I misinformed?"

"I have had cases. Quite a few clients, in fact. And I've done pretty well at finding some items that have gone missing, but it turns out the clients themselves haven't been so easy to find after I locate their objects."

I explained to her about Clive's unfortunate end and Winnifred's unfortunate social life.

"And then," I continued, "when I found Wordsworth's book, there were a couple of pages that had been torn out, and he says the book isn't complete without those pages, so he won't sign off on his contract until I find an intact copy of the book.

"If he had just signed, I would have had the paperwork for the application and it would have been on time, but he didn't and then the stupid calendar went off and yelled at me about the license being overdue. And I don't mean to blame others for my mistakes, but—"

I abruptly stopped speaking, flustered by my sudden bout of verbal diarrhea.

"Sorry," I muttered, "rambling." Then, trying to follow Runa's advice of minding my manners, I concluded with, "Thank you very much for listening,"

Olivia shook her head, causing the ends of her braids to sway and the small beads at the ends to clink together. I couldn't tell if the head shake was due to annoyance over allowing me into her office, commiseration at my bad luck, or frustration over something completely unrelated to my predicament.

"One moment," she said sharply.

Using her Tea-lephone — a tea kettle whose metallic surface served as a sort of video phone — Olivia pressed a few spots on the surface. I thought she might be calling Chester to have me thrown out on my ear, but a moment later, Wordsworth's imperious voice answered the call. I groaned. Why couldn't she have waited until I'd left? I certainly didn't want him to think I'd come here to complain about him. Although, I probably wouldn't have been the first.

Thankfully, the Tea-lephone's 'screen' faced Olivia, so if I stayed quiet during their conversation, the wormy librarian might never know I was listening.

"Hello, Wordsworth. Olivia here. Tell me, did Cassie Black ever find that book you were after?"

"Not exactly. The book she uncovered was compromised. Pages were missing."

"But your book was found. Surely, we could add the missing pages back in at some point." I wanted to say I tried that tack, but didn't want Wordsworth to know I was in the room. Or in the same city, for that matter. "It would only take a simple Duplex Spell on one—"

"I do not want to be disrespectful, Madame," Wordsworth cut

in disrespectfully, "but a true book aficionado would never consider that *his* book from then on. It would be forever tainted."

"But it's not *your* book. It's the property of Magic HeadQuarters. Miss Black has found what you asked, so technically, you could close her case with you."

"That is true. Technically."

"So," Olivia drew out the word in the manner of someone very tired of trying to extract information from the stubborn mule they were conversing with, "will you do it? Sign off on the contract, I mean?"

"Is she there?" I began emphatically shaking my head at Olivia and waving my hands in a way that screamed *Keep me out of this!* "Is she complaining about me, because—"

"No, no, nothing like that. It was simply something I heard from Rafi."

Okay, I didn't really like throwing Rafi under the Bookmobile, but better him than me.

"That's fine, then. But no, I cannot go against what is in the contract. It was very detailed as to the requirements for the condition of the book, and as it is a—"

"Magically binding contract," Olivia sighed. Then, to my questioning expression, she added, "It can't be altered in any way."

Sometimes you've just gotta hate magic.

"Exactly so. And that means, until an intact copy of the book is in my hands, there is simply no possible way I can sign off."

"I see. Well, thank you for your—" And before Olivia could finish, Wordsworth hung up.

CHAPTER FORTY-NINE
AN OFFER YOU CAN'T REFUSE

With a sharp flick of her fingers, Olivia conjured a knit cozy to cover the Tea-lephone. Or, who knows, perhaps to strangle it.

"He's not required to sign the bloody contract," she snarled, "but the slimy bastard certainly could if he wanted to. Gandalf's lousy beard, I hope the next librarian we get is more... *human*."

"How long do librarians usually stick around?" I asked.

"Wordsworth's already been here three hundred years. Most don't retire until at least their five hundredth anniversary." Even Olivia's braids looked dejected at the thought of this. "Now, as for you, apparently Wordsworth worded that contract quite thoroughly, and I can't force him to do anything that goes against a magically binding agreement. I also can't make him sign off on the case until it's completed per that contract. Which is only going to happen if you can somehow produce an intact copy of this ridiculous book."

Olivia pinched the bridge of her nose as if fighting off an oncoming migraine. Runa reached into her shirt pocket, then slipped Olivia a small packet of aspirin. Olivia shook out two of the pills and swallowed them dry.

"We really do need to get you licensed and on our detective

squad. Not today, perhaps. It's not an outright emergency yet, but certainly within—" Olivia looked from the files Fiona had brought to Fiona herself "—the next couple of weeks?" Fiona confirmed the timeline with a nod.

Olivia pondered something for longer than felt comfortable. My belly was flipping and flopping so much it's a wonder someone didn't ask about the Jazzercise class going on under my shirt.

Olivia then stood up, placed a pencil on the thick, stony ledge of a window, then returned to her desk and pulled a by-now familiar contract from her desk drawer. She began filling in all the boxes. I glanced to Runa, who was nodding her head encouragingly while also appearing rather astounded. Fiona, on the other hand, didn't look comfortable with what she was witnessing.

"There," said Olivia once she'd completed the sheet. "I'm hiring you to find that pencil."

"Wait. What?" I asked stupidly.

"This," she tapped the contract in front of her, "will give you what you need for your license. No more dealing with missing clients, dead clients, or persnickety clients. You'll start afresh."

Could it really be that easy? If so, why hadn't they just done this for me in the first place? Then again, my mom, with her own 'missing' pencil had tried, and I'd refused. At the time, I hadn't wanted a handout. I'd wanted to prove myself. But now…?

I got up, practically jogged over to the window, and reached for the pencil. Just take it back to Olivia, get a quick signature, and in a matter of a few seconds, I'd have what I'd been after for the past week.

I strode back to the desk and took a seat.

"Thank you," I said. "But, no."

Fiona shot me a proud-of-you grin. Olivia, after glancing over at the pencil still perched on the windowsill, fumbled with then dropped the pen she'd had poised over the license paperwork.

"No? What do you mean, no?"

"Do I really have to go into the stupid reasoning?" I groaned, like someone who's being asked to explain why they'd just rolled around naked in a briar patch. "It's very touchy-feely, and you know I don't—"

"Explain yourself," Olivia demanded.

I swallowed hard, brushed my palms along my skirt, then said, "I want my license. I want to have the agency and solve things and work with HQ on stuff. But if I take the easy route, if you hand me my license just like that, I won't have worked for it. I mean, I have worked for it, I suppose, but others won't see it that way. They'll see it as Cassie Black being moved up the ranks because of who she is and who she knows. I'll still be a flunky. In their eyes. And mine," I added, only just realizing how true that was. "I need to prove myself. To do this the right way."

Runa perched rigidly on her seat. Her body full of tension, possibly fearing how Olivia would respond, but from the corner of my eye I could see her lips twitching with a suppressed smile.

"That is insane," Olivia said flatly. She then snorted a laugh. "You truly never fail to surprise me."

"Proud to be consistent, ma'am."

Olivia twirled a braid around her index finger.

"I have one more proposal, and I highly suggest you take it. It will be your last chance."

I nodded, afraid to speak. What had I just done? I could be holding my license right now. I could be heading down to The Keys — the Yeoman's Warders' private pub — and celebrating with a pint. But no, I had to go all moral and introspective, and now I was facing ultimatums from a banshee who could kill me with a single scream.

"I can grant you an extension for the license application for two weeks," Olivia offered. "We do need you. Preferably sooner than that to get you up to speed, so I encourage you to move quickly on this matter. However, if that isn't enough time—"

"No. I mean, thank you. That's more than enough."

At least, I hoped it would be.

I will say here that the offer of the extension nearly made my heart burst with gratitude. Despite what Gwendolyn had told me, I was pretty sure that bending the rules wasn't something Olivia did every day. Her doing so filled me with an intense feeling of determination to show her I could pull this license thing off without a hitch.

Of course, it wouldn't be long before I was wondering what in the fiery depths of Hades I'd been thinking by not simply returning that pencil to her and taking the easy way out, but not taking it certainly felt like the right decision at the time.

"Now," Olivia said, "Wordsworth won't sign off for the copy of the book you found because the pages are missing, but he will accept any intact copy, yes?"

I said he would, but that I had no idea where another copy could be found.

"That is obviously a problem, but I'll see what I can do about it. Likely not much, I'm afraid. However, if you send me his contract, I will check it over thoroughly for any loopholes you need to be aware of.

"I'm also willing to use my influence to make sure that any other clients of yours are prompt in finalizing their contracts with you. You only need to ask. Does that sound like something that would help?" I said it did, thanked her, and was about to give her Mrs Oberlin's number when Olivia continued, "Good. Now, may I look at your application? I'd like to see where you're at with it."

"I, uh—"

"You haven't begun the application yet, have you?" I shook my head. Olivia drifted her hand along a blank piece of paper. It filled in with a facsimile of the form that had been sitting on my desk for the past week — although this one had far fewer tea stains and Pablo prints on it.

"Fill it in now. I'll send a copy with you, and the original can stay here as a show that you have begun the application process."

And so I filled in boxes. Name, address, clients, case work, my magic specialty… There was one box, though, that gave me pause.

"I haven't exactly settled on a name yet." Remembering Runa's advice, I added, "Please."

"Please?" Olivia asked as Runa rolled her eyes and shook her head.

"Sorry?" I tried, doing my best to work the politeness angle.

"Never mind. Just leave that blank. We can fill it in when you bring in a signed client contract. Now, this case that is close to completion…?"

I explained that Mrs Oberlin was my best bet. Not only did I have Winnifred's brooch, but Inspector Oberlin had confirmed it was indeed hers when he'd put me through that paperwork farce at the Academy.

"So," Olivia pointed to the Tea-lephone, an impish grin on her lips, "would you like that help now or later?"

Completely flabbergasted at the offer, I fumbled to say something, then Runa kicked the leg of my chair. To this day I wonder if she was aiming for my shin.

"Yes," I squeaked, hardly believing I might finally get a case settled. "I mean, now. Help. That'd be great. You're welcome."

Olivia, looking rather worried for my mental state, glanced at the client notes on my application, removed the Tea-lephone's cozy, and tapped the side of the teapot with her fingertips. I assume to dial Mrs Oberlin's number.

It rang. And rang. And rang. With an apologetic smile, Olivia tapped the pot again and the ringing stopped.

"I'll try again in a bit. Winnifred is known for not wanting to break away from any gossip sessions she's in the midst of. We'll get this sorted, and if all goes well, you'll have your license by tomorrow," said Olivia, with far too much relief in her voice for my comfort.

What in the world was this problem they were dealing with? And if it was so damn urgent, why go through all these silly steps to bring me onto the team? Magics, I thought with a mental *harrumph*.

Olivia then held a blank sheet over my paperwork and said, "Duplex." When she pulled the sheet away, it revealed an exact copy of my application. I reached for it, but she passed it instead to Runa, who immediately began looking it over. I guess privacy laws hadn't worked their way into magical bureaucracy. I gave Olivia a questioning look.

"Better for someone else to hold on to it. I've heard tales of your organizational skills. Now, any questions?"

"When I do get my license—" look at me sounding confident that I might actually pull this off "—you say you need as many agents as possible on something you're looking into. Can't I just get started on that now? At least get some background details?"

"I'm afraid without the license, we can't. But yes, it is pressing, so please do take this seriously. Unfortunately, while I can adjust due dates on matters such as this, the signed-contract aspect of the application can't be changed. Believe me, we've tried." Annoyance sparked in Olivia's eyes, and I swear the tiny universes contained in the beads at the end of her braids swirled with a little more vigor. "Tried recently, if you understand."

"Thank you," I murmured, and was pretty sure I'd gotten the politeness correct that time. Beyond that, I didn't know what to say. I mean, who'd believe that Olivia had tried to go against HQ's own policies for me? Which only further begged the question of how desperate they must be to get my insight into whatever trouble was brewing.

"Now, how about tea?" Olivia offered, closing the matter by switching from grave concern to welcoming cheer. "I believe the pixies have just gotten in something special from Fortnum's."

Olivia lifted her hand, fingers poised to snap, and my mouth was already watering at the mere mention of Fortnum & Mason treats. Just then, Runa's phone squawked. Reaching for the noisy device, she fumbled with my application, so Fiona took the sheet from her. Once Dr D was able to dig the phone from her pocket, she stepped aside to take the call.

Fiona began to explain to Olivia what organizational charms and collating spells she'd put on the files she'd brought, while I kept hoping Olivia would remember her manners and order up that tea for us. With all the trimmings.

My dreams of Chelsea buns and cheddar oat cakes were fully taking on a life of their own. So much so that I could practically taste the clotted cream. Runa then rushed back over to us. Her previously flushed cheeks had gone pale.

"Medical emergency. We've got to go."

We? Why *we?* There was still a chance of tea coming up. Scones? Sweets? Itty-bitty savories? I saw them all disappearing as my two companions started racing toward the door. I bolted from my chair, started to hurry after them, but then stopped to turn back at the threshold and thank Olivia for everything.

See, I can be polite when I try.

CHAPTER FIFTY
THE EMERGENCY

As we raced with her toward the portal, Fiona and I didn't bother to question if we should be following Runa. Olivia must have contacted Chester (I did notice he wore one of those Secret Service type earpieces now, probably Rafi's idea), because he had the portal open and ready for us by the time we reached it. At the last minute, Fiona remembered to grab my wrist, then the three of us were pulled and twisted from London to MagicLand.

Several people gave us curious looks as we burst from the portal and charged through the streets of Rosaria. Fiona kept asking Runa what had happened, but Runa was saving her breath for the effort of jogging as fast as her stout legs could carry her.

I wasn't even paying attention to where we were headed until we stopped.

No. No, no, no. Anywhere but here.

I nearly begged Runa to keep going. I wanted to insist that this couldn't be the location of the emergency call-out. But the five officers pacing along the walkway in front of the tidy home, the gawking crowd, and the crime scene tape strung across the shrubs to keep everyone back were clear signals she hadn't just stopped to admire the azaleas.

"Where is she?" Runa barked at one of the officers out front.

Responding with only a curt wave of his hand, he led her around the back to a lush garden full of flowers that splashed the yard with reds, yellows, pinks, and purples.

In all the rush and confusion and Runa's commanding nature, the cops must have thought Fiona and I had every right to stay alongside Dr D, because no one questioned us passing beyond the yellow strips of tape.

"Neighbor saw her through that window." Our police escort pointed to the house next door, to the second-story window that gave onto the garden. "Called it in immediately. Not sure what you can do, though," he said discouragingly.

Runa had already crouched down. In dumb shock, I watched her tend to Mrs Oberlin. I didn't even bother to scowl when the flash of a camera lit up the scene.

A second client attacked. Not to be selfish or unsympathetic, but this was really bad for business. Although, she was still breathing. At least there was that.

"Did the neighbor see anything?" I asked. "Any hint of who did this?"

"Saw someone she described as tall and slim letting themselves out the garden gate, but didn't glimpse their face. Doesn't do us much good unless the Inspector happened to have a Camera Charm on the garden. Which he doesn't," he added critically.

Fiona, not wanting to watch, was focused with great intensity on the paperwork in her hand, as if Mrs Oberlin's miracle cure could be gleaned from the HQ files.

Winnifred's mouth gaped open with a ragged gasp, like someone fighting for air. There were no obvious wounds, which likely meant a magic attack. Perhaps an Exploding Heart Charm that hadn't hit her directly, but had done enough damage to put her on the brink between life and death.

"Can you do anything for her?" I asked Runa.

"I don't know. Gandalf's gonads, where's a troll when you need one?" Runa began shredding chameleon skin, an antidote for poisons.

Mrs Oberlin's lips trembled, a look of fear in her eyes when they caught me. My first instinct was to step back, but I felt frozen in place as her right hand scrabbled in the soil. Inexplicably fascinated by this detail, I watched as her index finger drew two bumps, like the M a child would draw to represent a soaring seagull. Her finger remained poised in the dirt, but she added nothing to her doodle.

"Come on," Runa pleaded. Stupidly, I couldn't understand why.

Mrs Oberlin's body went rigid.

And then it relaxed.

"Is she dead?" I asked. No one answered me. Maybe I'd only mumbled the question to myself, or maybe the sudden buzz of panicked activity drowned out my words.

Still staring at the m-bird Winnifred had made, my legs stepped shakily back, the motion suddenly aided by someone pushing me up against the post of a pergola. Inspector Oberlin stared past me at his wife. No tears. No sobs. Then he glared at me and growled, "You're responsible for this. I don't know how, but I know she'd be alive if not for you."

His voice was loud enough for the large crowd gathered at the edge of the police tape to hear. Everyone who'd been watching Winnifred and Runa now fixed their morbid attention on me. They were pointing, whispering to one another, and likely taking the Inspector's accusation for fact. More fodder for the *Herald*, I thought.

Fiona stepped between me and Oberlin, then pulled me aside, tugging me by the arm until we reached a garden shed that shielded us from the worst of the stares. Medics in white rushed onto the scene with a stretcher, while Runa explained to them what she'd already tried.

Once the medics left with Mrs Oberlin's prone form, Runa reported to the officer in charge what she'd observed upon arrival. She then joined me and Fiona, looking irritated with herself and the situation. But there was something more in her expression. Something that made my gut knot more tightly than a string of Christmas lights.

"The application," she demanded, jutting out her hand.

Fiona instantly handed over my form. Runa scanned it, her jaw twitched, then she looked up at me with a mix of regret and fear. Someone pulled on the wrong end of the string of lights. The knot tightened and became more impossible to untangle.

"What?" I demanded, impatient with confusion. "What is it? I didn't do this."

"No, I know you didn't."

"Runa, what's wrong?" asked Fiona.

"Coppersmith. Oberlin. Both clients of yours."

Wondering if she was coming to the same conclusion Oberlin and the glaring onlookers had, I defiantly replied, "Like I just said, I didn't do it. I wasn't even around when Mrs—"

"No, but you found her brooch and Clive's marbles."

"I also found Wordsworth's book." I spoke harshly. Fully on the defensive. "And we know for a fact he isn't hurt or dead."

To many a library lover's dismay.

"That might be different," Runa mumbled this as if still sorting something out in her head. "He's not from Rosaria. Is that why?" Then, to me, she stated, "Your mom's pendant. You found it, and you were attacked."

"What does this have to do with anything?" I demanded, still not getting the point she was trying to make. Or maybe I was getting it, but just steadfastly denying it.

"Simon and Chloe have missed their last two appointments with me. *Missed*, you understand. Not cancelled."

She said this last bit softly, carefully, but that didn't stop a cold hand from gripping and twisting inside my chest.

"Cassie," Fiona whispered, as if she didn't dare speak the words too loudly, "when did you last see your parents?"

* * *

Cassie's troublemaking, trouble-creating, and trouble-finding continues in *The Unbearable Inspector Oberlin!*

BEHIND THE STORY
UNPLANNED ADVENTURES

Ugh, a cliffhanger, am I right?

This novel (just in case you didn't notice) is the start of a new trilogy featuring Cassie Black. And I promise I am cranking out the next two installments as quickly as possible so you don't have to spend too much time dangling over that cliff.

Those books (*The Unbearable Inspector Oberlin* and *The Unexpected Mr Hopkins*) will be full of Cassie sorting out strange jewels and missing Magics, trying to find Wordsworth's missing book, dealing with that pesky Inspector Oberlin, and learning more about that potential uprising… which you just know Cassie will get herself tangled up in whether HQ gives the okay or not.

But where did this story come from?

My own readers.

Seriously.

When the original Cassie Black Trilogy wrapped up, that was it. I was done*. Cassie Black had completed her hero's journey, she'd saved the world, she'd saved the cat, and she'd found her home and new family. I liked Cassie's story, I was proud of the work, but I honestly had no idea how popular the trilogy would become.

I also had no idea that readers would start hinting they'd like to see more of Cassie Black.

But what happens when you have a character without a story?

Well, I don't know what normal writers do, but I sat down with my list of Books I Want to Write to see if Cassie and the gang could fit in with any of the plots. There was a mystery series that had potential, but didn't quite suit the world I'd already built for Cassie.

Then one day, I was looking over a map of a museum in France. And on the map was a little square marked with what literally translated to "The Bureau of Found Objects." Which sounded like an amazing name for a detective agency. A detective agency that Cassie Black might be able to run, perhaps??

From there, it was a matter of sorting out what Cassie might need to find. Since books are always in my line of vision no matter where I am in my house, I figured, why not a book?

I quickly had a story idea in mind. A very simple story idea that centered solely on Cassie dealing with Wordsworth. Nothing else. No jewels. No brooches. No marbles. No attack goldfish.

If I would have turned my brain off then, there would be a fourth Cassie Black book and my writing life would have been *SO* much easier.

Unfortunately, by the time I got around to starting a first draft, my brain had gone wild with ideas. Ancient jewels, a grumpy police chief, the Elizabethan court, Tobey's exam anxiety, a suspicious mayor, and of course, an evil office chair.

I can't reveal too much just yet about how everything will play out, but layers upon layers kept getting added in. Some historical, some mysterious, and some just for laughs. And those layers meant the story couldn't be confined to one book (unless it was a VERY large book, indeed). It also meant that there would have to be cliffhangers.

As the trilogy moves along I will share a bit more of those layers and idea tidbits with you, because who doesn't love a peek behind the creative curtains?

For now, though, thanks so much for reading this book. I'd love to stay in touch, so please be sure to sign up for my monthly newsletter at *www.subscribepage.com/mrsmorris* (all lower case) to get a free story and to keep up to date on all my new releases.

And if you'd like to spend some more time with Sebastian at Bookman's Bookshop, you'll find him (and the magic of books) in *The Unwanted Inheritance of the Bookman Brothers.*

One last thing before I let you go, if you enjoyed this tale, and it has you itching for more, please be sure to tell another person you know who loves comic fantasy whodunits. A review on your favorite book retailer, Goodreads, or Bookbub would also be lovely.

By the way, if that itching continues, maybe go see your doctor. Just saying.

—Tammie Painter, April 2024

*If you notice some minor discrepancies between the "summing up" bit in Chapter 50 of *The Untangled Cassie Black* and the first chapters of this book (or the rest of Trilogy 2.0, for that matter), this is why. I really assumed that summing up would be The End.

And you know what they say about Assumed… it makes an ass out of U and Med.

Wait. That can't be right.

Anyway, minor consistency things aside, thanks for being forgiving in that regard.

ALSO BY TAMMIE PAINTER

The Humorous stuff

THE CIRCUS OF UNUSUAL CREATURES

Hoard It All Before, Tipping the Scales, Fangs a Million, Beast or Famine

It's not every day you meet an amateur sleuth with fangs. If you like comic fantasy whodunits that mix in laughs in with murderous mayhem and mythical beasts, you'll love The Circus of Unusual Creatures.

THE CASSIE BLACK TRILOGY

The Undead Mr. Tenpenny, The Uncanny Raven Winston, The Untangled Cassie Black, The Unusual Mayor Marheart

Work at a funeral home can be mundane. Until you start accidentally bringing the dead to life.

THE UNWANTED INHERITANCE OF THE BOOKMAN BROTHERS

A novella celebrating the magic of books. Wills often come with unexpected surprises. This one especially so.

THE GREAT ESCAPE

Peculiar pet shops. Troublesome dream homes. And robot vacuums that just want to be free Looking for a captivating (and quick) escape from reality? These fifteen tales of humor, myth, magic provide just that.

The Serious stuff

THE OSTERIA CHRONICLES

The Trials of Hercules, The Voyage of Heroes, The Maze of Minos, The Bonds of Osteria, The Battle of Ares, The Return of Odysseus

Myths and heroes may be reborn, but the whims of the gods never change. A six-book mythological fantasy adventure

DOMNA

The Sun God's Daughter, The Solon's Son, The Centaur's Gamble, The Regent's Edict, The Forgotten Heir, The Solon's Wife

Destiny isn't given. It's made by cunning, endurance, and, at times, bloodshed. A six-part historical fantasy tale filled with passion, political intrigue, betrayal, and familial rivalry.

THERE'S MORE...

To see all my currently available books and short stories, just scan the QR code or visit books.bookfunnel.com/tammiepainterbooks

ABOUT THE AUTHOR
THAT'S ME...TAMMIE PAINTER

Many moons ago I was a scientist in a neuroscience lab where I got to play with brains and illegal drugs.

Now, I take wickedly strong tea and turn it into comic fantasy whodunits full of mythical misfits and magical mishaps that I hope give you a giggle.

When I'm not creating worlds or killing off characters, I can be found gardening, planning my next travel adventure, concocting some sort of mess in the kitchen, or working as an unpaid servant to three cats and a guinea pig.

The quick-as-you-can story behind my books...

My fascination for myths, history, and how they interweave inspired my two historical fantasy series, The Osteria Chronicles and my second series, Domna.

But all those ancient myths and angst-ridden heroes got a bit too serious for someone with a strange sense of humor and odd way of looking at the world.

So, while sitting at my grandmother's funeral, my brain came up with an idea for a contemporary fantasy trilogy that's filled with magic, mystery, wry humor, and the dead who just won't stay dead. That idea turned into The Cassie Black Trilogy.

My latest humorous fantasy series, The Circus of Unusual Creatures, features cozy mysteries full of silly situations, confounding clues, oodles of omelets, and a detecting dragon.

You can learn more at *TammiePainter.com* or at that QR code, where you'll find probably more info than you could ever want or need.

MY NEXT BOOK
IS COMING SOON!

In fact, it might already be here by the time you read this, and there's probably been loads of exciting stuff you've missed out on. You know, like photos of my cats.

Anyway, I love staying in touch with my readers, so if you'd like to…

- Keep up-to-date with my writing news,
- Chat with me about books you love (and maybe those you hate),
- Receive the random free short story or exclusive discount now and then,
- And be among the first to learn about my new releases

  …then please do sign up for my monthly newsletter.

As a thank you for signing up, you'll get my short story *Mrs. Morris Meets Death* — a humorously, death-defying tale of time management, mistaken identities, cruise ships…. and romance novels.

Join in on the fun today by heading to www.subscribepage.com/mrsmorris

Printed in Great Britain
by Amazon